The Heir's Predicament

Center Point
Large Print

Also by Lorri Dudley and available from Center Point Large Print:

The Duke's Refuge
The Merchant's Yield
The Sugar Baron's Ring
The Captain's Quest
The Marquis's Pursuit

The Heir's Predicament

The Leeward Islands Series—Book 6

Lorri Dudley

CENTER POINT LARGE PRINT
THORNDIKE, MAINE

This Center Point Large Print edition is published in the year 2024 by arrangement with Wild Heart Books.

Copyright © 2022 by Lorri Dudley.
All rights reserved.

The characters and events in this fictional work are the product of the author's imagination. Any resemblance to actual people, living or dead, is coincidental.

Unless otherwise indicated, all Scripture quotations are taken from the Holy Bible, King James Version. Scripture quotations marked (NIV) are taken from the Holy Bible, New International Version®, NIV®. Copyright © 2011 by Biblica, Inc.™ Used by permission of Zondervan. All rights reserved worldwide. www.zondervan.com. The "NIV" and "New International Version" are trademarks registered in the United States Patent and Trademark Office by Biblica, Inc.™

The text of this Large Print edition is unabridged.
In other aspects, this book may vary
from the original edition.
Printed in the United States of America
on permanent paper sourced using
environmentally responsible foresting methods.
Set in 16-point Times New Roman type.

ISBN: 979-8-89164-358-1

The Library of Congress has cataloged this record under Library of Congress Control Number: 2024943145

The Heir's Predicament

*"Refrain from anger and turn from wrath;
do not fret—it leads only to evil.
For those who are evil will be destroyed,
but those who hope in the Lord
will inherit the land."
— Psalm 37:8-9 (NIV)*

Chapter 1

October 9, 1831
OLD ROAD, ANTIGUA

> Diary, you should have seen the color of the sunrise this morning. Oranges, pinks, and reds so vivid it increased a mighty disorder in me as if I might catch fire.
> ~ *Entry by Loretta Baxter, October 10, 1806*

"Shh. Keep your voice down." Maggie Prescott held her index finger to her lips. "Or this could become one big disaster." She'd seen Lord Granville standing on his balcony earlier that morning with his arms crossed and prominent wide-legged stance, surveying his grounds with a sharp eye. A prickling shiver walked up her spine. She'd avoided his notice during her first escapades to Greenview Manor, but the master of the house didn't appear to be someone she wanted to cross.

"I've done some foolhardy things in my past, but dash it, this beats them all." Her uncle's white linen sleeves flapped in the breeze, and his blue eyes shone brightly despite his dark scowl.

She still hadn't grown accustomed to seeing him with facial hair, his light brown scruff blending in with his tanned skin.

Maggie hid her slippers underneath the wild tamarind bush and tilted her head back to examine the feat ahead. The large breadfruit tree looked sturdy enough, and it had held her weight on prior attempts. Surely it could accommodate her uncle, Captain Anthony Middleton's, larger masculine frame.

She swallowed and planned her winding route among the limbs. There was no need to be concerned. Lord Granville was in the fields, directing his men until sundown as he did every day, even Sunday. She and her uncle would slip in, locate the diary, and be sailing back to London before nightfall.

"My gut's rolling like waves before a storm." Uncle Anthony shook his head. "Something doesn't feel right."

"Are you sure your stomach's not protesting the bottle of rum you finished off with the crew last night?"

"Such cheekiness." He glowered at her but then ruined the effect with a wink. "You get that from your uncle."

The tropical trade winds of Antigua rustled the palm branches and the dense green canopy of the large breadfruit tree that shaded the grand manor house. Maggie faced him and placed her hands on his shoulders. "I don't see another way. How else am I to regain my mother's diary?"

"My sister is your mother." He pointed a finger under Maggie's chin. "She's the one who raised and loved you and always will." Uncle Anthony's whispered tone sounded harsh, but he still went along with her plan, bending his knee and interlocking his fingers as a makeshift step to hoist her onto a branch.

Maggie silently whispered a prayer for patience as she blew a wisp of hair out of her eyes. How could she convey the importance of discovering the origins of her birth? Try as she might, she'd failed to make anybody, even her uncle, fully understand. "I will always think of Cilla and Tobie as my parents. I love them, which is why I need to learn the truth of my lineage." She placed a foot on her uncle's hands. "They've given me so much already, and I refuse to be a burden to them."

"You're too young to be worried about spinsterhood," he hissed in a sharp whisper.

"I'll be turning twenty this year."

He snorted. "As if that's ancient."

"Ready?" They'd dawdled long enough.

"I understand the *ton* puts all their stock in pure bloodlines." He exhaled and lifted her with a grunt. "But I still think using the front entrance would be easier."

Her shoulder brushed the thick weathered trunk, but the sturdy fabric of her gown didn't rip. "The butler slammed the door in our face the moment I mentioned the diary."

"Arrogant butlers are all the rage." He flinched as a piece of bark broke away and bounced off his cheek. "If it so happens that you're the heiress of this estate, I hope you sack him without a reference."

She gripped a low-hanging branch and readied to kick her leg up. "Please turn your back for a moment."

"For the record, I still think this is a terrible idea." Uncle Anthony grunted his displeasure but complied. "This entire debacle has been a wretched notion from the beginning. All this time, I thought you were at the local parish going through records, not invading houses. You're fortunate you haven't been shot."

Maggie hooked her leg around the branch, pulling herself until she rested on top. "We didn't sail across the Atlantic to get turned away by a butler. Besides, we'll be fine. I spent a week watching Lord Granville's whereabouts. He's a remarkably routine man."

She resettled her skirts. Tree climbing was an under-appreciated skill in England. Several of her governesses had lectured her on the inappropriateness of such a talent. One even fainted after discovering Maggie in the high branches of an oak tree. She'd revived Miss Fitch with smelling salts, only for the woman to quit on the spot. It was a pity. Maggie had liked the sensitive woman, and the governess's departure allowed for the austere Miss Van Hetters to accept the position.

The following branches proved easier to ascend as long as she kept her skirts from snagging on twigs and branches. She climbed until she stood on a limb extending toward the roofline near the grand house's second-floor balcony. She jumped to test the weight, and the branch barely swayed. It should hold Uncle Anthony.

She pushed aside some leaves obscuring her view of the grounds surrounding the grand manor. White canvas sails of the windmill where the sugar cane was crushed slowly circled in the breeze, and the sweet, medicinal smell of the boiling houses distilling molasses into rum mixed with the yeasty scent of the breadfruit tree. The estate lands sloped down the palm tree-lined lane, past the waves of green sugar cane, to Old Road. Just beyond that lay crystal blue waters, and if she squinted, she could see the main mast of *The Windward*, Uncle Anthony's ship, anchored in the harbor. This view could have been the exact one her mother witnessed from the veranda. A jitteriness rolled her stomach, like the feeling she'd gotten after she'd snuck the remainder of coffee this morning from the pot Uncle Anthony drank after his night of carousing.

"Psst!" she called to her uncle below. He didn't move, merely stood as he would at the helm of his ship, staring off at the horizon. His hair hadn't thinned, not even from the top view, although he would be considered middle-aged at nine and thirty. His sun-bleached locks fell in thick waves and added to his debonair appearance that drew the ladies' eyes, even if Uncle Anthony showed no intention of settling down.

She willed him to turn around and keep to the mission. Movement near the edge of the field startled her, and one foot slipped off the branch. She held tight to an upper limb and released a breath.

A group of five women returned from the field, balancing the afternoon cane bundles on their heads as they made their way to the windmill. Their emergence meant it was precisely three o'clock. Lord Granville ran the plantation like clockwork, allowing Maggie to plan this escapade down to the precise moment when the main house would be vacant.

Uncle Anthony leaned against the tree's trunk as the women strolled up the hill, their hips swaying back and forth. The workers would be inside the stone windmill for twenty minutes before returning to the field—time to hurry.

"Uncle Anthony, you can climb up now," she

whispered, but his only movement was his head shifting with the direction of the lithe slave women as they entered the mill to unload their burdens. Maggie leaned down. Was he too preoccupied admiring the ladies to remember why they were here? She plucked a breadfruit from a nearby branch and dropped it, hitting her uncle squarely between the shoulders.

He flinched and turned to peer up at her, holding his palms out as if to say, what was that for?

She waved him up.

The tree shook as he climbed, and Maggie tightened her grip on the upper branch.

"Are you certain the limb is going to hold my weight?" His whisper exaggerated the raspy tone of his voice. He stood barefooted on the branch just below hers.

"Indeed." She focused on her next climb. "Just don't go until I'm on the veranda." She stepped out like a tightrope walker and paused. "And don't look down." She didn't know whether she said the last bit for her benefit or her uncle's, but she sidestepped onto the branch, still holding onto the upper limb. The final few steps required her to release her overhead grip, but after multiple practice voyages, she no longer hesitated to disengage. She balanced the few remaining steps and leapt to the roof.

Wooden shingles bit into her hands as she

clung to the dormitory peak and eased to a seated position. Her palms tingled from the great height, but she scooted down a body-length to the roofline.

Uncle Anthony soared onto the gable end beside her with ease. His young adulthood spent scaling ratlines on his Majesty's Royal Navy ships quashed any fear of heights. "Your mother and father would have my head if they knew you were jumping onto housetops."

An all too familiar stab of guilt drained the moment's excitement at the thought of her adopted parents. "They've caught me climbing trees before. They may think nothing of it." Only because if discovered, their outrage over her disappearance and having her maid pretend to be Maggie at boarding school would supersede their anger at her climbing on a roof. She inched her way down the dried and curled wooden shingles. If her desire to discover the truth about her birth parents hadn't burned so great in her chest, she never would have done anything to disappoint her family. She could only hope that her plan would work and that they'd never find out about this adventure.

Her uncle snorted. "Your parents? Your mother boxes my ears if I indulge in one pint too many."

She hung her legs over the wooden gutter, finding the veranda railing below with her foot. "They'll be too busy ringing a peel over me and flying into the boughs for you sailing me across the Atlantic."

Her uncle paled and closed his eyes. "Don't remind me."

She dropped to the rail and lowered onto a small wooden chair next to a table that graced the balcony. Each morning as the sun rose, the master of Greenview Manor sat and read in that very seat as he partook of his morning coffee and a Johnnycake.

Part of her admired the man's strict schedule. She could set her watch pin to Lord Granville's daily routine. Her papa, Tobie, also abided by a stringent regimen with the men under him at the War Office, but at home, Maggie only knew Tobie at ease, laughing, joking, and playing with Maggie and her two younger siblings. Could Lord Granville also hold a softer side?

She swallowed. If they got caught, she prayed his lordship not only offered a softer side but a forgiving one.

Uncle Anthony jumped onto the terrace like a cat.

She slipped through the open balcony doors, peering around the meticulously kept room, listening for servants. The whole lot of them, even the surly butler, should be in the kitchen, off-set from the main house in case of fire, preparing for the evening meal. She breathed the fresh scent of lye soap and bergamot. The coverlet on the large

17

four-poster bed lay smooth and flat. Starched pillows lined the wooden headboard in tidy rows. Atop his hand-carved teak bureau sat a porcelain washbasin and a framed miniature portrait of a mature woman, likely his mother. On a nearby desk stood a candlestick, a silver tray with a stack of correspondences, a letter opener, inkwell, and a quill pen.

She stepped aside from the balcony door to allow room for Uncle Anthony to enter and peeked at the paper lying on the master's bed stand. His daily tasks were listed in neatly slanted script and meticulously marked off with bold strokes, except the last one.

- ~~Respond to invitations~~
- ~~Write a letter home~~
- *Find missing key to desk drawer*

In familiarizing herself with the layout of the grand manor in search of the hidden room housing her mama's diary, she'd grown acquainted with the man who frequented its halls without officially encountering him. He was fastidious in neatness and cleanliness. He organized his bookshelves by subject and title and his closets by color. The first time she'd dared enter the master's chamber, she hastily exited with guilt nipping at her heels. A young innocent shouldn't be snooping about a man's quarters, much less sneaking into his house uninvited.

Sweat trickled down her back, and she glanced at the clock on his bureau—quarter past three. The valet would return from pressing his master's shirts at quarter to five, when the men returned from the fields.

She had planned to take what belonged to her, namely her mother's diary, and be on her way, none the wiser. However, the hidden place under the stairs proved harder to locate than expected. Yesterday, when she was about to relent and conclude the instructions embedded in her mother's song were a childish fantasy, she saw the gap between the bookshelf and the wall. Upon closer inspection, she'd located the secret door under the attic stairs, but after several attempts to move the bookcase on her own, she'd had no choice but to involve her uncle.

"Which way?"

She borrowed the master's oil lamp from his nightstand and tipped her head toward the hall before striding around the massive bed. Cracking the door open, she listened and scanned the area before slipping from the master chamber. Her bare feet padded softly on the wooden floorboards. She moved aside, evading the one that squeaked.

Her uncle overlooked her intentional misstep, and the plank groaned its displeasure. Her breath caught as they both stood rigid, waiting for someone to call out, *Who's there?* But she heard only the distant singing of workers in the fields.

She slipped past the stairs, waving for her uncle to follow, and they stopped at a door on her left. Her fingers trembled as she lifted the latch and entered the room. This was it. She'd soon have the answers she'd prayed for. Flowered paper lined the walls, and the whitewashed furniture held a feminine quality. This must have been her mother's sitting area since the adjoining door led to a dressing room and bedchamber. The same reverent awe that had tickled her stomach the first time she entered remained steadfast.

"It's over here." She strode to a large bookshelf on the left side of the room flanked by two upholstered chairs. A nearby window spilled light into the small chamber, enticing inhabitants to curl up in the cozy seat and read. A door to the right of the chair opened to a flight of stairs leading to the attic. The bookcase rested an inch or so away from the wall, and rising onto her toes, she ran her fingers along the top edge and felt the casement molding of a hidden door.

Uncle Anthony rubbed his chin and eyed the object. "Let's try to shift it without removing the articles."

Rows of books lined the shelves. *The History of the Fall of Rome, Two Treatises of Government* by John Locke, and a volume of Lord Byron's poems presented a small sample of the collection. Were these her mother's books? Had her mother read them? Did she, too, enjoy the adventure of reading? If only Maggie had more time to peruse the content of these shelves, but answers to her questions could only be found within her mother's diary, which the song said rested in a room beneath the stairs.

Uncle Anthony gripped the corners, and his face reddened as he strained to lift. "Blasted pain..." It didn't move.

"Let me try and help. On the count of three." Maggie set the oil lamp on the floor and grasped the other side. "One... two... three..."

Uncle Anthony grunted and tugged while she attempted to wriggle the bookshelf away from the wall, but it wouldn't budge.

"I told you it was heavy." Maggie rubbed her reddened palms.

Uncle Anthony dragged in deep breaths from the exertion. "Confounded thing weighs more than a hog's head of sugar, and it takes four men to roll one of those up a plank."

"I merely need you to move the bookshelf enough for me to slide through the door." She pulled a handful of books off the top shelf and stacked them in a pile.

"There isn't time for this." He scowled and shook his head, setting a few books haphazardly onto the floor.

"Careful to keep them in order. They're alphabetized by title."

Maggie ignored the grumblings that followed as she removed a large conch shell with its polished pink center that served as a bookend for a series of Britannica encyclopedias. A flash of memory surfaced of wiping water from her face and holding up a similar conch shell for her mother to see. Her face was but a blurred image, but Maggie sensed her mother's pleasure and recalled her instructions on removing the conch.

This shell remained intact. Maggie forced her fingers to set it aside and remove the encyclopedias. Questions poured through her mind. She would have answers once they moved the bookshelf.

"Let's try again." Uncle Anthony didn't wait to clear out the bottom two shelves but bent to lift the casement, shifting it an inch.

"Wait." She set down the last volume and gripped the side of the bookcase. "Lift."

They struggled to drag aside the solid wood shelving. Her uncle's face turned from red to purple as he sidestepped in a waddle. With a whoosh of air, he stepped back.

Maggie rushed to the exposed wall and lifted the latch to the hidden door with shaky fingers. She bit down on her smile and inhaled a fluttering breath. Stale, dusty air tickled her nose, and she sneezed. The undainty sound bounced off the walls.

Uncle Anthony cupped a hand over her mouth, and she froze, not daring to breathe.

Chapter 2

Why must this war with France continue? I'm not too naïve to comprehend its atrocities. One need only open their eyes to see men faint in the fields, the women beg for food, and the horror of the half-burnt and fully drown bodies that wash up on shore.

~ Entry by Loretta Baxter, October 25, 1809

Samuel Fredrick Granville tossed the dead top of a sugar cane plant into the dirt.

"Da sugar borers have infected some of deese plants." Cuffee slit the sugar cane stalk and pried it open between his hands. He pointed to a black-headed sugar borer inside the pulp and held it out for Samuel. "Buggered pests."

The dull throb of a headache flicked the inside of his skull, and Samuel rubbed his forehead. "Is the crop ruined?"

"Da yield will be less." He eased out the larvae and squished it between his fingertips. "I think dey only got in da south field plants. Da other fields look healthy enough."

A successful harvest was necessary not only for the peerage to allow him to return to England but to prove Lucy had made a terrible mistake in jilting him the night before their wedding. His jaw clenched, and the all too familiar surge of heat flooded his limbs and burned the back of his neck hotter than the late afternoon sun. "If we need more resources, men, or fertilizers, let me know soon. A ship is to arrive in Montserrat in the next week or two." Samuel removed his watch from his breast pocket. He had just enough time to return to the house and wash up before the magistrate arrived.

The official seemed determined to pull Samuel into island politics. While having a say in the local lawmaking process could benefit him and Greenview Manor, he couldn't afford to lose sight of his goal—revive the neglected plantation and restore its income to the cash crop of a generation ago. After doing so, he could return to England, redeem his right to his inheritance and lord it over Harry—who'd gotten Samuel banished here—and the woman who gutted his heart.

"Increase the inspection of the plants. Have the workers trail each other, re-examining the leaves and removing any pests." Samuel stuffed the watch back into his pocket. "Make sure the workers get a good meal in their bellies and adequate sleep to keep their energy and spirits up." He clapped Cuffee on the arm. "I appreciate the update and keeping the workers at a steady pace. Carry on."

He caught a proud glimmer in Cuffee's eyes before Samuel turned and strode to the main house, ensuring his promptness for the magistrate's visit.

Maggie strained her ears for any indication of the servants having overheard her sneeze. Outside the window, a sugar bird's high-pitched chirp erupted then faded, leaving only the whisper of the breeze penetrating the house's stillness.

Her uncle lowered his hand and nodded.

Maggie lifted the oil lamp and slipped into the cramped darkness of the long-forsaken room her mama had sung about. She rolled the wick on the lantern to increase the flame and held it higher. Trunks lay stacked in the far corner along with a small child's table and chair. Had her mama sat there and played with her dolls or practiced her letters?

Maggie shook her head to focus. She inspected the floorboards, nudging each one with her toe. Beside the table, one shifted. She dropped to her knees and set the lamp aside. Her stomach tumbled like her younger brother when he raced their middle-sister down a steep hill.

Please be here. The words repeated in her mind like a mantra. Palms perspiring, her fingers traced the floor plank, seeking an edge to pry.

"Hurry up," Uncle Anthony hissed from the other side of the bookshelf. "I don't like this. A servant is bound to come by soon."

"Trust me. We have time." She couldn't get a good grip on the floor piece, so she removed the dagger Tobie had taught her to use and wedged the blade into the crack. It lifted. Her heart shouted a silent *huzzah*.

This was it. She set the board aside with trembling fingers and slid the oil lamp closer. She held her breath. A change in height in the trey ceilings of the salon below created a compartment inset into the floor, but it appeared empty. She squelched a whimper. It must be here.

She reached down, feeling the dusty space between the joists, praying she wouldn't touch a mouse or any other vermin lurking inside the recesses. Her fingers brushed something, and she yanked her hand back.

Wait. It had felt solid. Her hand slipped back into the hollow and traced a straight edge of . . . leather binding. She grasped the book and pulled it out, blowing off the thick layer of dust and wiping the remainder away. The binding crackled as she opened the cover. Her heartbeat thudded in her ears.

This journal belongs to Loretta Genevieve Baxter.

She sucked in a gasp. It was here, just like the song taught to her claimed.

A battle waged over cross and cane,

Underfoot, in a room beneath the stair, I stored my pain,

As the men, they came to blows,
Yonder where the sugar doth grow.

The grueling hours Maggie had spent focused on recalling the long-forgotten childhood memories paid off. And her paging through endless passenger lists in shipping logs for the name of the woman who'd been believed to have died in a shipwreck in the British Virgin Islands hadn't been for naught.

"Maggie." Her uncle's sharp tone pierced her thoughts. "Someone's coming in from the fields."

She quickly replaced the board and grabbed the lamp. How much time had passed? It couldn't be time for the men to return. Hugging the journal to her chest with her free hand, she squeezed back through the door.

"I found it." She held her prize out for him.

"Splendid." He bent to push the bookcase back into place, and she quickly stepped aside. "Now help me get this back in order."

"Right." She set down the oil lamp and stacked the books back on the middle shelves.

Her uncle shoved the books onto the top shelf.

"Those aren't in the proper order."

His eyes widened. "We need to leave. Now."

"He'll know someone has been here." She wedged the conch shell back in its place and scooped up her mama's journal.

A door slammed on the first floor.

Uncle Anthony yanked her to her feet and

pulled her by the hand into the hall. They rushed past the open stairs and into the master's chamber.

The oil lamp.

Maggie drew up short and yanked her hand free of her uncle's tight grip.

He whipped around.

"I left the lamp."

"Forget it."

She turned and fled back down the hall, feeling the whoosh of air as her uncle swiped at her back. It may take a few days for the master of the house to notice the books muddled order on the guestroom shelves, but he'll spot the missing lamp immediately.

She scooped up the lamp and winced as one knuckle brushed the hot glass globe. Booted footfalls clomped beneath her through the salon toward the foyer. She darted back down the hall and into the master's chamber just as the stairs creaked under the weight of the approaching footfalls. She set the lamp back on the nightstand and moved the handle to the proper angle. Her uncle beckoned her from the balcony. His eyes widened in a silent gasp, and he ducked out of view.

Maggie dropped to the floor and rolled under the bed. Hidden, for the most part, by the dust ruffle.

A pair of well-polished Hessian boots moved

into sight. Fabric swished as he flopped his jacket on the coverlet. Floorboards creaked under his footfalls to the bureau. The scent of hot, male skin blended with the aroma of boot polish. His movement stirred dust that tickled her nose. She pressed her hand against the lower half of her face to keep from sneezing.

Water splashed as he washed, probably his face, neck, and hands, but she couldn't see from her vantage point.

He cleared his throat, and the sound of patting with cloth meant he dried himself.

Please leave, her mind screamed, willing him not to notice her. Her breath caught. Were her skirts hidden, or did the hem hang out from under the bed?

Lord, get me out of this, and I promise to be good from now on. I will go to finishing school and be on my best behavior. Just please don't make anyone the wiser.

She slowly tucked her skirts under her body, and her left hand brushed a small, metal piece. The missing desk key on his task list. Her fingers closed around it, pressing the ridged metal against her palm.

He pivoted on his heel to face the bed.

She froze. Bile rose into her throat. Her mental chant of *please leave* changed to *don't throw up.*

He approached, stopping when the tips of his boots fell in line with the bed, so close her eyes crossed staring at them. The scent of oiled leather, vegetation, and dirt filled her lungs. He removed what must have been his jacket off the bed. Fabric slid against fabric as his arms pushed into the sleeves. The boots stepped toward the nightstand past her line of vision.

"Humph," he grunted. "Odd."

Odd? Oh no, the oil lamp. She hadn't turned the wick back down. Of course, he would notice. Why must he be so exacting? She squeezed her eyes tight. Would he have her arrested? Would she be left to rot in an Antiguan prison? Was the risk to discover her true lineage worth it?

I can't dance with you at the assembly. Mama says your blood may be tainted. She could still feel the crushing blow of Mitchell Trembley's words, the cool air hitting her palm as he dropped her hand.

The risk was worth it.

But what about the mistruth she'd devised to sail here without her adopted parents' knowledge? They'd shown her love and taken her in, treating her as if she were their own daughter.

Lord, please get me out of this mess.

The room grew eerily quiet. No footsteps. No grunts or swishing of fabrics. Only stillness. The kind that precedes someone jumping out and screaming—*caught you*. A whimper lodged in her throat. In this case, he'd be lifting the bed ruffle and reaching for her throat.

A knock sounded on the front door downstairs. Maggie jolted.

Booted footfalls traveled from the room, the squeaky board in the hall groaned, the stairs creaked as he descended.

She inhaled, and her lungs drew in glorious breath, expanding to full capacity to make up for the lack of air. That was close. She scrambled out from under the bed and reached back to retrieve her mother's journal.

Male voices greeted each other below. She must hurry while Lord Granville and his guest remained in the foyer. Setting the desk key on the nightstand, she stuffed the journal into her knapsack and moved to the balcony. She peeked around the white linen curtain. Colorful birds played among the breadfruit tree's branches, and the white sails of the windmills circled. Everything appeared normal, her escape clear. She stepped out into the trailing sunlight.

A hand covered her mouth, smothering her scream while an arm snaked around her waist, lifting her off the balcony.

"Granville, we need you at the assembly."

"Do come in, Mr. Langham." Samuel stepped aside as the portly magistrate wedged his way past Samuel's harried butler, Hawley, who in his rush to answer the door still donned the apron he wore while polishing silver.

Mr. Langham lingered in the entranceway. "It's good to see Hawley promoted to butler."

"Indeed. He's been at Greenview Manor since he was a boy. The prior overseer kept him as his valet, but I brought my own valet with me from England." Samuel fought down his impatience with the idle chatter.

Langham cleared his throat as if sensing Samuel's irritation. "I didn't set up this meeting to discuss the servants." He stepped into the foyer, removed his hat, and handed it to Hawley. "There are big decisions in the making. You'll want your say in these next few votes." He frowned and tilted his ear up. "Did you hear something?"

Samuel crossed his hands in front and forced a patient smile. "It's probably a macaw. Those birds can screech like the best of London's gossipmongers."

Langham peeked out the front door, left then right, before nodding to the butler as if signaling the all-clear to close the door. "One can never be too careful. The slaves are growing restless, especially with the rumors that the House of Lords will hold a vote on emancipation. We need everyone who has clout with the aristocracy to vote it down."

How could Samuel break it to the man he was only in Antigua until he made a profit? That was a goal he intended to accomplish in a single season.

"There's a lot at stake." Langham's voice strained as he eyed the large, imported chandelier in the open foyer that occasionally posed as a ballroom for parties. "I can't tell you how pleased we are that a Granville has returned to Antigua. We need more planters who see the truth of the island's happenings."

Samuel gestured for Mr. Langham to follow him to the back of the house. They entered the book-lined study, and the magistrate eyed the row of volumes as if estimating their value. Samuel sat in the highbacked chair behind his polished teak desk.

"More and more slaves are attempting to escape or overthrow their masters." Langham plopped into the cushioned chair, shaking his head. "It's a daily occurrence. Keep an eye out for runaways. We shoot on sight."

"What good does that do? I doubt the master who paid a hefty sum to purchase their laborer would want them dead."

Langham leaned forward. "It teaches the others a lesson."

Samuel's fingers curled into fists under his desk. He exhaled a steady breath to thwart the heat rolling to the surface in waves. He controlled his temper, not the other way around. Lucy's screams echoed in his ears along with the image of Harry—blood gushing from his nose. Samuel forced himself to remember the humiliation of standing in front of the House of Lords and Harry's father yelling, *"Granville is a violent criminal. Polite society upholds a level of standards, and Granville has abandoned these by taking up fisticuffs and pugilist behavior."*

How quickly could he send the magistrate on his way without appearing rude? "What exactly was the reason for calling this meeting?"

The magistrate scratched his sideburn as he collected his thoughts. "There's an assembly meeting this Wednesday, and we're asking all landowners to attend."

"Mr. Langham, as much as I appreciate your invite and acknowledge the importance of Antiguan politics, my intent is to return Greenview Manor to its former glory as quickly as possible. I cannot afford to divert my energies to . . ."

Mr. Langham leaned to the side to peek around Samuel out the window. His brow furrowed.

Samuel shifted in his seat to see outside.

Leaves rained down from the breadfruit tree like a windy day during the London fall.

The magistrate rose from his seat.

"By Jove . . ."

Maggie's heartbeat still hadn't returned to normal since her uncle had hauled her onto the roof. She clung to the upper branch of the breadfruit tree and walked hand over hand toward the trunk.

Uncle Anthony jumped onto the limb she stood upon, and it dipped low.

The sudden drop bounced her stomach into her chest. She gripped the branch above her and hung until he moved onto another branch.

"Quickly." Her uncle's scrambling shook the entire tree.

"I am hurrying." She swung her feet to another limb, but her skirt caught and left her bent at an odd angle.

Crack.

Uncle Anthony stilled. His gaze locked on her, and utter horror washed over his expression.

Snap.

The limb broke, and her uncle plummeted to the ground. Small branches, leaves, and breadfruit toppled after him. He landed with a thud on his back.

Maggie clung to her branch like a helpless kite tangled in a tree. She bit her lip to keep from crying out.

Uncle Anthony gasped for air.

Merciful heavens. Don't be hurt. "Are you all right?" Maggie kept her voice low.

He thumped hard on his chest and dragged air into his lungs. He shot to his feet and dashed to where he'd left his boots, hiding behind the tamarind bush.

"Who's there?"

Two men burst through the patio's French

doors. The unfamiliar portly man held a blunderbuss and poured powder down the barrel.

Blood rushed from her hands and feet, turning them numb, but somehow, she maintained her grip on the branch. She didn't dare move. If she and Uncle Anthony didn't make a sound, maybe the men would go back inside.

Uncle Anthony ran.

So much for hiding and waiting it out.

As if to impede the gun's aim, he zigged and zagged for the cane fields.

He left me.

"A thief." The man below hefted his blunderbuss onto his shoulder. "I'll shoot him for you."

Maggie bit her lip so hard she tasted blood. *God, don't let him get killed because of me.*

"Confound it." Lord Granville's livid tone jerked Maggie's attention back to the men below. "I told you, we're not shooting anyone." He ripped the blunderbuss up, and it discharged.

The shot exploded, jolting her body. Pain seared her thigh, and a scream ripped from her throat. Her grip on the limb slipped, and she fell. One branch after another snapped under her weight before the ground rose to meet her.

She hit the grassy dirt, landing on her right side and wrenching her arm. Thinking to make sure it wasn't broken, she rolled to her back. Piercing pain in her leg overwhelmed the ache in her arm, leaving her dizzy.

"Perdition!" Lord Granville dropped to his knees and leaned over her. His eyes searched her face, their stormy gray conveying his concern as his brow knit into deep creases.

The pungent smell of gunpowder surrounded her, and blackness circled her periphery. A steady ringing from the gunshot grew in her ears instead of fading. She struggled to push the darkness away, but she skirted a deep tunnel.

"Stay with me."

Despite the haze of pain, an oddly timed thought ruptured her fading consciousness.

Lord Granville has a fine face.

Chapter 3

Papa is in a dudgeon. If he catches me swimming in my chemise again, he threatened to send me to an English boarding school for proper ladies.

~ Entry by Loretta Baxter, November 8, 1809

Samuel cupped the fallen angel's face. Was her skin always this pale? Pain sliced through a pair of green-gold eyes he feared would haunt him forever before they fluttered closed. He clapped her ashen cheek. "Please, don't die on me."

He clutched a fistful of his hair and leaned back to examine her for injuries. Had she been shot, or did she merely startle and fall from the tree? Was he looking for a head wound or a flesh wound? The tiny burnt hole in the fabric of her gown and the blood staining the light-green material answered.

Behind him, Langham dropped his weapon. "Y-you shot her." He backed a step. "I-I was aiming for the bloke who got away."

Samuel twisted toward the house and bellowed for a footman. "John!"

Seconds later, he emerged.

"Fetch Dinah from the mill, quickly."

John yanked off the new buckled shoes Samuel had purchased for him the week before. If the situation weren't so dire, he would have smiled at the man's fastidious care for an item not many workers possessed. John sprinted to the windmill, and Samuel pressed his fingers to the neck of the unconscious woman, grateful a pulse thrummed.

His father's attorney had been accidently shot while fox hunting. Fortunately, the family physician had been among the hunting party. Samuel had been a boy of three and ten, but he remembered the physician applying pressure to the wound.

Her blood saturated a growing circle the size of his palm. He removed his jacket and pressed it to the stained area. What else had the doctor done? Samuel's stomach twisted as he looked for an exit wound. He gently rolled her onto her side. More blood soaked the backside. He fought down his queasiness and searched for a hole in her skirt. Sure enough, the shot had entered one side of her leg and exited the other. Was that a good thing? He laid her back once more. At least, they wouldn't have to probe her wound for a lead pellet.

His hands grew sticky from her blood, and bile rose in his throat. The bright crimson color and metallic smell brought forth memories of London he'd rather forget. His fiancée's screams, "You monster." She had cradled her lover's head in her lap. Blood from his broken nose had dripped onto her white gown. Samuel shuddered, returning his focus to the present.

He must stop the bleeding. How should he put pressure on a two-sided wound? On a man, Samuel would tie a bandage around the injury, but this was a woman. He couldn't very well lift her skirts. Samuel glanced over his shoulder at Langham, who stood a few feet back, his eyes wide with a dazed expression. He'd be of no help. What if . . . ? An idea struck.

He slipped his arm under her knees, lifting her enough to position his jacket underneath. He then tied the sleeves together in a makeshift tourniquet around both her legs, encompassing the outer wound. He leaned back. Was his bandaging tight enough to staunch the bleeding—or so constricting it would hurt her? She was a slight thing, lithe and thin. Her fall had shaken her hair from its coiffure, and dark waves spilled about her shoulders. A lock of hair draped her nose. With the curve of his finger, he smoothed it back. Her skin felt smooth against his work-weary hands, which had calloused in the past months. No fine lines marred her eyes, and with her small frame, he would have assumed her a child, except her figure curved and properly filled the gown.

He cleared his throat and turned to the magistrate hovering over his shoulder. "Help me get her inside."

Langham set his gun on the ground and wiped his palms down his trousers before squatting and lifting her legs.

Samuel carefully scooped his hands under her armpits and raised her body. She was lighter than a feather mattress. Her head lolled to the side, and her silken hair caressed his forearm. He traversed carefully, turning backward to enter the house through the French doors still open wide.

The magistrate shifted his hold, despite the woman's light weight.

"Careful with her." Samuel maneuvered them into the back salon, and together they laid her on the settee. As he wiggled his arms from underneath her, her limp hand dangled to the floor. He clasped her petite wrist and placed it gently across her midsection before stepping back.

"I didn't shoot her." Langham wiped the sweat from his forehead with the back of his sleeve.

"It was an accident." Samuel rubbed his face. Where was Dinah?

The healer slave woman darted into the room, appearing as if he'd conjured her. She stopped and bobbed a quick curtsy at her master before her gaze found the woman lying on the settee. "I knew it must be somethin' terrible ta pull me from my work." She kneeled by the woman's side. "Wat en heaven's name happened?"

"She's been shot in the leg. I'm not certain

about elsewhere." Samuel rubbed the back of his neck.

Dinah felt for the woman's pulse and inspected the body.

"Oh, and she fell out of a tree."

Dinah's head jerked back. Her eyes widened and locked on Samuel's. "Wat was a white woman doing in yer tree?" She shook her head. "Naw. It's none of my concern. You gentleman, please leave us be so I can treat her properly."

She shooed them out with the flick of her hands.

At the door, Samuel stole one last look at the strange beauty strewn across his settee. "Send someone for me if you need anything or her condition changes." He nodded to Dinah, closed the door, and turned, bumping into the magistrate. "Pardon."

Langham straightened the lapel of his twill jacket. "I also wonder why a white woman would be perched in your tree."

"Dashed if I know." He shrugged, but an image of the oil lamp with its flame burning high entered his mind. Had she been in his room? Why? To do him harm? To steal? To force him into marriage because he was to inherit an earldom? He held back a bitter chuckle. She'd have been out of luck on that account. Unless he turned his plot of land around, he'd become a displaced heir-apparent without any holdings back home—or two pennies to rub together.

"What about the other fellow who ran? Do you know him?"

Samuel shook his head. He'd only had a glimpse of the man before focusing on disarming the magistrate.

"Are they thieves? Smugglers? Pirates?" Langham folded his arms and arched a brow. "Aggressive fortune hunters? A husband seeking vengeance with his wife in tow?"

"I've never seen them before." His jaw tightened. "I haven't the foggiest." He didn't appreciate the implication in Langham's posture or tone.

"There'd better not be anything untoward going on at Greenview Manor." The magistrate pointed at Samuel's chest. "I'll be keeping a closer watch on things around here."

Samuel ground his back teeth together. "Make certain to leave your weapons behind. My staff and I appreciate our lives, and we don't need any more accidents." He spoke the last word with extra emphasis.

Langham blanched. "Good day to you, Lord Granville. I'll show myself out the back and see if I might locate and question the other intruder."

Hawley rounded the corner as if hearing his cue. He handed the magistrate his hat and gestured to the back door to see Langham out.

The magistrate retrieved his weapon, which remained on the ground under the breadfruit tree, but didn't load it before stalking off in the direction of the other man.

Samuel released a long whoosh of breath. How did this happen? How could he be chatting with the magistrate one minute and the next tending to a woman they'd shot out of a tree like a pheasant? The whole situation seemed surreal as if he should wake in his bed suffering from a nightmare brought on by the dreadful heat.

John returned and buckled his shoes. "If you don't mind me saying so, milord, that man doesn't seem right in the head."

Samuel didn't disagree. "Lord help us all. He's the judge and law enforcement of the island."

The washbasin water turned pink as Samuel cleaned the woman's blood off his hands. He massaged the muscles in the back on his neck and peered in the looking glass. His eyes showed tiny lines of strain, and dark smudges had formed underneath. Other than his weariness, which would be cured by a good rest that he couldn't afford at the moment, he appeared much the same as he had a year ago. Perhaps his face was a little tanner from the Caribbean sun, and his brown hair had lightened a bit. His life, however, was unrecognizable. In past situations, he would have dropped to his knees and prayed, but God seemed as distant and unapproachable as Samuel's homeland.

Those dark, sweeping lashes and vivid green eyes filled with agonizing pain flashed in his mind's eye. Who was she? He lowered his gaze to the bloodied water. Could Dinah stop the hemorrhaging, or would the fallen angel bleed out in his salon? Would another crime be added to the growing list on his conscience? Would the island gossips believe the shooting an accident, or would it, when word spread to England, add to his so-called violent actions that made him a criminal in the eyes of the peerage?

He should pray for the woman, but praying seemed like an admittance of guilt, or worse, weakness, as if he couldn't handle the situation. Once again, he'd been caught unaware—left to fit the puzzle pieces together. He remembered her small, limp frame draped on the settee, and he folded his hands to pray anyway. *Lord, don't let her die.*

Was he a hypocrite for beseeching God's help? A few months before, he'd cursed Harry Reginald to die after entering his mother's greenhouse. Choice words that shouldn't be said in front of a lady had spewed from Samuel's mouth, silencing the sounds of Harry's lovemaking. Harry had stuffed his shirt into his trousers as he turned.

"Before you fly into the boughs, let's talk about this."

Samuel's fists clenched, same as they had that night. Harry had been his closest mate. He'd had that facer coming. Samuel could still feel his fist connect with Harry's jaw, hear the satisfying smack of his knuckles against the man's nose. Only when Harry had refused to rouse and instead lay on the ground, motionless, had Samuel's rage dwindled.

Lucy's screams had pierced his eardrums.

The sticky red blood oozing from behind Harry's head had tossed cold water on Samuel's burning fury and sickened his stomach with dread. He couldn't have known Harry would fall back and hit his head on a stone planter, knocking himself unconscious.

Lucy had alternated between begging Harry to wake up and pleading with Samuel to keep the whole incident quiet. Thinking he might have killed his friend, Samuel vaguely recalled, promising to be discrete and locating the gardener, who revived Harry by waving ammonia under his nose like a smelling salt.

Keeping his word had never been so difficult as when he faced Harry's lies in front of the House of Lords and accepted his punishment. The only consequences Harry paid for ruining Samuel's carefully laid plans, dreams, and aspirations on the eve of Samuel and Lucy's wedding was a crooked nose and a splitting headache for a day.

"Enough." Samuel's voice silenced the already quiet room. His thoughts had strayed down that dark trail too many times. He shrugged out of his blood-smeared shirt and folded it over the foot of the bed. With the towel lying next to the washbasin, he washed his chest and stomach.

"Milord?" Carson, Samuel's valet since his youth and two years his junior, entered through the adjoining chamber. "I didn't expect you back so soon. You should have rung the bell pull. I was merely starching your shirts and finishing your correspondence."

He lifted Samuel's shirt, saw the blood stains, and drew back. "Did something amiss happen in the fields?" He dipped the stained fabric in the washbasin before plucking another ensemble from the wardrobe.

Samuel rubbed his temples. "Not in the fields. It was . . ." How could he explain what had happened? He exhaled a deep breath in hopes of releasing the day's troubles. "It's being handled."

"I'm certain it is." Carson offered a clean shirt.

Samuel accepted it, sliding his arms into the sleeves. He nodded to his prior clothes. "I can finish myself. You may see to salvaging the shirt."

"And the jacket, milord?"

"Is in worse condition, I'm afraid. I'll have Dinah bring it to you."

"As you wish." Carson lifted the washbasin and strode toward the door but paused by the nightstand. "I see you found the desk key."

Still buttoning his shirt, Samuel twisted around. "The desk key?"

Carson held it up.

"Right. Indeed." Perhaps a maid had come across it? He certainly hadn't located it, and if Carson hadn't . . .

The oil lamp rested on the same nightstand—the one where the wick hadn't been rolled down. The key rested next to his daily list of tasks, one of which stated, *find desk key*. Very odd, the desk key, the oil lamp, and the woman falling out of the breadfruit tree. Samuel tucked the tails of his shirt into his trousers and pushed through the French doors onto the balcony. Had she and the man who got away broken into his chamber? Had they read his task list? What had they been looking for?

Samuel returned to his chamber and out the door. "Carson."

Carson stopped in the hall and turned.

"Before you attend to the shirt . . ." Samuel tugged on his light cotton jacket. "Please do an account of my valuables. Alert me if anything is missing."

"Yes, milord. Right away."

Samuel stalked out the door. He had some questions for their uninvited guest.

"How is she?" Samuel rose from the chair in the hall as Dinah exited the salon.

The young woman brushed back the spiral curls that had escaped her topknot and jutted in all directions. His bloodied jacket was draped over her arm, and her bare toes poked from beneath the hem of her gown. "Considerin' dat could have been a lot worse." She made a sign of the cross. "Da shot didn't hit any main arteries, and her leg stopped bleedin'. It should heal nicely, but she must stay off her feet fer a few days. Da wound is deep and could easily reopen, and den we're back where we started. Also, I'll need ta watch ta mek sure no fever sets in."

"Did she awaken?"

"She came to fer a short time but is restin' now." Dinah glanced back into the room as if to make sure.

Samuel resisted the urge to peek around her and see for himself. "Did she say who she was or why she was here?"

Dinah shook her head. "Only murmured somethin' 'bout findin' her mama."

Looking for her mother. What did that mean? "Who's her mother?"

"I dunno, but dat girl has angels watchin' over her." Dinah slipped back into the salon. "Ya got ta see dis ta believe it."

With Dinah no longer blocking his view, Samuel placated his curiosity and peeked into the salon to the woman curled on the settee. Long waves of dark tresses spilled off the sofa and grazed the floor. Her skin held a slight olive hue, and her lips were rosy as if she'd eaten a peck of strawberries. He exhaled a breath, relieved a bit of her color had returned. Suspicions of his involvement in someone else's death would end his chance of returning home.

Dinah held up a book. "Look at dis." She ran her palm over the cover as she approached and offered him the tome. *Diary* was embossed into the leather cover with gold leaf.

He accepted the book and opened the cover. "This journal belongs to Loretta Genevieve Baxter." *Baxter*—he knew the name. Paul Fredrick Baxter was the prior owner of Greenview Manor, and he'd had a daughter. He glanced at Dinah. "Why would she take Miss Baxter's diary?"

Dinah shrugged. "Yer missing da miracle." She pointed to three small holes in the pages.

He leaned in closer to inspect. Pellet holes. Three small metal balls had embedded into the pages.

"If dis book hadn't been en her satchel and slung across her front, her injuries woulda been much worse, like intestine, liver, or kidney damage. Tat's one fortunate lady."

The woman's face, serene in blessed sleep, rested mere feet away. She could have died. Acid churned in Samuel's stomach. Why would she have risked her life stealing into Greenview Manor? Shooting her had been an accident, but theft was a punishable offense. Had her life taken a dire turn? She didn't look destitute. Her muslin gown was of fine quality, yet her feet were bare.

He lowered his voice to Dinah, impressed by her healing skills. He'd heard she'd learned the trade from her mother who died slowly of a wasting disease, but he'd yet to put them to the test other than his workers receiving a few minor burns and scrapes. "What else was in the woman's possession?"

"Not much. Da journal, a notebook, a quill, and an ink well." Dinah scratched her arm. "Da satchel looks like one dat could have been bought in town. I know I've seen some at the Sunday market."

"Milord?" Carson peeked his head inside the door. "All is accounted for upstairs. Would you like me to check the silver?"

"Hawley was polishing the silver earlier, yes?"

Carson bowed his head. "You are correct, sir."

"Nothing appeared to be missing?"

"No, my lord." Hawley's voice rang from the hall.

"No need to reinspect them." Had they planned to steal more and his meeting with the magistrate interrupted them?

"Here." Dinah pulled the bloodied jacket off her arm. "You're gonna want to soak dis in water." She handed it to Carson, who cupped it in his hands as if his best friend had died. He headed toward the kitchens.

"I'll be taking supper at my desk." Samuel nodded to Dinah. "Please notify me if she awakens or if her condition changes."

"Yes, milord." Dinah curtsied, her bare feet poking from the bottom of her skirts.

"Did the shoes I purchased not fit?"

"Oh, dey did. Thank you kindly." She dropped her skirts and dipped a little, hiding her bare feet. "I know how you prefer us ta wear dem in da house. I'll get dem on right away."

He held up a palm. "I was merely making sure the gift was acceptable."

"Thank you, kindly. I just didn't want dem to get ruined when I was in da boiling house. Not many workers have da privilege of wearin' shoes. It's been a nice change with you bein' here." She hurried away.

Samuel smiled and peeked once more at the curved form asleep on the settee. One arm lay folded at her bosom while the other was bent at the elbow with her slender hand resting under her cheek. Possessiveness tapped at the shell of his heart, but he had no business being stirred by an unknown woman. The odd stomach sensation was most likely due to hunger. He checked his pocket watch. *Six thirty*. Well past time for serving the evening meal unless one were keeping city hours—which he wasn't. Most days he returned from the fields ravished with hunger.

Exiting the room, he waved over a maid. "Keep an eye on her until Dinah returns."

"Yes, milord."

Samuel strode down the hall and settled behind his desk in his study. Had it been only a few hours ago that he sat here with the magistrate?

How did the day change so drastically? Couldn't something go according to plan?

From his desk, he withdrew the ledgers to drown his thoughts of sugar borers, island politics, and women falling from trees. Instead, he devised ways to return the plantation to its former profitable status. He'd summed the columns three times, as was his habit to ensure accuracy, but the numbers blurred before him as a pair of haunting green eyes emerged from his memory.

A diary was a strange thing to steal.

Chapter 4

I had the last fitting session for my gown to wear to the assembly ball. Although Papa finds Antiguan men unfit as suitors for his only daughter, I plan to dance until the soles of my slippers have worn through.

~ Entry by Loretta Baxter, January 25, 1810

Maggie clung to the peaceful nothingness of sleep, but it slipped away as a burning pain in her right thigh dragged her into consciousness. She groaned, expecting Cilla to be sitting by her bedside with a cool cloth as she always did when Maggie was sick or hurt. She opened her eyes, but Cilla wasn't there, and neither was she at home.

Where was she?

The burning sensation obscured her thoughts until she felt as if she were peering through a window with wavy glass. She tried to move, but a hand settled on her arm.

"Easy nuh. Ya don't want da bleedin' ta start again."

A female leaned over her. The woman's dark skin contrasted against her cream-colored serviceable gown and apron. The warm brown eyes with lashes that curled back seemed to communicate she was a friend, but her firm grip pressed Maggie back down.

"Where am I?" Maggie exhaled through tight lips as if she could blow the pain away.

"Greenview Manor." The woman released her and sat on a stool beside the settee.

Maggie's breath caught as the events from earlier jarred her memory. She pressed a hand to her head to think past the pain.

"I know yer leg's probably achin' somethin' bad." She held a cup to Maggie's lips. "Drink dis. It's willow bark tea wit a pinch of island ginger. It should mek ya feel a little better."

She drank a few sips.

"My name's Dinah." The woman set the cup aside and folded her hands under her apron. She nodded towards the door, and a footman turned and left. "If ya need somethin' stronger in yer cup, just hollah, and I can add a splash of rum fer ya."

Maggie shook her head, for she needed to keep her wits about her. *Merciful heavens,* she'd been caught. She gripped the edge of the settee. All she could remember was falling out of the tree and Lord Granville kneeling by her side. What must he think? Would the magistrate arrest her? Had Uncle Anthony gotten away, or had the magistrate already arrested him? If so, who would bail them out of this mess? Was finding her mother's diary worth all this?

The diary.

Maggie tried to push herself up but winced at the pain. She scanned her surroundings. Baroque period furniture graced the lavish room, and the walls were papered with hand-painted alternating pomegranates and palm trees. Thick crown molding accented the coffered ceiling, and wainscoting lined the walls. Her satchel lay on the floor near the highbacked chair.

"Lookin' fer your things?" Dinah passed over her bag.

Maggie accepted her belongings, but its lightness told her the diary was missing. She gulped back a groan.

Dinah lifted the journal from the floor and held it up. "Dis book saved yer life."

Maggie relaxed back into the settee.

She pointed at the cover. "See dem holes? Dat would have been yer middle. God's blessed me wit bein' a good healer, but dere's no comin' back from a hole in da stomach. You've got one keen guardian angel." She placed the book in Maggie's open hands.

Maggie's thumb traced the deep crevices, and tears sprang to her eyes. Her mother's journal had saved her life. Was she still watching over her daughter from heaven?

A forgotten childhood memory of being stranded on the island surfaced. Maggie had been crying and saying, "up, upie," because her legs were tired. She couldn't see her mother's face, but she remembered the feel of her mama's dirtied and ragged skirt in her hand, the cloth stiffened by saltwater. Her mama had hauled her into her arms, and Maggie'd buried her nose into her mother's shoulder, smelling of skin and sunshine. Her mama slipped, and Maggie's stomach rose into her mouth. They hit the ground, and Maggie's elbow scraped on a rock. Her mother had protected Maggie in her arms, but no one had protected her mother. The memory of her mama's legs bent in angles where they shouldn't bend rose bile into Maggie's throat.

Mama. The memory dragged a sob from her lips, and tears coursed over her cheeks.

Dinah's brow knit, and she ran her hand up and down Maggie's arm, taking the diary and setting it on a nearby table. "Dere now. Don't go upsettin' yerself. God's watchin' over you, and so am I."

Booted footfalls approached.

Dinah rose, and Maggie quickly wiped away her tears with the back of her hand.

Lord Granville entered the room, posing an intimidating picture. Was he friend or foe? His expression offered her no hints at his mood. His hair was combed forward in a Caesar cut. A fitted dark jacket snuggly constrained his broad shoulders and contrasted with his snowy-white shirtfront and neatly knotted cravat. He approached her with confident strides and stood at the foot of the settee. His tanned fingers curled around his lapels and rested in the V-cut as he peered down at her with steely gray eyes.

Maggie pressed her back deeper into the settee cushions.

This was the meticulous man who alphabetized his books, ran the plantation like clockwork, and wrote detailed daily task lists. Determined horizontal lines permanently creased his forehead even though not a single gray strand streaked his hair. The intensity in his gaze clearly stated he was ruler of his domain, in control, and would remain so no matter who challenged him. She braced for his interrogation.

"You're awake."

His statement of the obvious wasn't a question, so she didn't respond.

"What is your name?"

She cleared her throat. "Maggie. Maggie Prescott."

He dragged over a high back chair and sat, pulling up on the knees of his trousers before stretching out his legs. He leaned his elbow on the arm of the chair and rested his head in the L shape of his index finger and thumb. "How is your leg?"

The intense concern in those piercing eyes robbed her of normal speech. "Er . . . it's paining me at the moment, but I consider myself fortunate."

His gaze flicked to the journal and back. "As you should."

Maggie's jaw tightened, but she relaxed it. Perhaps he was once again stating the obvious and not lecturing her.

"I can assure you that you are in good hands with Dinah."

A hint of a smile touched Dinah's lips, and Maggie could tell the woman was pleased by the praise. She backed to stand against the wall to wait, ready when needed.

"You gave us a scare." He sat forward, placing his forearms on his thighs and lacing his fingers.

The stool where Dinah had sat rested between Maggie and Lord Granville, but it provided no cover from his powerful gaze, which crackled the air between them. She swallowed the urge to confess everything—how she'd lied to her parents about being in boarding school, how she'd sailed on her uncle's ship to the island, and how she'd snuck into his home. Would he understand her desperation to discover her lineage so she'd no longer burden her family? Would he help her or hand her over to the island authorities? Before the intensity of his gaze could loosen her tongue, she focused on his other features. His square jaw, straight nose, and eyebrows that sloped downward and added to her awareness of his serious temperament.

"Are you an islander?" He pressed his fingertips together into a pyramid shape.

"I was born on an island."

He blinked. "Which island?"

"One of the Virgin Islands." Maggie shrugged. "Which one is uncertain."

The corners of his lips twitched as if disappointed by her answer, but she'd grown accustomed to the disapproval of others.

"Where is your family?"

"England."

"Which part? Or is that uncertain, too?"

"Bristol."

He gazed up as if seeking the association. "The Prescotts from Bristol, you say?"

"Indeed."

His brows inched upward. "Are you hiding something, Miss Prescott? It is miss, isn't it?"

"Yes. I mean no." The pain in her leg clouded her focus. "I'm not hiding anything." *For the most part.* "And I'm not married."

"Then your father's full name, please."

Maggie hesitated. She'd been known for being truthful to the complaint of being blunt, but she'd lied to come here, and since then, the temptation to speak mistruths plagued her. Cilla had always warned her that one lie would lead to another. Her parents would be mortified if they knew she'd come to Antigua, but they were across the ocean. It wasn't as if gossip spread that far, right? She locked gazes with his and told the truth. "Captain Tobias Prescott is my father. Have you heard of him?"

He shook his head. "I don't believe I've had the pleasure." Lord Granville leaned back in his seat and crossed his arms. "How did you land in Antigua?"

"By ship." If she played the part of a ninnyhammer, maybe he'd grow frustrated and leave.

He didn't respond, merely stared her down. A splendid tactic she must learn to use on her younger siblings.

"My uncle brought me."

"The man we spotted running into the cane fields?"

"Yes. Captain Anthony Middleton."

"He left you behind, injured."

She swallowed around the lump in her throat. It wasn't the first time her uncle had done something cowardly. "It appears so."

He scratched his jaw. "What did you take from upstairs?"

Maggie stopped breathing. "I-I don't know what you mean?"

"Were you inside the house earlier?"

"I . . ." The throbbing in her leg coincided with her heartbeat, and she placed her hand on her upper thigh to ease it.

"I found it odd that the oil lamp hadn't been turned down."

She inwardly groaned.

"But I've never seen a thief who finishes the tasks off the victim's to-do list." He arched a questioning eyebrow. "Thank you for locating my missing desk key."

Foolish ninnyhammer. She'd found the key but hadn't considered the implications.

His gray eyes hardened to stone. "Did you steal from me?"

"No." She shook her head, but then her gaze landed on her mother's journal. "Only what was my mother's, and I figure it's mine by birthright."

"Your birthright?" His mouth tightened. "Explain."

Where should she start? What would he believe? Would he think she was here to usurp Greenview Manor?

He stood and walked toward the French doors leading to the stone patio. "Perhaps someone else might be more forthcoming, especially when the magistrate is already out looking for him."

A shadow shifted outside the window.

Lord Granville flung the door open. "Captain Middleton." He stepped aside. "Please do come in. We were just discussing your earlier visit."

"Is she . . . ?" Uncle Anthony entered, his body tense, holding his hat in his hands. His sleeves were torn, and his face scratched, likely from the sharp blades of the sugar palms. His countenance brightened when he spied her on the settee, and his shoulders relaxed. "Maggie, thank heaven you're alive. My sister would string me up if anything happened to you."

"Perhaps finding hobbies other than house thieving may benefit." Lord Granville strode to the sideboard.

Uncle Anthony blanched.

Lord Granville poured amber liquid from a decanter into a glass. He passed the drink to Uncle Anthony before resuming his seat. "Please sit." He gestured toward a matching highbacked chair.

Anthony raised the glass in a thank-you salute before sitting and swigging from the cup.

"Now." Lord Granville folded his hands across his lap. "Perhaps one of you shall be more forthcoming in answering my questions. Why did you enter the great house, and what was stolen?"

"She only wanted to learn more about her birth mother is all," Uncle Anthony burst out his plea. "Have pity on a poor orphan girl."

Maggie gritted her teeth and stared down Uncle Anthony with a look she hoped appeared threatening. She wasn't to be pitied. She'd survived alone on an island. She could take care of herself.

"Maggie and her mother were the only survivors when her ship went down in the Caribbean Sea." Uncle Anthony gripped his glass in both hands. "Her mother died on the island, and

Maggie was alone until my sister found her, brought her to England, and adopted her. I told my niece it was a bad idea to sneak into another's house." Uncle Anthony eyed her and shook his head as if she were a troublemaker.

As soon as she could return to his ship, she was going to toss Uncle Anthony's secret liquor stash into the ocean.

He ignored her scowl. "I told her to go about things in a proper manner by knocking on the front door."

Maggie started to sit up, but the shooting pain in her leg forced her back down. "You know very well that I tried the front door, but the butler refused to speak to me."

Lord Granville crossed his arms and called, "Hawley."

He appeared in the doorway. "Yes, my lord?"

"Did Captain Middleton and Miss Prescott pay us a call recently?"

"Indeed, my lord."

Lord Granville's brows drew together. "And you turned them away. Why?"

Hawley's cold gaze rolled over them from head to shoe. "I figured them for servants who should know enough to use the back entrance."

Heat flooded Maggie's cheeks. They'd been travel-worn and a little unkempt perhaps, but to be mistaken for a servant?

"I've never . . ." Uncle Anthony stood and

stepped forward as if ready to call the butler out.

"That will be all, Hawley." Lord Granville waited for him to leave the room. "My apologies for the confusion. I shall speak with him later." He cleared his throat. "So, because my butler turned you out, you decided your only option was to sneak in and take what you needed."

It sounded much worse restated.

"I told her that very thing." Uncle Anthony downed the rest of his drink. "She's as hard-headed as they come."

Maggie clenched her teeth. Forget his liquor. She was going to toss her uncle overboard. "I thought . . ." She softened her gaze and pleaded with Lord Granville. "I didn't think any harm would be done. You didn't even know that the diary existed. My mother had hidden it under the floorboards of the room under the stairs."

He tilted his head. "Your mother worked at Greenview Manor?"

"My mother was *heiress* to Greenview Manor."

Lord Granville stilled. His gaze drifted past her unfocused.

The ticking mantel clock Maggie hadn't even noticed earlier grew unbearably loud. Did he see her as a threat to his holdings? "We are only here to learn the truth of my lineage."

Uncle Anthony stood, reached into his pocket, and removed his change purse. "Name the value of the journal. I'll compensate you, and we'll be on our way."

Lord Granville blinked as if roused from a stupor. "That won't be necessary."

A smile broke across her uncle's face, and he stuffed his change purse back into his pocket. "You have my gratitude. We'll be on our way then." He approached from the other side of the settee and bent to help her up.

Maggie gripped the settee, bracing for the excruciating pain that would ensue.

"No." Lord Granville jumped to his feet. "Don't leave."

Uncle Anthony froze. They both peered at the man.

"Ah . . ." He scratched behind his ear. "I mean . . . She can't be moved." He nodded as if confirming his words in his own mind. He pivoted to face Dinah.

Dinah pushed off the wall and stepped to his side. "Would you like her brought to the hothouse?"

The small hospital near the servant's quarters would be the logical place for the lady to heal, but he shook his head. "Have Miss Prescott carried to the guest chamber, and settle her uncle into the room next door." He turned back to Maggie. "Dinah shall tend your wound but also serve as your lady's maid until a proper chaperone may be summoned from town tomorrow."

Stay here? Maggie's leg pain temporarily dissipated, and she squeezed the settee tighter to keep from floating from it. There wasn't a better excuse to stay and learn more about her mama. She flicked her gaze to the ceiling in a silent *thank-you* to God.

Uncle Anthony shifted his feet. "I have a crew to see to and cannot be delayed for too long."

"I'll send a footman with a message to your ship," Granville said. "If you could stay the night to maintain appearances until a chaperone arrives, then I'm certain you'll return to your ship tomorrow. Your niece will be safe with us, and I will do what I can to help her discover more about her mother."

"You'll help me?" Maggie forced her mouth to close so she wouldn't gawk at him.

He issued her a single nod. "I'll send in a footman and inform Hawley of the arrangements." He strode from the room.

Maggie stared at his back and the self-assuredness of his stride.

Who knew being shot in the leg would be a blessing?

Chapter 5

Oh Diary, how exhilarating it was to dance, but none of my dancing partners caught my fancy.
*~ Entry by Loretta Baxter,
January 28, 1810*

Samuel leaned his head against the leather backrest of his office chair and set the letter to his solicitor aside. He stared at the five-by-four inset squares of the coffered ceiling. What were the chances that the beautiful young woman who'd broken into his home could be the heiress to Greenview Manor? The plantation had fallen to their family due to its former owner passing away without any living relatives. Many absentee planters had resigned or handed over their failing plantation to overseers or bankers. Whose property claims would stand if challenged?

Samuel or his solicitors would need to discover the truth and quickly. He rubbed his lower jaw. If Miss Prescott could claim Greenview Manor, he'd lose not only his plantation but also his chance to return to England. He'd be a lord with no home to lord over. His hope of refilling his family coffers would be dashed, along with his petty attempt to prove to himself and to Lucy that he, not Harry Reginald, would have been the better marriage choice. He scooted his chair closer and removed another sheet of paper. First, his conscience demanded he inform the poor chit's adopted parents of what had transpired. Perhaps they'd send for her, and Miss Prescott's threat to his livelihood could be forgotten. He dipped his pen into the inkwell.

> Dear Captain and Mrs. Tobias Prescott,
> I feel obliged to inform you regarding an incident involving your daughter. She is healing and in good care in Antigua. I'll allow her to explain the particulars, but I wanted to assure you of her health and wellbeing after being shot in the leg . . .

He described the incident and informed her parents that he'd keep them apprised of her condition. He tugged on the bell pull. When a footman arrived, he handed over the two missives along with a blank sheet of paper.

"Please give Captain Middleton the paper and then take the note to his ship. He'll provide the name and location. The other two need to sail on the appropriate ship."

"Yes, milord." The footman bowed and strode off.

The sun lowered on the horizon, casting its evening sunbeam onto the looking glass. Samuel opened his pocket watch. Half-past seven. Time to begin his nightly routine.

He rubbed his eyes with the heel of his hands. It had been a trying day between the discovery of sugar borers, a wretched meeting with the magistrate, and unwittingly shooting a trespasser whose face he couldn't seem to put from his mind. Exhaustion weighed his feet as though his boots were filled with sand. Perhaps he could skip his nightly perimeter walk?

Skip it? Are you mad? What if the dinner fires weren't extinguished properly and the sugar fields burned? Or worse, his new guest's tales were false and Captain Middleton's crew hid awaiting his signal to raid the plantation and neighboring town? What if slaves were gathering to revolt, like Langham stated? What if . . . ?

Samuel silenced the errant thoughts that plagued him nightly by donning his jacket and exiting his study into the back hallway. Servants bustled, carrying fresh sheets for the guest beds and airing out the guest chambers. They paused and moved aside as he passed to exit through the side door on his way to the stairs. The groomsman had his horse saddled and ready for Samuel's inspection.

The nightly breeze blew the day's heat out to sea. The few remaining beams of sunlight highlighted the fields and palm trees in a golden glow. He galloped past the great house along the edges of the garden and in between the north and west fields to the perimeter of the plantation's grounds. The underbrush had worn into a path since he'd begun his inspection routine when he first arrived six months before. He turned onto Old Road and spotted the blue livery of John, his footman, on his way to the harbor to pass Captain Middleton's message to his crew. He listened carefully for the lilt of the sea's shanty in the distance. The rumble of rolling waves washed over him as easy as breathing. The soothing rhythm indicated good wellbeing. Ragged waves or breathing meant problems ahead. The cane fields lay still except for the occasional tickle from the wind. Thankfully, no pirates lay in wait to plunder his hard work and its proceeds.

Old Road was also clear except for a passing cart carrying several barrels of sugar. The driver touched the brim of his straw hat as he passed.

Samuel returned the greeting with a dip of his chin before riding east to the boundary of his fields.

He slowed to inhale the sweet verdant scent of the growing cane and the mineral musk of freshly fertilized soil. The new plowing method and lime fertilizer appeared to be working. Lush green sugar cane rolled in the breeze like ocean waves. With such a hardy-looking crop, he had doubted Cuffee's suspicions of sugar borers until Cuffee cut open the stalk and showed Samuel the destructive little devils, killing the hearts of the young cane stalks with their voracious appetites.

Samuel had already invested in new plows, drainage systems to run rainwater into holding ponds, and better clothing, food, and medicines for the workers. Some other island planters treated their slaves worse than chattel, which never made sense to him. Wouldn't healthy slaves and better working conditions keep the workers from succumbing to disease and injury? The more hands to plant, cultivate, and harvest meant a better crop in the end. It seemed reasonable and compassionate to make their best interests a priority.

His mount's ears perked up, and a worker emerged from the sugar cane field with his machete resting on his shoulder. The golden sun highlighted the ridges and valleys of the slave's scarred back from a whipping. Samuel's own back ached at the mere sight.

"Good evening." Samuel called after the man.

The worker turned, and his Adam's apple bobbed as he swallowed. "Evenin'."

Samuel recognized him as one of Mr. Hennion's slaves. He'd worked the adjacent fields of Samuel's neighbor and had a long walk back to the slave quarters.

On several occasions, while inspecting the fields and in town, Samuel had run into Hennion. He'd seemed like a decent fellow, friendly, well-dressed, with a fondness for drink and finer things, as told by his rounded middle, ruddy complexion, and the brightly-patterned waistcoats he often sported. It seemed unlikely such a cordial man would allow his overseers to treat his slaves so poorly. Mayhap the man was unaware?

Samuel turned and trotted uphill to the north fields, where the cane fields led up to and stopped at the thick jungle foliage of Boggy Peak. He rounded back, stopping to admire the land. Smoke from home fires drifted on the breeze, and dots of firelight flickered among the cottages of the slave quarters. He rode back down to complete his route. The scent of burning wood mingled with the aroma of fish, beans, and rice. In their mix of African-island accents, women chattered and stirred supper pots while children laughed, chasing one another.

A loud bird call swiveled the heads of the women and children. Samuel slowed his horse. The day's events and the magistrate's talk about slave revolts tensed his muscles.

A toddler squealed and ran barefoot toward the fields.

A man set down his tools and wiped the sweat from his brow with the back of his hand before scooping the child into his arms. "Yer too heavy fer a lit' pickney. I can't be carryin' sucha big boy afta workin' en da fields all day." He set the child down and kissed his wife full on the lips before leaning over the pot to sniff or inspect the food.

She slapped him on the arm in a coy manner, but even in the dimming light, Samuel could see the love shining in the woman's eyes.

Samuel moved the reins to his left hand to rub away the tense ache in his chest. He'd once thought he was going to have a woman to come home to, a woman whose cheek he'd press a kiss onto. Lucy would have dressed for him and had the children lined up for a kiss goodnight before their nanny herded them to bed. What a naïve fool he'd been.

He tore his gaze from the intimate family moment and focused on the grand manor home on the crest of the hill overlooking the acres of fields. His family home, Ywain Manor, in England was even more luxurious. His father had groomed him to run the large estate, and once able, he'd resume his coveted position as heir to the earldom, but he couldn't shake the empty feeling of doing it alone.

His simple fantasy of marrying Lucy and having her children died. It now twisted into a wishful scene of him running into Lucy at the opera. Gone would be the expensive furs Samuel had bought for her and the sapphire necklace he'd purchased the night he arranged their engagement with her father. Lucy would admit she'd made an awful mistake and beg him to take her back.

He'd turn to the lovely woman on his arm and

ask her to excuse Lucy's impolite behavior before steering his new fiancée through the curtain to their private, luxury box.

It was a petty dream, but satisfying, and an improvement over the rage he used to feel whenever he thought of that night and the consequences it wrought. His control over his temper was improving. By Jove, he would not turn into his father.

Samuel spurred his horse with a click of his tongue to where he usually met Cuffee between the boiling house and the windmills. Cuffee would be finishing his own nightly inspection before closing up the boiling house, and right on time, he exited and raised a hand in greeting. The repetitive swoosh and squeak of the turning sails played in the background as Cuffee went over the day's tasks, how many bundles of cane had been cut, how many threshed into sugar, and how much boiled into molasses or distilled into rum.

Cuffee wiped the back of his neck with a rag and stuffed it into his belt. "Not bad for a day's work."

A rare grin cracked Samuel's lips. "Not bad at all." He clapped Cuffee on the shoulder. "Let's do it again tomorrow."

Cuffee shook his head and backed away with an upward twist to the corners of his mouth.

"Be thinking of some incentives to motivate the workers. Something that would make a nice prize and impress their women." Samuel folded his arms. "I think we can get more out of them with some healthy competition." The scarred back of one of Mr. Hennion's slaves came to mind. "More so than the whip."

"I'll be thinkin' on it." Cuffee spun on his booted heel and strode toward his separate quarters.

Samuel crested the hill of the main house. The sun, retiring for the evening, backlit the manor in vivid orange sky that settled into indigo. Greenview Manor's lower windows shone bright with candles. Even the second-floor guest-wing window glowed with yellow light as his new uninvited guest settled in. Who was this mysterious woman with wide green eyes who fell from the sky, this disturbing yet enchanting Maggie Prescott?

Mosquitoes emerged in swarms, buzzing about his head. Samuel spurred his horse to the stables, his mind working to put these new puzzle pieces together. If Miss Prescott's lineage proved true, did that make her the rightful owner of Greenview Plantation? Was Miss Prescott's presence a threat? He weighed the pros and cons again, ticking them off one by one, and still came to the same conclusion. It was best to keep his potential foe close.

Maggie held her breath and dove deep. Tiny fingers of a six-year-old cupped the conch and pushed off the sandy bottom, breaking through the surface and holding her prize high for Tobie to see. She spotted another shell through the crystal waters. It was farther away, but Tobie would be impressed with her catch. She swam deeper, past the waving fan coral. A shadow passed over her, sending a chill down her spine—*shark!* Breeching the waves, she called for Tobie or Cilla, but instead, her mouth cried out, "Mama!"

There was no one there. Her mama had died and couldn't save her. Maggie paddled the water, barely keeping her nose above the surface. *God, I'm sorry. I shouldn't have lied. I never should have left Tobie and Cilla.*

A shadow drew her gaze upward. A hand reached into the water, it squeezed her arm and pulled her. *Tobie?* Did he find me?

She blinked the seawater from her eyes and gulped in a deep breath, but it wasn't her adopted father's face she saw but a younger man's. He had a severe expression and stormy gray eyes that bore into her, weighing who she was and judging whether she would be saved or allowed to slip back under the waves. She parted her lips, intending to scream, *Pull me in,* but the words lodged in her throat. He tightened his grip as if to haul her into the boat, but then his eyes widened. Pain seared her leg as sharp jaws clamped down, tearing into the flesh of her thigh. Blood darkened the water.

She jarred awake, sitting up straight. White-hot pain shot through her body. She grasped her leg. The remnants of her dream-turned-nightmare swirled, clouding what was real and what was a figment of her imagination. She was in a bed. There was no shark. But the man with the serious expression who'd held her suspended—he was very real.

A creak sounded outside her door.

Maggie stilled her breathing.

Booted footfalls retreated down the hall, followed by the click of a latch opening and shutting.

She lay in the strange bed and listened around her thunderous beating heart, which pounded in sync with her throbbing leg.

The mysterious Lord Granville was very real indeed.

Chapter 6

Papa claims we are safer now that Britain has claimed the last remaining French-controlled island of Guadeloupe. The French Privateers who've raided our ships will have no place to anchor.
> *~ Entry by Loretta Baxter,*
> *February 6, 1810*

Maggie eased onto her back, careful not to trigger the burning pain in her leg. The lilt of Creole accents drifted in through the open window as men and women headed to the fields. Sunlight streamed into the room past white cotton draperies fluttering in the breeze.

"Yer awake." Dinah sat in a chair pulled next to the bed. Her hands stilled, the needle held in midair, before she pulled a thread through a pair of breeches she mended. "How's da leg dis morn?"

"Better, as long as I don't move." The fitful sleep left her feeling groggy and unrested. She hadn't realized how often she shifted in bed until she couldn't without pain.

Daylight illuminated the quaint room. A colorful quilt lay folded at the foot of the bed. A braided rug decorated the wooden floorboards.

A bureau large enough to hold a selection of gowns stood in the corner. Her stomach fluttered. *Had her mama stored her extra gowns in that very wardrobe?* She'd slept in her mama's childhood home. Granted, not in her mother's chamber or bed, but soon she'd try to explore. If given the choice, she would start in the nursery and schoolroom on the third floor and eventually move to the bedchamber with the room under the stairs. As she'd been carried upstairs last evening, she'd been tempted to plead to be assigned to her mama's room, but even she knew better. It wouldn't be proper for an unmarried woman to reside so near the master's chamber. She must figure a way to learn about her origins. The song her birth mama had taught her as a small child on a deserted island led her here. There must be more clues as to why she left Antigua and the identity of Maggie's papa.

Now if she could just hobble down the hall past three doors to her mama's former bedchamber on the right. Maggie wiggled the toes on her left leg and sucked in a sharp breath. Blast her injury. It would not keep her from her purpose. She needed to learn the truth of her lineage. Without knowing if her birth had been noble or baseborn, she would remain forever stuck between worlds. It didn't matter how hard her parents tried to have her act gently-bred, the question would always remain. Was she illegitimate? Until she could decisively prove the answer, she would remain a burden to those she loved.

Knowing her lineage would direct the course of her future.

Dinah placed her mending back into the basket and rose. "Mind if I tek a look at yer wound? I stitched da skin closed on both sides while you were unconscious yestaday. Da hole looked clean, and da bleeding had stopped, but I want ta change the dressin' and mek sure da cut didn't reopen or become infected."

She nodded, and Dinah folded Maggie's borrowed nightshift in a way to expose the least amount of skin. She untied the bandage, lifted the dressing, and nodded. "It's a good sign dat the skin isn't an angry red. Dat's when I know infection is settin' in."

She eased Maggie onto her side, evaluating the exit wound. "The pellet didn't hit any arteries or bones, just went clean through a bit of muscle." She whistled. "Der are angels watchin' over you. I'm sure of it."

While Dinah reapplied a clean bandage. Maggie stared out the window. In the yard beyond the small walled flower garden, Lord Granville stood beside a mulatto man who must be the overseer. He directed the workers rolling barrels out of the boiling houses. It took several men to maneuver the heavy barrels up a plank onto a cart.

Lord Granville stood with his legs apart and his

hands fisted on his hips. His jacket off, the breeze ruffled his sleeves and plastered his shirt to his muscled back. He pointed toward the windmills and motioned over to the curing house. Another wagon cart stopped, and men unloaded bushels of crushed cane. He greeted them each with a nod as they entered the boiling house, reminding Maggie of the orchestra conductor she'd seen when Tobie had taken her to the opera last year. She'd been awed by the singers' voices and instruments that moved in unison at the queue of one man, who directed them with the slightest gesture. As the conductor was the master of the orchestra, Lord Granville acted as the maestro of Greenview Manor.

Why was she so fascinated with this man? She'd attributed it to him residing in the house where her mother used to live, but her curiosity had only grown after meeting him in person. She'd assumed someone so regimented would be old and set in his ways, but Lord Granville didn't appear as if he'd yet reached thirty. He stalked over to the windmill with young, virile strides, shielded his eyes from the sun, and peered up at the spinning sails. He yelled something to the overseer in a deep baritone voice. She couldn't discern the words, but it brought back the image of his face suspended above hers as she lay on the ground.

Stay with me, he'd commanded. His stormy

eyes had peered down at her with force as if he intended to shock her heart into rhythm. Lord Granville may look younger than he behaved, but in the depths of those gray eyes, she glimpsed an older soul, a survivor—much like herself.

"Until tat muscle heals, yer gonna have a terrible time gettin' around, but as long as you tek it easy, you'll be good as new in no time." Dinah covered her back up with the sheet and chuckled to herself.

Maggie carefully eased into a seated position. "What's so funny?"

She pressed her lips tight. "It's nothin'." She waved. "Nothin' dat needs mentionin'."

Maggie touched the woman's shoulder. "I could use a little levity this morning."

Dinah shook her head, but her smile broke through. "I was just thinkin' about yesterday. Poor thing, when I came in da room, you were hog-tied."

"Hog-tied?" Maggie smiled. "Truly? Did he think I would make a run for it in my injured state?"

Dinah's grin widened. "I think da master knew ta stop da bleedin', but I don't think he knew how ta go about it—proper-like."

Maggie struggled to picture the measured Lord Granville at a loss for what to do, and it welled up laughter that released in an inelegant snort.

"His heart was in da right place." Dinah relaxed

as if she'd found a kindred spirit. She slapped her knee and cackled, "But I've never seen da master so beside himself while you looked like prize-winning game ready to be served on a platter."

Maggie burst out laughing, gripping her hip to keep her leg from shaking.

Spying Maggie's movement, Dinah subdued her own mirth. "Now I'll be in a heap of trouble if ya re-open dat wound on account of me makin' ya laugh. Masta Granville will ring a peel over me if he finds out I told you dis story."

"Never fear." Maggie placed her hand over her heart. "Your story is safe with me." She peered back out the window.

Maggie's smile fell.

The object of their discussion was staring up at them.

Melodious laughter floated down from the second floor. Samuel's gaze snapped to the open guest-chamber window, and a smile twitched his lips at the sweet ringing sound. He exhaled, puffing out his cheeks. Thank heaven, his guest was awake and hale. His muscles tightened. It sounded as if she were having a jolly good time—without him.

Cuffee cleared his throat, awaiting the rest of Samuel's sentence.

Blast. Gossip would be circulating among the staff after yesterday's events, and now here he stood, acting like some besotted fool, gazing up at the window and frowning like a jealous beau. "The heat will be unbearable today. Rotate the men in the boiling house every hour with those in the mill to give the workers some relief."

"Dat's kind of ya." Cuffee removed his hat and bowed his head. "I know dat ya get an earful from da other plantation owners, but da workers are much happier now dat yer in charge and not dat Mr. Fines. I think yer gonna see da workers produce more cause dey respect you. 'Cause you treat dem with dignity."

He nodded his thanks. The conditions in which his father's overseer had run the plantation had been horrifying. Tossing Mr. Fines out on his ear was the first and best decision Samuel had made since arriving in Antigua, even if Mr. Fines stirred up trouble in town for Samuel. He peered back up at the second-floor window. If Fines learned of a woman disputing Samuel's rights to the plantation, what other dissension would the man create?

"Keep the men hard at work. Hardest worker gets to pick out a new pair of shoes for him and his family from Sunday's market." He inhaled the sweet Caribbean air tinged with fresh-crushed cane and boiled molasses. "I won't be joining you in the fields this morning. I have something to tend to in the great house."

Cuffee glanced at the second floor and hooked his thumbs into the waistband of his pants. "You go on and tek yer time. I'll keep everything on schedule fer ya." He backed toward the boiling house. "Don't ya worry."

Samuel strode toward the great house, covering the ground with long strides. His skin tingled, eager to discover how his houseguest fared but wary Cuffee had received the wrong impression of why a woman's laughter rang through the courtyard.

Hawley swung the French door wide as Samuel approached. "Good morning, my lord."

Samuel nodded and strode past him. He scaled the stairs to the second floor two at a time and bounded into his chamber.

Carson jumped to attention with brush in hand. He swept the master's clothes, ridding him of dirt and dust. Samuel washed his face, neck, and hands, and dried with the towel Carson folded and left next to the basin. Behind him, the rhythmic motion of Carson quick-shining Samuel's boots swished.

Female voices drifted down the hall, Dinah's boisterous and Miss Prescott's melodic. He strode toward the sound, rounded the corner to the guest wing, and stopped at Miss Prescott's door. Samuel raised his fist to knock. Should he wake her uncle before visiting? At least his houseguest wasn't the type who slept the day away. Unlike Captain Anthony, whose snores rumbled from behind the door across the way. Their volume rattled a picture hanging on the wall.

In London, it would be inappropriate for Samuel to enter a woman's bedchamber, but they were in Antigua. It was his duty to check on his guests, especially the injured ones. His curiosity had little to do with it. He rapped on the solid wood.

The voices quieted.

Chair legs scraped the floor, and the boards creaked under footfalls. Dinah swung open the door. "Good mornin', milord." She stepped aside.

Miss Prescott sat abed. Waves of long dark hair cascaded over the white pillowcases. A matching pair of long eyelashes blinked but firmly held his gaze, lowering slightly as if taking in his full height and dress. *Curious little house guest.* He couldn't resist pulling back his shoulders and lifting his chest the slightest degree. His father had demanded excellent posture, and it wasn't in his nature to slouch. "I hope you found everything satisfactory?"

Her cheeks held a reddish hue, but whether it was from sleep, a reaction to his comment, or a fever, he couldn't tell. "Indee—" Her voice squeaked, and she cleared her throat. "Forgive me." Her cheeks reddened even more. "Indeed." She glanced at Dinah. "The accommodations and my care have been splendid. I appreciate your hospitality."

He stepped further into the room, but not too far. She was dressed in the same gown she'd worn yesterday, but there was something more intimate about standing near a bed as opposed to the settee upon which she had laid the day before. He leaned against a tall dresser and crossed his arms. "How is your leg?"

"Better today." A shy smile played at the corners of her mouth.

His chest tightened, and he rubbed it. His breakfast of blood sausage with eggs and cream must be giving him indigestion.

"It only hurts when I move." She attempted to sit up further.

He flipped his palm out to still her. "Don't move on my behalf."

She froze, and an awkward silence fell between them.

He'd come here for a reason, but for the life him, he could no longer remember what it was.

Her smile widened, and a lighthearted giggle fluttered past her lips. "Are you ready to start already?"

"Start?" He blinked.

"To seek more information about my mother." Her smile faded at his non-reaction. "You said you'd help. Is it still your intention?"

"Quite right." He pushed off the dresser and paced in front of the bed. "I didn't forget. It has merely been a busy morning, and I figured you wouldn't be up for anything strenuous with your injury. I knocked to see how you were faring"—

he stopped and faced her—"and to ask if there was anything you needed to retrieve in the way of possessions?"

She placed a finger on her bottom lips. "My trunk, but it's still aboard my uncle's ship. I'm certain Anthony will get it for me."

From the wracking snores shaking the picture frames outside the man's room, it may be a while. "If he doesn't, I'll send a footman to retrieve it."

"I appreciate your generosity." Her hand rubbed her thigh.

"My pleasure. Please make yourself at home and take the time you need to heal." Perhaps fewer of the island folks would hear about the incident if she stayed abed. Lord knew Samuel didn't need to blacken his reputation further by harboring an unrelated and unattached female in his home—one that had been shot on his lands. He doubted the magistrate would cast him in a favorable light if he had to retell the story.

"And for letting me stay and learn more about my mother."

His interest peaked. "Have you started reading her journal?"

She closed her eyelids, and her dark eyelashes curled up. "I'm afraid not." Her eyes opened, and her face relaxed on an exhale. "My leg stole my concentration."

He pushed down his guilt.

"I wanted to absorb every word. I daresay . . ."

She winced as she reached for it on the nightstand, but it was beyond her fingertips.

He intervened, handing it to her. The sweet scent of orange blossoms teased his senses.

"Thank you." Her smile appeared again, spreading over white teeth. One incisor on the bottom was a bit crooked, but the imperfection only made her more appealing.

He backed away a step and straightened. Was his nervousness due to the fact that he'd accidentally shot Miss Prescott, or a lingering apprehension of women after Lucy's betrayal?

She clutched the journal to her bosom. "I plan to spend the day pouring over its pages."

"Very good." He removed his pocket watch and inspected the time. Minutes ago, the desire to see his houseguest drove him to abandon his regular schedule. Now he was happy for an excuse to leave. "I'll return this evening to learn what you've discovered, but at the moment, I'm—"

"Headed to the boiling houses." She peeked out the window. "It must be nearing ten o'clock."

"Indeed." Strange. He strode to the door. He had planned to inspect the boiling house, but how did she know that? He stopped and glanced back at her.

Her head bowed, and her fingers reverently ran down the leather cover binding and flipped open the cover page.

She wasn't one of those mind readers, was she?

He didn't believe a wit in that superstitious stuff the workers and islanders put so much stock in.

Maggie glanced up at him, her wide-set eyes filled with questions.

"How did you"—he cleared his throat—"know that I was going to the boiling house?"

Her head tilted. "You are a very routine man," she said in a matter-of-fact tone.

"You've been observing me?" To break into his house and steal from him? Had he been a fool to invite in a stranger?

She lowered her gaze.

Heat rushed through his body. Her careful calculation of watching his every move, invading his privacy, and infiltrating his personal space—uninvited—reached a new high on his disturbance scale.

He gripped the door frame to keep from capitulating to his father's rage. Blind anger had had him banished to Antigua, but he would fight it. He would not become his father. "How long?"

"A week." She peered up at him with solemn eyes. "At first, it was out of curiosity. I wanted to stand where my mother had stood and see the world how she saw it. But you were so fastidious in your comings and goings—disciplined—predictable, it became apparent I could sneak in and retrieve my mama's diary, and you would be none the wiser."

"So predictable. I made it easy—"

"You fascinated me."

"—for a thief . . ." *Wait.* Fascinated?

Her gaze lowered. "My adopted father is also regimented." She peeked from beneath those dark lashes and studied his reaction. "But I could set my watch to your daily routine. You make lists and check them off each night. You alphabetize your bookshelves and color-code your wardrobe." She rolled the bedsheet between two fingers. "I know I've overstepped and invaded your privacy. I'm truly sorry, but I couldn't help but be awed by your tendencies."

Awed? His anger evaporated like the morning dew under the tropical sun. Who was this woman? Thieves didn't typically use words like *fastidious* in their vocabulary. She could read and sounded well-educated.

She held his gaze. "I've never seen the like."

Was this some coy move meant to gain his affections? He'd witnessed women and their wiles before. In hindsight, Lucy had used hers aplenty on him until Harry returned from the West Indies. Miss Prescott didn't seem like the cunning type. In fact, the way she studied him suggested she was more curious than coy. Those wide green eyes searched his expression as if desiring to explore the inner workings of his mind.

He blinked and looked away to shut her out. "Very well then. Enjoy your reading." He patted the door frame and pivoted on his heel. "I will check back later."

Halfway down the hall, the corners of his lips twitched involuntarily.

She found him fascinating.

Chapter 7

Diary, is my life not my own? Papa has informed me I am to be wed to a man I have never met, and he sails for Antigua in under a month.

~ Entry by Loretta Baxter, March 2, 1810

After breaking her fast, Maggie used her hands to move her leg into a more comfortable position. Yesterday, she'd heard Lord Granville say he believed her to be a thief. He wasn't wrong. Technically, she had broken into his house and taken her mother's diary. But wasn't it rightfully hers? Still the guilt unsettled her stomach. How had she turned down such a dark path? She or her uncle could have been killed or sentenced to serve time in an island prison. She didn't even know what sort of punishments were issued on Antigua for thieving. Hanging? Indentured servitude? Loss of a limb? Her morning meal threatened to make a reappearance. Cilla and Tobie would be devastated. How could she do that to them when they'd sacrificed so much for her?

She couldn't fully explain the burning desire to know her lineage. Not in words. Discovering who and what she truly was would justify everything in the end. She'd tried to explain to Cilla the need to know about her parents, but a sadness had shadowed Cilla's eyes. She retold the story of how God had used a storm to toss her and Tobie into the sea and brought them to an island just so they would find her. Their tale always warmed Maggie's heart. She never doubted God and her family loved her, but as a child, Maggie hadn't understood fully how one's past affected one's future.

When she reached a marriageable age, the importance of her birth came to light. If she were legitimate, she would finish boarding school and enter English society with her head held high no matter what Mitchell Trembley's gossipmonger mama whispered. But if she were illegitimate, she would be unmarriable among the upper classes. She'd become a burden to her parents, or she could move to America, where one's background wasn't of consequence. But to do that, she'd be forced to leave her family behind.

Dinah had left to return the dishes to the kitchen and attend to some chores. Uncle Anthony still snored in the room across the hall. Maggie cracked open the cover to her mother's journal and reread the first page.

This diary belongs to Loretta Genevieve Baxter.

Her mother. Maggie had discovered as much by researching passenger logs of ships that had wrecked near the island chain where she'd been discovered around the approximate year of her birth, which her parents figured to be in 1812. Only one ship had listed female passengers. A Mrs. Ethel Moravian, who would have been four and fifty years, and a Miss Loretta Genevieve Baxter, who would have been around eight and ten traveling from Antigua to America—similar in age to Maggie's now. The ship Loretta had sailed upon sank due to a storm in 1811, and Tobie recalled seeing the ship's name, the *Rutherford*, branded into wood remnants of crates that had washed ashore. From Antigua's St. John's parish annals, Maggie discovered that her mother was the only daughter of a wealthy sugar baron, Paul Fredrick Baxter, who resided at Greenview Manor. It verified the song lyrics her birth-mother had taught her. Over the years, more and more stanzas pushed into her memory. At first, only words or phrases surfaced. She wrote them down, and like composing music, a song materialized.

I was born in the land of sugar sweet.
At the spot where John and
   Mary did meet.
Over yon where the wind in the
   mill's sails blow.

"Mama." She whispered as she turned the page. "Who were you? What were you like? Who was or is my father? Let me find the answers here."

Maggie inhaled a steady breath and stared at the neatly looped script.

> I must write my words, for I dare not say them aloud. I have much to be thankful for. The sugar crop has been good this year, and Papa has sent for more fabrics to make into gowns. One dress shall be completed for the upcoming assembly ball and another will be my wedding gown when papa decides whom I shall marry.

Maggie used a finger to mark her place and stared at the ceiling. Her lungs contracted as if out of breath. *This is it.* She would soon find the answers she'd been craving.

> I look forward to the dance. It is the island's biggest event to celebrate the harvest, and planters return from England to be in attendance. The reel is my favorite dance, and I've practiced the steps well.

Maggie fought her eagerness to discover the identity of her father so that she could absorb the insight into her mother's life. She studied each word, hoping to not only read what was on the page but also between the lines straight from her mother's heart. Loretta spoke of the servants as if they were friends, noting when the footman had a toothache or the maid was laid up in bed from a spill on the stairs. She knew at least some

French, for she would substitute sentences for their French translation. And she must have had an artistic side, for she spent pages describing the beauty of a sunset or the color of the ocean waves lapping the sand.

Dinah brought Maggie tea at high noon and a meal at midday. She checked Maggie's bandage on both accounts but left her to read in peace. The hall clock chimed the one o'clock hour as Uncle Anthony strolled into the room, stretching his arms. "If it weren't for the blasted heat, this plantation might actually make island life enjoyable. I slept like a babe." He dropped into the tufted chair, where Dinah usually sat to do her mending, propped his feet up on the small stool, and laced his fingers behind his head. "The sleeping arrangements here are much better than aboard my ship." He peered heavenward. "The men's snores could fill a mainsail and carry us back to England."

"You don't say?" If her uncle recognized the sarcasm in her tone, he didn't comment.

"I shall have to reconsider Lord Granville's kind offer for a continued visit."

She narrowed her gaze. "We are not here to take advantage of his hospitality."

"Yet he hasn't produced a suitable chaperone thus far, now, has he?" He leaned over and plucked a remaining scone from the tray beside the bed. "I can't be having my favorite niece sleeping in an unmarried man's house unchaperoned." He slathered the scone with mango jam, ate a bite, and closed his eyes to savor the delicious sweet bread. "I'd only be extending my stay to uphold your reputation."

"Like you did for the banker's daughter?"

Uncle Anthony choked and pounded his chest with his fist. "Who told you . . . ? How did you hear about that?"

"I do not condone your actions. You're too old to be playing the part of a rogue, and mark me, you are going to find yourself looking down the barrel of her father's gun."

He grumbled and ate another bite of scone. "How's the reading? Find what you were looking for?"

She ran her fingers over the holes left in the cover from the pellets. The damage impeded some of her understanding, but for the most part, she'd been able to fill in the missing or incomplete words. She exhaled a deep sigh. "Not entirely, but I'm getting to know who my mother truly was, and it's stirring up memories. For instance, I think I sat in her lap once and watched the sunset. It's more of a sense of her presence and a haze of colors, but it makes me feel closer to her. I'm ready to read more."

Uncle Anthony swallowed the last bite of scone and rose. "Well then, I'll let you get back to it." He ruffled her hair and strode to the door. "I must check on my crew, but I'll be back before nightfall."

He opened the door just as Dinah entered.

Maggie yawned and rubbed the ache in her thigh. She flipped open her mother's diary.

Dinah approached and reached for the book. "I'm gonna tek dis and set it aside fer now. I can see yer knackered, and its time fer you ta rest. Yer leg needs ta heal."

"It was a small yawn. I'll pull through." She tried to stop Dinah from taking the diary, but the effort increased the throbbing in her leg. "I've only just started to read again."

"And it will be here fer ya wen ya wake." She set it on the nightstand before picking up her mending and resuming her spot in the chair Uncle Anthony had vacated.

Maggie opened her mouth to protest, but Dinah eyed her in a way that clearly stated they'd reached the end of their discussion, so Maggie eased onto her good side and closed her eyelids.

The ocean breeze rustled the curtains and lulled Maggie into a dream. She stood in a tidepool beside a shadowy image of her mother, her dirty gown hiked up on one side so as not to get wet. Mama sang as she pried oysters from off the Mangrove tree's roots and dropped them into a basket. Her voice was as lovely as a freshwater stream.

Maggie inhaled a deep breath and dove under the water. She moved her arms and legs the way her mama had taught her and opened her eyes to search for a moving shell. Saltwater burned and blurred her vision. She heeded her mama's warnings and avoided the red spiny creature. Her lungs compressed, screaming for air, but movement caught her attention.

A conch grazed on algae, pushing its large shell along the sandy bottom.

She scooped it and swam for the surface, exhaling a trail of bubbles. Gasping in a deep breath, she held up the shell. "I got un." She kicked her feet until she could stand in the shallows. "Wook mama, I got un. I got un conch."

She couldn't see her mama's face, but she could feel her mother's smile as bright as the sun. "Very good, mon trésor."

Maggie wiped saltwater from her face and pushed her wet hair from her eyes. She set the conch in the shallow water to play with it until time to eat. Her mama's voice floated over her.

"A plantation built of white gold.
In all the isles, there's no such hold.
Over yon where the sugar doth grow."

Maggie chimed in, repeating what she knew.

"He wood me out in da summer night.
Spoke sweet words ta my heart's d-tight.
Over yon where plants sew."

Maggie's eyes sprung open, and she rolled over in bed, gritting her teeth at the pain.

"Somethin' da matter?" Dinah set her mending aside and half rose.

"I need my satchel." She scanned the room. "Where is it."

Dinah gingerly strode to the wardrobe until her knee joints cracked, and her normal sauntering gait returned. She removed Maggie's bag and handed it to her.

Maggie yanked open the drawstring and pulled out a notebook with a quill pen and ink well. "He wood me out into da summer night." She murmured the words so the abyss, where all dreams disappear, wouldn't steal the memory from her.

She didn't want to drip ink on the bedding, so she pushed her injured leg over the side of the bed.

"Wat do ya tink yer doin'?"

Maggie ignored Dinah and limped over to a small writing desk, wincing with each step.

Dinah rushed over and pulled out the chair. "Ya shouldn't be walkin' on yer leg. You'll re-open da wound." She aided Maggie into a seated position.

"I have to write something down. It will only take a moment."

She flipped to the end of her notes, uncorked the ink, and dipped the quill into the well.

"He wood." Pausing with the pen in midair, she frowned. "Wood isn't right." *But I was only* a child. *He wood me into the summer's night.* "Wooed. He wooed me into the summer's night."

She scribbled the sentence across the page. "My heart's d-tight . . . d-tight." She gasped. "Delight. I bet it was my heart's delight." She wrote the next line in her notes.

Dinah crossed her arms. "Who's dis heart's delight, and why is he wooin' a young woman like yerself inta da night?"

Maggie giggled at the concern lining Dinah's expression. "It's a song my mother used to sing to me. I'm trying to remember it. I was young and didn't quite understand the words." She pressed the end of the quill to her lips. "Over yon where the plants sew."

Dinah chuckled, and her shoulders jiggled. "Plants can't sew."

"Plants." Maggie peered out the window at the men working the field, inspecting their labor. She straightened. "Not plants, planters."

A snort escaped through Dinah's nose. "I've never known a planter ta be good wit a needle and thread."

"Not sewing with a needle but sowing as in planting a field."

"Well now, dat meks more sense." Dinah nodded.

Maggie re-read what she wrote. "He wooed me out in the summer night. Spoke sweet words to my heart's delight. Over yon where planters sow."

"And it rhymes." Dinah placed a hand on her hip. "How does da rest go?"

She set the quill down and leaned back in the chair. "That's the problem. I only remember bits and pieces. I have the first and second stanza and now a third, but there's more. Something about Papa and too great to pay . . . cross and cane . . . underneath the stair she hid her pain." She held up her index finger. "Which is where I found her diary."

Dinah's voice changed to an awe-filled whisper. "It's like one of dem riddles." She circled a finger. "Let me hear da whole of it. Mayba I can help."

Maggie sang what she knew.

"I was born in the land of sugar sweet.
At the spot where John and
   Mary did meet.
Over yon where the wind in
   the mill's sails blow.

A plantation built of white gold.
In all the isles, there's no such hold.
Over yon where the sugar doth grow."

Dinah joined in the last known stanza with a harmony.

"He wooed me out into da summer night.
Spoke sweet words ta my heart's delight.
Over yon where the planters sow."

"Well, I'll be." Dinah shifted to meet Maggie's eyes. "Yer mama was singin' about here. Da land of sugar sweet is da islands. Wind in mill's sail's blow—she's talkin' 'bout windmills, and dere ain't another island dat has more windmill den Antigua."

"That's what I figured, too, but who do you think John and Mary could be?"

Dinah paced the length of the room.

Maggie murmured the line once more, "At the spot where John and Mary did meet."

"Dat's it." A large smile grew across Dinah's face. "Antigua is divided inta six parishes, and Greenview Manor is close ta da boundary line of St. John's and St. Mary's. Dey meet at da top of da north field over by da church."

"That confirms it." Maggie clasped her hands to her breast. "My mother is Loretta Baxter. She must have taught me this song to lead me to Greenview Manor and her diary hidden in the room beneath the stairs." Maggie once more stared out the window. Her mama had attempted to pass down her legacy the only way she could to a toddler—through song.

The sun hovered just above the horizon. Where had the day gone? But, though her leg throbbed, Maggie wasn't disappointed, for they'd accomplished much. She should return to the bed, but she needed another moment to ponder in wonder. Her mother'd had the foresight to use song to teach her young daughter so that she would stand a chance of remembering it. If only Maggie had known it held clues to her heritage, she would have worked harder and earlier to remember the words and decipher their meaning.

She ran her fingers over the now dry ink of the lyrics she'd jotted down. Soon she'd understand her past, and it would unlock her future.

Chapter 8

I know two things about the man whom my father arranged for me to marry: he is well-inlaid and holds a fierce temper. I'm supposed to pray for his safety, but I find myself praying for his ship to be delayed.
~ *Entry by Loretta Baxter,*
April 4, 1810

A mongoose scurried across the path, a racer snake dangling from its mouth. Samuel's horse reared, balking at the creatures. He leaned forward and loosened the reins, regaining control by turning his horse in a half-circle. "Whoa. Easy, boy."

The creature darted into the cane field to enjoy its feast.

Samuel whispered encouragement to his steed and patted its neck to calm it. This had been another trying day. A bead of sweat ran down the curve of his lower back, and he wiped another from his brow. Streaks of grime lined his forearm and probably crossed his forehead. His skin itched with the dried salt of his sweat.

Cuffee's hawks circled above the north field, likely looking to make a meal of the black rats that had been spotted gnawing at the cane and killing the precious shoots.

Samuel inhaled the scent of fresh cut cane, using the break to enjoy the view from partway up the peaks of the Shekerley Mountains. From a distance, all stood calm in Greenview's fields, but it was the little pests that attacked without ceasing, eating away at the profits of his labor.

Tree frogs had already begun chirping as the cooler, humid air settled in for the night. The sun hung on the horizon where the island dipped into the bay, coloring the fields in a green-golden light, similar to the color of Miss Prescott's eyes. The day's events had taken a turn as he was called to settle a dispute among the field workers and an issue of a leak in the boiling house cauldron, which had spilled molasses. He'd never returned to check upon Miss Prescott's condition or learn if she'd discovered any information from Loretta Baxter's journal. When he passed by the great house earlier, he'd heard women singing. It seemed to emanate from the second-floor window. The women carrying bundles of cane heard it, too, and slowed to listen. The melodious sound held a lovely quality as if sung by a courtesan. Miss Prescott must not have been suffering unduly from her injury, which helped ease his guilt for not checking on her wellbeing. She was in good hands with Dinah. At least, that was what he told himself.

Although he hadn't been able to discern their words, the rich sound reminded him of a nightingale's song, much like the one that sang the evening his father had asked him to join him in surveying their lands. He spurred his horse past the north field boundary marker as memories surfaced.

Samuel had ridden tall beside his father past thatched-roof cottages and tenants who stood at attention and removed their hats or bowed. The muscles in Samuel's legs and stomach tightened for he didn't dare fall out of step after witnessing his father unload his temper upon his steward. Already his thighs and back ached. His father slowed to a stop and pointed to a boundary marker beyond the fields of English barley. "See that?"

Samuel leaned forward on his mount, eyeing the ground in the direction his father pointed.

"No, boy. Look up." He held out both his hands with his arms widespread. "Do you see this?"

The evening light glowed brightly over the heads of grain. Waves of the golden crop stretched into the valley below. "Yes, Papa."

A rare smile spread over his father's lips. "All of this shall be yours one day."

Samuel's breath had caught. As the firstborn son, he would inherit Ywain Manor and its lands.

Until that moment, at the young age of seven, the grand scale and magnitude of his birthright hadn't hit him in full. His skin had tingled with the rush of potential. He'd be fair to his tenants and earn their respect. God would bless him and expand his territory because he'd be a generous landowner.

Samuel would make his father proud.

His father's smile flattened into a grim line. "From this day forward, you will bear the weight and responsibility upon your shoulders so that, when I die, you will be ready to seize control."

Samuel's mare danced beneath him as if sensing his fear. His father watched him, judging his response. Samuel tightened the reins and controlled his horse before he gave his father reason to burst into another one of his fiery, uncontrolled tirades that sent witnesses fleeing for safety. "I will do you proud, Papa." No one would work harder to ensure Ywain Manor prospered. That night changed Samuel into a man, and he strove to work as hard as it took to achieve the desired result.

And one slip had lost it all.

He spurred his horse toward the great house to meet Cuffee for their nightly assessment.

He wouldn't allow for another.

The dwindling light blurred the pages of her mother's diary.

Dinah had left to help with the evening meal and would bring Maggie a tray as soon as it was ready.

Maggie's backside ached from sitting for such a long period and her muscles, unaccustomed to a life of repose, screamed to move about. She set aside the book and eased her legs over the edge of the bed. Her injury protested but didn't throb as it had earlier. Perhaps that was a good sign it was healing. Careful not to apply pressure on her wounded leg, she stood, leaning heavily on the other. She gripped the bedside table for support and pushed off it, hobbling to the window. Fresh air filled her lungs, a blend of salty ocean and sweet molasses drifting from the boiling house. The sun had begun to set, casting long palm tree shadows down the lane.

Lord Granville would be returning from his nightly ride soon.

Right on schedule, he appeared, walking his steed toward the stables. He paused and stared off in the distance. She leaned further out the window to glimpse what he saw.

A red-orange sun shimmered on the horizon, splashing its vivid color upon the waves in the distance. It hung there for a suspended moment, and Maggie caught her breath as if seeing God's hand hold it in place. Rays of orange light sprayed upward, turning the scattered clouds a bright pink before the sun yawned a deep breath and retired for the night.

While his horse munched the grass, Lord Granville remained frozen as if in awe.

Maggie's palms tingled as they had the time she'd snuck out of bed to watch her parents' party from the landing with her face pressed against the railing spindles. This was a version of the estate's owner that she hadn't witnessed. For all his discipline, regimented regulation, and logical authority, it appeared Samuel Granville had a sensitive, romantic side—one that stopped to admire a sunset.

The sun dipped below the horizon, and twilight settled over the island. Lord Granville strode with smooth, long strides to the stables, his horse in tow.

Her heart twisted. Even with his calculated plans and preparations, and despite the self-assuredness with which he carried himself, he seemed . . . lonely. As if he, too, were a misfit, much like herself. He merely hadn't realized it yet. She stared out her window until the sky changed from orange to purple. The stars appeared, and the chorus of tree frogs, crickets, and cicadas clamored to be heard.

She hobbled back to the bed and touched her mother's diary. Soon she'd know to whom and where she belonged, but why would a man who knew his lineage and had lands and people who respected him, seem lost? What had brought him to Antigua when most planters were returning to their homelands? What had driven him to revive Greenview Manor to its former glory when other Englishmen were abandoning their properties?

The room darkened, and she turned up the lantern on the side table. Her stomach growled for the evening meal. Her family had eaten at country hours, but Lord Granville operated somewhere between country and city hours.

A knock sounded.

Dinah balanced a tray in one hand as she pushed open the door and stood aside.

Lord Granville's frame filled the doorway. He'd changed into his evening attire—a dark jacket and trousers with a white cravat. Gone was the relaxed manner in which he'd enjoyed the sunset just outside her window. A formal, polite, and well-respected man stood in her presence. "Might I join you for supper?"

All the proper training, studying of Debrett's, and the coy rules for how a gently-bred lady should accept an invitation flashed through her mind, but she quickly dismissed the formal rules. She wanted to see more of the man who'd admired the sunset, and her injury had sapped her strength for the drudgery of proprieties and protocols. "Please do." She gestured to a seat nearby. "As long as you don't mind my being casual."

He hesitated as if uncertain of expectations. Goodness, what if he found her words to be too forward? Had she already embarrassed herself? She sighed and smiled at how ridiculous she must seem. It was probably too late to redeem her respectability after being shot from a tree.

Dinah unfolded the legs of the tray and situated it upon Maggie's lap as Lord Granville sat. A footman set his tray on the table, snapped the folded napkin, and draped it over his lordship's lap. Lord Granville rested his elbows on the armrests and studied her down his straight, Grecian nose.

A smile tugged the corners of her lips. His intense scrutiny touched her nerves and ignited such a need to laugh that she had to bite the inside of her cheek to contain her giggles. A distraction often helped. She inhaled a deep breath filled with the tangy spice of pepperpot stew. Beef, dumplings, and okra floated in the thick broth. Her mouth watered.

"Please go ahead and eat." He smoothed wrinkles from his napkin and set the tray on his lap. He straightened his utensils into perfect parallel lines before selecting the soup spoon. Stirring three times, he let it briefly cool and sipped a taste. Without being called, the footman rushed over carrying the salt-seller. Lord Granville used the salt-ladle to pinch three dashes into the soup, stirred three additional times, and sipped again. He nodded, and the footman backed against the wall.

Cilla would have been impressed by his manners. She was forever instructing Maggie not to dive into her food once the blessing was completed. "Will you bless the food, or shall I?"

He blinked and cleared his throat. "Forgive me. I've grown too accustomed to eating alone in my study." He bowed his head and closed his eyes, "Dearest Lord God Almighty, creator of the heavens and earth, bless Thy bounty to the nourishment of our bodies, and we beseech Thee to bestow your favor upon the harvest. Amen."

"Amen." She hadn't expected such a flowery prayer. He undoubtedly would have found hers simple and straight to the point, but she'd always been that way with God. Since God could read her innermost thoughts, there didn't seem a reason to put on pretenses.

Lord Granville scooped the steaming soup away from him, letting it rest in the spoon to cool instead of blowing off the steam.

She picked up her utensil. "You said you generally eat alone?"

"Indeed." He swallowed a bite of the stew. "Unless I'm invited to dine with some of the planters and their wives. I find eating while working to be efficient."

"I would find it lonesome. Dining is quite an event in my household. My mother and father insist we eat as a family, but I have two younger siblings, Sophia, who is six years of age, and Michael, who is three. They are always getting me to laugh with their antics." She chuckled to stave off the homesickness. "Michael detests Brussels sprouts. He once stashed them into the table's center pedestal so he wouldn't have to eat them. It took weeks for the maids to discover where the awful smell was coming from." She laughed and shook her head. "But it was nothing like the time he used Uncle Anthony's pint of dark ale to stash the others."

The barest hint of a smile formed on Lord Granville's mouth, emphasizing the squareness of his jaw and the firm sensuality of his lips, but he continued to assess her as if determining whether she spoke the truth.

"Uncle Anthony downed the pint and choked on a sprout, spitting it across the room." She giggled, holding her leg to keep it from shaking.

A snort escaped Lord Granville's nose, but he pinched his lips tight, keeping his smile in check.

She gained control of her mirth and tilted her head. Her mouth ached from smiling so wide. "You don't laugh often, do you?"

He didn't answer, but the sparkle in his eyes dimmed.

"I beg your pardon, that was rude of me."

She'd spoken out of turn. "Cilla is forever telling me to consider my words before I speak them."

"Have you adapted to island cuisine?" He changed the subject. With his spoon, he dunked an okra slice into the broth.

"Quite." Her food remained untouched. She'd been so carried away with the conversation, she had forgotten her hunger. "But I think it is in my blood because it turns out my Mama listed some of her favorite meals in the diary, and they are also some of mine." She ate a bite without allowing it to cool. Tears pricked the back of her lids, and she drank a gulp of lemonade to cool the burn.

He eyed her above his napkin and wiped his mouth before spreading the cloth neatly back in his lap.

So much for a casual dining experience. "Do you have any siblings?"

He sipped from his drink and set it down before speaking. "One brother."

"How lovely. Are you of a similar age? I always wondered what it would be like to have a sibling close in age. Someone to talk to, attend balls or soirees together, exchange books or gowns, that sort of thing."

"I'm five years Bradlee's senior."

She flashed him a smile. "I'm certain you are a splendid big brother."

His expression remained stoic, but his eyes darkened. Tension built as silence settled between them. Maggie focused on her stew, not about to let his high-in-the-instep arrogance ruin her meal.

He buttered his bread. "How did your reading go? Did you learn anything definitive about your family?"

She swallowed a bite of okra. At the opportunity to speak about her mother and all she'd learned, the food in her stomach rolled. She set her spoon down and pushed the bowl farther back on the tray so she could lean forward. "I discovered my mother was a wonderful woman. She loved the island and its inhabitants, and she especially enjoyed the island's sunsets, writing lengthy descriptions regarding them."

"Island sunsets are a sight to witness."

Should she mention that she'd seen him admiring one?

She bit the inside of her lip. Best to keep that to herself until she understood him better. "My mother was also fascinated with England's upper classes, a debutant's coming out before the king, and dancing at balls. Alas, she never had an opportunity to visit her homeland."

"Nothing concrete?"

Her mouth dropped at such bluntness, and she had to force it closed. And to think, she was the one forced to attend finishing school—well, almost. Did he fear she planned to dispute his rights to the plantation? Why else would he use the words definitive and concrete?

"That was in bad form." He scratched the peak of his hairline. "It appears I'm rusty in exchanging pleasant conversation. I daresay it has to do with working day and night to ensure this plantation produces. Please, do continue."

"I must reassure you, I'm here only to discover my lineage. I've learned from a young age not to worry about material things. God provides all that I need."

"Indeed." Lord Granville nodded but continued to critically assess her. A long pause built into an awkward silence, until his gaze slid to her mother's diary on the bedside table.

Concrete discoveries. "I learned that my mother was her parents' only surviving child. My grandmother died in childbirth, and my grandfather tried to remarry, but his second wife died in a storm at sea in route to Antigua from England. They had no other living relatives."

"That is consistent with what my father said. He was gifted the land by a dying friend who had no other living relatives. Was there any information to tie your birth to Miss Baxter?"

"What information do you mean?"

He shrugged. "Like the mention of your birth or the name Maggie Baxter? Or would it be Margaret?"

"It could be anything."

His spoon stopped midway to his lips. "Like Madalene?"

"No, I mean any name. My adopted parents gave me the name Maggie, Maggie Prescott. I don't have a middle name."

His straight brows dipped, slanting toward the bridge of his nose.

The footman removed her unattended tray.

"I bet you have several names." One thing Debrett's taught her was that most of the peerage had not only multiple names but also multiple titles.

"Lord Samuel Fredrick Harcourt Granville, son of the Earl of Cardon."

"Of course." Inappropriate laughter welled, and she didn't bother to restrain it.

"You mock my title?" He half rose, but the tray blocked his movement. The footman swooped, removing his tray.

She shook both hands to stay him. "My apologies. It merely struck me as funny how different our lives are. While your name is your legacy and reputation, and might I add a mouthful, mine is simple and arbitrary—just Maggie. You see why learning even the slightest bit of information about who I am and where I came from is so important?"

He rested back in his chair, his eyes awash in confusion and something else. Sympathy? She stopped guessing before reading the obvious conclusion she was tired of witnessing when people looked at her—pity.

"I beg yer pardon." Dinah stirred in the far corner. "I don't mean ta interrupt, but tell his lordship about da song. I believe tat might just be yer proof."

Samuel's gaze snapped to the healer. A song? What proof? What did it prove?

"Quite right, my mama's song." A light melodic giggle floated from Miss Prescott.

He struggled to keep his pulse at its regular tempo. Miss Prescott's presence threw his life and normal functioning out of synchrony. Her propensity toward laughter set him off-kilter. Only on rare occasions had he ever heard his mother or father laugh. His brother Bradlee had a hearty guffaw but primarily displayed in front of friends, not so much his family. Bradlee steered clear of father's critical eye and escaped the worst of their father's admonitions as a second-born son. The lilt of Miss Prescott's laughter flipped his stomach and left him craving more—but unsure how to draw it from her.

"A song my mother must have taught me while we were stranded on the island is coming back to me a few stanzas at a time. At first, I didn't understand what it meant, but with Dinah's help, we believe my mother created it to teach me about her and her life, like a riddle."

A warm glow lit her eyes and heightened the color in her cheeks.

He crossed his ankle over his knee and laced his fingers over his chest. "Please, do me the honor."

Her gaze lowered, and her hair slid forward like a curtain. She swept it back over her shoulder and looked past him out the window, where the stars had begun to twinkle in the night sky. She sang with beautiful clarity. Her rich tone rippled a current under his skin and lifted the fine hair on his arms. Her breast heaved as she poured her heart into the song, and her eyes glazed over as if lost in a memory.

The words warmed him like a hot spring, bubbling up images in his mind of windmills, sugarcane fields, and summer nights such as this. She sang of Antigua. Of that, he knew with certainty.

The last note hung in the air. The song ended unfinished, like following the smell of baked sweetbreads but finding the oven empty.

Dinah clapped, and Miss Prescott sank back into the pillows behind her as if having exhausted her energy.

"You have a remarkable singing voice."

"You are too kind." Her eyes sparkled. "I've had little formal training except what Tobie taught me. As a captain, he sang sea ditties mostly. Cilla can't carry a tune, so I was tasked to sing my younger siblings to sleep at night." Her face shone with love for her younger brother and sister. "Tobie purchased tickets to a musical at Covenant Garden, and I was enthralled, but the chords of one song sounded familiar. I'd heard the tune before. After that night, I'd wake remembering lines from a song my birth mother taught me. Initially, I brushed it off, but it became a reoccurring dream. I'd be digging in the sand with a woman I knew was my mama, and she'd be singing. I started writing the words down because what was so vivid in my dream would quickly fade once I woke." She exhaled a sigh so deep it squeezed air from his lungs. "It's the song that led me to Antigua. I just wish I could remember the entirety of it."

"You will." The determination in his tone shocked him. Did he want her to learn the truth? As long as it didn't draw into question his ownership of Greenview Manor. He rose and moved to stand beside her bed. It was past time he retired for the evening. "We can discuss your dreams and their meanings more tomorrow."

"It's not a dream." Her wide eyes pleaded for understanding. "It's a memory."

He placed his hand over hers. It bordered on what was acceptable, but it was far better than what he desired to do. He itched to run his fingers through her silken locks, trace the smooth angle of her jawline, feel the softness of her lips. "Tomorrow." He withdrew his hand. "Tonight, it's best for you to rest. Perhaps more will be revealed while you slumber."

Why was he encouraging her? What had he been thinking, offering his help? Especially if her revelation called into question his future?

Chapter 9

French privateers still raid our ships despite British control of the Leeward Islands. Papa grumbles under his breath about those blasted Bonaparte frogs but insists I maintain my French lessons.
~ *Entry by Loretta Baxter,*
April 4, 1810

The following evening, Maggie sat upon the bed in her mother's room. She'd had the footman carry her there since her leg still hurt too badly to bear her full weight. It only seemed fair to see the room in which her mother transcribed the diary. Dinah joined her, and Maggie pointed out things referenced in her mother's journal. "It says here that she spilt her watercolor palette and paints on the floorboards but hid the discoloration under the rug."

Dinah rolled up the far side of the rug, and sure enough, faded stains of blues, yellows, greens, and red had sunk into the woodgrain.

"It doesn't sound like my mother was much of an artist even though she longed to be. She complains that even the best colourman couldn't tint paints bright enough to compare to the color of an Antiguan sunset."

As Dinah returned the rug to its rightful position, Maggie beckoned her to her side. "Oh, and listen to this." She tapped the page with her index finger and read, "'I finished reading Gulliver's Travels and enjoyed it very much.'" Maggie peeked up from the diary. "I saw that book on the shelf earlier."

Lord Granville passed on his way to the guest room with two footmen in tow carrying trays with their evening meal. He stopped at the sound of her voice, and the footman maneuvered as not to crash the tray into his master. "What are you doing in here?" Lord Granville poked his head in the doorway. "Was something wrong with your accommodations?"

Maggie grinned and waved him in. "Join us." She spread her arms wide. "This is the room where my mother slept, played, and wrote her diary."

He scanned the space as if seeing it for the first time.

She gestured to the window and its faded flora chintz curtains. "She wrote about staring out this window and seeing boats in the bay." Maggie sat up straighter and motioned for Dinah to flip back the rug. "And look. She was trying to paint the scene from her window one rainy day and accidentally knocked over the easel and palette onto the floor."

He strode closer and leaned over to inspect the stains.

Her fingers slid around his hand. "See this."

His gaze met hers and held for a moment, crackling the air. Did he understand her excitement? Did he know what it meant to her to be connected to her mother's life even if it was only reading about her and standing in the same spots she'd once stood?

"There's a silver coin wedged in between the bed and the bureau." She pointed to the sliver of silver between the boards. "It fell out of her reticule and rolled into the crack. The more she tried to pry it out, the deeper it wedged. And do you know what my mother wrote?"

One side of his mouth lifted in a crooked smile. "What did she write?"

"C'est la vie. It's French for 'such is life.'" She laughed and squeezed his hand. "She'd figured it was safe there, and she'd know where it was if there ever was an emergency." Maggie inhaled, winded by the excitement.

He eyed her. "Such an occasion must not have risen if it's still there."

"That's not the point. The thing is that I would have reacted the same way."

Lines folded the middle of his brow. "You'd disregard the coin's value that easily?"

She shook her head. "I'd consider my abilities and resources, and if there were nothing to be done at the moment, I wouldn't fret about it. There are worst disasters than a stuck coin, especially when you know where it is and that it's not going anywhere."

The wrinkles in his forehead eased.

"Don't you see?" She squeezed his hand again. "I'm like her. I'm not odd."

"Who said you were odd?" He glanced at their clasped hands before meeting her gaze. His gray eyes darkened, and his Adam's apple bobbed.

She released his hand as heat rushed into her cheeks. Hadn't he found her forwardness odd? Most others would. "No one of consequence." Just the young men and women in whose circles she ran. The peerage kept rules for everything, and now she regretted not learning such ridiculousness. He must think her a pea goose for in her excitement, she hadn't realized she'd taken his hand nor that she'd held it for so long.

He reached into his pocket and removed a small knife. Wedging it under the coin, he pressed. A muscle flexed in his jaw as he exerted pressure. The silver piece dislodged, shooting straight up. Lord Granville snatched it out of the air with his free hand.

Maggie gasped.

He shifted to face her with the slightest upturn curving one side of his mouth. He held the silver coin out.

"Oh no, I couldn't take it. It's your house, and you are now the rightful owner. Besides, you've been generous enough already."

He slid the knife back into his pocket. "I think she would have wanted you to have it." He gripped Maggie's wrist and gently turned her palm up. The brush of his thumb on the sensitive underside sent tingles coursing up her arm.

He dropped it into her hand.

She stared at the silver piece her mother had once owned. Did his words mean that he believed her? She still had no indication of who her father might have been, but the way Samuel regarded her made her feel as if her legitimacy wasn't in question.

"What did you mean by odd?" he asked.

She eased her leg over and scooted up so that he could sit at the foot of the bed.

He sat but kept his gaze firmly locked on hers, demanding answers with the arch of his brow.

"Perhaps different would have been a better word." She ran her fingers down a lock of her hair and absently braided the end. "I'm not like other women my age." She sighed. "While genteel ladies fuss over the latest fashion trends, how to perfectly execute flirtations with their fans, and the financial worth of every gentleman of the peerage, I couldn't have been less interested."

"Truly?"

Was the surprised look on his face genuine or mocking? "If my gown was a bit wrinkled or my hairpins slipped, I wouldn't rush to my lady's maid declaring the night a disaster. I found it silly for a footman or maid to follow me about carrying my items and dressing me like a doll every hour. It's ridiculous." She leaned forward for extra emphasis. "Did you know that the average woman during the season changes her gown at least five times a day? And that each change in wardrobe takes over an hour? That's a tremendous amount of time wasted. Not to mention that they rarely wear the same gown more than once. It's a frivolous squander. Maybe real life isn't always scavenging for food, but it's certainly not changing from a morning dress, to a riding habit, to a day dress, to a formal gown."

"You remember the island?"

"The one where we were deserted was much smaller than Antigua but had some freshwater run-off."

The footman cleared his throat, reminding them that their dinner trays were growing cold.

Lord Granville instructed him to bring in another chair so he could continue his discussion with Miss Prescott. The footman returned with a low-back chair and set it beside the bed. While they dined, Maggie spoke of what she could remember from the island, how Tobie and Cilla rescued her and taught her to speak, sing, and dance until a ship arrived and brought them to England.

He spared his sliced mango and root vegetables from drowning in the gravy seeping over the mutton slice. "Your parents, Mr. and Mrs. Prescott, they let you sail with your uncle to learn about your birth parents?"

The bite of root vegetables soured in her mouth, but she swallowed it. "Not exactly."

"What do you mean?"

She lowered her gaze and pushed her least favorite vegetable into the gravy to mask the taste. Her cheeks heated, and her fingertips numbed. Should she tell him the truth? Lie again to save face? Her gut twisted, and bile rose in her throat. She was so close to learning her heritage. Would she jeopardize everything she'd set out to discover? They'd come so far. What if he tossed her out on her ear? How dreadful to have to leave and not be here to find the stains and coins her mother left behind. Would she be relinquishing clues about her father's identity?

He waited for her to speak, his eyes softening, coaxing her to confess. The lies needed to stop. This whole mess had started with a falsehood told to her parents. She might be able to justify her actions to herself. But upon reconsideration, she could see how these events could be mistaken for housebreaking, even if the stolen item was technically hers. Lord Granville already extended her mercy, but would he continue to do so after learning her recklessness wasn't a momentary lack of judgement but premeditated? She lifted her chin, ready to face his contempt at her actions.

• • •

Samuel marveled at the brave and independent beauty before him. Despite having endured so much, she'd held onto optimism and hope. He was fascinated by her spirit. She was sure enough to climb a tree and leap onto his roof to obtain a diary. She didn't cower in his presence, as some did, nor did she vie to win his favor. Instead, she'd reached for his hand out of excitement and held it as if he were a cherished friend. Maggie Prescott was comfortable in her own skin, and he felt drawn to her ease and enthusiasm.

He'd meticulously worked hard at everything not to disappoint his father, his peers, and even himself. Yet, Miss Prescott didn't care a wit about appearances. She hadn't so much as asked for a spare gown or for Dinah to do her hair. She hadn't requested a looking glass or an opportunity to freshen up before he entered the room as Lucy always had. Miss Prescott didn't need to. Her natural beauty magnified an inner joy that radiated outward. She marveled over every discovery about her mother, and seeing her happiness eroded the weariness of his day. He was drawn to her with a craving he hadn't known he had until the dish was set before him.

Something, however, was upsetting her. His question regarding her adoptive parents changed her demeanor. Uncertainty teetered in her expression. Her gaze jumped from the bedspread to her hands to the floor and back again. Whereas, only moments before, her eyes had shone bright with love whenever she spoke of her adoptive parents and siblings, now they seemed dull and frightened.

"Where do they think you sailed?"

Her green eyes turned to liquid remorse. "They don't know I sailed," she blurted. "They believe I'm at finishing school." Her shoulders slumped as if no longer burdened by a heavy weight. "I'm supposed to be learning how to better fit amid the quality and gentry. My disregard for proper etiquette has caused them concern."

Stifling a snort of laughter, he sympathized with her parents, regarding not only her lack of propriety, but how Miss Prescott must have been a handful.

Need he point out the holes in her plan? "Wouldn't the headmistress notice and report your absence?"

She combed her fingers through the ends of her hair, undoing the prior loose braid. "I sort of sent my lady's maid in my stead."

He rubbed his hand across his lower jaw to hide his shock. "They wouldn't recognize that she's not you? Has the headmistress never seen you?"

"I was beginning my first of two years training, and I'm adopted, so the school wouldn't expect me to resemble my parents."

"How did that work?" He couldn't imagine a

maid impersonating a lady. "She knows enough to impersonate you?"

"Well, I was sent there to learn etiquette." Her fingers combed faster. "I know it's not common practice, but she and I are of a similar age and were fast friends, so I taught her to read and do sums. It only seemed fair. She couldn't help her social status, and there wasn't much differentiating us except that an upstanding family had rescued me. She was happy to attend finishing school, for she longed to be something other than merely a lady's maid. With her learning, she might be able to advance to being a governess or a lady's companion."

He scratched his head, unable to stop his mind from running through various scenarios for weak points in her plan. "Wouldn't your parents expect letters or want to visit?"

"I wrote out five months' worth of letters in advance." She shrugged a shoulder. "Ruth posts one per week."

He snorted a chuckle, amazed by her ingenuity—or evil genius.

"And I plan to return to England before holiday." A telling quaver entered her voice. "Which is why I must work fast to learn everything, or I'll be found out, and my parents will be terribly disappointed in me."

His letter. A chill froze the blood in his veins. Egad, he'd posted a letter to her parents informing them of the shooting incident and instructing them not to worry.

"You look stricken." Her eyebrows crinkled. "You're thinking I'm wretched for disobeying. I shouldn't have betrayed their trust."

He cleared his throat. "It's merely indigestion."

"It's too late. It's done. I'm already here." She gripped the diary to her chest. "I never meant to disappoint them."

He had to stop the letter before the ship sailed. Setting aside his tray, he rose with one fist pounding his chest. "Cook has a quick remedy for it. I'll be but a moment." He strode from the room with the footman in tow carrying his tray.

Once out of earshot, he rounded on his footman. "The missive I gave you to post the other night. Did you?"

John nodded. "I brought it to da postmasta yestaday mornin' cuz his office was closed da night before by da time I'd gotten dere."

"Run and wake the postmaster on my behalf. Tell him I must know if that letter has sailed or not. If it hasn't, retrieve the letter and bring it back." He patted the footman on the back. "And do hurry."

The plate rattled on the tray as John dashed down the stairs.

Samuel rubbed his face with both hands. If that letter had already left for England, he would suffer from indigestion for the next several months. Should he tell Miss Prescott? They were still on tentative ground, considering she'd broken into his home—and he'd shot her out of a tree.

Her easy smile surfaced in his mind. He'd not upset her needlessly. What were the odds that the ship had left port that day?

Decided, he turned back toward the room where her mother had slept but stopped at the stairway to the attic. He'd stored some trunks that had once been in that room. They should still be there. Could they give her more insight into her birth mother's life? Would she act as awestruck as she had with the coin?

Could he make her eyes flash again as if he'd conjured magic?

He retrieved the oil lamp from his chamber and strode up the attic stairs. The trapped heat of the day hit him like a solid wall. He could already hear Carson's sigh when he spied dust and cobwebs on his master's clothing. Samuel could have rung for a servant, but he didn't want to share the glory if he located the trunk.

A broken bureau sat in one corner with a rusted birdcage on top. Several old rugs had been rolled and stuffed under the attic ridge, and chests were stacked in the other. He ducked his head under a beam and held the lantern closer to the trunks, looking for the carved heart engraving he remembered from the trunk in that room. He found it, of course, on the bottom and set the lamp down to remove the top two compartments, setting them aside in another stack. With his handkerchief, he wiped off the dust and lifted the lid.

A faint lavender scent still lingered within the ruffles and lace. He closed the trunk and lifted it, hooking his pinky finger through the top ring of the oil lamp, and cautiously picked his way down the stairs. His smile grew, thinking of Miss Prescott's reaction. Did she always approach life with such exuberance or only in regard to her lineage?

Why did it matter to him?

He rounded the corner and kicked the attic door closed with his boot.

Dinah and Miss Prescott stopped their conversation as he entered the room. The beaming smile Miss Prescott met him with tripped his step. Her wide eyes flittered over the trunk before once again meeting his gaze.

Dinah rushed over and took the lamp from his fingers. "Wat have you brought from da attic?"

He set it on the side of the bed and cracked open the lid. "I came across these while searching for some old ledgers a while back."

Miss Prescott scooted closer, craning her neck to peek around his arm.

The hinges creaked as he flipped the top open.

Her pink lips parted, and her fingers covered her mouth. "Are these . . . ?" Her gaze searched his for answers.

He shrugged. "I can't be certain, but the gowns are too nice to have been a maid's, and there's no indication that your grandfather"—if they truly were related—"remarried."

"They're my mother's." She spoke in a reverent whisper. Her hand reached to touch the fabric and retracted. "May I?"

He pinched back a grin. "Of course."

She lifted some sort of lace overlay gown slightly yellowed from age and held it up to admire the cut.

"Lordy." Dinah moved closer. "Dat sure is lovely."

Miss Prescott couldn't hold the gown up to see it in its entirety from her seated position, so Dinah draped it over her.

Miss Prescott's eyes became glassy. "It's beautiful, and it looks as if it might fit. Perhaps she was a bit taller, but we would have been close in size." She blinked away tears as she met his gaze, and his heart thrummed a wild beat. "This is why I had to come." She ran her fingers over the fabric. "Not knowing my past feels like living in a house without a foundation. One doesn't know how long the structure will hold or what will cause it to come crashing down. Everything I learn is like setting footings and stones to build the ground formation." She licked her lips. "Thank you for showing me this."

He bowed his head. "There's more in there."

"Truly?" She leaned forward.

Dinah selected a silky green gown with layers of those ruffly-looking things. Samuel squeezed his eyes closed. What did the ladies call those things? Flu . . . no . . . flounces. He chuckled at the impractical waste of fabric.

"They don't look as if they've ever been worn." Miss Prescott inspected the flounced dress while Dinah held up another made of muslin so pale he couldn't tell whether it was off-white or pink. Dinah lay it over the headboard and picked another. This plain-cut cotton dress showed signs of wear—a bit of grass stained the hem, a tiny blot of what resembled berry juice on the cuff—but it had a colorful sash that belted around the waist in a blend of vivid oranges, reds, pinks, yellows, and light indigo.

Miss Prescott gasped. "This must have been her favorite because she wore it often." She fingered the belt. "It's the colors of an Antiguan sunset. Oh, how she loved sunsets."

Samuel leaned against the bureau and crossed his arms. "Has your uncle returned with your trunks? I haven't seen him, but Hawley informed me he returned last night to sleep. Rather on the late side."

A pink flush stained her cheeks. "He was a bit

detained." She waved a hand. "Managing a ship's crew can be quite a chore. Unfortunately, he forgot my trunk, but he did promise to retrieve them tomorrow."

"I see." What he saw was that Captain Anthony Middleton was a sluggard. "If these gowns fit you, then I'll have the staff freshen them up."

Her whole face lit like the morning sun. "Truly?"

Something popped inside his chest. He gave her used clothing that only held sentimental value, and she acted as though he'd gifted her emeralds. He'd purchased a sapphire bracelet for Lucy worth more than his thoroughbred horse, and although she'd immediately donned it, he'd only received a polite kiss on the cheek and a perfunctory thank-you.

"I noticed you didn't wear shoes. See if there are any slippers or boots in the trunk. If not or they don't fit, I'll purchase you some from the shoemaker in town tomorrow."

"I have shoes." She peered up at him with all honesty. "I merely left them under a bush."

He hadn't meant to embarrass her by his comment, thankfully, she didn't appear phased. More than half of the islanders didn't own a pair of shoes or walked around without them.

"I shall leave you two to explore the remaining contents." He nodded to Dinah. "Please see that the dresses are cleaned and pressed."

Dinah curtsied. "Right away, milord."

He bowed to Miss Prescott. "Good night, Miss Prescott."

"Good night, Lord Granville."

Her infectious smile curved the corners of his lips. Tomorrow, he'd buy her a fine pair of slippers, and it would be worth every shilling merely to witness her reaction.

Chapter 10

News arrived that Napoleon has wed an Austrian princess by the name of Marie Louise. While the princess and I are of a similar age, I'm encouraged that at least my betrothed is not so advanced in age as Bonaparte.

~ Entry by Loretta Baxter, June 20, 1810

The following morning, Samuel mounted his horse and held her steady as he addressed Cuffee. The sun heated his back, warm for this time of day. Undoubtedly it would be a scorcher.

He nodded toward the mill. "Better to get as much of the hard labor done while it's still cool. Make certain those cane bundles are crushed, and then meet me in town for supplies. Bring the cart because we're running low on fertilizer. If the wind doesn't pick up, then yoke the bull. Let's not let any of those bundles start to ferment."

Cuffee tipped his wide-brim hat and set off toward the mill.

With a click of his tongue, Samuel's horse broke into a gallop toward Old Road, where he steered his steed toward the oceanside route. John had returned last night with news that his letter to

Miss Prescott's parents had already sailed with a ship bound for England. A tightness dwelled in Samuel's chest, and he rolled his shoulder to ease it. Since he was out this way, he'd visit with the postmaster himself to confirm.

The interior roads might have been shorter, but the coastal winds along the bayside offered a cooler, more pleasurable ride. He'd pay a call to the Kellys and ride the rest of the way into town with George. He glimpsed Middleton's ship anchored in the quay. Not much activity on board this morning. Samuel had woken to the stumbling footsteps of Middleton creeping up the main stairs at Greenview Manor an hour past midnight. Samuel and Hawley had cornered the captain, believing him to be an intruder. "I thought you were sleeping on your ship."

"I remembered you saying something about a chaperone." Middleton's breath reeked of rum. "I figured it'd be best if I stayed." He grasped the door of the chamber in which he'd previously slept and cracked it open. "Fer my niece's reputation and all." He pointed an index finger in Samuel's direction. "Although I don't have to worry about the little mite much. Her papa taught her how to wield a knife like the best of 'em." He slipped into the room and shut the door.

Samuel held the lamp higher to see Hawley's expression. He had appeared as annoyed as Samuel. Hawley murmured something about turncoats who associated with the ne'er-do-well French and set off to bed.

By Jove, it had been one o'clock in the morning. If Samuel had wanted to ravish Miss Prescott, he would have had ample time. Fortunately for Miss Prescott and her uncle, he was a gentleman. He shook his head at the memory.

A passing islander dipped his hat, and Samuel returned the gesture. Some guardian Middleton was. The first thing Samuel had done when he woke this morning was to add, *seek chaperone for Miss Prescott,* to his list. Three full days had passed since Miss Prescott fell into his life, and he was overdue to find a proper companion for his houseguest, but issues in the fields had kept him from heading into town.

Samuel rode his horse along the scalloped white beaches as gulls screeched their staccatos overhead. He spied a nest of newly hatched sea turtles paddling their flippers through the sand to get to the ocean and slowed his horse. The hovering gulls picked off many, but a few determined baby turtles made it to the surf and freedom. A small crystal wave swept up one of the tiny creatures and pulled him deeper. In the shimmering sunlight off the water, Samuel caught the shadow of a tiny head pop out and take a breath before heading on his journey into the deep blue waters.

Palm branches rustled as the wind picked

up. He'd toured the continent after finishing university, but nothing compared to the savage beauty of Antigua. The island was wild and carefree, yet he harnessed the wind to crush the cane and fought to make the land produce, to once again squeeze a profit out of the white gold. Harry would someday know Samuel Granville was more than his title. He'd revive the land Harry believed to be a vile waste, and Lucy would regret jilting him. He'd be the one sea turtle who persisted and pulled through, surviving to show English high society and the crown that he was the better man.

Spying the stone marker of the plantation owned by George Kelly, Samuel turned his horse up the lane. George and his wife, Theadosia, sat out front sipping lemonade, and from the looks of it, enjoying each other's company. Every time Samuel witnessed the love George and Thea held for one another, envy struck a chord in his heart. Samuel's parents respected one another but never acted in an outwardly loving way. He'd longed for a marriage like the Kellys', but as he'd courted Miss Lucy Tilly, he'd realized he didn't know how to go about creating one.

"Good morning, Samuel." Thea rose and waved.

An image of Miss Prescott entered his mind. If Maggie were Thea and he were George, Maggie, spying him returning from the field, would wave from the porch with her sunny grin. The ocean wind would billow her skirts and whip her long tresses about her face. He'd step onto the porch and scoop her into his arms. She'd bubble with laughter, and he'd tip her back to claim her mouth, kissing the smile off her lips.

Samuel jolted and mentally shook himself. He dipped the brim of his hat. "Morning to you, Mrs. Kelly."

"You well know that you can call me Thea." She planted her hands on her ample hips.

She reminded him every time. At first he'd refrained from using her first name for the sake of propriety. Now, he called her Mrs. Kelly just to get a rise out of her.

Samuel dismounted and joined them. Setting one foot on the stair, he leaned against the rail.

"Would you care for some lemonade? Shall I ring for another glass?" Red spirals of hair danced about her tanned and freckled face.

"Another time, perhaps." He removed his hat and held it to his chest.

George rose. "Are you on your way to the assembly?"

He shook his head. "No, I only plan to be in Antigua for a couple of growing seasons. I'd prefer to avoid island politics." He cleared his throat. "I do have a question, and I was hoping Mrs. Kelly could help with an answer."

"Me?" She glanced at George and raised her eyebrows before turning back to Samuel and straightening. "Well now, how may I help you?"

"I was hoping you could recommend a chaperone."

"A chaperone?" Her expression lit. "Is there a romantic interest visiting? If so, I absolutely must meet her."

"Not exactly."

"A relative?"

"No."

Her brows snapped together. "Then why are you in need of a chaperone?"

"I have an injured woman staying with me."

"Injured? How so?"

Samuel scratched behind his ear. "I sort of shot her out of a tree."

Both George and Thea's heads jerked back.

"You what?" Thea stared at him.

"How did you . . . ? *Why* did you . . . ?" George couldn't seem to finish his sentence.

He gestured for Samuel to pull up a chair and tell the whole the story. They all sat, and Samuel explained the situation as they listened with rapt attention.

"Poor thing." Thea twisted a loose curl about her index finger. "You say she broke in to discover information regarding her mama?"

George shifted in his seat. "I remember old man Baxter—ornery fellow. I'd heard he had a daughter but turned bitter after she was gone. I'd assumed she'd died of the fever, not from a shipwreck."

He rubbed his hand down his beard, and his expression grew troubled. "What does that mean for you? Has she found anything conclusive?"

"Not yet." If George so quickly understood the implications of questioning ownership of his land, other islanders were likely to infer the same. All the more reason to quickly get to the bottom of whether Miss Prescott held any claim to Greenview Manor. "I know I can trust you to stay quiet on the matter. I don't need island gossip to get out of hand."

They both nodded as a clock chimed somewhere inside the house.

"Gracious." George set his empty glass down. "I'm going to be late for the assembly." He rose.

Samuel followed, but Thea stopped him with a hand. "I bet Widow Morgan would be happy to chaperone, and it might help her get past her grief to care for someone."

"Splendid idea." Samuel thanked her and mounted his horse.

A groom walked George's mount over and held it for him. George pecked a kiss on his wife's cheek and pulled her into his embrace. Samuel turned his head to give them a moment of privacy, and when he dared to look back, George had released his wife but slid his hand down her arm, giving her hand one final squeeze. Samuel circled his horse in place while he waited for George to finish his farewell.

George kicked a leg over his saddle and blew his wife another kiss. His horse whinnied and trotted forward as if aware of his preoccupied master.

Samuel maneuvered his horse so that George didn't ride straight into him.

"Sam." Thea was the only person who called him such. "You're welcome to join us for the noon meal."

"You are most kind, but I must postpone for another time."

"Next week then." Thea didn't take no for an answer. She was half Irish, half African from the island of Monserrat, and claimed the stubbornness came from the Irish half.

He nodded his consent.

George chuckled. "She'll hunt you down and force you to take an occasional break from your work now and then."

He'd tried to get the Kellys to understand his reasoning for needing to work and revive the plantation, but they insisted he take time to relax. He'd rest when Greenview's profits allowed him to return to England. Better to change the subject. "Fill me in on what has transpired this week and during the last meeting."

George's expression grew serious as they cantered down the lane. "Word from England is that Parliament will pass the bill to free all slaves on the homeland and on the islands. Some of us feel like we should get on top of it and pass our own regulation so that it will be a smoother transition when the decree comes down.

"Langham's wholeheartedly against that." Samuel turned his horse toward St. John's.

George followed alongside. "Fines and your neighbor, Hennion, too."

"They're merely voting to discuss the matter tonight?"

"That's correct."

"Surely these men aren't threatened by entertaining a discussion?"

George exhaled a long breath filled with exasperation. "We could use someone with a level head in our midst." His expression begged for Samuel to come. "It will be mostly over by the time we arrive. You can just raise a hand or not and be on your way." He held Samuel's gaze. "What do you say?"

The Kellys had been very generous to him since he arrived on the island. He owed it to his friend. "I still believe it's best to stay out of these things, but"—he sighed—"fine. I'll go."

"Huzzah!" George pumped his fist over his head.

They crested the hill and gained a view of St. John's Cathedral's spires and the masts of ships docked in St. John's Bay down near Red Cliffe Quay. The closer they traveled to town, the busier the streets turned. Oxen pulled loads of barrels or wares toward the docks. Donkeys hee-hawed, weighed down with heavy packs. African children chased each other across the street, giggling and yelling in thick accents. A buzz roared from the market, but Samuel continued on past rows of colorful shopfronts. At the wrought-iron gates of the courthouse, they dismounted and tied their horses to a hitching post. Samuel followed George through the center arch of the stone entryway, into the lobby, and upstairs.

In the assembly room, the meeting had already started when they entered from the back. Sticks propped open the windows to allow for a cross breeze. Eleven men of the plantocracy sat with their arms folded as a minister stood next to the lead council and spoke. "Gentlemen, we are merely asking to open a discussion."

Grumbles murmured from half the room.

Mr. Fines, an eastern planter from St. Philips and overseer, slammed his fist against his palm. "What is there to discuss? Freeing slaves will drive sugar prices higher than London is willing to pay. Many of us are already in debt due to the last drought."

More murmurs followed.

The minister raised both hands, quieting them. "London and American abolitionists are threatening to boycott our sugar products if we continue to use slave labor."

"They'll reconsider when they're drinking

plain tea and don't have any confections to serve for desserts." Fines's voice rose to a shout. "If we free our slaves, they'll refuse to work. We'd be ruined, and the whole island would be ruined too."

Rumors hinted that England's House of Lords had used Samuel's punishment as a warning for all the entitled young bucks of the aristocracy. The stipulation for him to return to his life was that Greenview must turn a profit and his reputation must become impeccable. His father agreed, threatening to pass his inheritance to his brother, Bradlee. Greenview Manor held his only hope. Could freeing slaves send everyone into debt? Would it ruin his chance? Those landowners who couldn't pack up and leave, would they end up facing starvation? Would he? His workers were in his care. He hadn't asked for this responsibility, but he must see to their wellbeing nonetheless.

"All we're asking for is to open it up for debate." The minister held his palms out. "Antigua won't be ruined over a discussion. We're talking about people made in God's image, people who have rights. Freedoms can be given in steps."

Cuffee, Carson, and Dinah, although slaves, were people Samuel had come to respect. He may own the land and assume the risks and rewards of whether it failed or prospered, but he couldn't do anything without them. He'd seen firsthand how much harder they worked with a bit of incentive. Perhaps they'd work harder if they were paid wages or a percentage produced. The cost per barrel would go up, but if there were more barrels, the extra cost would even out as long as demand remained.

"We've already been told to offer slaves religious education and recognize their marriages as Christian unions." Fines shook his fist as if ready to battle the minister. "We had them start honoring the Sabbath, and they retaliated for our kindness by burning our cane fields."

Samuel's jaw clenched.

An islander Samuel hadn't met stood and raised his voice. "The assembly closed the Sunday market, and you know as well as I that they misrepresented scripture to say slaves weren't keeping the Sabbath holy. The market isn't only for slaves to barter for food and things they needed. It's a crucial social interaction for them. Those acts by the assembly doomed Antigua to unrest."

"Unless we keep them in line," Fines said, his voice rising a pitch, "they'll burn our fields and kill us in our sleep."

A gavel strike pounded. The head council brought the room back to order. "Sit down, Mr. Carver and Mr. Fines."

"Without any rights, they have no other

recourse." The minister held his palms out. "If we offer them a voice—a vote—a say in matters—"

"Votes!" Langham thundered. "You're asking to make them equals?"

"All I'm saying is that there is a peaceful solution, but if we don't open it up for debate, then there will continue to be unrest."

Langham rose. "Is that a threat?"

The head council's gavel pounded again on the wooden podium.

Sweat trickled down Samuel's lower back as the upper chamber heated.

The room quieted, and to Samuel's surprise, George stood. "I believe our worries are unfounded. Our island is small. Other than our sugar plantations, there are limited means for employment. Our slaves aren't going to prefer starvation over work. If we are fair and just and provide them enough to put food on their tables, they will willingly continue to work for their survival and the island's."

A cacophony of rumbles of agreement and grunts of disapproval filled the room.

"Enough talk." The head council clapped the lid of his pocket watch closed. "It's time to vote." He peered around the room. "For those of you willing to entertain further discussion about emancipating slaves, show your hand."

Fines and Langham shifted in their seats to scan the room.

Six of the thirteen planters raised their hands, including George.

Langham and Fines eyed Samuel, their look clearly demanding he side with them.

Samuel's heart pounded. It came down to his vote. He hadn't wanted to get involved, yet here he sat as the tie-breaker, still weighing his decision. The only way to return to England with any dignity was to fill his coffers, but he held the weight of responsibility to those he housed, fed, and employed. What would his vote mean for the worker whose child ran and hugged him after returning from a hard day's work. How wretched it must have felt to have been uprooted from his homeland and sent here to an island. At least Samuel had had a property and clothes on his back. He'd understood the language. These were people. God's children, as the minister had stated. Made in God's image.

"Are all the votes in?"

By not involving himself, he was choosing a side in which his heart couldn't find rest. Samuel raised his hand and held it high.

Langham's head jerked back as if discovering Brutus with a bloodied knife in Caesar's back.

Fines hit Samuel with a long, icy stare.

George leaned in and whispered, "I do believe we've made some enemies."

"Seven to six brings a vote in front of the assembly, further discussion it is." The councilor dropped the gavel, and men rose from their seats amid loud grumbling from the dissenters. "We'll reconvene in one month after discussions for the official vote on emancipation."

George nudged him. "I think it best to make a hasty exit."

One glance at Langham and Samuel agreed. They left the same way they'd entered.

Standing under the stone arches of the front entrance amid the hustle of the street, George clapped him on the arm. "Thank you for taking a stand in there."

"So much for staying out of island politics." Samuel forced a shaky smile.

"Thea will be proud of your decision. I bet she'll even make your favorite tarts when you join us for supper." George's expression grew solemn. "I'm afraid you made some adversaries today."

"I just hope it doesn't hurt sugar profits." Samuel sighed. All he did was vote to continue a discussion. Certainly, that wouldn't cause harm. He tipped his hat to his friend. "I must be off to see to my real reason for coming into town."

Langham exited the courthouse arguing with the head council.

George nodded toward the magistrate. "Keep your wits about you. We may have upset the wrong people."

Chapter 11

Dearest Diary, I found my father perusing your pages, so I've taken to hiding this logging of my private innermost thoughts under the floorboard in the room under the stairs.

~ Entry by Loretta Baxter, June 21, 1810

Maggie wobbled on one leg as she peered into the mirror. Her mother's walking dress of Indian muslin with appliquéd lace adorned at the hem, bosom, and sleeves fit her perfectly except for a two-inch alteration to lift the hem. She stared at her reflection and tilted her head. Had her mama looked like her? Perhaps there was a portrait or miniature of her somewhere in the house. She must ask Hawley and hope he's in a better mood and not railing about Napoleon Bonaparte.

"Ya look lovely, Miss Prescott." Dinah whistled.

Would Samuel think so? Maggie blushed. She shouldn't entertain such thoughts until she discovered the truth of her lineage. Then she could discern for whom it was appropriate for her to set her cap.

"And look how it fits, like it was made fer ya." She swished the material back and forth. The pale gown, although of the finest quality, lacked something. Her green eyes glowed in contrast with the white muslin.

Personality.

She yanked the vibrant scarf off the bed and tied her hair back with an oversized bow. A smile swept across her lips. "You're right. It suits me."

Dinah bent down and stuck pins into the hem. "Hold still now. I don't want ta stick ya by accident. Dis will just tek a minute."

Maggie ran her hands down the sides. Something crinkled. She felt for a pocket and located one among the dress folds. She slid her hand in and removed a yellowed piece of paper. She unfolded it and held it up to read.

Ma tres chere Loretta,

She gasped. The note had been written to her mother—*my dearest Loretta.*

Could this be from Maggie's father?

Her mouth opened, but words wouldn't come. She'd read the last page of her mother's diary today. Although it alluded to her wanting to marry and her papa's preferences for a family alliance, nothing confirmed Maggie's lineage. Did this letter hold the answer? Her free hand felt around for Dinah, crouching and holding pins in her mouth. Her fingers connected with springy hair.

Dinah peeked up and murmured something with the pins still between her teeth.

"Dinah." She held out the worn paper. "Look what I found in the dress pocket. It's a letter to my mother."

She removed the pins from her lips. "I'll be. Who's it from?"

Maggie flipped over the page and skipped to the signature. She reread it. "I don't know. It's written in French." She concentrated on the translation. *De tout mon coeur, Ton Loup.* "With all my heart, signed, Your Wolf?" Wolf? She snorted. Her French was rusty. *Wait.* She heard Miss Fitch, her governess's voice teaching a lesson on France. Wasn't mon loup or my wolf a male term of endearment? She gripped the letter with both hands. Her stomach somersaulted as she met Dinah's curious gaze.

"I think it's a love letter."

Samuel slid the wrapped bundle of slippers into his saddle bag, but didn't mount his horse, needing to check his list of tasks. His impulse purchase of a lady's walking cane wouldn't fit, so he'd have to ride with it tucked under his arm. He should have had Cuffee take it with him in the wagon, but Samuel didn't want to miss Maggie's look of surprise. She'd been delighted by receiving the coin from the floorboards and overjoyed by some musty gowns from the attic that held sentimental value. He couldn't shake the longing to see those green eyes light up. And the mere thought of her easy smile shining for him bubbled his insides like boiling molasses.

Samuel whistled an island tune he'd heard the workers sing in the field and pulled out his task list. He'd spoken with Thea & George—*check*—confirmed with the postmaster—*check*—loaded Cuffee up with lime for the fields—*check*—met with Widow Morgan, who agreed to stay with them as a chaperone until Maggie's leg healed—*check*.

Maggie. When had he begun to use her given name? He hadn't received permission, but now that he knew her better, calling her Miss Prescott seemed too formal. Maggie suited a vivacious, unconventional, and free-spirited woman. The tingling bells of her laughter rang in his ears. *C'est la vie. It's French for "such is life."* She'd taken his hand and squeezed it as if it were the most natural thing in the world to do. His hand tingled where her fingers had touched. *Don't you see? If I'm like my mother, then I'm not odd.*

He ground his teeth. If someone dared to call Maggie odd in his presence, he'd . . . His neck burned hotter than the island sun in July. He shook his hands to keep his temper in check. He wouldn't be drawing anyone's cork, because he refused to become like his father. Not anymore, at least. He was in control, and if some greenhorn didn't see Maggie's natural beauty both inside and out, then it was that fool's loss.

Samuel snapped the drooped list straight. Widow Morgan would be joining them in two days because she'd promised to visit her sister, which meant he needed to convince Maggie's uncle to stay for two more nights. Middleton was a cad, returning at absurdly late hours smelling like a distillery. Why the British Navy set him in charge was beyond Samuel's comprehension.

Boisterous laughter erupted from the tavern across the way—only sluggards drank at midday. One voice shouted above the others, followed by more laughter, confirming Middleton was where Samuel figured he'd find him. *Speaking of sluggards and cads . . .*

Better to ask Middleton to remain at Greenview Manor now instead of waiting until the wee hours of the morning when he stumbled in as drunk as a wheelbarrow. Samuel waited for a wagon to pass and crossed the street to the *Black Parrot Tavern*.

The sickly-sweet scent of stale rum hit Samuel before he pushed the door open. Voices silenced, and he could feel wary gazes on him even though his eyes hadn't adjusted to the dim room. The stench of unwashed males mixed with pungent spirits and clung to the humid air.

Chair legs scraped across the wooden floor, and he turned his head.

"Lord Granville." The volume of Captain Middleton's voice proved him already half-sprung. "Fancy seein' you here."

Samuel recognized Middleton's outline as the man gripped his arm and led him over to his table.

"A glass of yer finest kill devil for my generous host," he shouted to the tavern owner.

Samuel had opened his mouth to decline when the shadows came into focus, and Mr. Fines's grimace stared at him from the adjacent chair.

Middleton clapped Samuel on the back and sat. "I was just talking to Fines here about my niece's search for her parents."

Fines's lips compressed into a sinister line. "Indeed, but I must beg your leave." He nodded to Middleton. "Enjoy your stay in Antigua. I appreciate your answering my inquiries. I do hope your niece finds the information she seeks." He pinned Samuel with an ominous glare.

Samuel's throat tightened. The question about whether he'd made an enemy of Fines today was answered.

Sliding a few coins onto the table, Fines rose and strode from the tavern. He recoiled slightly from the bright sun as he exited, donning his hat for shade.

"Fines seems like a good enough bloke, but something tells me the man could be a rapscallion." Middleton swigged from his half-empty glass. "I'd keep an eye on him if I were you."

The tips of Samuel's ears burned. "Yet you

willingly offered him information regarding your niece."

"Mags?" Middleton swatted his hand. "She's a good girl with a quick mind. She wouldn't have anything to do with the likes of Fines." He leaned on his elbow. "Is that jealousy I hear? Mayhap it's you I need to keep an eye on."

The burning sensation spread to Samuel's cheeks. He lowered his voice so the other customers couldn't hear. "How do you plan to accomplish such a task when you arrive at two in the morning and sleep until noon?"

Middleton straightened. "I don't see you keeping your word to provide my niece with a proper chaperone. Need I remind you that she's in this condition because of you."

The *Black Parrot's* patrons passed curious glances at Samuel. "I've located a chaperone, and need I remind you, Miss Prescott is injured . . ." He emphasized the last word so that listening ears couldn't confuse what kind of "condition" Miss Prescott was in. He didn't need any black marks to his reputation in Antigua. The only way back into the peerages' good graces was to prove himself capable and above reproach. "Because the two of you were trespassing where you shouldn't have been."

Middleton's grip tightened on his glass, and a muscle twitched in his jaw. He stared Samuel down for a long moment before bursting into laughter.

Samuel shifted in his seat. What was so confoundedly funny?

The captain tossed back the rest of his drink as the tavern owner set new glasses in front of them. "Granville, you are bang up to the mark." He raised both hands as if in surrender. "From now on, I shall take my duenna duties seriously and return by eleven."

"Dusk."

His grin fell. "Dusk it is then." He tapped his fingernails on the glass. "When does the chaperone arrive?"

"The day after tomorrow."

Middleton rubbed the lower half of his face. His gaze flicked to the far corner of the room, and he mumbled what sounded like a mild curse. Samuel twisted around to glimpse a banker partaking of his noontime meal and scowling at the captain above his paper. Middleton swallowed another gulp of his grog.

Samuel narrowed his eyes on Middleton. "Why are you here—in Antigua? It's hard to believe a slip of a woman convinced a captain to use his leave time to sail her across the Atlantic unbeknownst to her parents to discover her lineage." He lowered his voice. "What is your intent?"

Middleton met Samuel's glare and pounded

his fist on the table, spilling rum over the rim of Samuel's cup. "God's truth, she's my niece." He leaned in closer. "She's a sweet girl and as innocent as a lamb, but she's also a survivor. Maggie has the street smarts of a Sunday market huckster."

Middleton leaned back, raising a finger. "She thinks she convinced me to come by promising to put in a good word for me with a rich and lovely young widow who'll be in mourning until Christmas. Maggie knows the woman from church and has helped with her children's parties. Although the widow Simmons is enticing, that's not what got me to sail Maggie here. Truth is, I've had a soft spot for the little mite since my brother-in-law carried her into the War Office. Mags was as thin as a switch with wide eyes that encompassed half her face. Even though she was a scrawny thing with broken English, she demanded in front of a British lieutenant to see Cil-a—my sister, Priscilla. Maggie's tougher than she looks. It's what makes her a survivor."

Middleton cupped his glass in both hands but didn't drink. Instead, his eyes took on a far-away look. "Maggie may not find much information regarding her lineage, but I'm surprised by what she's discovered already. Determining the full truth and her father's identity will be more challenging and may confirm our fears that she's . . ."

Middleton didn't have to finish the sentence.

A bi-blow. An illegitimate child. Base born. Beneath him.

Muscles tensed throughout Samuel's body. Was the truth better left unknown? Unless there was enough proof Miss Baxter married a proper gentleman, to society, Maggie would be considered a woman of ill-repute and relegated to the fringes. His own parents would eschew her as ill-suited.

A year ago, he might have felt the same, but circumstances and the island had humbled him. He deserved being cast aside due to not controlling his temper, but she'd done nothing to warrant being cast out other than being born and surviving.

"I understand why it means so much to her." Middleton's face sagged with a haggard expression, and he lowered his voice. "Her parents don't comprehend her desire to know her lineage the way I do. Everything I have is because I'm the firstborn son of a naval lieutenant. I'm a wretched screwup and a coward. I don't deserve the honor of captain. I acquired the position because of my father."

He paled as if pained by the admission. "Maggie's been through a lot, and not merely from being deserted on an island as a small child. My sister puts on a good front and has forced society to accept Maggie by her connections.

Ladies of enormous consequences like the Duchess of Linton have offered their influential support for her coming out, but when it comes to marriage, few are willing to risk their bloodlines being seen as tainted."

He sipped from his glass. "It's most obvious at the local dance assemblies when no one will ask Maggie to dance. I'm dragged to these hideous events to step in as a dance partner for my niece so she doesn't become a wallflower. It's agonizing to watch the hope in her eyes dim." His fingers curled into fists.

Samuel's grip tightened on his pant leg.

"She loves to dance and is quite good at it, but her only partners, other than her dance instructor, have been her father and me. It takes all my energy not to walk over to one of those undeserving young bucks and plant a good facer."

He could relate to Middleton's frustration, the desire for justice and turning to fisticuffs. However, drawing Harry's cork didn't land Samuel the justice he'd been seeking. Quite the opposite.

Middleton exhaled and flattened his palms on the table. "I'll do everything in my power to help her discover the truth, even sail during my leave to some godforsaken island."

Samuel grimaced. Everything in his power? "How is getting foxed in a tavern helping Maggie?"

"At least they serve good rum." Middleton stood, walked over to a man sitting near the bar, and waved Samuel over. "There are two things taverns are great for—good grog and local gossip." He clapped the man on the back. "Right, ol' chap?"

The man raised his glass. By his weathered skin and fine-tailored but worn clothing, Samuel guessed he'd worked as a plantation overseer.

Middleton rested his elbow on the bar. "Tell my friend here what you told me about Miss Loretta Baxter."

The man swiveled on his stool and cast his gaze to the ceiling. "Miss Baxter, now she was a good soul and as beautiful as an island sunrise. Her light shone just as bright too."

Maggie's sunny face and eyes, glowing with delight, floated through Samuel's mind. She sounded like her mother, and if being joy-filled was odd, then he'd take odd any day.

"Until her papa snuffed it out."

Chapter 12

Try as hard as I might, I cannot retrieve my half-pence. My attempts merely wedge it deeper into the crack. I shall not fret over the stuck coin for at least I shall know where to find it.

~ *Entry by Loretta Baxter, June 26, 1810*

Samuel returned to the Greenview Manor later than anticipated. After meeting with Cuffee and inspecting the boiling house repairs, he scrambled to make up for lost time. He checked his watch as Carson knotted his cravat. It was time for the evening meal.

"Please hold still, milord." Carson started again on the proper knot.

He couldn't wait any longer. Already, he'd have to wait until after supper to present Maggie with his purchases. He stepped back and, to Carson's horror, yanked out the cravat and unbuttoned the top button. "I believe I'll dress casually this evening."

Carson's mouth opened and closed like a fish's. "Y-yes, certainly, milord." He draped the tie over his arm.

"For a change." He patted Carson on the

shoulder. "Nothing to concern yourself over." He pointed to the cane and package lying on the bed. "Have a footman bring these over once we've finished eating."

"Yes, milord." Carson stared as if Samuel had grown horns.

Samuel left his jacket still hanging and rolled his sleeves.

The footmen holding trays from the kitchen entered, and Samuel followed them to Miss Loretta Baxter's old room. They set the trays on a side table and moved to the perimeter, affording him a view of a stunning beauty in repose.

Maggie sat propped up against the pillows. Her dark tresses were pulled back with an overly large bow that framed her face in a vibrant array of colors. Fine French muslin fabric trimmed with lace displayed her womanly curves in a way her prior loose-fitted dress hadn't.

A playful smile spread across her lips and illuminated her face.

Samuel leaned against the door frame, unable to move, for his knees had turned to water.

"You look different." Her lighthearted giggle rippled the air. "It suits you."

Miraculously, his knees solidified, and he pushed off the door jamb and crossed his arms over his chest, hoping to appear nonchalant. He nodded at her. "The gown suits you too. Quite lovely, I might add."

The color in her cheeks heightened.

He dared to test his legs and strode to the nearest chair, but his gaze kept straying to Maggie. *You have no future with someone of such precarious lineage. What are you doing?*

She eased her injured leg over the side of the bed and stood, hopping to the set of chairs.

Samuel rushed to her side. "There's no need to get up."

"Don't be silly. I'm going to sit and dine with you."

He cupped her elbow and provided a steady arm to lean her weight upon. "Need I remind you that you are an invalid who is recovering from being shot in the leg."

"Have I warned you I make a wretched patient?" She flashed him a jaunty smile before spoiling the effect with a wince.

They settled into the set of chairs, and a footman placed a small table between them. Another footman lifted the canteen lid. The smell of coconut soup wafted under Samuel's nose.

There was no harm in enjoying the company of a lovely woman. Nothing untoward would happen. Didn't he deserve a moment of happiness? Especially after all he'd been through with Lucy? Why should he feel guilty when he'd worked himself to the bone, every day, to squeeze a profit from this sugar plantation?

Hadn't he earned a respite? Besides, a good host attended to his guests. It couldn't be helped that his houseguest turned out to be a lovely woman.

Maggie leaned over the soup and inhaled. "It smells delicious." Folding her hands, she bowed her head.

He jolted and quickly did the same, fumbling through a formal prayer.

She picked up her spoon. "Of course, the night I decide to dress properly, you'd choose to be casual."

"I was running a tad behind schedule."

"You, running late?" She raised her brows. "Has the Caribbean Sea frozen over?"

He chuckled at her sarcasm. "I can be a bit exacting when it comes to time." He stirred his soup thrice around, and the footman held out the salt-seller. Samuel dished out a pinch and swirled it in with three quick rounds. Maggie studied him across the table. He resisted the urge to feel his chin for stubble. Did she like what she saw? He should have taken time for a quick shave.

She tasted a spoonful of spiced soup. "I was starting to wonder if you'd be joining me for the evening meal or if you'd become otherwise engaged."

Never. The unequivocal thought jarred him. He ate a bite, stalling to sort through his thoughts. "I enjoy your company very much. Dining with you has become a routine."

She gulped as if the soup tasted sour.

He'd just paid her a high compliment. Why then did she wince?

"Oh." She wiped her face with her napkin and sat up straighter. "You wouldn't believe what I found in this very dress."

Though her words invited him to regard her gown and figure, Samuel forced his gaze to remain on her face.

She twisted, lifting her hip to reach into the side pocket.

Her womanly curves tightened the muscles in his midsection, so he bounced his gaze to the ceiling.

She removed a piece of folded paper. "There was a love note for my mother in French. My father could have written it, but it was signed with the nickname, *ton loup*."

His spoon stopped halfway to his lips. "Your wolf?"

Her face lit. "You speak French?"

"*Je parle un peu.* A little, but I'm afraid I'm rather rusty."

She held out the letter. "Would you please confirm my translation?"

He unfolded it and stared at the slanted script.

Maggie pointed to a notebook on the writing desk, and the footman handed it to her. She opened the cover. "Here it goes . . .

My Dearest Loretta,

I pray you may deeply believe in my love when you read this, for the pang of your absence is too great for me to bear. I count the days until I may again look upon your lovely countenance."

Maggie glanced up as if to gauge his reaction. His eyes locked on hers, and her throat convulsed before she peered back down at the page. A strange sense of rolling thunder rumbled deep in his chest. He'd never experienced such pangs around Lucy. It had to be the letter. The Frenchman was adept at conveying his sentiments.

She cleared her throat.

I shall not be persuaded to end my pursuit of you. You are my own heart, and the moment we part, it is ripped from my chest. I have been in acute torment since my departure. I beg you to gratify my wishes. Think of me with every breath, and may you too be filled with secret longing. May we both impatiently await my return, and may God speed the wind in the sails of my ship. A fortnight is an eternity. Meet me at dusk the day you spy my mast pulling into port. I spoke no falsehood. I hold the letter in my breast pocket close to my heart. I shall remain true to my promise.

Until then, my treasure, I pray for your unchangeable affection.

With all my heart,
Your Wolf

Frogs' whistling outside the window permeated the chamber. The humid, night air felt thicker to breathe than it had moments before.

"Did I misinterpret anything?" Her pink lips remained parted, and her dark lashes swept down to glance at the notebook and swept up again.

He clutched the underside of the table as if it were a life raft keeping him from drifting to the beautiful siren seated in front of him.

She closed the notebook, placing her slender hand on top. "I had to look up a few words in the French-to-English dictionary. Thankfully, Dinah found a volume in your library. I hope you don't mind that I borrowed it."

"Not at all." He cleared his throat to remove its squeaky tone and gulped his drink. "Your interpretation sounded accurate."

The footman refilled his glass, and Samuel used the distraction to shake himself mentally. What on God's earth had come over him? He focused on his soup.

"I'm getting closer to the truth. I can feel it. Do you think he was a French sea captain? Have you heard of anyone with the nickname Wolf?"

"I haven't, but I also haven't been in Antigua long. There are some friends I can ask. In fact, they've invited us to dine with them."

Her chest lifted . . .

"But I declined because of your injury."

And fell.

Did she look forward to meeting others? Perhaps he should invite the Kellys to dine at Greenview?

"You'll be happy to note that my leg is improving." She stood.

"Careful." He set down his utensils, prepared to catch her if she toppled.

Using the table for leverage, she limped to the window. "See." She lifted her chin and flashed him that easy-going smile that flowed so naturally from her countenance. "I can stand and move a few steps, albeit slowly."

He longed to reel in her happiness—absorb it into his parched bones.

How could she act so at ease? He'd been the firstborn son destined to inherit his father's fortune, lands, and title, yet he always felt pressured to fix his weaknesses, improve, do better. From the sound of that letter, she could have been the result of some vile libertine's conquest to despoil her mother's innocence with his smooth talk of ardent passion. Yet, her joy hadn't diminished.

Was she a naïve believer in love? Samuel didn't want to crush her spirit, but among the *ton*, marriage was a business dealing. Some couples came to appreciate one another, as had his parents, or in rare cases, fell in love. More often than not, ardent passions were expressed to a man's mistress or a woman's cicisbeo, not a spouse. Lucy and Harry hadn't the discipline to wait until after Samuel and Lucy exchanged vows to begin their sordid affair. Harry had probably fed Lucy a similar line. *I have been in acute torment since my departure. I beg you to gratify my wishes.*

His fingertips dug into the armrests. The acidic sting of their betrayal still burned his insides. He wouldn't be such a fool again.

You are not your father. Focus and calm yourself. His stomach churned with acid. Time to change the topic. "You are getting around quite well, but don't overdo it." He nodded to the footman to retrieve his presents for Maggie. "I brought you something to aid you as you become mobile."

She clasped a hand to her chest. "A gift?"

Samuel crossed the room to meet the footman at the door and hid the cane and slippers behind his back. "Sit and close your eyes."

Her face shone brighter than the vibrant colors donning the ribbon in her hair. She hobbled back to the chair and did as asked. "I'm the one who should be repaying you for your hospitality, but I'm not sure how."

He had shot her. She wasn't taking advantage of his generosity. His mouth opened to say, *think nothing of it.* But what came out was, "All I ask is to be the recipient of your beautiful smile."

Confound it. Where did those words come from?

Her rosy lips curved and revealed rows of pearl-white teeth.

He shifted his chair and sat facing her, holding out the cane between them. "Open your eyes."

Her lids sprang open, and she gasped as if he'd shown her a diamond the size of her palm. "It's lovely." She tentatively reached out, and he passed the cane to her. Her fingers ran over the polished wood and porcelain head. She stood and leaned her weight upon it, hobbling to the window and back. Stopping near the foot of the bed, she angled the top of the cane away from her and posed as if to have her portrait painted. "It's the perfect height."

A fuzzy warmth spread through his midsection, bubbling up until he felt lighter, almost giddy.

She straightened and swung the cane as he'd witnessed many fops do to draw attention to themselves, and pretended to tip a make-believe beaver skin hat. She laughed at her own impersonation.

He joined in, but his laughter sounded strange with those muscles underutilized.

"It's perfect." She held it up to examine the

smooth top but winced as she put too much weight on her bad leg.

He jumped up and aided her to sit on the foot of the bed.

"And thoughtful. Just what I needed."

"There's more." He pulled the package around and set it on her lap.

She peered at him with disbelief twinkling in her eyes.

He grinned, savoring the moment. His heart pressed against his breastplate.

She patted the coverlet on the spot next to her for him to sit, and he complied while she peeled back the paper. Her smile faded. "Slippers," she whispered.

Did she not like his gift?

"Dancing slippers." She reverently touched the satin fabric. "How did you know?"

Dancing shoes? Weren't all slippers the same?

"I love to dance." She faced him with bright eyes. As if on impulse, her arms wrapped him in a side hug, and she pressed her cheek to his.

He relaxed into her embrace inhaling the soft scent of orange blossoms and the lavender sachet from her mother's trunk. She fit perfectly against his side. He savored the soft, smoothness of her skin against his cheek. His hand slid up her spine and curved around the nape of her neck, where silken wisps of hair teased his senses. The perverse desire to whoop like a soldier staking his claim filled Samuel's ribs to the point of cracking. Was this how sheer joy felt?

"Thank you," she whispered, her breath hot against his ear. She pulled back, and his nerve endings cried out with dismay.

He should warn her about the letter he posted to her parents. As much as he despised ruining the moment, now was his chance.

"I see I arrived in the nick of time." Middleton's voice boomed from the doorway.

Samuel straightened, waiting for the captain to call him out. He could hear the paces being counted off for a duel.

"Uncle Anthony, don't be dramatic. I was merely expressing my gratitude over Lord Granville's thoughtful gesture."

Thoughtful, yes. Samuel stood and leaned his hip against the dresser to add some separation between himself and Maggie.

She held up the cane and slippers. "See what he purchased for me?"

Middleton paused in scowling at Samuel to assess the gifts. "Shoes? What happened to the ones you had?"

"They were under the bush, but someone found them."

Samuel crossed his arms. "How do you know?"

"I saw a worker wearing them." She pointed at the window. "Outside. I didn't have the heart to yell that they were mine."

"They should be returned." The crease between Samuel's eyebrows deepened.

"No, I couldn't do that to her. You should have seen the young girl. She strutted around like she believed she was Queen Elizabeth."

Not being concerned with the loss of her shoes meant she must be more well off than he'd initially judged. Not that her financial situation mattered, since she was still of questionable lineage. But what if she did discover her father's identity, and he was a planter or gentleman? Could a future together be possible?

Middleton sniffed Maggie's tray and picked up the barely eaten bowl. "Did you tell Maggie what we learned today?" He wandered over to sit on the foot of the bed.

Maggie's wide eyes honed on him. "You have information? On my family?"

Samuel cleared his throat. "Indeed. We spoke to a gentleman who's lived in Antigua for forty years, and he knew your grandfather."

She gripped the edge of the seat cushion, peering at him with rapt intensity.

"Mr. O'Malley used to tailor your grandfather's clothes," Samuel said. "He knew of your mother and spoke of her fondly. Your grandmother died in childbirth, and your mother grew up under the care of servants and your grandfather's watchful eye."

Middleton circled his index finger. "Get to

the interesting part." He ate several greedy bites from her soup.

Maggie frowned at her uncle.

"Mr. O'Malley mentioned how your grandfather had arranged a marriage between your mother and some titled fop—his words—arriving from England."

"England?" A crease formed between Maggie's brows.

An English groom didn't coincide with the love letter written in French, but perhaps it was meant to keep its content secret. "He couldn't remember the groom's name but thought perhaps it started with the letter C or K. O'Malley was commissioned to make new clothes for the celebration and to spare no expense."

Samuel massaged the back of his neck, pressing the tension from the strained muscles. "O'Malley also believed a rift had grown between your grandfather and mother but couldn't say if it was due to the marriage arrangement. Only that Mr. Baxter's bullheadedness drove his daughter to board the ship that sank her in a watery grave."

Samuel ticked a mental list of all the man had revealed. "Oh, and he thought a visit to St. John's parish would provide more answers. Reverend Doyle passed a few years ago. The new reverend hasn't been around long but should be able to dig something up from the annals."

Maggie blinked as if trying to piece together

jumbled bits of information. She gripped her cane and rose. "I have to heal, so I can visit the parish." She hobbled in a circle around the perimeter of the room.

Middleton wiped his mouth, and his napkin muffled his words. "Hold on now. The parish will still be there in a few days."

Samuel pushed off the dresser and guided her back toward the bed. "Take it easy."

"But we have leads now." Although she protested, she didn't resist his touch as he turned her and settled her back down. "And I'm certain there are others who would have known my mother. We must speak with them."

She twisted to view her uncle. "And I need you to ask about any records of French ships docking in the year 1810 or 1811. See if you can get access to the shipping logs."

Samuel's fingers itched to start a task list. "I can request a meeting with the new reverend."

"Splendid, and I can . . ." Her countenance fell. She rubbed her thigh, and guilt pricked Samuel's side once again for causing her injury.

He lifted her chin with a curved index finger. "You'll continue to scour the diary for more clues."

She nodded, but her lashes lowered, and her enthusiasm appeared to wane. Was being stuck inside the house wearing on her? Although she didn't complain, keeping Maggie's natural exuberance confined to an upstairs chamber was like hiding a light under a bushel.

He rose. "The hour grows late, and there are a few items I must complete before I turn in for the night."

Middleton's mouth was full, so he raised a hand in a silent wave.

A bemused smile curved Maggie's lips. "Still items to check off the list."

He chuckled at her teasing as he strode down the hall. Lucy had never teased him. He and his Eton classmates had taunted each other, especially Harry, and all in good fun, but it often left him ill-at-ease. Maggie's playful jesting bonded them as if they held a special secret.

Selfishly, he wanted to keep her all to himself, but it wasn't possible. Was it?

Not once her parents received his letter. Surely they'd come for their daughter or at least send someone. He needed to tell her, but how? When? Her parents having to cross the Atlantic would bide him some time. At least, until he could find the right moment. Would her beautiful smile become a frown of disappointment? Would she resent his interfering?

Samuel descended the stairs and locked himself in his study. He dipped his quill in ink, pausing before putting pen to the clean sheet of paper. His hand scribbled the number one and proceeded to list the tasks he should be concentrating on instead of Maggie. He needed to snuff out whatever had taken hold of him, but her expressive smile interrupted his thoughts. How velvety soft would her lips feel under his?

He snorted.

She'd probably smile against his mouth, for he'd never known anyone so quick to laugh or grin even in the face of a challenge.

He rubbed his mouth with the back of his hand, wiping away his musings. He may not have attended church in an age, but he hadn't forgotten that lusting after a woman was a sin.

Especially desiring after a woman of questionable lineage—one that would put him in an unfavorable light with the peerage and his father.

And that was all these stirrings were—lust.

Anything else would be most unfortunate.

Chapter 13

I shouldn't listen to island gossip, but my lady's maid hinted that a storm has driven ships off course. Could I hope my intended's charter was one?

~ Entry by Loretta Baxter,
July 3, 1810

Her reading complete, Maggie closed her mother's diary and flopped back against the bed pillows. The book rested upon her chest, but its weight wasn't what pressed the air from her lungs. "God, that can't be all. I thought Mama's diary would hold the answers I need." She swallowed around the lump in her throat. "But it just ended." Peering at the ceiling tiles, she listened to Uncle Anthony's snoring rumbling from across the hall. "Coming here couldn't have been all for naught."

The last thing her mama had written was about the newly appointed Governor of the Leeward Islands, some man named Hugh Elliot. "While I'm grateful to learn that my mother shared Governor Elliot's abolitionist tendencies, it leaves no clues as to who my father was. Where do I go from here?"

Her throat tightened. "I've risked so much,

and time is of the essence." She had a month remaining to learn all she could before she chanced not returning in time for her school holiday and the ball that started the season.

She reread the love letter written to her mother. *I shall not be persuaded to end my pursuit of you. You are my own heart* . . . "Lord, please help me learn whose child I am." Dreaded tears burned the back of her eyelids. She blinked them away, refusing to succumb to despair. God had helped her through worse. A solution would come. She glanced heavenward. "Lord, give me wisdom."

A breeze ruffled the curtains, but it didn't provide relief, only circulated the warm air with more warm air. Her muscles twitched with the need to move. Fresh air and sunshine beckoned her. She'd always preferred the outdoors. A ceiling and four walls suffocated her over time, even during England's cold winters.

She flipped back the covers and carefully shifted her injured leg off the bed. Stiffness attacked her limbs after lying abed for several hours. She gripped her cane and pressed half her weight upon it. Though Dinah had been called to help dress the burned arm of one of the boiling house workers, Maggie could hear Dinah's motherly warning, "Tek it easy."

She should probably wait for Dinah's return before attempting to venture outside.

A bold Carib grackle landed on her windowsill.

Its black feathers shone a blueish hue in the sun, and its yellow eyes glanced at her before hopping to face outward. It puffed its feathers and squawked. A return cry from its mate echoed. The bird peered back one last time as if to say, *follow me,* before flying away.

It was all the incentive Maggie needed.

She ached for the outdoors. It was another thing that made her different from the ladies of the *ton*. While they spent their days indoors, changing gowns countlessly, writing correspondences, or taking callers, Maggie preferred to breathe fresh air and feel the sunshine on her face. Which meant she had to break another ridiculous etiquette rule—wearing bonnets and always carrying a parasol.

How often had her governesses berated her for falling asleep lying in the grass? The open air was where Maggie felt most at peace and could relax. It had taken years for her to adapt to sleeping on a soft mattress. Throughout her childhood, she'd wake from nightmares of being sucked into quicksand and only be able to return to sleep with hard floorboards beneath her.

Leaning heavily on the cane, she limped to the exit, opened the door, and hobbled to the steps. *Now what?* The steep central staircase loomed before her. Could she make it, or would she tumble and break her good leg? She spied the curved banister. Could she slide like she had as a young child? What would her host think of such inappropriate behavior? Or the butler for that matter?

As if producing him from her thoughts, Hawley appeared at the bottom of the steps.

"Hawley." She gripped the railing for support and limped down one stair. "I'm afraid I could use your assistance in descending the stairs."

The proper butler scrunched his nose and eyed her with a scowl. "It's an act of treason to aid Bonaparte lovers." He stomped off toward the kitchens.

What in heaven's name was that about?

Carson emerged from the master's chamber. "May I be of service, madame?"

She hesitated only a moment. "Would you be so kind as to carry me down the stairs?"

"Most certainly." The valet stopped in front of her.

She placed a hand on Carson's shoulder and gripped the cane tight. "I think if you—"

He scooped her up as if she weighed nothing and traipsed down, curving around the banister into the downstairs hall. "Where to, Miss Prescott?"

She grinned. "To the garden. If I'm not mistaken, there's a bench under the tamarind tree."

Hawley, who'd stopped to reprimand a maid, looked up and glared at Maggie with pinched lips.

Carson chuckled. "Not sure what's put him in a dudgeon. I guess helping a lovely lady in distress is above his station."

Lovely? Did Carson mean to flatter her? Her governesses had always told her she was much too thin to be considered pretty.

He strode down the hall while a footman, who'd been polishing the mahogany floors with coconut husks, scurried to open the door.

Sunshine welcomed her with its warm embrace, and she inhaled a deep breath filled with the scent of molasses and the yeasty scent of the breadfruit tree.

Carson's shoes crunched along a pebble path to the tamarind tree and the bench resting in the shade of its branches. He set her down. "Shall I ring for a glass of lemonade to help with the heat?"

"That would be splendid."

He spun on his heel and trekked back toward the butlery.

A hymn sung by the workers tending the sugar cane drifted in from the fields. She stretched her legs and lifted her hair to allow the cool prevailing winds to tickle her neck. Hibiscus plants brightened the garden with their pink flowers, and in the sun, sharp green leaves parted to reveal black pineapples. Aloe plants grew naturally inside and outside of the quaint garden's whitewashed fence.

The ocean breeze tickled a lock of hair, causing it to dance in front of her face. Maggie could hear Cilla reprimand, saying she'd grown too old to wear her hair down, so she slid her mother's scarf from around her waist and used it to tie the length of it back.

Her foot tapped to the rhythm of the workers' song. She recognized the tune from singing at church in England and hummed along. The humming slipped into a melody, and the lyrics flowed from her lips. She closed her eyes and let her earlier frustration melt away at each bar of the heart-filled praise.

Forgetting the exact words of the last stanza, she once again hummed and opened her eyes.

Samuel stood with his hip leaning against the fence post. His arms were folded, one leg crossed in front of the other. How long had he been listening?

"What are you doing out here?" He pushed off the fence and strode toward her with measured steps. He glanced at her cane. "Maybe I should take back my gift." His tone sounded like a jest, but his expression turned serious. "You shouldn't be venturing this far."

Carson approached behind Samuel, carrying her lemonade on a tray.

"Oh, don't fret." She shrugged. "I didn't walk."

He frowned at her. "Then how did you get out here?"

She ignored Samuel's black mood. "I was carried."

"By whom?" His frown deepened.

"Carson was kind enough to aid me."

Carson skidded to a stop, and lemonade splashed on the tray.

Samuel rounded on him. "You carried her?"

"N-no." He shook his head. "I mean, yes, my lord." He backed a step. "I-ah . . . She asked for aid, and I offered it." He balanced the tray with one hand and pulled down on the bottom hem of his jacket. "I'm not certain as to what you would have had me do."

"He did as I asked." Her chin raised in the way her governesses called defiant. "Which was the right thing to do."

Samuel pivoted on his heel and glared at her.

Carson's confused expression and the absurdity of the whole thing hit her, and an inelegant snort erupted. She pinched her lips together and covered her mouth with her hand, but her mirth couldn't be contained.

"You find this entertaining?"

Samuel's serious face only heightened the hilarity, and she moved her hand to her stomach.

His lips twitched, and he glanced away to hide his laugh, but she heard it gurgle in his throat.

"You must admit"—she tried to contain herself—"it is rather funny."

Carson's shoulders relaxed.

Samuel's face contorted as he fought for control. Laughter won.

Their guffaws mellowed into chuckles, and Maggie reached for the lemonade.

Carson passed the glass to her.

Samuel stretched his mouth as if his cheeks ached and waved Carson away. "That will be all."

The poor valet scurried off as if escaping punishment.

With the praise song from the field replaying in her heart, laughter tingling her lips, and the fresh air and sunshine reviving her spirits, she scooted over and patted the bench seat. "Care to sit?"

Samuel settled on the bench and lounged against the backrest.

A grackle, perhaps the same one from her window, perched on one of the pineapple leaves and bobbed up and down. The song in the field finished, and the workers started a soulful melody.

Samuel leaned forward and rested his forearms on his thighs, tapping his thumbs together.

Another giggle bubbled up inside. Samuel was too much the busy type to sit and enjoy the lovely view of the garden, but here he was staring straight ahead at the hibiscus plant.

He rubbed his forehead.

Could he not enjoy a brief moment before the weight of his responsibilities plagued him?

The breeze fluttered the end of her scarf into her eyes, and she pulled it away. "The blossoms are lovely, aren't they?"

"Hmm." He glanced her way. "Er . . . indeed." He nodded toward the plant. "What are they called."

"Hibiscus."

"They are rather pretty." His brows pulled together. "Why did you come out here?"

Emboldened by the moment, she flashed him a jaunty look. "I was hoping to see you and enjoy your company."

"You couldn't wait until supper?"

"I could have." She eyed him askance. "But since I was becoming a part of your routine, I thought it best to mix things up a bit." She spread her arms. "Be spontaneous."

His spine straightened, and tension flowed from his body. "Where's Dinah?"

"She's tending to a burn."

"Does she know you're here?"

"I'm certain someone will be kind enough to direct her to my whereabouts." Leary of his clipped speech and change in mood, she crossed her arms. "I don't believe I need caretaking every waking hour."

"No, definitely not."

She didn't appreciate his sarcastic tone.

"You only sailed to an unfamiliar island without your parents' knowledge, stole into my house, got shot from a tree, and now I find you've snuck out of your room."

It was her turn to frown. "Hawley and Carson were aware, and your footman. What's his name . . . ?" She snapped her fingers. "Weston."

"I guess it makes you much like your mother, who also snuck away, but for clandestine meetings with some Frenchman."

"We don't know the full situation." Her stomach balled like a fist. "She probably had her reasons. It sounds like they truly loved each other."

He snorted.

She narrowed her eyes. "I believe it was well-intentioned."

"Ha."

"Ha?" She sat up straighter and shifted in her seat. "Don't you remember? He wrote, 'I shall not be persuaded to end my pursuit of you. You are my own heart.'"

"The man was a libertine. He didn't even sign his name." He eyed her. "You are naïve in the ways of men. Your idea of pursuit and what he was truly after may differ."

"But it claims that he spoke no falsehood and would remain true to his promise. There's a good chance that promise was marriage."

His gray eyes darkened, and a muscle in his jaw twitched. "He also begged her to gratify his wishes and be filled with secret longing. Mark me. The rogue wanted to have a tryst with your poor enamored mother. I can only pray she didn't fall for the lies from his silvered tongue." He gripped the bench back with white knuckles.

She recoiled. What had brought on such accusations? Why was he so upset? Shouldn't she be the one angry over his insinuations of her mother's lack of morals? Her mama's hazy silhouette backlit by sunlight floated in her memory. Maggie was alive because of her mama's sacrifice. Nothing Maggie had read in the diary indicated her mama was a naïve greenhorn who would be seduced by a man with flowery speech.

Beads of perspiration formed on her forehead. The sun had moved so they no longer sat amid the shade.

"Noon tea shall be served soon, and the men will be returning from the field for a respite." He rose. "It's best if you go back to your chamber."

"I'll wait for Carson to return."

"Carson shouldn't be carrying you."

"Why?" She gasped. "Does he have a bad back?" He should have told her. "I did see him brace it once after inspecting the polish on your boots. I'll ring for a footman."

Samuel glanced heavenward as if petitioning God. "I will do the carrying."

"But you have a meeting with Cuffee at noon."

"I'll be tardy."

"You hate being late."

Careful not to jostle her injured leg, he scooped her into his arms.

She yelped and clung to him. "Don't be ridiculous."

"Ridiculous?" He stomped out of the garden and through the gate. "You're being naïve."

"Naïve?" She glared at him as the footman swung the door open for them to pass.

Samuel inclined his head back toward the bench and addressed the footman, "Fetch her cane and bring it to her chamber after she's rested and finished a nap."

Her voice rose. "You're the one acting childish."

The footman lowered his gaze as if not wanting to overhear the conversation, and Cilla's voice rang in her head. *Proper ladies don't argue or gossip in front of the staff.* She gritted her teeth. Why did the *ton* equivocate being proper with hiding one's emotions? It was one more reason why she'd never fit in.

The bunched muscles of Samuel's arms tightened into solid rock beneath her, and a fierce frown darkened his face. "You have no idea the scoundrels who are out there, who encounter a beautiful woman who doesn't know the ways of men and takes advantage of her."

"I'm not like other women. I can handle—"

"You may think you can outsmart a rogue, but they'll take one look at that inviting smile, your innocent look." He rounded the stair newel post and ascended the first couple of steps. But he paused on the landing. "They'll sweet talk you and tell you how exotic your eyes are with those thick sweeping lashes." He set her down to face him. His eyes glittered like ice, but his thumb gently stroked her cheek. "They'll say how smooth your skin feels, and how you're a rare jewel."

Her breath quickened, and she fought down the hope that he meant those very words.

His gaze darkened. "The way you run wild and snub your nose at society's standards, will only encourage them."

She glanced at the ceiling with a sarcastic appeal for mercy. "Enough, for heaven's sake."

He pressed her back into the corner of the stairwell. "To do this."

She sucked in a gasp before his lips ambushed hers.

Instinctively, her hand dropped to the knife, and she thought about Tobie's instruction on fending off an attacker. *Soft places wound the deepest.*

His hand slid behind her head to cushion it from the hard wall.

This wasn't an attacker. It was Samuel, who'd bought her slippers, laughed with her in the garden, shared his roof and now her first kiss.

His firm mouth moved over hers, demanding acquiescence.

Samuel wouldn't hurt her, but he wanted to frighten her. Teach her a lesson. Why?

His unrelenting kiss molded her lips, fusing them with the sour-sweet taste of lemonade and befuddling her senses.

What if he was the only man ever to kiss her? It wasn't inconceivable, not with her unknown linage. She was caught between above and below stairs literally and figuratively. The highborn believed her beneath them, the working class believed her above them. What if she assuaged her curiosity—just this once?

Her arms wound around his neck, her fingers threading into his hair. She kissed him back with a hunger of her own.

Samuel had intended to educate Maggie so that men wouldn't sway her, men like Harry, who'd lured Lucy away with his flowery words. He meant to frighten Maggie so she wouldn't be caught unawares when cornered by a libertine or tempted, as Lucy had been.

Satisfied he'd successfully taught her a lesson, he resolved to release her.

But she pulled him closer, and the heady scent of orange blossoms invigorated his senses. Her lips conformed to his, and the anger he'd struggled to reign in evaporated until all that remained was a desire to please. He coaxed her mouth, kneading and pressing until she melted in his arms.

Lost in sensation's haze, he set her on her feet,

trailing kisses along her jaw and nuzzling her neck before returning to reclaim her mouth once more. His lesson had taken a wrong turn. She wasn't supposed to kiss him back, nor release a soft moan and draw him closer. He shouldn't be succumbing to the dizzying cravings of his passions. Yet, his heart stretched as if emerging from hibernation, longing to bask in the warmth of her sunshine.

He absorbed her impulsiveness and lived the moment, unhinged by the smoothness of her skin, the softness of her mouth, and the way her body perfectly fit his. Was this how the Frenchman had felt when he'd composed those words? When he'd begged Loretta to think of him with every breath, knowing acute torment at their departure?

You are no better than Harry.

He tore his mouth from hers.

Passion darkened Maggie's eyes to a deep, jungle green. Her lips were red, swollen, and her cheeks flushed. The brightly colored tie had fallen, lying limp on the stair landing.

He staggered back, and her dark tresses slid off his shoulders and trailed down his white linen shirt as if not wanting to part.

Bile rose in his mouth. He'd allowed his anger to best him once again. He was a cad. Not only had he injured Maggie, but now he'd taken advantage of her, a guest in his house. Was he going to add despoiler of innocents to his list of crimes?

He backed up another step and lost his footing over the edge of the landing. Maggie reached for him, putting weight on her bad leg, and winced.

He grabbed the rail and steadied himself. "That was uncalled for." He cleared his throat and tugged on the bottom of his shirt to straighten it. "Forgive me."

Her hand rose to her cheeks as if to feel their heat, then to her swollen lips.

His own still tingled.

Blast. What had he been thinking?

Her eyes searched his face.

Did she think him a blackguard? A proper woman would slap him across the face, and he wouldn't blame her. A weak woman would crumple into a mass of tears or fly into hysterics. An offended woman would call for her uncle, still lying upstairs abed from the sound of his snores, and demand retribution. She could force him to the alter or to the dueling field.

Maggie inched closer. She placed a hand over his heart, the other over hers. His muscles leapt at her touch, and his heart banged against his ribs. Her gaze met his, filled with wonder and confusion, shaking him to the core.

He had to get away from her—far away. He couldn't trust himself not to pull her into his embrace once more. His passion, like his anger, had taken on a life of its own, and he couldn't cave to the temptation. He half pivoted and stopped. *Blast.* Maggie stared at him from the corner of the landing. He couldn't leave her to hop up the stairs in her injured state. Gritting his teeth, he scooped her up and darted up the remaining stairs two at a time. Upon entering the guest chamber, he unceremoniously dumped her on the bed. Her grimace of pain only deepened his guilt.

He stormed out of the house and into the stables, demanding two horses to be saddled. One groom held the reins of Samuel's horse as he mounted while another groomsman climbed into the saddle on the other. Samuel clucked his tongue and galloped away as if the headless horseman chased in pursuit. He glanced back once only to spy Cuffee standing near the windmill scratching his head, waiting for their meeting.

Blast and double blast.

Chapter 14

Lady Boyle has met my betrothed in England. He is fair of face and runs in the upper-most circles but is in need of an advantageous marriage. It seems my future has been whittled down to a financial transaction.

*~ Entry by Loretta Baxter,
July 7, 1810*

Maggie stared at the ceiling. Her mind knew she'd passed into dangerous territory, but her heart secretly swept into a waltz. She shouldn't have allowed him to kiss her. A proper lady would have shown outrage, not kissed him back.

She pressed her palms against her eye sockets. *God, I want to do what is right, but I keep doing the wrong thing. I tried to be a proper lady. All those tutors, governesses, and lessons couldn't change the fact that all society's rules seemed ludicrous, especially after surviving on an island. Who cares which direction one dips their soup spoon? Why can't we eat faster when we're hungry? What was so wrong about letting my bonnet dangle on my back?* When she spoke her mind, she was deemed a hoyden. If she showed emotion, she was considered *"too lively."* Anyone witnessing her display in the stairwell would have certainly labeled her a hussy.

Society's rules may seem preposterous, but she possessed a new respect for why God required certain things in a specific order. *God, forgive me for acting like a wanton woman.* One sin seemed to lead to another. With a groan, she rolled onto her good leg. In the heady moment, the justification for her desire seemed clear. Samuel had initiated the kiss, not she, and she'd figured she'd not have the opportunity to be kissed again. Why hadn't she done the right thing and trusted God with her future?

The pain of the local country dances had reopened fresh wounds. She could still hear Mitchell's chiding. "You really thought I'd be able to dance with you?" He glanced in his mother's direction. "You're pretty and all but . . ." He'd looked both ways, grabbed her hand, and pulled her into a darkened corner of the assembly hall behind a large potted plant. He pressed her into the corner, blocking her from view with his body. "I can't dance with you in public. You could be the daughter of a slop seller or the rat catcher." He stepped closer. His hand cupped her waist, his thumb rubbing the bottom of her corset along the sensitive skin of her stomach. "But I fancy you."

Despite his earlier hurtful statement, her heart had skipped a beat. He fancied her?

"Can you sneak out of your house?"

Warning alarms sounded in her mind, but she nodded.

"Good." A wicked smile twisted his lips. "Meet me in the Ruger barn at midnight."

Her spine stiffened, but she kept her tone light. "What shall we do there at such a late hour?"

He peered behind him as if to double-check no one noticed them.

With a shaking hand, she reached into the side pocket of her gown, praying for God's protection.

Mitchell's gaze returned with a sultry over-confident expression. "A little of this." He closed his eyes, and his lips descended toward hers. His chin met with the tip of her cutlass.

"I highly doubt my father was a slop seller. More likely, he was a pirate because I know how to gut a man." She didn't, not really, but thanks to Tobie's lessons, she could defend herself. She'd never understood what had come over her, stating her father was a pirate, but the panicked expression on Mitchell's face was worth all the taunting, shunning, and ridicule she'd faced later.

Mitchell had blanched and backed away with raised hands before darting off to stand behind his mother.

Maggie snorted. A full-grown man, heading to University, ran to his mother because a young barely five-foot-tall woman dared fend off his advances.

Uncle Anthony found her after spying Mitchell's hasty retreat. He questioned her, but her humiliation was too great to reveal what had happened.

Why hadn't she reacted the same in the stairwell with Samuel? When had her wounded soul become so desperate for attention? Samuel didn't love her. He wasn't about to ask for the hand of an orphan with questionable bloodlines. He might have initiated the kiss, but she was the one who'd made it intimate.

Something had changed then—in his kiss—in him. He'd relinquished control, becoming a man who desired a woman.

His kisses had sated her need to feel wanted, worthy, desirable, but being away from the headiness of the moment doused her with reality.

She'd overheard Uncle Anthony talk about some of his exploits with females to his crew members. Drink and passion caused a man to lose his wits. To a man in the heat of lust, she could have been the upstairs maid, a tavern wench, or a paramour.

Her cheeks and ears burned. Her stomach sank like a ship with a damaged hull, and she curled into a fetal position so she wouldn't retch. She should have stopped his kiss, shown some outrage. She might not be a harlot, but she'd acted like one.

Bile rose in her throat.

How would she face Samuel? He'd certainly

seemed disappointed. He tossed her in her room and fled, not only the house but the plantation grounds, too, as though there hadn't been enough space to distance himself.

She pulled a pillow over her face. *You ninnyhammer.*

Should she pack her things and return to the ship? What about learning more about her mother and father? Had she ruined her chance to discover the truth? Yet, even the diary had led to a dead end. Had she risked everything for naught?

How long she lay there in torment with her thoughts, she didn't know, but the sun grew low in the sky. There must be something she could do. She limped over to the desk and pulled out a sheet of paper. Perhaps someone from St. John's rectory would be willing to meet with her or search the public records.

She picked up a quill and dipped it in the ink well.

Dear Rector,

My name is Maggie Prescott. I must ask for your help, for I'm injured and unable to leave the premises. I'm seeking the identity of my father and was hoping there might be something documented in the annals regarding my mother, Miss Loretta Genevieve Baxter, daughter of Paul Fredrick Baxter.

Samuel had said he'd meet with the rector. Was she overstepping her bounds? Would she even be staying at Greenview Manor after today's events? She placed pen to paper.

> I would appreciate your confidentiality in this matter. All correspondence can be made through Captain Anthony Middleton aboard The Windward.
> With sincerest appreciation,
> Miss Maggie Prescott

A knock sounded, and Maggie jumped. Dinah wouldn't knock. Had Uncle Anthony returned early? How would she explain to him why they had to leave? "Come in."

A footman swung the door wide and stepped aside with a bow.

"Well, here you are, my dear." A woman dressed in mourning blacks swept around the footman, who backed out and returned to his duties. A crooked black cap sat atop a severe bun of blond hair from which a few escaped tendrils framed her face.

She set her embroidery hoop in the chair. "Lord Granville said you'd be here."

The woman smoothed back the tendrils, re-pinning them underneath the righted cap. Her acute gaze surveyed Maggie. "He told me your leg is injured."

Maggie pushed herself into an upright position and nodded.

The woman walked the perimeter of the room, peering at the oceanscape painting on the wall and fingering the silver-handled brush that lay on the bureau. "At least, that's what I was able to discern while I clung to my side saddle for dear life."

She glided to the window and pushed aside the drapes for a better view outside. Her face held a mature countenance, not yet lined with wrinkles, but her skin was no longer plump with the fullness of youth. Maggie guessed the woman to be around Uncle Anthony's age. She appeared equally confident in her own skin.

"Oh, goodness." She spun around so fast her black skirts twirled about her feet. "Forgive me. I haven't introduced myself." She curtsied. "I'm Judith Morgan, but some call me the Widow Morgan, Mrs. Morgan, or just Judith is fine too."

Maggie forced a wobbly grin. "Pleased to meet you. I'm Maggie Prescott."

"The breakneck gallop at which we rode here has me out of sorts." She flounced into the nearby chair but then neatly arranged her skirts over her crossed ankles. "I'm to be your chaperone."

Maggie's smile fell. So that was why Samuel had left in such a hurry. From the state of Mrs. Morgan's hair, flushed cheeks, and flustered words, he must have ripped her from her home and escorted her here in haste. Had he been that affected by their kiss? A current ran over Maggie's skin like the warm Gulf Stream at the thought of their intimate embrace. Or was the disciplined man sickened by the temptation of lust and acted accordingly? Her skin chilled.

Mrs. Morgan eyed her intently.

"I'm sorry about your husband."

"Franklin was a good man, but he dipped too deep in his cups." She pursed her lips. "It was only a matter of time."

"He was ill?" Maggie covered her mouth. "How dreadful."

"Franklin was a drunk." She blinked away tears. "I don't mean to speak ill of the man, but it's true. He had a good heart, but the kill-devil had a hold over him. He stepped in front of a moving carriage and was trampled." She inhaled a deep breath and released it. "Long before he did so, I had to stop worrying and start planning on how to care for myself after he left this world."

Maggie blinked. "I'm terribly sorry. It must have been horrid for you to endure."

"I'm a survivor. I've lived on this island all my life, seen my share of death." A weary expression aged her. "As a rule, I make it a point not to get too attached." She notched up her chin, and her youthfulness returned. "It would serve you well to do the same."

The image of Samuel laughing in the garden

appeared in her mind's eye, and Maggie sank back into the pillows. "Um . . . well . . . thank you for sacrificing your time to aid us as a chaperone . . . with appearances and all." How would Cilla act in this situation? She sat up straighter. "Lord Granville has been kind enough to take me in until I've recovered."

Mrs. Morgan folded her arms and tapped her index finger on her forearm. "How is it that you injured your leg? I assume a twisted ankle has you bedridden."

Samuel hadn't explained, apparently. "Actually, I was shot."

Her new chaperone startled, grabbing the arm rests of her chair. "My word." She leaned forward. "Why? Who, who shot you?"

"It's a long story. Either Lord Granville or the Magistrate. I'm not certain which. They were wrestling over the gun, but it went off by accident. They didn't know I had hidden in the tree."

"In a tree?" Mrs. Morgan's eyes widened, and Maggie explained her tale from the beginning.

Dinah entered the room carrying tea, and Mrs. Morgan served it, all the while grilling Maggie with questions. Maggie finished the tale by reading the letter found in her mother's gown pocket. She didn't mention the argument she and Samuel had had in the garden, nor their interlude on the stairs.

Mrs. Morgan sipped from her cup. "I remember hearing about your mother."

"You do?" Maggie choked on her tea. "Please, I'm desperate for information."

"I'm afraid it's not much. I was a wee bit of a thing, barely out of leading strings when she disappeared. Rumor had it she either ran off with a lover or threw herself into the sea to avoid marrying her papa's choice of a suitor. I guess that if you're her daughter that would rule out the latter."

"Indeed." Maggie kept her gaze on Mrs. Morgan's expression while she set her teacup on the bedside table. It teetered on the edge, but Maggie pushed it to the center. "Did the islanders speculate who the gentleman might have been?"

Mrs. Morgan pressed her index finger to her lips and glanced at the ceiling. "All I can remember is that your grandfather's heart stopped one day out of grief. I'd never heard of such a thing and panicked that it could happen to me." She placed a hand over her heart. "I used to stop and make sure mine was working properly. Granted, I had likely only seen four years."

Maggie chuckled and imagined a much younger version of her chaperone.

"My sister is two years my elder. I will see if she remembers more." Her dainty eyebrows inverted. "Surely your mother's diary mentioned the Frenchman or the other gentleman who arrived from England?"

"I'd hoped so, but I just finished the last entry, and it left more questions than answers. Her last entry was trivial, rambling on about a new governor." The sick pain returned, leaving her heart wilted. "I thought she'd mentioned the diary in her song because it held answers, but it didn't. It just ended." She shook her head. "While it was interesting information, I'd hoped for more. It just seemed so inconsequential for her last entry."

"Could there be a second volume?"

"Maybe." She had been in a rush retrieving the diary. "It was dark. Perhaps I merely grabbed the first one I discovered." She aided her bad leg over the side of the bed. "We must go look."

"Now?" Dinah stood.

"I love a good mystery." Widow Morgan set her tea aside and clapped her hands. "This shall be splendid fun." She rose from her seat. "Wait until my sister hears about this. She thought her news about our second cousin's engagement to a viscount was exciting."

A warning alarm rang in Maggie's mind. She'd grown accustomed to being the topic of gossip, but for some reason, this seemed personal. She could laugh off being the daughter of a pirate because her lineage was unknown, but would she be able to laugh off the truth? First, she had to learn it. She silenced the foreboding and reached for her cane. "We'll need to summon a footman to move the bookshelf."

Perhaps she hadn't reached a dead end after all.

Samuel wiped sweat from his brow and handed Cuffee the wooden stepladder to carry back to the tool shed. The cistern was running dangerously low on water—one more thing to add to his growing list of problems. Thus far, he'd kept the sugar crop viable by hand watering the growing shoots, but he couldn't risk leaving the plantation without enough drinking water to survive the upcoming dry season.

He needed a plan. What did the islanders do to obtain fresh water? George may have some answers, and Thea had invited Samuel for a meal, but it would be easier on Maggie if they joined him at Greenview Manor. He'd have a footman carry over an invitation to dine with them in the next few days.

Samuel dusted off his hands. "Keep an eye on the North field. Hennion's workers were congregating there again. They dispersed as I rode by, but it's suspicious." He hadn't seen them as he'd ridden the property for his nightly inspection, but he'd heard voices, and when he approached, the cane rustled as they ran off in different directions. He would have to alert Hennion and the magistrate, but the idea of such a meeting left a bitter taste in his mouth.

Unrest at the neighboring plantation, sugar borers eating the cane plants, water running low, and a chance that all his work would be for naught because a mere slip of a woman had appeared . . . His life had somehow turned upside down.

What else could come his way?

Maggie's teasing smile and her lighthearted, sarcastic tone filled his memory. *It's remarkable. You do laugh.* Laughing was a luxury for second sons. His brother Bradlee jested and laughed at will, but Samuel had always endured life with a critical eye. He not only had to live up to the standards of an earl and the peerage, but he also had to live up to his father's specifications. None of that left time for laughter. Samuel had chuckled a few times with his friends at university, more so because they were funning someone other than him. He'd guffawed at scaring his brother by locking him in the crypt, but looking back, treating Bradlee like that hadn't been funny.

However, laughing in the garden with Maggie had felt . . . pleasant.

He grunted, picturing Maggie holding her stomach with a smile as warm and bright as the noonday sun. *Better than pleasant*. The freedom had felt extraordinary, like a day where they produced twice as much as expected. But then, he and Maggie had argued over that ridiculous love letter. And to make matters worse, he'd gone and kissed her, becoming the rogue he'd meant to warn her about.

He slapped at a mosquito. Last night, he couldn't wait to return to see her beautiful smile. Now his feet dragged with the uncertainty of what lay ahead. He could only hope Widow Morgan would not only diffuse the situation but douse it with ice water.

The indigo sky turned black, and he could no longer delay returning to the main house. He'd ask for his evening meal to once again be served in his office. Maggie had said she hadn't wanted to be part of his routine, so he would oblige her. Besides, it would give her and Widow Morgan more time to get acquainted.

His rationalizations didn't solve his restlessness.

He entered the house through the French doors and greeted Hawley.

"I'll have a bath drawn and brought up to your room."

Samuel paused. He should ration their water, but a glimpse in the hall mirror showed how badly a bath was needed. "Half the normal amount is fine."

Carson met him in his chamber and gaped at his haggard appearance before aiding him.

Samuel passed him his shirt for cleaning, and Carson patted the cloth as though soothing a child. Samuel dismissed him to care for the attire.

A footman rolled a wooden tub into the master chamber, followed by maids carrying pots of lukewarm water. He would have preferred cooler, but his spirits lifted as he rinsed away the filth. All he needed to do was strategize, formulate a plan, and keep pushing harder and moving forward. He was the same man who had smoothed over tensions between the tenants in Northern England, arranged the finances for the renovations to Ywain Manor, and saved a pretty coin by overseeing the projects himself. If he could do all that, he could revive a sugar plantation.

Harry hadn't the fortitude to work a single day much less save his family's island holdings. His friend had lived off his father's allowance until the man had threatened to cut him off. He issued Harry an ultimatum—marry rich or move to the wretched, blistering West Indies to re-establish his father's sugar plantation. Harry stayed a week on his father's plantation in Northern Antigua before he'd boarded the next ship to England. The day he returned, he'd asked Samuel to meet him at the local tavern.

"It's an impossible task, I tell you. It can't be done. No one can revive that horrid place." Harry signaled the alehouse keeper to pour them each a mug. He held his glass high. "To getting leg-shackled." He clanked Samuel's glass. "May she be rich as sin, and may the lights be dim when I crawl into her bed."

He tipped back his mug and downed his drink.

Samuel had worried about how Harry would take the news of his own engagement to Lucy. Thinking back on it, Samuel snorted. He'd actually worried his bachelor friend would have felt abandoned, left out, or angry that another potential conquest had got away. Shaking his head, he sank lower into the water and let the memories surface.

"I have an announcement."

Harry had slammed down his mug and wiped his mouth with his sleeve.

"You'll have one less gent to compete with on the marriage mart."

Harry blinked.

"While you were in the islands, I made an offer of marriage to Miss Lucy Tilly."

Harry stared at him for a long moment. "Congratulations, old chap." He signaled for another round. "Miss Tilly is one lucky chick-a-biddy." He leaned on the bar top. "Do I know this chit? Tell me about her."

"I met her the night you sailed. We danced at the Travis ball." The opportunity had arisen because Harry hadn't been there to woo her first with his silvered tongue. "She's demure and polite, and my father approves of the match."

Harry clapped Samuel on the shoulder. "She seems like the perfect wife."

He'd thought the same until Harry had ruined

her. Samuel splashed water over his face. Only looking back did Samuel remember the odd glint in Harry's gaze—the competitiveness in his smile.

When the House of Lords decided to dole out Samuel's punishment for breaking Harry's nose, Samuel knew for certain that Harry had used his father's influence as second cousin of King William IV to persuade the peerage to his side.

"One year to cool your heels in the Leeward Islands. After a year, you may petition for your return."

Samuel snapped the towel off the rack and rose from the tub with renewed determination.

Tomorrow he'd visit with Hennion and warn him about the suspicious activity among his field workers, then he'd speak with George about the water supply. Samuel dried and donned his breeches. He removed a paper from his desk and scribbled a new checklist.

Carson returned.

"Nothing fancy. I shall be taking my meal in my study."

The valet laid out Samuel's supper attire and aided him into the shirt and jacket.

A thud in the hallway froze Carson's fingers in tying Samuel's cravat.

Samuel strained to listen. It sounded too heavy for Miss Prescott to have suffered a fall. She'd been so light in his arms. He pushed the errant thought aside.

Only the still of the evening filled the room. Carson finished tying the neckpiece.

Samuel stepped into the hall and followed the murmur of voices into a sitting room, where a bookshelf half blocked his way. He scooted around it and past a cluster of servants with their backs to him. They held lanterns illuminating an alcove under the attic stairs. A female body lay sprawled on her stomach on the floor. The waif-like form was none other than Miss Maggie Prescott.

Her head was twisted to the side, with her eyes closed, and face scrunched up. "How far under the floor does this go?" She wedged her shoulder deeper into the hole where his floorboard used to be. "I feel something."

The group, consisting of Dinah, Widow Morgan, and his footmen, leaned in closer, their backs to Samuel.

"I can't quite reach it though." Her eyes sprung open, and she rolled to her side. Her gaze met his over Dinah's shoulder. Maggie gasped and jolted, wacking the back of her hand on the hole's opening. The group spun around and straightened.

Miss Prescott winced.

He crossed his arms and leaned against the narrow side of the bookshelf. "What, pray tell, is going on here?"

Chapter 15

Oh, Diary, my heart swells within me. The most glorious and troublesome thing has happened. I saved a wondrously handsome man from certain death, but Papa would never forgive me if he learned the truth.

*~ Entry by Loretta Baxter,
July 14, 1810*

Samuel's muscles wound into tight coils. *Confound it.* What trouble was Maggie—er—Miss Prescott getting herself into now? "Why are the floorboards removed?"

She wiggled her arm from the cavity and sat up. Dinah gaped at him.

Widow Morgan clasped her hands and pursed her lips.

His footman straightened and inched back into the shadows.

Miss Prescott scanned his face. Her natural ease around him had disappeared. "We . . ." She glanced at the nervous faces and amended. "*I* think there might be another volume of my mother's diary." She brushed the dust off her arm, and the particles floated in the air. "I thought I felt it." She sneezed.

He grunted and stepped forward.

His footman bowed out of the cramped room, and the others cowered in a corner.

Berating himself for not going straight to his study, Samuel squatted next to her. He clenched his teeth and slid his arm around her waist, elevating her to her feet. She hopped on her good leg, and he steadied her, trying to ignore how nicely she fit against his side.

Dinah handed Miss Prescott her cane, and Miss Prescott stepped from his embrace. As soon as she was gone, his body craved her soft warmth and delicious scent. *Don't be a fool.*

"Allow me." Samuel bent down and lay on the hardwood. Sliding his hand into the dark abyss, he roved through the dust coating the space between floors.

"I felt something a little to the right."

He twisted his head to find Maggie—Miss Prescott—leaning over him. Her long hair cascaded over her shoulder and swung only a few inches above him.

The hole constricted his bicep, but he forced his arm inside to his shoulder. His hand moved left and bumped something. A leather binding?

"Do you feel anything?" Her voice shook with what sounded like nervous anticipation.

It was slightly out of his reach, but he hooked his middle finger in the binding and spun it until he could grasp a corner. This was definitely a book. He drew the volume forward and another book slid off the top. Were there more?

He froze.

Was this a wise course of action? If he removed this volume, could its contents negate his claim to Greenview Manor? Was there a chance? He had yet to hear back from his attorneys.

Maggie leaned closer. Her dark hair pooled around him, and her lips parted as if in a silent gasp.

There was another possibility.

Would this volume confirm Maggie's illegitimacy? Would it ruin her chances to marry within her class? Maybe it would be best for it to be read in private before publicly announcing its existence. He'd be protecting her from island gossip. Besides, he had to consider his reputation and that of his family. The diary involved his future too. Against all odds, if Maggie turned out to be the rightful owner of Greenview Manor, maybe he could control when the information was divulged. He wouldn't keep it secret for forever, but perhaps he could strike a deal with Maggie to hold back the announcement until after he'd restored his reputation and rightful claim as heir and returned to England. He wiggled back and pulled on his arm.

Stuck.

Her brow furrowed. "Is something wrong?"

He shifted his position for better leverage

and twisted his shoulder to yank out his arm. It wouldn't budge.

"What's the matter?"

He gritted his teeth and struggled to free himself.

She shifted to the side for a better view, and her silky hair swept over his face, leaving a trailing scent of orange blossoms behind. "Is your arm stuck?"

He growled, "I'm fine. I merely need a moment to adjust." He wrenched his arm. Still nothing. *Devil take it,* he wasn't going to sleep with his shoulder wedged in a hole tonight or any other night. Using his other hand, he dug his fingertips into wood, attempting to pry up the floorboard, but he couldn't get adequate leverage in his awkward position.

"Oh, dear." She frowned, but he couldn't determine whether it was due to his tone of voice or the situation.

"Dinner is ready to be served in the dining room." His footman's voice sounded behind them.

Maggie turned, and her hair tickled his nose with its scent. "We'll be down in a moment. Please keep it in the warming tray for now." Her hair lifted as she stood. "Actually, James?"

His footman's name was James? How had she learned his staff's name so quickly? He'd been here almost a year and still floundered with knowing the house staff other than Dinah, Hawley, and Carson.

"If you could fetch us some butter, that would be lovely."

Footsteps retreated down the hall, and Samuel could feel the vibration of the floorboards squeezing his shoulder.

"Don't fret." She touched her slender hand on his free arm as if to reassure him.

"I'm not fretting." He ground his teeth and twisted one direction then the other to wring his arm loose. Carson and another maid joined the curious eyes, wondering about the commotion. "There's nothing to see here." He could feel the veins in his neck throb, and his words rumbled in his chest like a growl. "Everyone get back to work."

The staff bumped into each other in their haste to leave. Only Maggie and Widow Morgan remained. The chaperone seemed to be enjoying the entertainment.

James returned and handed a butter container to Maggie before darting back the way he came.

Seemingly unperturbed by his anger, Maggie dipped her fingers into the jar. "My younger brother, Michael, got his arm stuck up the downspout. To this day, I don't know why he reached up there, but a good greasing did the trick."

Her nearness aroused the same unwanted

stirrings he'd experienced on the stairwell. "I can free myself on my own. Step away."

She ignored him.

He tried to locate a stud to push his arm free but met only cavernous space. A fine red mist filled his vision, and he yelled, "I said, step away!"

The widow Morgan's eyebrows raised, and she side-stepped around the corner and out of view.

Maggie sat down with a grunt of pain next to him.

The woman was ignoring her injury to help him, and all he could do was shout at her.

Her fingers rubbed butter into his cambric shirt and along the floorboard. Her gentle touch and massaging motion soothed the beast inside. He closed his eyes and allowed her loving hand to ease the tension of the moment and the weighty problems of the day. She hadn't run like the others, and she didn't recoil at his temper. Why did that comfort him?

When everyone else cowered, a mere slip of a girl courageously held her ground. In that aspect, Maggie truly was remarkable. She'd crossed the Atlantic on her own with only an unreliable, half-in-his-cups uncle to protect her. She'd been shot, but she hadn't once complained. She'd witnessed his ugly temper get the best of him on several occasions, yet she didn't shrink back or run away.

She shifted, her fingers probing around the back of his shoulder and the sensitive underarm skin. He met her gaze, and in those incredible green depths, he saw a brave explorer and a confident blossoming woman who'd dared to kiss him back. But he also saw a beautiful youth standing on the perimeter of a dancefloor, hoping for an opportunity to dance.

She was magnificent.

But not for him.

He was heir to an earldom. There were expectations and responsibilities. Good breeding was a requirement—not because it mattered to him, but because polite society would only accept their own.

He'd understood this since birth. Why then did his future seem bleak without her?

Her fingers stopped moving. "Now try."

He pushed the diaries up near his elbow for him to retrieve at a later date.

She gently squeezed his shoulder.

He twisted while raising his arm, and it slid out from the tight hole's grip, scraping along the sides.

She clapped her hands, a genuine smile aimed his way.

He propped himself up on his elbow and rubbed the area where his shoulder had scraped. "Thank you." Holding her gaze, he willed her to hear the sincerity in his voice. "I apologize for my rude behavior." His chest constricted, and he cleared his throat, refusing to let his gaze drop to her full mouth. "Just now and earlier. Please forgive me."

A veil shuttered her eyes, and color rose in her cheeks. "Think nothing of it." Her face brightened, illuminating the small alcove. "I'm grateful your supper won't have to be brought to you in here."

Widow Morgan sashayed into view. Had she been listening to them the whole time? *Criminy.* He frowned. Proper chaperoning was what he was paying her to do.

"You found nothing?" The widow's sigh rung with disappointment. "How I'd hoped to continue searching for clues on this treasure hunt."

Samuel sat up straighter. How dare she be so flippant about something so important to Maggie's future.

Maggie peered at Mrs. Morgan with a thoughtful expression—or perhaps fondness. She didn't appear to be the least bit offended.

He shrugged off his defensiveness and rose to his feet before aiding Maggie to stand.

Widow Morgan passed Maggie her cane. "I do believe our supper is growing cold. Shall we?"

Samuel eyed the vibrant beauty before him, and the idea of dining alone seemed dull. He offered Maggie his arm and walked slowly for her comfort as she limped down the hall after Widow Morgan. "If you would wait one moment," he said, "I must change my clothing."

"Carson is going to be devastated to discover

you've ruined another shirt." A teasing grin twisted one side of her mouth. "Go on and change."

"Are you certain?" Perhaps he should escort her to supper first?

"Quite." She shooed him with her hand.

He strode into his chamber, removed the buttered shirt, and pulled on a fresh one, not bothering to don his cravat for the second time. His parents would have been horrified by his lack of decency, but they weren't there. He stretched his neck, feeling less burdened and free, at least for the moment.

He exited into the hall expecting Maggie to be waiting for him at the top of the stairs, but with her cane in hand and holding the rail, she'd descended the first two stairs while Widow Morgan cheered her on from below.

"What do you think you're doing?"

Maggie flashed him a smile over her shoulder. "Getting a head start to supper."

He bounded down the first three steps and stopped in front of her. "Oh no, you don't."

"I don't think that's such a—oh!"

He swept her into his arms, and she clung to his neck. Once again, he was amazed by the lightness of her lithe form. He'd picked up bundles of cane heavier. "Is your leg all right?"

She nodded, but a slight flush crept up her neck, and she averted her gaze.

He descended the rest of the steps and glided past Widow Morgan, who raised an eyebrow but said nothing. Instead of setting Maggie down in the foyer, he continued into the dining room and set her in the chair the footman pulled out for her.

The footman turned to Samuel. "Shall I set a place for you in 'ere instead of yer study, milord?"

"Please do"—he cleared his throat—"er, James."

The widow accepted the chair the footman pulled out across from Maggie and twirled a finger above her head. "Miss Prescott, your hair."

Maggie's eyes widened, and she scraped her long hair back, twisting it into a bun and tying it in place with her mother's scarf.

Samuel remembered the feel of her silken hair tickling his skin. Her mother's versatile scarf came in handy, but he preferred her hair loose.

James dished the cracked conch with rice and black-eyed peas and pork cooked in lime and Samuel stumbled through saying grace. How had he fallen so far out of practice? He'd grown accustomed to a quick *thank you for the provisions* when he ate by himself in his office. Sometimes, he forgot to pray at all.

As if the smell of food had summoned him, Captain Middleton arrived after meeting with his crew. "The delicious aroma started my stomach rumbling the moment I reached the house." He drew up short. At the sight of Widow Morgan, his countenance changed from arrogant sluggard to sophisticated gentlemen. "I beg your pardon. I didn't know you had company."

Samuel held back a snort. "Mrs. Morgan, may I present to you Captain Anthony Middleton of *The Windward*."

Anthony bowed. "It's a pleasure to make your acquaintance."

The widow assessed him.

"What special occasion grants us the presence of one so lovely?" He sat in the empty chair to her right, and her look turned scathing.

"I'm here as chaperone to your niece to prevent her from falling for men who think they can woo her with flattery."

Maggie pressed her napkin to her lips as if holding back laughter.

Samuel caught the subtle warning in her words and held back an approving smile. Thea had been wise in recommending Widow Morgan. He nodded for the footman to fill Middleton's glass and plate.

Middleton appeared unperturbed. "A married woman chaperoning?"

Mrs. Morgan exhaled as if growing impatient. "I'm recently widowed."

"Is that so?" Middleton's hand froze midair with a forkful of rice. "I mean . . . my condolences."

The widow nodded at Samuel. "I'm grateful for

the opportunity, and I do believe Miss Prescott and I have hit it off splendidly."

"Indeed." Maggie's hand stilled as she finished her last bite of the conch and seconded with a smile.

He blinked at her finished plate. Widow Morgan stared also.

A rosy flush crept into Maggie's cheeks, and she wiped her face with her napkin. "I beg your pardon. Decorum states that I should have eaten slower, but . . ." She shifted her fork and spoon to the top of her plate. "Seafood is one of my favorites, especially conch, and well . . ." She glanced at the faces peering back at her and shrugged. "Propriety is impractical when one's stomach is growling."

Samuel smothered his laugh with a cough but couldn't hide his grin. She wasn't wrong. There were many etiquette protocols he abided by that made absolutely no sense. His smile widened. If only he had the freedom like Maggie to live by feelings and reason and not expectations. Her scoffing attitude for social norms, however adorable, would incite criticism and scorn from the elites, which was probably why her parents had ushered her off to finishing school.

Tell her about the letter you sent to her parents.

Samuel's stomach dropped with his smile, and he sipped from his glass to hide his expression.

Middleton said something that lightened the

mood, and Maggie's laughter bounced around the room. The musicality of it reverberated in Samuel's chest, tickling his rib cage. If he had his way, she would never attend boarding school. He wouldn't allow society to quash her open nature. He admired her abandon to enjoy life and push aside petty trivialities. Maggie was a fresh breeze in a stale room, rain in a dry land. Her smile raised his spirits, and her laughter set him at ease, and from the looks on Middleton's and Mrs. Morgan's faces, she had a similar effect on others.

Why ruin the moment by bringing up the letter? The ship wouldn't even have reached London yet. There was plenty of time to break the news to her—*later.*

A bell from the tower pierced the night air, souring the bite of pork in Samuel's mouth.

At the table, everyone swiveled their gazes to the window, where a distant light flickered on the horizon.

"Fire!" Cuffee's voice bellowed from outside.

Chapter 16

Oh, Diary, he returned to me. I stood on the bluff trying to save the disaster I'd made of my watercolor landscape when hands covered my eyes, and a kiss was pressed to my cheek.

~ *Entry by Loretta Baxter, August 10, 1810*

Maggie fumbled for her cane as Samuel and Uncle Anthony pushed back from the table and made haste out the door.

Judith ran to the widow and clung to the drapes, peering into the dark. Men rushed outside carrying shovels and buckets.

"How bad is it?" Maggie tried to decipher their thick accents as she hobbled to stand beside her chaperone. "Are we in danger?"

"It's too early to know." Candlelight illuminated the woman's stricken face. "The orange glow looks small, but I don't know if it's because the fire was caught early or because it's in the distance. Pray for the former." She pressed her interlaced fingers to her lips. "With the lack of rain, the bigger the fire, the faster it will sweep through an area, leaving devastation in its wake."

A prickle tightened the muscles around Maggie's

shoulders and threatened to suck the air from her lungs. "Can they stop it from spreading?"

"They will try, but it will take God's intervention."

Maggie stared at the orange glow. *Lord, protect the field workers and their families, save the sugar cane crop that puts food on their tables, and God, please protect Uncle Anthony and Samuel. Don't let any harm come to them.*

More shouts filled the night air.

Curious servants emerged from the kitchens and other corners of the house. The scullery maids wrung their hands in their aprons or clutched a footman and wept in fright. Dinah grabbed supplies for burns and exited through the patio doors.

Maggie's spine steeled. "There must be something we can do to help."

"You're injured, and my job is to keep you and your reputation safe." Judith shook her head. "The best thing is to stay put."

She closed her eyes. *God, I can't sit still while lives and livelihoods are in danger.* She recalled Uncle Anthony retelling a story about his being called on shore to battle a blazing fire. The men would need water to combat the fire and their thirst. Her eyelids sprung open, and she scanned the room. She grabbed a nearby vase and removed the flowers. Holding it out, she hailed one of the maids. "Use this and any other containers you can find. Fill them with water and take them to the men fighting the flames."

The girl's hands trembled, but she took it.

"The rest of the women should do the same." She eyed Hawley. "Take the men and find shovels, rakes, or even metal pans that can be used for digging, and find Lord Granville and help dig a trench that the fire can't jump. Carson, you and James stay with me."

Hawley folded his arms as if about to refuse her orders. Instead, he nodded toward the footmen. They stormed into the smoky night air.

Judith raised her thin brows. "Well done. You will make a grand mistress of your own house someday."

Leaning on her cane, Maggie hobbled toward the door. "I'm not done yet." James opened the door for her.

Carson bowed. "Allow me, madame." He scooped her up into his arms. "Where to?"

"The wagon."

Judith scurried and caught up, grabbing an oil lamp and hitching up her skirts with her other hand. "If all this transpired on my first evening, what shall happen by week's end?"

The humid night air hung thick with smoke that blocked the stars from view. The moon, still low on the horizon, illuminated the plume of smoke billowing into the dark sky.

"James, find some empty barrels and bring them to the stables."

He dashed off to tend to his instructions.

Lines of worry furrowed Judith's brow. "But your leg. If you ride to the fields, you'll only be in the way."

"We won't be riding to the fields. We'll be riding to the ocean."

"The ocean?" Judith held up the lamp as if to assess the sincerity of Maggie's words. She blinked. "For water?"

"Exactly."

Carson entered the musty stable and aided Maggie in the wagon since the groomsmen had left to fight the fire.

Maggie adjusted her leg to a comfortable position. "Do you know how to hook a horse to the cart?"

Judith passed Maggie the lantern. "I do." She opened the latch to a horse's stall and went about harnessing the mare to the cart, instructing Carson on how to help.

James appeared with several more footmen, each carrying a barrel. There were five in all. That would have to do.

Maggie held the reins as the men loaded the barrels into the back of the wagon. "Set the last one in the back and then please help Lord Granville in the fields. He'll need every available hand."

"Why don't you let me drive?" Judith climbed onto the buckboard.

"This is something I can do with one leg." Praise God, Tobie had relented to her nagging and taught her how to drive a team. "You will need to be my legs once we get to the sea."

Judith set fisted hands on her hips. "I don't have the strength to carry an empty barrel, much less one filled with water."

"You won't have to." Maggie snapped the reins, and the wagon jerked forward. "I know where we can get help."

Samuel shoveled another blade full of earth onto the blaze and yelled to the men doing likewise, "Make certain the line is wide enough that those flames can't jump it."

The fire had started in the far corner of Hennion's fields, where he'd seen the slaves lingering in the cane paths during his nightly walk-around. Hennion's men battled on the opposite side to contain the fire but weren't making much progress.

The fire continued to spread.

How much cane would be lost tonight? Samuel peered at the men without shovels, who slapped the flames with the shirts from off their backs. How many lives would be lost? They'd already worked a full day. Sweat glistened along hardened muscle in the light of the fire as they strove to control the flame's direction. Fatigue had to be setting in. The cistern was already low on water. If the blaze didn't take their lives, the lack of water would.

He shoveled harder and faster, doubtful he was making a dent. Smoke burned his eyes and lungs, and sticky embers of ash covered his shirt but didn't catch fire, probably due to the sweat drenching his clothing. The muscles in his right arm grew hot and complained, so he switched the shovel to his left. With every shovel-full, he feared he wouldn't be able to keep this up, but what other choice did he have? If he lost the crop, the plantation would become insolvent. He'd never be exonerated. He'd never be able to return to England. He wouldn't even be able to feed himself and his workers here in Antigua.

They'd probably only been fighting the flames for an hour, but it felt like an eternity. The fire jumped the line in the north field, and men left their posts to battle that section. The slave quarters, where the workers' families resided, stood closest to that area. Samuel remained with a few other field hands, digging a trench to keep the east field from burning, but the fire was spreading faster than they could shovel. His muscles protested his every movement, and the top layer of his skin felt crispy like the skin of a roasted goose. His throat was scratchy and parched from the smoke and unable to generate any saliva.

The cane behind him rattled, and a maid emerged like a godsend, carrying a pitcher of water. "Here's da water." The girl's voice shook as she stared wide-eyed at the flames.

Samuel yanked the pitcher and swallowed one gulp. The cool refreshment soothed his throat and rejuvenated his overheated body. "Cuffee." He offered the pitcher to the overseer, who'd worked steadfastly by his side. "Take a drink and pass it down."

Cuffee's expression turned to one of relief as he too downed a gulp.

Samuel gripped his shovel and started once more hefting dirt onto the flames to smother the fire. He yelled over the crackle to the girl. "Who instructed you to bring water?"

The girl appeared in a trance from the dancing light devouring the crops, but she answered, "Miz Prescott."

He grunted and hefted another load. The woman never ceased to surprise him.

The girl retreated for more water, taking the empty pitcher with her. Shrieks rose above the crackling din coming from Hennion's fields, and Samuel prayed his neighbor's men weren't losing ground. To stop this fire, there needed to be a two-frontal attack. He coughed on the ash of burning sugar which seemed to stick to the inside of his lungs and wiped his brow with his already blackened shirt sleeve. The smoke plume above shifted westward toward his plantation, and he yelled to Cuffee, "The winds have shifted. Unless we finish this control line, the east field and the house will burn."

The worker on the other side of Cuffee fell to his knees and keeled over on his side.

Cuffee dropped his shovel and dragged the man a safe distance from the fire. "He's fainted from da heat, is all." Before Cuffee could return to his spot, a shirtless Carson ran up and lifted the man's shovel and started digging.

There wasn't time to pause, so Samuel continued to shovel but allowed his disbelief to ring in his voice. "Did you use your shirt to battle the flames?" The smoke scratched his throat and irritated his lungs.

"Yes, milord," Carson tossed a load of dirt onto the flames, "and I'll be heartsick about it tomorrow, but right now, we must do what we must do."

The show of loyalty brought new life to Samuel's weary limbs, but after ten or so more yards of digging, the shovel slipped from his hands. He shook out his arms and removed his handkerchief to bind his bleeding palms before resuming shoveling. He peered down the fire line. It appeared to be holding, but they had much farther to go. So much farther.

He stumbled, his knees weakening. He leaned on the handle of the shovel to shore himself up. How much longer before he too fainted?

The ground rumbled.

An earthquake? He glanced up at the smoky night sky. Was this island determined to break him?

The smell of smoke, ash, and burnt sugar hung thick in the air. Maggie slowed the team. Yellow flames twisted in a wicked dance of life and death, billowing clouds of smoke, reflecting a dark orange color against the black sky. Even though she leaned on her good leg, her injured one protested. She stopped the wagon above the line of fire so the water from the barrels could run downhill and pushed the horses as close to the action as possible without spooking them. As it was, they neighed and pranced nervously.

Two crewmen from *The Windward* jumped out of the back. Maggie twisted and pushed the long wooden plank the sailors had wedged between her and Judith toward the sailors, who used the board to roll barrels of seawater from the wagon.

Judith pressed a hand to her cheek. "My Word. It's a bigger fire than I thought." She climbed down from the wagon. "I'll calm the horses." She held the bridles and spoke soothing words to the frightened animals.

The fire's stifling heat overrode any relief the cooler night air might have brought. Greenview Manor's workers from the fields and house staff appeared only as dark shadows against the bright blaze as they dug a trough between the flames and the cane field. The angry yellow light illuminated the exhaustion and fear in the men's faces, yet they continued their tasks, knowing the lives of their families depended on stopping the blaze.

Maggie yelled to the sailor named Dregs, "Drill holes in the top like I said and then carefully roll the barrels down the hill near the flames."

"Aye-aye, little Maggsy." He removed the long metal corkscrew drill and went to work.

Maggie rubbed the pain in her leg away and cursed the red stain where one of the wounds had reopened, ruining her mother's gown. At least she'd donned the serviceable one.

The sailors rolled the barrels, spraying the flames with seawater as they passed. Cheers from the men fighting the blaze rang out. She caught sight of Samuel. His fine cambric shirt was stained black with ash, and smudges of soot donned his forehead and cheeks. Instead of merely commanding the slaves, he worked alongside them, matching them shovelful for shovelful. He paused as one of the sailors passed, rolling a barrel, and used the moment to wipe the sweat from his brow. He leaned heavily on his shovel but saluted her by raising his fist and shouting in a scratchy voice, "Huzzah for Miss Prescott and *The Windward*'s crew."

The workers echoed with a chorused, "Huzzah!"

Maggie's chin lowered as she fought to hide a grateful smile. Her heart went out to Samuel and his men in such exhausted states.

"Dregs." Uncle Anthony's voice piped above the crackle of the fire. "You are a sight for sore eyes. I should have known my men would come to the rescue."

She couldn't hear Dregs's response, but several heads swiveled in her direction, including Samuel's. She lowered her gaze, and her fingers gripped the buckboard tighter. There must be something she could do besides sitting and staring at the flames.

Something stuck out from amid the canes in the field. Were those feet? She gasped. Did someone faint from exhaustion? The heat? A combination of both?

She tied her hair back tight with her mother's scarf and carefully climbed down, trying not to put weight on her injured leg. Thank heaven she'd brought her cane along with her. She grabbed it and hobbled over. The dark-skinned man lay in the dirt shirtless, revealing lithe muscles. She averted her gaze, having never witnessed a man in a half state of dress so close. She eased into a kneeling position beside him and attempted to wake him by patting his cheek. His skin was hot to the touch. Her hand hovered under his nose, feeling for his exhale of air. The man was still breathing. Praise God.

"Judith." Maggie waved to her chaperone manning the horses. "I need water or a wet rag."

The widow stayed the horses with a calming voice, backing away slowly. She stopped one of the sailors unloading the last barrel. The sailor removed the bandana from his head and, after corkscrewing holes in the lid, overturned the barrel. Water sprayed out, and the flames hissed in retreat, fading into a cloud of smoke. The sailor dipped his bandana in the water and passed it to Judith.

Judith hurried over and knelt on the other side of the immobile slave and blotted his forehead, cheeks, and neck. The man's eyes fluttered open, and Judith aided him to a seated position. He whispered something to her, and she lifted the rag and wrung water droplets into the man's open mouth.

The man needed fresh water, not salt water from a dirtied rag. Where were the servants she'd ordered to bring water? She rose halfway, gripping her cane for balance. Her leg had become an anchor keeping her chained to one spot. People needed help, but her leg limited her actions. In the dim lantern light coming from the main house, she spied a shadow of a woman scurrying up one of the paths. Maggie lost her among the sugar cane only to catch her movement as she drew closer. The woman hurried as best as she could with a water jug balanced on her head.

Maggie stood on her good leg and waved her cane. "Over here," she yelled, but there was no way of knowing if the woman heard her over the crackling fire.

Judith returned to blotting the man's face. Samuel and the other men worked with renewed vigor now that the water barrels had lessened the flames a bit. The man rolling the first barrel had run out of water and waited for Maggie halfway down the hill.

The woman with the water jug slowed. The poor thing appeared exhausted. If the path weren't too narrow to fit the wagon, Maggie would have ridden to help.

"Judith." She waited for the chaperone to look her way. "There's a woman with water about fifty yards down this path." She pointed the way.

Judith patted the man's chest before she jumped up, hiked up her skirt, and ran to the woman. She removed the jug from the weary servant, who sank to her knees for a brief moment of relief before following Judith back to the man and offering him water.

Judith had to pull the jug away to slow the man's drinking or else he'd retch.

"Can the two of you get him to the wagon?"

The man overheard and rose but swayed on his feet. Judith held him steady under one arm, the servant woman under his other. They staggered under the man's weight but aided him into the back of the cart.

The servant woman ran back for the jug and brought it to the rest of the men still fighting the fire. Maggie hobbled back to the wagon and climbed into the seat.

"Get him to the infirmary."

She recognized Samuel's voice, but he didn't break stride in his shoveling of dirt. He remained in command even with all the commotion.

"This probably isn't the chaperoning job you expected," Maggie said as Judith slid onto the bench seat next to her. Sweat beaded on Judith's skin, and bits of ash clung to her hair and smudged her cheeks.

The widow stared at the glowing fire. "In the islands, hardly anything is as anticipated."

Maggie snapped the reins and got the horses moving, stopping the cart only to give a lift to the servant with a now empty jug and once more to pick up the seamen and load their empty barrels. She dropped the workers off at the main house, and the servant woman aided the ailing man to the infirmary before Maggie drove the crewmen back to the seaside to refill the barrels.

In all, it took five trips before the fire was extinguished. The holes in the lids of the barrels made them harder to unload from the wagon without spilling. The sky had turned from black to purple with the hint of dawn approaching.

"Men." Samuel leaned on the handle of his shovel with the blade stuck into the overturned dirt that formed the line between black ash and smoldering cinders and the lush green of the unharmed field. He addressed the sweaty ash-smudged men slumped on the ground too weary from their fire-fighting efforts to stand. "Thanks to your relentless efforts tonight, your families were saved, and we still have beds and our livelihood." He wiped the soot from his forehead with his sleeve and winced at the movement. "Go home." He waved toward the slave quarters. "Use the morning to get some rest. Cuffee and I will assess the damage and see what can be salvaged."

Several men groaned as they slowly rose. They trudged back to either the slave quarters or the main house, dragging their shovels. Most of them no longer wore a shirt, for it had been taken off and used to beat out the flames since there weren't enough shovels to go around.

Maggie slumped on the wagon's bench, her eyelids heavy and threatening to close. Judith had nodded off beside her. Her head had rolled to the side, and her mouth hung open. She'd probably be horrified at her unladylike manner, but the poor woman had earned a rest.

Samuel and Cuffee developed a plan for the workers' wives to watch for any embers that may spark back to life and let the men rest.

Uncle Anthony and his crewmen had crawled into the back of the wagon and promptly fell asleep. Dregs and her uncle alternated their snores.

Maggie yawned, inhaling a bit of ash. She coughed it out, closing her eyes in the effort. The wagon groaned and sagged on the driver's side under a new passenger's weight.

Samuel climbed onto the bench seat. "I'll drive." He nudged her over and took the reins.

She didn't have the energy to argue, nor did she want to. She scooted to the left, careful not to wake Judith, but Samuel's broad shoulders spread outside of the driver's area and into her space. She had no choice but to allow his shoulder to rest against hers as he drove to the main house.

He reeked of sweat, smoke, and burnt sugar, but the comfort of his form beside her welled irrational tears. All that had been done . . . how hard they had worked . . . everything that had been at risk . . . She blinked furiously.

Samuel had worked tirelessly, fighting for their lives, their livelihood, his home, and her mother's home. So many people depended upon him, herself included. If the main house had gone up in flames, her lineage and ancestry would never be known. She blinked away the unwanted tears, attributing them to being tired, but she couldn't brush off the overwhelming desire to throw her arms around Samuel and cling to him.

She longed to kiss him and convey her gratitude and her appreciation of his leadership, to express her joy. Part of her admitted that she desired to feel the power of his lips move over hers once more.

But that would only lead to trouble. If she turned out to be a nobody, desiring Samuel would be like trying to reel in the moon. The need for his closeness persisted, so she settled for resting her head on his shoulder. She felt his head turn to peer at her.

Had her gesture been too brash? Why did she always fail where proper etiquette was concerned? *Please let him think I've nodded off.*

He leaned his head against the top of hers.

Her breath caught. Was he also in need of comfort?

Other than Tobie, she'd never witnessed anyone work as hard for his survival and that of others. Samuel wasn't like the other men back in London. Work wasn't above him. He may look pretentious, but his actions spoke the truth. He could be in charge, but if needed, he would bend down alongside his field hands and plant ratoons, wield a machete and harvest the sugar crop, or pick up a shovel and battle a fire shoulder to shoulder with his slaves.

The wagon drew close to the main house. Samuel straightened, and Maggie did the same. He reined the wagon to a stop, and Judith awoke with a start.

"Goodness." She rubbed her eyes. "What a first day. My sister won't be able to top this."

The smell of bacon frying floated from the kitchen, and Samuel lifted his nose and closed his eyes. "I'm not certain whether I'm more tired or famished."

The bacon scent woke the men in the cart as if raising the dead. They followed their noses, trudging into the house. Uncle Anthony paused to help Judith alight from the wagon before his stomach took the lead.

Samuel eased out of the wagon like an elderly man with a bent back.

"Are you hurt?" Maggie grabbed her cane and scooted along the bench toward him.

He rolled his shoulders and grimaced. "Merely sore from shoveling."

She turned to climb down, careful not to put much weight on her bad leg, which throbbed from overexertion.

"Allow me." His warm hand curved around her waist.

She leaned away. "I can do it. You're exhaust—Oh."

He lifted her into his arms and carried her to the main house. The smell of fire wafted around them with each step, and the comfort of being cradled in strong arms overrode the pain pulsating through her leg.

"Would you prefer to—?" He turned his head

and coughed. "Pardon me." He cleared his throat. "There's still a bit of smoke in my lungs. Would you care to break your fast or retire to your chamber?"

"That bacon smells delicious." Judith swept past them into the dining room, where maids were bringing out food as fast as it was coming out of the pan. Seamen formed a line holding plates ready to bombard the next maid. "Men," Judith addressed the crowd, "be seated as gentlemen and guests. Let the staff have some room to work."

"Mrs. Morgan." Uncle Anthony's voice held a gravelly tone. "Please come and join us."

Maggie's stomach rumbled. "Perhaps a full stomach might . . ."

Samuel's frown furrowed deep creases in his brow.

"What?" She tracked his gaze to her thigh.

"You're bleeding." He scanned the room, but the footmen who had helped battle the fire were still returning from the field. "Hawley?" He spun, and her grip on his neck tightened.

The butler hurried out of the dining room, a coffee carafe in hand and an apron tied about his waist.

"Fetch Dinah. Miss Prescott is injured."

The butler's nostrils flared.

"Be quick about it."

"It's nothing." Maggie fell limp with a sigh.

"No need to drag Dinah away from people who truly need help."

Hawley hailed a footman from the dining room and delegated his task.

Ash smudged James's cheek and dotted his hair, but he darted off out the French doors.

Maggie opened her mouth to call him back, but Hawley sliced her with a cold glare before returning to serving the men coffee. What she'd done to offend the butler, she couldn't fathom, but he'd been put off by her presence from the start.

Samuel pinched the fold of her mother's gown between his thumb and index finger and pulled it straight to inspect the blood-stained fabric. "This is nothing?" He hefted her away from the delicious smells and into the salon, lowering her onto the green brocade settee.

"You shouldn't have been driving the wagon." His voice increased in volume with each sentence. "You should have been upstairs in your chamber, resting your leg and healing."

"I'm supposed to lie around while a fire rages?"

He widened his stance and folded his arms as if daring her to dispute his authority. "You should be abed, not putting yourself in harm's way." He shook his head. "Come to think of it, two lone women, riding to the docks after dark—that wasn't safe either. I'm beginning to wonder if you seek after trouble."

"Your men were needed in the fields to battle the fire." She shifted onto her good hip to face him. "And if there is one thing sailors hate, it's fire. Granted, that's when it's aboard a ship, but they were eager to help fill the barrels with ocean water and load them into the cart."

He paced the length of the settee.

"Besides I sailed with those men from England. They're my uncle's men."

"Another ludicrous stunt." His pitch lowered to a growl, and his face reddened to a burgundy color. "Of all the reckless, foolhardy . . ."

Ah.

Samuel's anger spoke his sentiments loud and clear. Maggie suppressed a grin at his concern for her. A life with Samuel may not be a possibility in England, but things weren't as stigmatized in Antigua. If he planned to stay in the islands, could she see herself with him, as his wife? Her emotions were getting ahead of reality, but marriage to Samuel, who'd work hard to provide and protect those he loved seemed like a splendid dream. She may not hold his heart, but his care was a good beginning.

Chapter 17

Nary a moment passes that I don't think of his smile, the exhilarating roll of his laughter, or the velvety feel of his lips as they brushed my knuckles.

~ *Entry by Loretta Baxter, August 10, 1810*

Samuel's insides rolled like molasses in the copper cauldrons of the boiling houses. His chest heaved with each breath, and his muscles coiled, impatient to release the tension.

You're just like your father.

He leaned over Maggie, gripping the arms of the settee. "You are done taking unnecessary risks. You are my responsibility."

She blinked, her long lashes sweeping up and down. "I am?"

Red mist clogged his thought processes. He couldn't tell if her question was sincere or meant to be defiant. His arms bent until their faces were a hands-width apart. "The moment you stepped foot on my property, you became my concern." He should stop, calm himself, but the fire inside had already jumped the trench. His heart pounded with the need to make her understand. "And I will not let anything happen to you while you are under my roof despite your attempts to get yourself killed."

Her hand slid along his jaw, and her fingers splayed as she pressed her palm to his cheek. "Thank you."

He sucked in a breath at her gentle touch, and the tension plaguing his body dissipated into steam as if she'd thrown water on his fire. He lowered to his knees, and she shifted to face him. Her thumb stroked his cheek, and his lungs stilled. How was she doing this? How had she soothed the rage he'd fought his entire life with a single touch?

"Thank you for saving my mother's house."

Her legacy. She merely wanted to preserve the house that held the answers to her questions. Understanding her motive allowed him to breathe again.

"Thank you for your leadership, for instructing the men how to battle the fire." Her fingers caressed the side of his face and lowered to rest over his heart. "You saved all of our lives."

His heartbeat responded with a rapid knocking on the walls of his chest, screaming for her to be let in. How many years had he worked to please his father without receiving a single acknowledgment for his efforts? Yet here stood a slip of a woman who appreciated him.

"You care for these people." She pointed with her chin toward the door as if to show she meant everyone at Greenview Manor.

Every inch of his being craved more, but he wouldn't show it. He couldn't let anyone see how weak he was.

Her gaze returned to his, and the golden flecks in the depths of her green eyes glittered.

The muscles in his back knotted, restraining against his impulse to beg her to affirm him with more honeyed accolades and seal them with the sweetness of her kiss.

The cords of her neck convulsed with her swallow. "Thank you for caring for me." Her front teeth tugged on her bottom lip.

His reserve crumbled, leaving him a humbled mass. "I thought . . ." He forced out a strangled whisper. "I thought we were going to lose it all—the fields, the house, my chance to ever return to London."

"God granted us His favor." Her thumb rested in the dip of his clavicle where the knot of his cravat usually tied. The intimate touch brought a tingling sensation that spread through his chest and down his spine. "He gave us the wisdom to know what to do and the energy to sustain us."

He nodded with a small snort. "I could barely lift the shovel but somehow kept going."

Sympathy softened her gaze. "You fought bravely."

He ran his hands up her arms and gripped her shoulders, itching to pull her into his embrace. She'd praised him, but he was the one who should be grateful. Despite his outburst, he was amazed by the woman he'd witnessed tonight—one who wasn't afraid to take action even in her injured state. She didn't ask for accolades for her part in subduing the fire. Instead, she offered them to him.

"I was angry because you risked much and put yourself in harm's way." He stroked her hair, amazed it still felt silken under his palm after all the smoke and ash that had floated through the air. "Men would have died if you hadn't had the forethought to instruct the women to bring water." He wound his hand behind the slender curve of her neck and dipped his fingers into the hair at the base of her head. "And it would have taken twice as long to contain the fire if you hadn't recruited the men from the ship."

"Are you saying we make a good team?" The lighthearted glow returned to her eyes.

Blood rushed through his veins. Not like the jolt from the shout of fire, but like a riptide current sweeping him out to sea. She left him disoriented, but her gaze was his anchor. He adored how she remained positive, how she hadn't feared his anger. She instinctively knew how to quell what he struggled to subdue, how to tame the beast within him.

His thumb brushed her lower lip. The warmth in her eyes compelled him to lean in closer. His mind was too exhausted to list all the reasons why doing so would be a bad idea. His mouth hovered above hers, absorbing her gasp. He swept his lips over hers—testing, teasing—and a different kind of fire ignited between them.

"I came as fast as I could." Dinah burst into the room.

He jerked away.

Dinah turned to face the wall. "I didna see a tang," she said in a winded voice.

A becoming blush spread over Maggie's cheeks.

Samuel rolled back onto his haunches and rose, his leg muscles protesting as much as his heart. "Miss Prescott has reinjured her leg. She's bleeding."

Dinah kneeled on the other side of the settee, frowning. "I'll need ta have a look." She fingered the hem of Maggie's bloodstained gown and eyed Samuel.

"Of course." He bowed, hating to be bereft of Maggie's presence, but wisdom warned to escape before he landed himself in a sticky mess of his own doing. "Please excuse me."

"No need." Dinah crossed the room. "You can sit right there." She returned with a folding screen and set it between them. "James?"

The footman poked his head into the room.

"Have someone bring da master and Miss Prescott something to fill their stomachs."

He bowed before disappearing as fast as he'd appeared.

Behind the screen, fabric rustled. "If ya want ta heal, yer gonna have ta tek it easy nah," Dinah fussed.

"Exactly what I told her." Samuel nodded to the screen even though they couldn't see him.

A latch clicked, and a lid opened. "Good tang I brought my kit wit me."

Samuel swallowed and stuck his hands in his pockets. Dinah's shadow moved behind the screen while he walked to a nearby chair. Gripping the arms, he lowered his aching muscles into the cushions.

Dinah leaned around the screen. "Might Miss Prescott have a small taste of spirits to boost her courage and clean da wound?"

Samuel leapt from his seat. "Of course." In two strides, he reached the small bar, where he uncorked the decanter of rum, pouring the amber liquid into a crystal glass. He held up the bottle after and peered into it. Someone had been helping himself.

Anthony Middleton's burst of laughter bounded from across the hall.

Samuel recorked the decanter with a good idea of the culprit and passed the glass to Dinah.

"I don't partake of spirits." Maggie's voice sounded strained.

He, too, had sworn off the stuff. Best to keep a clear mind.

"Suit yerself." Dinah's shadow moved. "But

I'm gonna use it to clean da wound. Dis is gonna burn a bit."

Maggie's inhaled hiss of breath jarred him even with the warning. He swallowed and resumed his seat, running his palms over his thighs.

"It's gonna tek justa few stitches to sew ya up so dat ya stop bleedin'."

A restrained whimper choked out of Maggie, and Samuel's fingers dug into his knees.

"Dat's one."

Maggie released a ragged breath and sucked in a few more in succession. He leaned forward and rocked slightly, bracing for her cry. Maybe they should wait and let her rest up first, or perhaps they should force her to drink the glass of rum. Or a couple? He raked his hair.

She gasped out a tiny moan before sucking in another breath and holding it. She didn't scream. He'd heard grown men cry like children while getting stitched. For such a frail-looking mite of a woman, Maggie had the inner strength of an ox.

He stood and paced. His legs protested, but his concern for Maggie's pain overrode his aches. "You shouldn't have driven that cart."

"We went over this." She bit out the words through what he guessed were clenched teeth.

His cravat had already been removed, but he ran his finger under his collar. "You won't stay in your bed and insist upon moving about the house." He pivoted on his heel to face the screen.

"You're making"—the long pause screamed her agony—"too much of this."

The air in the room grew stifling. He opened the window sash wider. "I never should have given you that cane." He raised his voice, "I'm taking it back."

"You can't take back a gif—ahhh."

His chest rose and fell, fighting to hold back a roar, and his control slipped. She needed to see reason. "Then stop acting carelessly."

"You think I'm careless?"

The rushing of blood in his ears drowned out whether her tone sounded offended or shocked. "Only a thoughtless person—"

"Thoughtless? You believe me thoughtless? Everyone was helping. How could I sit back and watch as others risked their lives, while everything you've worked so hard for burned?"

The edge in her voice rang clear. He didn't want to argue, and he hadn't meant to raise his voice, but she was misinterpreting everything. Dash it all, he was trying to protect her for her own good.

"All finished." Dinah folded the screen and carried it back to where she'd found it.

"You will stay in your bed. Do you hear me?" He glared at her.

Her green eyes flashed. "I hear you quite clearly." Maggie's coloring was high, the tendrils of hair around her face damp with sweat.

Her full lips had thinned into a tight line and the cords of her neck taut as if restraining from wringing his neck. She looked exquisite reclined on the settee, composed like a regal queen who'd just returned from battle, blood staining her gown and a smudge of ash on her forehead.

His puffed chest deflated like a collapsed soufflé. Hadn't getting shot taught her a lesson? She wasn't immortal. She was vulnerable, delicate . . . precious.

He rubbed his face. His seven and twenty years felt more like seven and seventy. How could he keep her safe if she found her foolhardy acts justifiable? What could he say to get through to her? "Just because you survived alone on an island as a child doesn't mean you are invincible. I've witnessed strong, healthy men who've died from an infection from wounds less serious than yours."

She exhaled a breath as if her patience waned. "I appreciate that you are trying to keep me safe, but none of us is promised tomorrow, and I will not live in fear."

If she wouldn't see reason, then he had no choice but to tighten the reins. "You are my responsibility, and I can't have you reinjuring yourself or getting your wound infected. Until your leg has healed entirely, you are to remain off your feet and in your chamber."

"You're making me a prisoner?" Her eyes widened. "You can't be serious."

"Quite." He lifted one eyebrow to emphasize the sincerity of his command.

Her lips parted. Had he finally rendered her speechless.

He turned to leave, and the relief of reestablishing a semblance of control lightened his chest.

Widow Morgan stood in the doorway with crossed arms and a frown.

How much had she overheard? Did she find him as unreasonable as Miss Prescott? Did it matter? He paid her wages to act as chaperone, not judge.

"Your meal is ready," she said as he passed.

"Have a tray brought to my chamber."

He skirted the dining room, and Hawley met him at the stair. "Mr. Cuffee would like a word with you regarding the cane fields."

Samuel glanced up the stairs where his bed beckoned. "Have a groom drive the sailors and Captain Middleton to their ship. Tell Cuffee to meet me in my office and have two trays brought there."

"Right away, my lord." Hawley bowed and left to speak to Cuffee.

Samuel spun and strode toward his office. Passing by the salon, he glimpsed Maggie, her hands folded and her head bowed as if in prayer. Did she seek a higher power to get what she wanted? Surely God understood the importance of keeping His child safe.

Samuel entered the solace of his office, sat behind his desk, and picked up a quill to start a task list for tomorrow. The wall clock showed the early hour. It was already tomorrow.

A knock sounded.

"Enter."

Cuffee strolled in, his hat between his hands. "I inspected da cane. It's hard ta believe, but I tink da stalks protected da sugar. Dere's a way to salvage wat was burned. Everybody's mighty tired, but we'd have ta act fast."

Samuel gestured for Cuffee to sit and listened to his plan. When the overseer was finished, Samuel rubbed his eyes. "Are you certain it can be saved?"

"Yessir." Cuffee coughed and pressed a fist to his sternum. "I'd stake my good name on it."

"I gave the men the day off." Samuel grimaced. "I can't go back on my word, but if we can save it, we need to try." He slumped in his chair and stared at the wall clock. "See who's willing to work for pay. I'll give them a cut of what I can sell. The option is theirs. They'll not be punished for saying no."

A twitch of a smile grew on Cuffee's lips. "Tat should motivate dem, but we need ta get ta work right away."

Hawley and a footman carried in two trays, but Samuel raised his hand, stopping them, and stood. "All right then. Let's not waste time if there's work to be done."

Hawley's normal scowl deepened.

Samuel swiped two bread rolls off the tray and tossed one to Cuffee before exiting the room and then the main house through the French doors.

Through the window, Samuel caught Maggie's surprised expression. She could beseech God's intervention, but he'd work to regain control of the plantation's yield, his temper, and his desires. His legs protested every step, but he'd fight to his very last breath to make this island produce. His future depended on it.

Maggie awoke to footsteps stumbling up the stairs. Had Uncle Anthony forgotten he was staying aboard the ship and instead staggered into the house after a night of carousing? It wouldn't be the first time he'd humiliated himself, and her by default. If discovered, he'd embarrass them all by his foxed state. Daylight streamed into her room, but she didn't have the foggiest idea of the time. She threw back the covers and slipped into her robe.

She knotted her sash and limped to the door. Her thigh still throbbed from the stitches. The house lay eerily still, but after last night's events, most of the staff had probably dropped into their beds and slept like the dead. She hobbled down the hall, keeping an eye on Samuel's closed door since he'd forbidden her from leaving her room. She stopped at the top of the stairs. A man lay sprawled on the staircase unconscious, but it wasn't Uncle Anthony.

Her hand flew to cover her mouth.

Samuel.

Chapter 18

His hair is black like a raven's and his eyes as green as the sugarcane fields. They twinkle with laughter and mischief, but when he looks at me, their beautiful depths darken, and I find myself lost in the jungle of his passion.

~ Entry by Loretta Baxter,
August 10, 1810

Dear Lord, let him be all right. Maggie scrambled down the few stairs as best as her leg would allow and knelt beside him. She shook him, but he didn't respond. His back rose and fell with his inhale and exhale. Thank heaven he was breathing. Leaning down, she whispered in his ear, "Samuel, wake up."

A weak half-groan, half-whimper gurgled in his throat.

She shook him harder. "Please, I can't pull you upstairs myself."

Nothing.

She needed help, but her uncle must have stayed on his ship, for his door was open and his bed empty. Who else would be close by that didn't require her traipsing all over the house?

A valet would sleep on a pallet in the master's changing room. *Carson.*

She limped up the steps and crept into the master's chamber. Samuel's bergamot cologne lingered in the room, welcoming her like a warm cup of Earl Gray tea. She eased around the neatly made four-poster bed. Last time she'd entered, this chamber had served as her hiding spot. The hulking bed held her gaze. It was only a piece of furniture, but after having tasted Samuel's kiss, it now seemed intimate. A sacred place she never should have invaded in the first place.

Reaching the changing room, she tapped on the wooden paneled door. A muffled snore responded. She lifted the latch and peeked inside, identifying the lump asleep in the far corner.

"Carson," she whispered, tiptoeing closer. She shook his shoulder. "Carson."

The man jolted awake and sat up. "I'm sorry, milord. I only closed my eyes for a second."

She waved her hand. "It's me, Miss Prescott."

He blinked. "Miss Prescott?" He threw off the blanket and stood. "Is something amiss? Is it the master?"

"Indeed." She beckoned for him to follow her. "I need your help."

He followed her around the bed and into the hall.

"Egad." He drew up short, spying Samuel.

"I think he passed out from exhaustion."

Carson trotted down the stairs and crouched next to his master. She limped down after him. "Can you help me carry him into bed?"

"Shall I wake Hawley?"

Maggie paused. The last person she was in the mood to see was the ill-natured butler. She shook her head. "I think it would be a blow to Lord Granville's pride for anyone to find him in such a state. I daresay, we should get him to bed and not mention this."

The valet nodded and eased Samuel over onto his back. Samuel's eyelids fluttered but didn't open.

"You get his top half." She maneuvered to pick up his boots. "And I'll take his feet."

"Are you sure you can manage?" Carson scooped under Samuel's armpits and lifted.

"He wouldn't want anyone to see him like this. I'll make do. Just go slowly." She grabbed Samuel's boots and tucked them under her arms. Carson held the brunt of the weight and edged up one stair at a time, for which Maggie was grateful. She staggered up the few steps, and Carson wiggled around the corner of the railing, grunting.

Maggie readjusted her hold on Samuel's legs, which grew heavier by the moment.

Samuel's eyes fluttered open then closed. "Stop," he murmured. "Leg. Hurt."

She halted. "You hurt your leg?" She lightened her grasp as much as she could without dropping him.

"Your leg," he mumbled with his eyes closed. He followed it with a light snore.

She snorted. Samuel issued commands even while he slept. Well, he had a lesson to learn if he thought she would comply. She shuffled into his chamber.

Carson indicated with his head for her to swing around so Samuel's feet would be at the foot of the bed, and they lined him up parallel. "On the count of three. One . . . two . . . three . . ."

She hefted the lower half of Samuel's body onto the bed and clenched her teeth to bite back the pain in her leg. The smell of burnt sugar billowed around her.

Maggie leaned against the bedpost and caught her breath.

A weak cough lolled Samuel's head to the side. His square jaw and straight nose were marred with dirt, and bits of ash clung to his mussed hair.

Her fingers tingled with the urge to stroke his tousled locks.

Carson frowned. "He's filthy. Should I attempt to wipe his face or change his dress? He'll dirty the bedspread."

She reached over and pulled the other half of the coverlet over him. "He needs his rest right now."

His valet's frown deepened.

She touched his shoulder. "It's going to be fine. A little dirt will wash out."

Carson retreated to his makeshift bed in the

closet, muttering, "Ruined. The third shirt this week."

Samuel's mouth slumped open, and another louder snore rumbled. In rest, his face held a boyish quality. She brushed her fingers gently over the curl at the tip of his widow's peak. He had given his all to save his livelihood and that of many others, to the point of collapsing.

"You are a good man, Samuel Granville," she whispered and plucked out a bit of ash caught in his hair. *I think you need protecting, too.* She pressed a kiss to her fingertips and smoothed the disheveled tendril above his temple.

She limped back to bed. He was the one who had needed help, but even in his weakened state, when she'd carried the bone-weary man to bed, his concerned utterances had been for her. She chuckled and shook her head.

Samuel's temper may be formidable, but it was all bluster.

Samuel woke the next day and groaned. His muscles objected to the slightest movement and stiffened his body. His head pounded, and his eyelids felt weighted with bricks. His yawn turned into a cough, and he wrapped his arms around his midsection to stop the agonizing movement while his lungs cleared ash residue.

"Good morning, milord." Carson entered and set out fresh clothes.

Brighter light than usual streamed in from between the parting of the curtains. "What time is it?"

"Half-past ten."

Carson had to be mistaken. Midmorning? Samuel never overslept. The fire and a rapid harvest of the damaged cane plants slammed into the forefront of his mind. Samuel threw back the covers and jumped out of bed, grunting at the pain. He leaned over the wash basin and splashed water over his face and wiped his chest and arms with a towel to remove the filth. Cuffee will be wondering why Samuel missed his morning perimeter walk and his review of today's agenda. Due to offering the men a day off, the plantation was half-staffed. Was the harvested cane being juiced? Were the boiling houses staffed and managed? If the fields weren't limed today and the cane leaves inspected for sugar borers and other insects, how badly would the plantation be set back?

"I'm late." He stuffed his arms into his shirt's sleeves that Carson held out for him and donned his trousers.

Carson fumbled with Samuel's shirt buttons. "I daresay I can button faster when you're still."

Samuel paused for a moment, and Carson moved to knotting Samuel's cravat. Samuel sat and tugged on his stockings and boots.

"You could use a shave this morning."

Samuel felt the scruff already forming a

beard. He hated being unshaven. "There's no time."

Carson turned with the razor and washbasin in hand. "But you've callers this morning."

Blast. Of course, the fire would draw every busybodied gossip on the island. He'd be expected to greet them, and before he welcomed guests, he'd need to shave. Both of those tasks would only delay him further from seeing to his property.

Maggie's words emerged from his memory. *Propriety can be impractical.*

He snorted. She was right. He grabbed his jacket and folded it over his arm before bounding down the stairs. The townsfolk would have to suffer his unshaven state.

Hawley greeted him at the bottom. "The magistrate and Mr. Fines arrived earlier and are requesting a meeting with you and to interview the field slaves."

"They want to question our workers?" Samuel furrowed his brow. "Where are they now?"

"They've gone to meet with Hennion but will come calling again after."

Samuel was hardly in the mood for the likes of Fines and Langham.

"Also, my lord, your attorneys arrived with important information."

Wretched timing. "How long have they been waiting?"

"Twenty minutes, sir. Miss Prescott and Mrs. Morgan are entertaining them over tea in the blue salon."

The pounding in Samuel's head increased, and he squeezed his eyes tight. Not only were his attorneys socializing with the very person he'd assigned them to investigate, but Fines and Langham, the two men on the island most determined to undermine him at every turn, would be returning soon. *Double blast.*

Should he tell Maggie they were researching her past? He'd promised to help her, but her optimism and laisse faire attitude gave him pause. Touchy subjects that could forever ruin one's reputation needed to be handled discretely. She believed the best of people, but society worked the other way, assuming the worst until you proved them wrong.

A murmur of feminine voices drifted into the hall. His lawyers should keep client privilege sacred, but he'd better get in there and monitor the situation. "Notify me the moment Fines and the magistrate return."

"Yes, my lord."

Samuel rounded the corner and paused just before the open doorway to the blue salon. Through the crack in the door, he caught Maggie's profile as she sat on the sofa, demure with her ankles crossed and her gown fanned out around her. Her hair had been pulled up in a coiffure of soft curls, and she'd donned a pair of white gloves. She drew a teacup to her lips. "Come now, Mr. Stanhope." She smiled as if teasing the man. "I'm certain your sister has many redeeming qualities that will benefit the marriage mart."

"She's quite good at talking a man's ear off." Stanhope scratched under his chin.

"Perhaps you could introduce her to a hot air balloon pilot." A glint lit Maggie's eyes. "He might appreciate the extra lift."

The two men burst into laughter. Mr. Stanhope slapped his knee, and Mr. Pierpont held his stomach. Miss Maggie Prescott was full of surprises, and it appeared she could rival any of London's society hostesses. He stepped into the room. "Gentlemen."

Maggie's head swiveled in his direction, her pink lips parting.

Widow Morgan looked up from her embroidery, and the attorneys started to rise, but Samuel waved them back. "I see you've met my houseguests, Miss Maggie Prescott, and her chaperone, Mrs. Judith Morgan."

Mr. Pierpont nodded. "Delightful company. The pleasure was all ours."

"I don't mean to interrupt, but gentlemen, if you'll follow me to my office, we can let the ladies get back to"—what was it they'd been doing?—"their other engagements."

The lawyers excused themselves and exited into the hall. Before Samuel turned to guide them to his office, his gaze locked with Maggie's. She issued him a look that seemed to say, *You should still be in bed.*

As if she had the right to lecture him after reopening her wound.

He arched a brow, wanting to stay and tease her into presenting him with one of her smiles, but the attorneys were waiting for him.

"Right this way." He strode down the hall. The men followed, their boots clapping on the stone tiles. Samuel held open the door to his study, and he gestured for them to take a seat in the low back chairs before Samuel sat behind his desk. "Thank you for coming. I must apologize for my haggard appearance and brisk behavior. Last night . . ." He frowned. "I guess it was the night prior. There was a fire in the fields, and it required all hands to combat the blaze."

"Miss Prescott apprised us of the terrible situation." Mr. Stanhope pursed his lips. "I hope it didn't cause much devastation."

"We were able to contain it, but I'm rather put out at the moment, so I must get down to business. What information do you have for me?"

"Certainly," Pierpont murmured and removed a folder from his case, handing it to Stanhope.

Stanhope pulled spectacles from his breast pocket and wrapped them around his ears. "We looked into your request." He opened the folder. "The succession of Greenview Manor to the Granville family is legitimate. The property and holdings were not entailed so the property could be passed outside of the family line."

Samuel leaned back in his chair and mentally sighed a breath of relief.

"There's one caveat. Primogeniture takes priority, so if Mr. Baxter's sole daughter,"—he peered through his spectacles at the paper before him—"a Miss Loretta Baxter, married and sired a legitimate child, then the land, holdings, and property would go to either her husband or their firstborn son." Stanhope trailed his index finger down the page. "If only daughters were sired, then the inheritance would go to whomever the firstborn daughter married."

He peered at Samuel above the rim of his spectacles as if to check if Samuel had a question before he continued.

Samuel nodded for him to keep reading.

"If the firstborn daughter never married, then the land and holdings would go to the second daughter's husband and so on down the line. If Miss Loretta Baxter had no children, or if none of her daughters married, then the holdings could fall to her husband's siblings or male cousins. However, since Miss Baxter's marriage is still in question and any legitimate children are unknown, her father's gift of the lands to Lord

Henry Granville, Earl of Cardon, stands. And upon his death shall be inherited by you, his firstborn son. Unless the House of Lords reverts the holdings to your brother for the incident with Lord Reginald."

The muscle in Samuel's jaw twitched. The trial before his peers had been a farce. The Tilly family had used its influence to forbid their daughter's name from being spoken to protect the family's reputation. Harry had used his loose relation to the King to bribe or blackmail members to his side. A single vote ruled in Harry's favor, with Lord Seaton abstaining.

Samuel's jaw tightened at the memory of his former friend passing a note to Lord Wheaton, who whispered its contents to the speaker. They deliberated aloud, and blood had drained from Samuel's face and hands. In the melee, the terms banishment and exile had been tossed around.

Several young bucks he'd regularly played cards with at Whites gentlemen's club demanded his inheritance be stripped from him. Samuel had stood helplessly on a precipice in where men he would have called his mates laughed about handing Samuel's future, and all his life's work, to someone else.

The Duke of Linton was the only fellow to speak reason. "Indeed, we cannot have a peer of the realm attempting to take the life of another peer, but I hardly believe Lord Reginald's nose being broken warrants such a stiff penalty as losing all of Lord Granville's lands."

Shouts had rung out, and the final determination was that he would be sent to cool his heels in Antigua. It wasn't fair that he'd been punished as an example for the aristocracy's heirs, but he'd prove he could remain an upstanding servant of the monarchy and aid his homeland by turning a profit. He'd be allowed to return after harvest for a lesser sentence consisting of a fine. If he couldn't follow the decree, then the House of Lord's influence, both financially and socially, would revert his inheritance to his younger brother. Samuel's one saving grace was that his title would remain with him and his bloodline.

Samuel exhaled a steady breath and refocused on what his attorneys were saying. "Did you find any documentation in the annals regarding Miss Baxter having married?"

Mr. Pierpont cleared his throat. "We've written the rector at St. John's parish requesting he pull whatever he can find from the annals on Miss Baxter, including birth, death, and marriage certificates. He has yet to respond."

"And if Miss Baxter had a child—" Samuel leaned on his elbows and laced his fingers. "How would that child go about proving their legitimacy?"

The attorneys exchanged glances. Mr. Stanhope

spoke, "They would need to produce a birth certificate or that of the child's christening."

"And if such certificates couldn't be located?"

Mr. Pierpont stroked his tightly trimmed beard. "Then a case would be brought before the assembly, and witnesses would be called to prove beyond a reasonable doubt that the child was the legitimate heir."

"It's best not to allow it that far, if possible." Mr. Stanhope slid his spectacles to the tip of his nose and peered over the top. "Messy rot that turns out to be. People show up in droves to gossip about exposed secrets and other speculations, whether true or not. Even if legitimacy is determined, reputations can suffer."

Samuel conjured Maggie's image in his mind, her easy smile speeding his pulse. He couldn't abide her enduring such invasive scrutiny. His stomach knotted, but how could he convince her to end a search that would only result in heartache? That letter written to her mother by some rogue, implied her illegitimacy. Weren't her opportunities in life better with the truth left unknown than confirmation of an unfortunate circumstance?

Stanhope cleared his throat. "Obviously any illegitimate children wouldn't pose a threat to your ownership since illegitimate children cannot inherit per English law. At least, not without specifically being named in a will or final testament, and even then, it's often successfully contested."

Samuel rose. "Thank you, gentlemen." He bowed to Stanhope and Pierpont. "I need not remind you of the confidentiality of this information, including our meeting." He didn't want Fines or Langham questioning his ownership.

"Of course." Stanhope nodded as he and Mr. Pierpont rose. "If I may venture a guess, your inquiry may regard a certain young houseguest who informed us she is here to research her ancestry."

Samuel didn't respond.

Stanhope nudged Pierpont with his elbow and nodded at Samuel. "If the rector finds proof of a legitimate parentage, then my sage advice would be to haul that lovely young lady to the altar as fast as possible."

The men chuckled at their jest but smothered it when Samuel didn't participate.

"Good day, gentlemen." He saw them to the study door, where Hawley waited to see them out. Samuel returned to his desk and jotted notes for his task list per their conversation. He waved the paper for the ink to dry.

Marry Maggie.

His insides leapt at the prospect like a dolphin jumping alongside a ship. Marriage would be the obvious solution if she were the legitimate daughter of a sugar baron or the natural daughter of the Prescotts. However, her questionable lineage was problematic. She'd continue to be shunned by elite society. His title and status wouldn't have swayed their favor even before he'd set himself in a precarious state. If he married someone base-born, he'd become an outcast too. Banks would no longer loan to him. Businesses would turn him away. His family and everyone under his care would suffer.

He slid the paper into the top desk drawer as a knock sounded.

Hawley stood in the doorway.

"Are Fines and Langham back?"

"No, my lord." Hawley straightened his lapel. "Mr. and Mrs. Kelly have arrived and are awaiting you in the blue salon."

Of course they'd heard about the fire and come to check on him.

"Mrs. Morgan's sister has also arrived to see about her wellbeing. They too are seated in the blue salon, along with Miss Prescott."

"Very good. I will join them." Samuel rose. "If anyone else comes calling"—which they most certainly would, as gossip spread quickly over the island—"tell them we aren't receiving any more visitors today."

"Yes, my lord." Hawley bowed and returned to his station.

Samuel followed the sound of women's laughter into the blue salon. He'd planned to introduce Maggie to Thea and George, but his gut told him the men would have met their match if those two got together. He quietly stopped and stood in the salon's entryway.

Maggie and Thea had already seemed to hit it off, for they were huddled close. Maggie pointed to something in a journal and Thea nodded.

George had picked up the book on agricultural practices that Samuel had left on the end table and perused its pages.

Mrs. Morgan and her sister sat in the far corner, probably discussing recent events if her sister's shocked expression were any indicator.

"Ah, there you are." George closed the volume and set it aside. "I'm glad to see you're hale. Thea was beside herself after hearing about the fire." George moved to rise, but Samuel stayed him with a wave.

Samuel sat in the seat next to Maggie. She cast him a sideway glance, and heat pulsed through his extremities. An image of her leaning over and drawing the covers over him flashed through his mind. Where had that come from? His lack of sleep was making him delusional.

Thea's voice interrupted his thoughts. ". . . beside ourselves with worry." She pursed her lips. "You look wretched."

Samuel snorted. "Why, thank you."

She waved her hand. "You know what I mean. As long as I've known you, I've never seen you go without a shave, and the smudges under your eyes are darker than black pineapples."

He felt Maggie's gaze upon him, and the roots of his hair tingled as if her fingers had combed the front. Heat crept up his collar, and he mentally shook himself.

"I haven't tried one of those." Maggie glanced at Thea. "Are they delicious?"

"Quite." Thea pivoted into the new topic. "When you join us for dinner, I will make certain to have some black pineapple. I think you'll love it." She faced Samuel. "I took the liberty of mentioning our invitation to Miss Prescott. I shall be expecting you this Friday, and do not use the fire as an excuse. You of all people need to relax and enjoy the company of others. You work too hard."

He looked to George for support, but his friend's expression told him it was best to go along with his wife's demands. "Why don't you dine here?" Samuel suggested. "Miss Prescott isn't ready to travel yet with her injury."

"Miss Prescott told us about the fire and all that happened." Thea shook her head. "Dreadful, quite dreadful. What a blessing that no one was hurt."

George leaned forward. "How much was lost?"

"We were fortunate." Samuel preferred this turn in their conversation topic. "The field that caught fire was ready to be yielded in a few weeks. Cuffee discovered the sugar preserved within the stalks. The fire forced us to speed up our harvesting so it wouldn't turn while lying in the field, but we got it done."

"By Jove." George pressed his hand to his head. "You spent the night battling a fire and the morning harvesting cane. No wonder you look haggard."

"Your insults are too kind." Samuel laced his tone with sarcasm.

A giggled snort burst from beside him. Maggie covered her mouth with the back of her hand.

"Pish posh." Thea clucked her tongue. "You know it's out of concern. How many hours of sleep have you gotten in the last forty-eight?"

He summed them in his head. "Three."

Thea gasped.

"Ghastly." George shook his head. "Your workers must be exhausted. If you're in need, I can lend you some of my men."

Samuel understood the kindness of his friend's offer. Every hand was needed this time of year, and losing workers, even for a day, would be putting him out. "I appreciate that. If the need arises, I will take you up on your aid. My plan is to break the men into shorter shifts so they can rest between rotations."

"I will not be sent away a second time." The magistrate's blustery voice echoed from the front entrance. "I demand to see Lord Granville."

Widow Morgan and her sister paused their murmured conversation, their eyes wide.

Samuel rose. "I beg your pardon." The gossip mongers would get their fill that day.

George aided Thea to a stand. "We should let you get back to your duties."

"We're just pleased to know you're well." Thea leaned her head against her husband's shoulder. "It was lovely to meet you, Miss Prescott, and we look forward to seeing you this Friday."

"Indeed." Maggie smiled, and the room brightened. "I cannot wait." She gripped her cane to rise.

"Wait here." Samuel clasped her shoulder. "You should stay off that leg."

"Stand aside." The magistrate commanded from the hall, presumably to Hawley.

At Samuel's gesture, George and Thea exited into the hall.

"Mr. and Mrs. Kelly." The magistrate's tone eased, and pitch increased with surprise. "I didn't see your carriage outside."

"We chose to ride instead." George bowed to the magistrate. "Splendid to see you, Mr. Langham, Mr. Fines. I don't mean to be brief, but we must be getting back to the plantation. Good day." Hawley handed them their hats, and they slipped out the front door.

Samuel widened his stance, bracing for trouble. "How may I help you, gentlemen?"

Fines pressed around the magistrate and poked Samuel in the chest. "We've spoken to Hennion and have questions for you."

"Indeed." The word came out as a low growl, and he locked his jaw to keep his temper in place.

Fines's gaze slid over Samuel's shoulder. "Who is this?"

The magistrate leaned and whispered in Mr. Fines's ear.

Samuel pivoted to see what was behind him and his growl turned to a groan. He strode to where Maggie stood in the salon doorway and shooed her back inside.

Her gaze locked on his, and she gripped his sleeve. "I recognize the magistrate, but not the other man. May I help? I might be able to calm matters, especially since it was the magistrate who shot me."

His lips twitched, grateful she believed the best of him. "I'm afraid any conversation with Mr. Fines won't be fit for a woman's ears. Please stay here. I will deal with them." He pleaded with her to do as he bid—for once.

She nodded and stepped back while Mrs. Morgan and her sister sat alert, likely eager for more gossip.

Samuel turned back to face his accusers but held his palm up to keep Maggie put behind him. He didn't have the time or the patience for Fines's schemes and faradiddles. He stepped back into the hall, lowering his arm to his side. "It has been an exhaustive few days, and I have much work to do. What is it that demands my immediate attention?"

Fines puffed his chest as if ready to fight. "We have reason to believe your slaves started the fire."

Chapter 19

Every curse Papa utters regarding the French stabs a dagger into my heart.
> ~ *Entry by Loretta Baxter,*
> *August 26, 1810*

Maggie gasped. Who was that man? How dare he accuse Samuel's men of setting the fire. What evidence did he have? At the time of the fire, the men had just come in from the fields for the evening meal. If men had been missing, Cuffee would have noticed and brought it to Samuel's attention. Not to mention that Samuel had just come in from his evening inspection. Surely, he would have seen something.

"You're mistak—" She tried to step out into the hallway but met with Samuel's extended hand. His glare over his shoulder warned her, hard and insistent, to stay out. A muscle twitched in his cheek. The man had raised Samuel's hackles, and she could tell by the coiled tension in his arms that he was fighting not to draw the man's cork.

She touched his arm to calm him and show her support. "What he's saying is preposterous."

"Let me handle this."

"Entertaining ladies again, I see." The stranger's tone had turned snide. "And so soon after your fiancée crying off."

Samuel's nostrils flared and his hard stare focused back on Fines. "You overstep." His fingers curled into fists. "You know nothing about what you speak."

"Oh, you thought word wouldn't travel here from England? That your reputation was safe here in the islands? I, too, have contacts in London, and they believe you are a danger to society. I've already alerted the assembly."

Samuel's eyes narrowed, and his face turned a reddish color.

"I am, of course, concerned for the lady's safety." He crossed his arms and sauntered a couple of steps closer.

Mr. Langham followed on his heels.

Through the salon's door, Maggie glimpsed both Judith and her sister leaning their ears toward the action.

The accusing man stopped an arm's length away. His upper lip curled, and his gaze slithered over Maggie's form. "Assuming she *is* a lady."

Maggie's mouth dropped open.

A low growl rumbled beside her. Samuel wound back, braced to launch himself at the disreputable man.

She gripped his arm with both her hands. He stepped toward Fines, dragging her along with his momentum. Her slippers slid across the tiles, and she crashed into his side.

He shook her off.

If she didn't intervene, they most certainly would come to blows. Maggie poked her head around Samuel and eyed his accuser. "Maybe you should speak to Mr. Langham about why Lord Granville ended up with me as his houseguest in the first place?"

The man twisted to look at his cohort with a puzzled expression, and Mr. Langham fumbled for his pocket watch. "I fear our time is precious. Perhaps we should be getting on with questioning the slaves." He exited the way they had come, and his wretched companion followed.

Take that. Maggie's lips curved.

Samuel lifted her with a vice-like grip on her upper arms, and she swallowed a startled scream.

"I can handle this," he ground out through clenched teeth. Samuel walked her back into the blue salon and set her down, fixing her with a steely glare before turning to Widow Morgan.

Judith jumped up, hooked Maggie's elbow, and tugged her over to where she sat with her sister. Maggie peered over her shoulder as Samuel strode back into the hall toward the foyer.

God, I don't trust those men. Give Samuel your wisdom for what to say and keep his temper under control so they can't use his anger against him.

"Why is it that you always get the excitement?" Caroline fussed at her sister, "while I have to abide with dull and boring?"

Movement outside the salon window caught Maggie's attention.

Cuffee crossed in front of the mill on his way to meet Samuel and the men.

Maggie leaned over a chair's low back and out the open window that overlooked the garden. "Cuffee." She waved him over.

He glanced off in the distance to where Samuel stood and hustled toward her. "Miz Prescott, do ya need sometang?"

"I believe the men meeting with Lord Granville are trying to trick him. I specifically think they are trying to goad him into losing his temper so they can spread lies about him."

Cuffee's head drew back.

"I need you to help him not give way to his anger."

"How am I suppose ta do dat?" He mopped the back of his neck with his handkerchief.

"If Lord Granville starts to get angry, I want you to distract him."

"Wit wat?"

Cilla and Tobie always used to use ridiculous words or a code phrase to de-escalate high emotions. "I want you to say something silly like whatever makes Lord Granville laugh."

"Da master doesn't laugh much."

Her heart twisted. "Then say something ridiculous that would make others laugh. Something out of context."

Cuffee leaned in closer. "Like . . ."

"Like . . ." She scanned the garden just outside the window where she and Samuel had discussed the name of the flower. "Like hibiscus blossoms."

He peered at her like she'd gone a little mad.

"It will work, you'll see."

He straightened. "If ya say so, Miz Prescott. I will give it a try." He bowed and strode over to Samuel, joining in step behind the magistrate and his friend. The group marched toward the slave quarters.

God, please let it work.

Judith clucked her tongue, and Maggie turned to find the sisters perched on either side of the chair's arms. Judith shook her head. "I agree their motives seem far from honorable."

"Oh, tosh." Caroline leaned in for a better view. "Mr. Fines and Mr. Langham are merely looking to discover how the fire started. The women in town think there have been more than a few cases of slaves intentionally starting fires to hurt their masters as part of an uprising."

Maggie stared at the retreating men's forms. Mr. Fines must be the unpleasant man's name. He appeared to be the same age as Samuel and of a similar build. However, Samuel was sophisticated, polished, and a man of character. Mr. Fines appeared . . . What was it about him that seemed different—the cut of his clothes, the jumpiness in his eyes, the jealousy in the twist of his lips?

She scooted to sit properly in the chair and face the sisters. "Tell me about this Mr. Fines fellow."

A spark lit in the sisters' eyes as if a log had been added to the gossip fire. They glanced at each other and smiled before ringing for more tea and pulling up their chairs.

Judith started. "Mr. Fines manages plantations for absentee planters, and he managed Greenview Manor until Lord Granville arrived."

Caroline leaned closer. "Lord Granville's first act upon arriving was to terminate Mr. Fines. He didn't take it well. Went straight to the tavern and dipped deep into his cups. Then he stumbled over to his paramour's house and locked himself in there tight."

"No one heard a peep from him for an entire week." Judith's lips pursed.

"I've never been jealous of one of the muslin company women." Caroline arranged her skirts with a coy smile. "But Mr. Fines is nice on the eyes."

Judith harrumphed. "Comments like that are why I received the chaperone position and not you."

As the women continued with their hearsay, Maggie's stomach knotted. Mr. Fines's hatred toward Samuel ran deep. Samuel must watch his back. Or perhaps, she should watch it for him.

Tension, like a crank, wound Samuel's shoulders toward his ears. Loathing for Fines cramped his stomach. If Maggie hadn't stopped him, he would have pummeled Fines, probably landing himself in jail at the magistrate's instructions, having witnessed the entire debacle.

They stopped at the boiling house, and Fines stood, legs widespread and his hands on his hips, observing the workers. "Just as I suspected." He turned around and glared at Samuel. "The boiling house is running at full capacity. A fire should have slowed production down or halted it entirely, but you seem to be doing quite well despite the fire."

He rounded on Cuffee. "Speak the truth, boy. Did your master instruct you to burn the fields because he found a way to cheat the harvesting?" The man jabbed his finger at Samuel's loyal overseer, who happened to be a freeman.

Samuel's vision narrowed on the ugly lines marring Fines's face. "You will not speak to—"

"A fire that could have put the whole island in danger?" Fines stepped toe-to-toe with Cuffee.

"—my overseer in such a fashion." Samuel wedged between Fines and Cuffee, ready to defend his employee. "You don't need to answer him."

"Either he answers me here"—Spittle flew from Fines's mouth—"or he answers me in front of the assembly."

"You're looking for trade secrets so you can steal them." Samuel clenched and unclenched his fingers. If Fines laid a hand on Cuffee, this encounter would end in punches being thrown.

Fines faced Samuel. "You're the one who's trying to disrupt a system that's been in place since the island was discovered. You're the one voting for giving slaves rights and freedoms that don't belong to their kind." He turned back to Cuffee, "Answer me, boy."

Samuel eyed Fines's cravat, his fingers twitching to grab the man by the collar and toss him off his property.

Cuffee straightened to full height, cleared his throat, and said, "Hibiscus."

"What?" Fines drew back.

Samuel's gaze jerked to his overseer.

"What did he say?" Fines's brows lowered.

"Hibiscus," Cuffee replied, a little louder this time.

Samuel gave his head a hard shake. He needed more sleep, and Cuffee did, too, for that matter. Maybe they were both delirious.

"Is he an idiot or something?" Fines waved his fist. "Do you take me for a fool?"

The men working the cauldrons paused in their stirring and stared at the commotion.

Samuel rounded on the magistrate. "Am I supposed to stand by while this man insults my overseer and me? If this were England, we'd be choosing barking irons at dawn and walking ten paces for lesser insults."

Mr. Langham pulled at his collar with his index finger. "We can't be having any of that." He tugged on Fines's arm. "Maybe there is someone else we can speak to?"

Fines pointed at the nearest man, who shrank back at the sight of Greenville Manor's former overseer. "You."

The man's eyes widened. What was the worker's name? Maggie had him learning things he'd never bothered with before. *Seban. That was it.*

"Yes, you." Fines waved him over. "Come here and be quick about it."

If Samuel's memory of the ledgers served, Seban had been purchased by Fines at least five years before, yet Fines hadn't bothered to learn the man's name.

Seban wiped his brow then passed his stirring stick to the worker beside him. His gaze jumped between Cuffee and Fines as he hurried over and stood at attention.

Fines jabbed his finger against the worker's chest. "Did your master instruct someone to burn the fields so you could reap the harvest easier?"

The worker started to shake his head but glanced at Cuffee, who issued him a curt nod. The worker cleared his throat and swallowed. "Hibiscus?"

"Hibiscus blossoms," Cuffee corrected him.

Mr. Fines spun and stomped his foot, spewing foul curses.

Samuel snorted, leaned toward Cuffee, and whispered. "What are you doing?"

"It's Miz Prescott's doing. She told me if ya got upset ta say Hibiscus."

"Why that?"

"I don't rightly know."

Fines and Langham stalked out of the boiling house, and Fines kicked the dirt. "Find me someone who works in the field."

Cuffee led them into the fields, and this time Samuel followed. Either Maggie was half-crazed or a genius. As ridiculous as it sounded, her outrageous attempt to keep him calm appeared to be working. He'd been stunned out of his fury. *Hibiscus? Really?* An image of her sitting on the garden bench enjoying the sunlight and fresh air as she commented on the beautiful blossoms crossed his mind. He hadn't even known what they were called until she'd told him. He shook his head. *I won't forget from now on*.

They approached a group of workers bundling the burnt stalks of sugar cane and loading them onto a cart. Cuffee spoke to the men in the thickest island accent Samuel had ever heard, but the word "hibiscus" was discernible. The men stopped their bundling and stood. They stared at Cuffee with puzzled expressions.

"You, there." Fines pointed to the man on the right. "Come here."

A worried look crossed over the man's features, and he plodded over.

"Do you speak English?"

"Yessir." The worker nodded.

"Were you or any of the workers instructed to start the fire the other night?" Fines's shoulders had risen and remained around the man's ears.

"No, sir."

His nostrils flared. "Hennion's slaves said the fire started in your fields and cost him half of his crops and ten of his slaves that either died battling the blaze or ran away."

Samuel's workers removed their hats in honor of the dead, and Samuel did the same.

"Put your hats back on." Fines stiffened, and his hands curled into fists. "We don't honor deserters."

Samuel stepped forward. "We honor those who fought bravely and died for it." His jaw tightened. "You're done here."

Fines's body shook, and he screamed. "I'm done when I say I'm done."

"Well now." Langham held up his palms. "I don't know about that."

Heat pulsed through Samuel. He'd had enough of Fines and his wheedling.

The field hand squared his shoulders, plopped his hat on, and said in a firm voice, "Hibiscus."

Fines's mouth opened, and his lips quivered, but no sound emitted.

The other field workers donned their hats and said the same.

Fines reared back to strike the field worker, but Samuel stopped the man's fist with his hand. "You will not touch my workers."

The magistrate jumped between Samuel and Fines. "Whoa. I think it's time for us to be going." He gripped the back of Fines's coat and tugged him toward the main house.

The entire way Fines shouted at Samuel. "You think you can make a mockery of me, do you? I'm going to make your life miserable. You just watch."

Samuel ambled in their wake. "Is that a threat?" A twitch of a smile tugged on the corner of his mouth. "Langham, I think you should take note that I'm being harassed and threatened on my own property."

"When I'm through with you"—Fines struggled against Langham's firm grip—"England's not going to take you back, and Antigua's going to spit you out like bad rum."

Cuffee glanced at Samuel and shrugged. "Hibiscus blossoms."

A snort of laughter burst out of Samuel, which sent Fines into another furious rant as he and Langham stomped away.

More laughter erupted until Samuel's stomach and cheekbones ached. He clapped Cuffee on the shoulder. "I'm not entirely sure what all that rot was about, but you put on a jolly good show of it."

"Ya have Miss Prescott ta thank. She put me up to it."

Samuel shook his head and tried to wipe away his grin with the back of his hand. "She's most unexpected, isn't she?"

Cuffee slapped his thigh and laughed. "You can say tat."

They meandered back, still chuckling over the incident and Fines's reaction. Samuel sent Cuffee to check on the men at the boiling house while he headed toward the manor.

He needed a word with Miss Prescott.

Chapter 20

Oh, Diary, my heart races at every sound. I'm a mass of frayed nerves. I long to see my love once more, but he risks his very life. If spotted, he'll surely hang.
~ Entry by Loretta Baxter, August 26, 1810

Maggie wanted to weep with delight when she spied the men returning from the field. Not only because it meant they hadn't attacked one another, but because Caroline's gossiping about the local islanders grated on Maggie's nerves. She didn't need to know that much about Mrs. Webster's errant son or the kind of houses he frequented.

Caroline's neck craned, spotting Mr. Langham and Mr. Fines headed toward the stable. She excused herself with a hurried farewell and chased after them to see if they would be kind enough to escort her home.

Judith pursed her lips and let the curtain fall back in place. "From the look on Mr. Fines's face, I don't believe my sister will find him fit company on the ride."

Was Mr. Fines's unpleasant mood a good sign or a bad one? Was Samuel able to keep his temper in check? Maggie fiddled with her mother's scarf, which she'd tied today around her waist. The stuffiness of being indoors pressed in around her. Stay in her room. *Bah.* "Would you care to move outside to the garden where we might find more of a breeze? It's shaded this time of day."

"Splendid idea." Judith rose and picked up Maggie's mother's diary to carry for her. "You can read another excerpt of the journal to me." She tucked the book under her arm. "In case I might be able to find any clues that only a local person would know."

Maggie picked up her cane and hobbled outside. Her mother's diary was personal and reading it to another person felt like a betrayal, but Judith had a good point. She may know something only a local would know, like Dinah's understanding where Mary and John did meet meant the border of St. John's and St. Mary's.

Maggie settled on the bench, and Judith spread a blanket under the tree. She'd opened the diary to start reading when the rusty latch of the gate creaked.

"There you are." Samuel entered and closed the gate behind him.

Maggie squinted against the sun haloing his head, which made his expression unreadable.

"I was hoping to have a word with you."

His soft tone didn't warn of the authoritative lecture on why she shouldn't interfere that she'd been expecting. She scooted over so he could sit next to her on the bench, resuming the same spots where they'd sat previously—her pulse thundered at the thought—the day he'd kissed her. She flicked a glance at Judith, who leaned back against the tree trunk and pulled out her embroidery.

The wooden slats sank a bit under Samuel's muscular form as if conspiring to slide them together. Maggie set the diary down to grip the armrest, reprimanding her imagination, for there was no fear of her sliding into his lap. Not to mention that, as chaperone, Judith's position was to interfere before Maggie could make any more mistakes she'd later regret.

Samuel tugged the fabric of his trousers and crossed his ankle over his knee. He rested his arm on the bench backrest behind her and nodded toward the flowers with his chin. "Hibiscus, aye?"

She licked her lips. "Cuffee told you I put him up to it?"

"Rightly so."

Neither his expression nor his tone offered any indication of his mood. She should never have involved herself. What had she been thinking, telling Cuffee to say such a ridiculous thing, especially when a man was in a provoked state? She stared at her lap and braced herself for the tongue lashing she deserved.

"Thank you."

Her gaze snapped to his profile. "You-you're not angry?"

"Angry?" He shrugged a shoulder. "A little, but that word doesn't suffice."

Was his relaxed position a cover to control his fury?

"I'd say shocked and stunned are better descriptions." A glint sparkled in his eyes. "Along with baffled, amused, and perhaps amazed." A hint of a smile twisted one corner of his mouth.

Was he teasing her? "It worked?" She couldn't keep the disbelief from her voice.

"Splendidly." He chuckled. "It was genius. How did you know to use such a distraction?"

She fiddled with the corner of the diary. "Cilla, my mother, often uses outrageous things to distract my father."

"Like what?" He shifted toward her. "So I can prepare myself."

He believed there'd be another time. Her stomach whirled. "Often, she'll change the subject to something amusing." Maggie pressed her lips tightly to hold back a smile. "Or she'll sing, but Cilla"—how to put it nicely?—"Cilla can't carry a tune. It sounds silly, but it makes Tobie laugh."

His grin spread, showing a crack of white teeth and the masculine quirk of his mouth. Mesmerized by the memory of those firmly molded lips pressed against hers, she tried to focus on the conversation. "She's also been known to redirect his anger with a kiss."

His smile wavered, and a nervous chuckle escaped.

She sucked in a breath. Why in heaven had she brought that up?

His gaze shifted to Judith, and hers followed. Judith's head rested against the tree trunk, her eyes closed and lips slightly parted. How had the woman fallen asleep so quickly? Her chaperone had certainly picked a terrible time to fall asleep. Maggie's grip tightened on the armrest, and she squeezed against it. "Hibiscus blossoms merely popped into my head. It seemed like Mr. Fines was trying to bait you with his accusations, and I cannot abide bullies. I know I shouldn't have interfered, but—"

"You're right, you shouldn't have."

She swallowed at his terse statement.

The corner of his mouth twitched. "But I'm glad you did."

She exhaled a sigh of relief. "Were you astonished? What did you say?" The need to know the details pressed against her breastbone. "How did Mr. Fines react? Pray tell." Merciful heaven, had the sisters' gossiping habits worn off on her?

He raised his palm. "I thought the lack of sleep had hindered Cuffee's faculties until he mentioned that you put him up to it. Mr. Fines reacted as if we were shamming him and threatened to make us regret it."

"Mr. Fines grew upset?"

"He had an apoplectic fit—to put it mildly."

"I didn't mean to make the situation worse." She hugged her arms.

"It was a ripping good show."

"For such a regimented man"—she frowned at him—"you're very unpredictable."

He tilted his head back and laughed, a boisterous sound that seemed to vibrate the bench seat beneath her. Women carrying bundles of cane faltered in their steps and stared in his direction. He held his midsection as his laughter subsided. "I haven't laughed this much in one day, ever." He sighed as if searching through memories. "Not even at Harry's silly antics."

"Was Harry a friend of yours?" She knew very little about Samuel's life in England. She craved to understand more about the fascinating man beside her and the people who'd influenced him.

"He was." The light in his eyes dimmed.

Her hand flew to cover her mouth. "Is he . . . Did he die?"

Samuel shook his head. "He's alive." He uncrossed his ankle and tugged on the knees of his trousers. "We had a disagreement of sorts."

Fines's statement echoed in her mind, *Entertaining the ladies again, so soon after your fiancée crying off.* "A disagreement over a woman." Maggie pressed her lips tight, wishing she could recall her words.

"Indeed."

Even though their bodies didn't touch, she could feel him stiffen. She remained quiet. If he didn't wish to speak of it, she wouldn't press him.

He scratched the peak of his hairline. "Fines's accusations, while hateful, weren't entirely wrong. Miss Lucy Tully and I were engaged, but the story of her crying off is not the truth."

Maggie drew back. "You're still engaged?" *She had kissed an engaged man?*

"Definitely not."

She exhaled a quiet sigh of relief.

"I . . ." His lips worked for a moment as if he tried to decide upon the right words. "The night before our wedding, I discovered Harry and Lucy in the greenhouse . . . together."

Maggie blinked, imagining a couple strolling through aisles of orange blossoms.

"In a lover's embrace."

The memory squeezed Samuel's chest, but Maggie's innocent, wide-eyed expression lessened the pain.

"Oh, my." She gasped. "He was your friend." Her eyebrows snapped together. "And she was your fiancée. How could they hurt you in such a manner? It's . . ." She paused as if fumbling for words. "It's . . . well"—she notched up her chin—"wretched."

He snorted his agreement. Her reaction confirmed her parents did a good job protecting her innocence even from the sordid gossip of indiscretions among the *ton*. "Your methods of distraction would have come in handy." He closed his eyes to blot out Lucy's screams and the sight of blood. "I let my temper get the best of me." He opened them to find two green pools of concern honed upon him. "My reaction was the reason I was sent to Antigua."

She crossed her arms. "If the man is still alive, then you were merciful."

He appreciated her loyalty. Even his father had lectured him on how the heir to an earldom doesn't resort to fisticuffs. The irony of his father's anger wasn't lost on Samuel. His father's temper could cut a man to the bone, but striking a man was dishonorable. Many a time, Samuel would have preferred the physical blow over the verbal.

"May I ask what happened?"

His back muscles twisted into knots. He could still see their entwined bodies nestled in the far corner of the greenhouse between his mother's prize gardenias. Heat surged through his veins at the thought. "I lost control."

He gritted his teeth. "Lucy gasped when she

spied me, Harry turned, and I planted a facer." The memory of the sickening crack of Harry's nose flushed any residual rage into the pit of Samuel's stomach, where it ran cold. "I broke his nose. Harry covered his face and cursed before peeking down to find his hands covered in blood. He fainted at the sight, fell and cracked his head on a flowerpot."

"Oh my goodness."

"Lucy's grandparents own Coutts bank and threatened to refuse my father credit if word spread and ruined their granddaughter's reputation. Harry's father, the Earl of Creighton, had the ear of the king and demanded retribution for his son's near-death injury. Harry might have been concussed, but there was no indication he suffered any long-term effects other than a crooked nose. I was thrown in jail for a week and tried by my peers in the House of Lords."

"They banished you to Antigua?"

"They demanded that I apologize publicly to Harry. They wanted me to get on my knees and grovel. I was supposed to look upon my so-called friend—who'd seduced my fiancée the night before our wedding—and say I was sorry for breaking his nose. 'It's just two words. How hard could it be?' That was what everyone told me, but as I peered into Harry's smug face and he smiled his arrogant smile, my body went up in flames. Rage filled me to the point where

I couldn't speak, much less apologize. All I could think of was how he'd ruined my fiancée and my life." Samuel exhaled to calm his rapid breathing.

"The Duke of Linton was the deciding vote. He moved to hold a stay until after my 'heels had cooled.' Harry demanded I be sent to Antigua for his safety, which I knew was due to him not being able to make a go of it here on the island. He called Antigua an 'infernal, destitute isle full of mosquitoes and vermin.' I was determined to prove myself if it meant I could forgo conceding to my betrayer. I had been wronged and part of my drive stems from a desire to show Harry and Lucy that I am the better man."

"This odious Harry fellow could use a lesson from you in hard work and loyalty."

Her defense spread warmth to a dark and lonely place in Samuel's heart. Maggie didn't demand he be more—or better. She accepted his demeanor, his person, even his temper. Instead of condemning his faults, she believed he was capable of change. He laid his hand on top of hers. "Thank you."

She tilted her head in that adorable way of hers. "For what?"

"You believed I could control my temper when even after I'd given myself up as a lost cause. That's why you gave Cuffee a distraction word. You defended me against Fines and didn't denounce my actions toward Harry when others have."

"And I would again a thousand times over." She nodded as if for emphasis.

He drew his eyebrows together. "Even when I unleashed my temper on you yesterday, you didn't judge me as some monster."

A bright smile swept across her lips, and the world melted away until all he saw was her exotic beauty before him. She might have been raised in England, but Maggie carried a savoir faire of effortless attraction.

"If you think you were cross, you should have met my first nanny, Miss Dodd. She could stop a person cold with the raising of an eyebrow." Her light laugh tripped up his heartbeat, and the mesmerizing green pools of her eyes caught him in their swirling tide.

"I don't know what fate brought you to me." He slid along the bench seat, closing the distance between them.

She searched his gaze. "God brought me here," she said in a feathery whisper. "He placed it on my heart, even though I went about it the wrong way."

Samuel hadn't thought much about divine intervention. To him, God seemed a judgmental father waiting for him to slip-up so he could be punished, but in the moment, her earnest expression had him believing God had sent Maggie to him as a gift of hope.

She sucked in a breath as if realizing his intention to kiss her once more.

He shouldn't take such liberties, but she was so tempting, so open, so near. His arm curved around her back to draw her closer.

Her green eyes widened.

You are no better than Harry.

His conscience doused him with years of gentleman's training. Her ripe lips hovered so near that he could feel the quickness of her breath. Harry would have a bit of sport without any recourse, but he wasn't Harry. Samuel had done the right thing as far as women were concerned, but it only got him a fiancée who'd tupped with another man the eve of their wedding.

Didn't he deserve a bit of happiness?

The angry fire in his gut stoked back to life, and his fingers curled around Maggie's shoulder, drawing her to him. He glanced at the Widow Morgan and found her watching them with one eye, which she quickly closed.

Some chaperone she turned out to be.

Maggie pressed a small hand to his chest. The color in her cheeks had heightened, and her breathing exhaled in ragged puffs.

Blast. He was a cad. Maggie didn't deserve such treatment.

He moved away and scraped his hand through his hair. "My apologies. I don't know what came over me."

"There's something between us." She stared at the hibiscus plant. "A push and pull I don't understand either, but until I know my true linage, I'm between worlds. I'm too highborn to be a commoner yet too lowborn to be of a marriageable class. I'm untouchable."

She was very touchable. Too touchable, and that was the problem. *By Jove,* the island must be getting to him. Since when was he tempted to become a despoiler of innocents? "It sounds despicable, but a part of me envies Harry."

"Truly?"

"He doesn't hold the weight of being a firstborn son. His family fortune wasn't made in the islands, and he's bent on spending it. He's glib and flirtatious with the ladies. When he's in the room, he's the center of attention. Part of me was relieved to go unnoticed in the wings, but another wished I could be charming like he was."

Her forehead wrinkled as if doubting his statement.

"Only when Harry's father sent him to Antigua to mature him was I noticed. Lucy singled me out, and I wasted no time in speaking to her father to ask for her hand in marriage. I figured I needed to snatch the opportunity before Harry returned. In a way, I was right. Harry lived up to his rogue reputation, in spite of our friendship."

"It was fortunate you learned of their infidelity before you married. You averted disaster."

"I don't know why I'm telling you this."

"Because you need a friend."

The word repelled him like a cat from water.

"I've never met Harry, but I know without question that you are the most fascinating man I've ever met, and if the two of you stood side by side, this Harry fellow would blend in with the wallpaper."

If she was trying to drive his desire into a frenzy, she was doing a splendid job. He conjured Harry's image to cool his ardor. Maggie could say such words because she hadn't met Harry, but she endeared him with her loyalty.

"Besides your appealing traits, as noted by a friend"—she emphasized the last word—"you certainly hold something over him now."

What would Maggie know about Harry?

A perky smile rounded her cheeks. "A straight nose."

His laughter erupted, causing the Widow Morgan to jolt upright and a worker yards away to drop her bundle of cane.

Chapter 21

My love is near. During my morning stroll, I discovered a heart drawn in the sand. I must figure a way to elude the watchful gaze of the chaperone Papa hired to keep up appearances.

*~ Entry by Loretta Baxter,
August 31, 1810*

A stiff breeze ruffled Samuel's hair as he rode in from his nightly inspection. All seemed quiet. Most men had recovered from the fire and the quick harvest it caused. The cooking fires had been snuffed out early, and the sound of snoring men resounded through the slave quarters as the last ray of sunlight dwindled into twilight.

"How low are the cisterns?"

Cuffee wiped the sweat from his brow and stuffed the linen cloth into his back pocket. "Too low. A week. Maybe ten days if da Lord smiles upon us."

God smiling wasn't an image Samuel could conjure. Action needed to be taken. He wished Cuffee good night and strode into the main house to wash and change for the evening meal.

The house seemed quiet until he reached the second floor landing. Furniture had been rearranged, drawers removed, and books pulled off shelves. Every lantern was lit, illuminating the upstairs as if it were day. Footmen and maids crouched to feel inside and underneath furniture. Some shook out books and scoured cracks and crevices.

The chaos smelled of Maggie's doing. "What is going on here?"

Footmen and maids jumped to attention.

Widow Morgan set down the book she was shaking. "Good evening, Lord Granville." Her gaze flicked to the adjoining chamber.

He strode to the open door. His eyes scanned the room for the source of all this commotion and located Miss Prescott lying under a writing desk, feeling the underside. The colorful scarf that had become a daily part of her wardrobe protected her long dark tresses from dust.

"Is it already that late?" She flipped around and crawled backward out from under the desk gingerly, watching her head.

He moved to her side and lowered his hand. He'd grown accustomed to her using his routine as a time clock of sorts. "May I ask why my household is turned inside out?"

She placed her slender hand into his, and he leaned down, sliding an arm around her waist to ease her to a stand without further injuring her leg. "I found another letter written in French, this one was in a book." Excitement sparkled like emeralds in her eyes, and dust smudged her left cheek.

"Indeed." He removed his handkerchief from his inside breast pocket.

"We were looking for others."

He wiped the dirt from her cheek.

She tugged on her bottom lip with her top teeth and glanced around the room. "You're not upset by the mess, are you? I promise we'll put everything back in place."

Strange, but he wasn't angry. He was growing accustomed to Maggie setting her mind to something and seeing it through. He too had such determination but lacked her quirky uninhibited way of going about her plans. Normally, this much disarray would have put him in a dudgeon, but perhaps he'd mellowed. "What did the letter say?"

She stuffed her hand into her gown pocket and pulled out a yellow sheet of paper. "Let me read it to you." She favored her injured leg as she strode to the bed and sat, unfolding the letter. Although her focus remained on the paper, her hand patted the coverlet beside her, inviting him to sit.

The pink hue of her gown matched the rosiness in her cheeks. She sat erect with perfect posture, her slight form taking up little space on the mattress. Yet this woman had shown incredible inner strength. She glanced his way to see what was delaying him.

He crossed the room in two strides and lowered

beside her. He leaned in to read the letter, allowing their shoulders to touch.

If she objected, she didn't voice it. Instead, she translated.

> Dearest Loretta,
> My love. I hope this letter finds you. I've had to pay off several servants for their continued silence. If only your father would be reasonable. A decade of war has hardened his heart toward the French, but I will not be deterred. My ardor for you is too great. We will find a way with God's blessing, whether in the islands or America.
> I read your concerns in your last letter even though you did your best not to voice them. I know you well enough to hear your thoughts. Do not fret, my love. We will be together again. Do not lose hope. I will fight to the bitter end for you.
> Think of me, for there is not a moment that passes that I don't think of you and our union.

Maggie lowered her hands with the letter into her lap. "He still signed it, 'your wolf.'" Her chest rose and fell on a deep sigh, but then she brightened. "He mentioned a union. He could mean a marriage union."

"If they had married, the islanders would refer to your mother by her married name, but every islander and official I've spoken to calls her Miss Baxter." He hated to speak the truth. "The wolf may be speaking of another sort of union."

She lowered her chin. "I thought we'd run into a dead end when no significant mention of my father was revealed in the diary and there were no others to be found."

Pain pierced his chest. He tried reading the other two volumes he'd pulled from beneath the floorboards when no one was looking and had hidden in his desk drawer. But with the fire and Loretta Baxter's detailed flowery writings combined with his long days overseeing the fields in the hot sun, had him dosing off every time he determined to read them. Maggie had turned his home inside-out, looking for clues when he possibly held the answers. He was only trying to protect her from herself. What if her father wasn't someone reputable? Wouldn't it be better for her father's identity to remain unknown than to discover she was a bi-blow?

The guilt ate at him. His reasons weren't so noble. He was protecting her but also his own interests. Her questionable lineage made the idea of asking for her hand in marriage near improbable, but the truth of illegitimate birth made it impossible. He vowed to read the other volumes this evening.

"But there's still hope." She blew the tie of her scarf, which had fallen in front of her eyes, out of the way. "Maybe more letters remain hidden, and we just have to find them."

He adored her optimism. "Indeed." The pesky tie of her scarf drooped again, and she blew it back once more.

"Allow me." He swept the tie away and leaned closer to tuck it under the knot. When finished, he lightly trailed his knuckle down the back of her neck, feeling her shiver.

"I love a good mystery." Widow Morgan spoke from the doorway.

He pushed to a stand. "Dinner should be ready." He bowed to Maggie. "I must change before we dine. I shall see you shortly." Striding across the room, he nodded to the Widow Morgan as he passed but felt her gaze upon him until he shut his chamber door.

With her good leg, Maggie kicked under the table, hitting Uncle Anthony's shin. Her Uncle's tendency to visit around suppertime, checking-in on his beloved niece, no longer rang true. It seemed he'd come for the food but the way he flirted with Judith left no doubt he came to call upon her.

He rubbed his leg and scowled back at Maggie. However, he no longer leaned so close that the cuff of his sleeve nearly dangled into Judith's dessert.

Judith's pursed lips deepened into a frown aimed at the captain.

Maggie would talk with her uncle later about minding clear indications that a woman is not interested. Never had she witnessed him behave like a cursed rum touch to gain a woman's attention. Could he not understand that Judith was recently widowed? Did he not see she was still dressed in mourning blacks? Why didn't he realize her cutting remarks showed her disinterest?

"Middleton." Samuel's voice cut through the awkward glances at the table. "I'd like to commission you and your crew for a task."

Her uncle issued her one last glare before picking up his glass and turning with rapt attention toward Samuel. "Commissioned, you say? What kind of task did you have in mind?"

"To retrieve fresh water from Montserrat."

Uncle Anthony's glass stilled halfway to his lips, and Judith's eyes widened.

Maggie forced her voice to sound light. "Are we running a little low?"

"Nothing to worry over"—Samuel's voice lowered—"yet."

"It's been an age since I've visited Montserrat." He glanced at Judith. "I can sail with my crew at week's end."

Samuel cleared his throat. "On the morrow would be preferable."

His guests blinked at him in silence.

It hadn't rained in a couple of weeks, but had the situation grown that desperate? Maggie sucked in a breath. She'd instructed the women to bring fresh water to the men battling the fire to drink. Had she dwindled their drinking water supply and put everyone in jeopardy?

Samuel paused in raising his fork to his lips. "Truly. We are fine." He nodded toward her uncle. "We are fortunate to have a readily available ship to depart and assist us in this matter." He ate the bite of bread pudding, and the rest of the table finished their dessert in silence—even Uncle Anthony.

Maggie swallowed her last bite of pudding. If she didn't ask now, she wouldn't get a chance again until tomorrow night, and then she'd lose another day. The rector had replied to her letter but had stated with the quantity of annals to peruse it would be best for her to come in person when she was able. She straightened in her seat. "Lord Granville."

Samuel looked up from his dish.

"Thanks to the fire, you haven't had the time to visit the parish annals, but I would like to ride into St. John's tomorrow with Mrs. Morgan and speak with the registrar. I'd written the rector and a letter from him arrived, inviting us to visit. I'm growing anxious to know the truth."

"Not tomorrow." He ate another spoonful and swallowed. "Nor this week."

She placed her hands on the table and pushed back. "Whyever not?"

His gaze flicked to her uncle then Judith as if looking for support to back him up. "I won't allow it because of your leg."

"But my leg feels much improved." She turned her palms over. "As you have seen, I'm moving up and down stairs, and I can get around short distances without the use of my cane."

Uncle Anthony leaned back in his chair with a smug smile, as if amused to have her arguing with someone other than himself for a change.

Samuel set down his spoon and dabbed at the corners of his mouth with his napkin. "Which is precisely why I forbid you going into town. You are overdoing it." He snorted. "I arrived back from the fields only to discover you've been carrying on around the house when you are supposed to stay abed as instructed."

Her face heated, as it often had when her parents forbade her to do something. She forced a mild smile. "And I'm telling you that I feel well and able enough for a short visit. For heaven's sake, I'll be riding in a wagon. There's nothing strenuous about that."

"You were riding in a wagon when you last reopened your leg wound."

Touché. "I was driving the wagon. Tomorrow, I will be riding."

"You are under my care. You should rest."

"I daresay that Uncle Anthony is my guardian in this circumstance." She turned to her uncle, demanding his approval.

"Ah, quite right, but . . ." Anthony paled and rearranged his silverware. "Tomorrow I leave for Montserrat, at which time your guardianship shall temporarily pass to Lord Granville in my absence." He glanced at Samuel as if seeking his approval.

Samuel issued him a curt nod. "Well then, the matter is resolved." He pushed back from the table. "We shall adjourn to discuss travel to Monserrat. Good evening, ladies."

Her uncle wasted no time in fleeing the dining room, but Samuel pinned her with a *so-there* look before vacating the dining room.

Maggie lifted her chin and murmured, "Tyrant," perhaps just loud enough for him to overhear.

Maggie's fingers gripped the window molding. As Samuel and Cuffee crested the north field, she stepped back, and the curtain fell back into place.

"It's time." Judith handed Maggie her cane. "Let's go."

Maggie hesitated. Another deception to add to her list. Hadn't she learned her lesson yet? "Maybe Samuel will give us permission tomorrow."

"Will you be healed fully by tomorrow?"

She delicately felt the stitches in her thigh. "No."

"It's your decision." Judith shrugged. "You're the one who must return before your parents uncover your farce."

If she returned knowing she hadn't tried every means possible to discover the truth, it would haunt her. "Very well then." She limped to the door.

Judith rubbed her palms together. "I haven't had this much excitement since my drunken husband stole the neighbor's horse and I had to sneak the animal back into the stables before the neighbor returned."

"How awful."

Judith had endured a lot with a husband who dipped deep in his cups.

Dinah met them at the bottom of the stairs. "I had da carriage brought around."

"Thank you, Dinah." Maggie and Judith snuck out the front door while Hawley polished the silver in the butler's kitchen.

Maggie's insides quaked like they had the day she'd arrived in Antigua. Today could be the day she discovered her true lineage. Would she be relieved? Disappointed? More curious? The beautiful landscape of white sand beaches and turquoise coves soothed her jumpiness as they rode into town.

She pushed her insecurities aside and absorbed the tranquil ocean water so clear that she could see colorful fish floating about and a ray gliding under the crystal waves even from this distance. Judith peered straight ahead as if unfazed by the beauty around her. Would Loretta Baxter have also been so accustomed to the island that it had become commonplace?

Antigua's cove spreads its lush arms out to the teal ocean waters, drawing them to her breast, welcoming all life teeming within to her bosom.

The vivid descriptions recorded in her mother's diary revealed her mother held a similar reverence and awe of beauty as Maggie.

The wagon jostled, and Maggie gripped her leg to hold it steady.

Judith weaved around a couple of braying donkeys loaded with bundles of cane, sauntering along the dirt path that served as a road. Their liquid brown eyes blinked at the wagon, and their master dipped his hat at Judith and Maggie before he urged the animals along.

The wagon topped the hill and bumped down the road toward the valley next to the harbor, where the bustling town of St. John's rested. The spires of its namesake church stood tall and proud in the distance.

Islanders shouted greetings to Judith and tipped their hat toward the wagon, their curious gazes lingering on Maggie. Judith remained focused on their intended goal but nodded or waved in return. She drove the wagon up to the church's side yard and yanked the team to a stop.

"Good morning, Mrs. Morgan." A mulatto man hurried over to aid the widow down from her perch. "I heard about the fire. Glad to see you are safe and well."

"You are too kind, Mr. Andrews." She waved him off. "Be a dear and see to my charge. Her leg is injured, so take care with her."

"Yes, indeedy." He scurried around to the opposite side and caught Maggie backing down of her own accord. He clasped her about the waist, lifting her and setting her down on the sidewalk.

She stiffened, uncomfortable with a stranger's touch, but turned and thanked him.

He tipped his hat. "My pleasure, Miss—"

Judith shoved Maggie's cane into her hand and scooted her in the direction of the church's side door. "I'm afraid we're in a bit of a hurry, but thank you kindly for your aid."

Mr. Andrews gaped after them.

Judith held the door open, and Maggie stepped inside the dimly lit rectory. The smell of dusty books and faint incense met them in the front hall. The parish clerk sat behind a thick oak desk. He looked up and lowered his spectacles to the end of his narrow nose and peered over the top at them.

"Ah, Mrs. Morgan." He rose. "Lovely to see you. I heard about the fire. Praise our Heavenly Father that he spared His children and there weren't many deaths."

"Indeed. We were fortunate." She curtsied. "Thank you for your prayers on our behalf."

"It has been quite some time." He adjusted a long sleeve of his robe. "I'd hoped to see more of you after your husband's passing."

Judith squirmed at the priest's reprimand. "Reverend Tynan, this is my charge, Miss Maggie Prescott. We're here to review the annals for information regarding her mother, Miss Loretta Baxter."

"Blessings, my dear." The corners of his eyes crinkled with his smile. "Follow me." He shuffled down the hall, conveniently at a speed Maggie easily followed, to a locked room on the right. He raised his arm, sliding his billowing sleeve down his arm. He fumbled with the key ring, testing several before locating the correct one. The door swung wide, and he entered, pulling back the curtains. Bright morning sun streamed in, highlighting floating dust particles.

Maggie inhaled the scent of old pages and glue. She stepped into the archive room lined with rows and rows of bookshelves. Her stomach swirled like a dog chasing its tail. Were the answers she sought here?

"The books are ordered by date." He gestured to the left side of the room. "Oldest." He swung back to the right. "To newest."

The reverend turned and frowned at several stacks of books on the floor. "If you're looking within the last five years, it would be among these. We've run out of shelves and require more space, I'm afraid." He sighed. "I will leave you two ladies to your hunting. If you have any questions, I will be at my desk." He bowed and exited the room but paused at the door.

"I hope to see the two of you here tomorrow morning." He raised a sharp brow but didn't wait for their answer.

Her mother had mentioned her age and birthday in one of her entries—March of 1793. Maggie located the set and trailed her finger across the book's spines. *1785 . . . 1790 . . .* She moved to the next bookshelf and rose onto her toes, feeling only a slight twinge in her injured leg. *1793.* She removed the volume and flipped to the correct date.

> Baxter, Loretta Genevieve, baptized March 21, 1793, born St. Mary, Antigua March 12, 1793, legitimate daughter of Sir Paul Fredrick Baxter and Mrs. Mary Frances Baxter, residents of St. Mary, Antigua.

Maggie's fingers hovered over the entry. "She's here."

Judith pushed up the cover to read the date on the back. "Do you know when she would have been married or when you would have been born?"

"Unfortunately, no." Maggie shook her head. "My parents guess my age to be around twenty years, but I've always been smaller than most."

Judith pressed the tip of her index finger to her lips and stared at the annals. "She could have been married anywhere from age fourteen to age twenty-eight, but in the islands, twenty-eight would be on-the-shelf, a definite spinster."

"I was rescued in 1814. So I'm guessing an entry could be anywhere between the years 1804 until then, but most likely between 1809 and 1813. How about you start in 1814 and work backward, and I'll start in 1809 and work forward. We're looking for either my birth and baptism or her marriage."

Judith pulled out a yellowed volume and flipped it open.

"There you are." Caroline entered the room.

"I hope you don't mind." Judith glanced at Maggie but waved her sister over. "I figured my sister could help."

"Not at all." She could use all the help she could get, but would Caroline prove to be more of a distraction than an aide?

"Reverend Tynan has aged." Caroline peeked over Judith's shoulder at the volume she perused. "I thought for certain he was going to oversee the church in Bristol. I wonder what happened?"

"We don't have much time." Judith nodded toward the bookshelves. "Grab a volume and look for the name Loretta Genevieve Baxter."

"Wouldn't it be easier to look for Maggie . . . ? What is your last name again?" Caroline blinked at Maggie.

"Prescott."

"It doesn't matter." Judith released an exasperated sigh. "We don't know the christened name given to her by her mother. Her adopted family calls her Maggie Prescott."

"Oh, of course." Caroline grabbed a volume and flashed a giddy smile. "You're right. This is exciting." She pivoted from facing her sister to Maggie. "One scribbled line in one of these dusty old books will decide whether you are highborn and able to associate with elite society or lowborn and meant to scrub floors and pinch pennies for a living."

Maggie swallowed and pulled the volume marked *1809 and 1810* from off the shelves and ignored her shaky nerves. The three women moved to a small table near the window's light.

Several hours passed as they poured over the ledgers. Church bells chimed the eleventh hour. The ink blurred. Her eyes had grown weary, and her ears ached from Caroline spying a name she recognized and reciting every bit of gossip she knew about the person.

"Patrick David Fennel." Caroline clucked her tongue. "I knew it." She pointed her finger at an entry. "He's sired at least twelve children with four different women—two in Antigua, one in England, and another in Barbados—the rogue." She slid her finger down the page. "Oh, this was the family who was buried in a mudslide." She shook her head. "A bloomin' shame. Only the middle son and daughter survived because they ran to the attic and got onto the roof. Everyone else was buried alive." A hush fell over the room.

For the past four hours, Caroline had recalled every story of disaster and child's name born out of wedlock, and Maggie cringed every time Caroline gasped, thinking it could be her name read. How would the sisters treat her if she were a known bi-blow? Maggie steeled her spine. At least she'd have discovered the truth and where she fit on the social ladder.

Would her mother have done something so reckless? Through reading her diary, Maggie better understood the woman who birthed her and cared for her until her dying breath. Maggie fingered the colorful scarf at her waist. Her mother seemed as vibrant as an Antiguan sunrise. She was full of life, spontaneous, whimsical, and passionate.

Was Samuel right in believing a rogue with pretty speech had preyed upon her mother's innocence? Would her mother be such an easy victim? Heat rose into Maggie's cheeks. She'd returned Samuel's kiss in the stairwell without considering the consequences. Had her mother also been swept up by the moment?

Judith slapped her volume closed. "Nothing noteworthy in 1813 to 1814."

"Unless you count Mr. Fenwick's little surprise." Caroline nudged her sister. Someone passed outside the window, redirecting Caroline's attention. "Excuse me for a moment." She passed the ledger to her sister and left the room.

Maggie and Judith leaned toward the window to catch a glimpse of who Caroline sought, but they'd already passed.

Maggie flipped the page and scanned the list of names, but Loretta Genevieve Baxter didn't appear there or on the following twenty pages.

"Nothing." Judith closed her volume. "I'm terribly sorry." She rubbed Maggie's arm with a sad smile and stood. "It looks like you're almost finished. I'm going to check on my sister. Meet us out front when you're done."

She exited the room, and Maggie concentrated on the few remaining pages, willing her mother's name to appear. Her index finger was stained black from tracing line after line, to no avail. She blinked away the prick of tears and closed the book. "Nothing. Not a single clue."

She tilted her head back to keep her tears from spilling over. "God, why? I thought you wanted me to know the truth?"

Only silence rang off the thick beams of the rafters.

Maggie rose and slid the books back onto the

shelves. She'd risked everything in coming here, not just to this parish but to Antigua itself. How could she return still uncertain? She notched her chin. There must be more clues. She just needed a few more pieces to the puzzle. "I'll continue to search the house. Lord Granville's arm had gotten stuck under the floorboards. Maybe there's another journal that was beyond his reach. Maybe there's another letter." The surety of her words didn't keep her heart from sinking and creating a dull ache in her chest. Would she ever find her answers in time?

She exited the annals and hobbled back down the hall. Reverend Tynan looked up from the Bible spread open across his desk. "If your disappointed expression is any indication, then it appears you didn't find what you were seeking."

Maggie shook her head.

The reverend squeezed her hand. "Pray on it some more. God will reveal what you need to know in time, and if He doesn't, then you still need to trust He's bringing all things together for your good."

He picked up his quill and pushed a scrap of paper in front of him. "Mrs. Morgan said you're looking for information on your mother. I was transferred here seven years ago, so I never knew her or your grandfather, but tell me her full name? Perhaps I may come across something."

"Miss Loretta Genevieve Baxter."

He blinked. "Someone else brought up her name." He jotted it down in neatly formed script.

"Lord Granville?" Had Samuel found the time to inquire for her?

"No, it was a different name." He shook his head. "It will come to me."

She thanked him and exited the rectory.

"I will be praying," he called after her.

The sisters stood across the street with a gentleman dressed in gray. A carriage carrying a load of crated chickens blocked Maggie's view. It passed, leaving a trail of floating feathers, and the sisters crossed the street toward her with the man in tow.

Maggie stilled.

Mr. Fines.

Chapter 22

Woe isn't a strong enough word to describe my despair. My betrothed's ship has arrived. Papa said our banns would be posted beginning next week.

~ Entry by Loretta Baxter, September 15, 1810

At the moment, Mr. Fines was the last person with whom Maggie wanted to interact. She addressed Judith, who reached her first. "We must be getting back."

"Of course." Judith shooed her in the direction of the wagon. "There will be plenty of excitement if Lord Granville discovers you disobeyed his commands."

"You poor dear." Caroline's color was high, her eyes overly bright. "I had no idea you were being held prisoner." She pulled Maggie to her chest in a tight embrace.

"I don't know what you're talking about." Maggie balanced on her good leg and pulled away.

Mr. Fines removed his hat. "You are a brave woman. My business associate in London has informed me of Lord Granville's temper and the situation. Do not fear. I will find a way to rescue you from that fiend's clutches."

"You're quite mistaken." Maggie frowned.

"We got off to a bad start yesterday." He bowed. "I let past hurts taint our introduction, and I sincerely apologize. Let me aid you into the wagon." Mr. Fines touched her lower back, guiding her. "It's the least I can do, especially with your injury."

His expression appeared sincere. Had she been hasty in her judgment of him? Could he be a decent fellow? She didn't know the circumstances surrounding Mr. Fines's termination, but it was easy to understand how animosity existed between him and Samuel.

Before she could agree, his hands slid around her waist, and he hefted her up, gently placing her on the bench seat.

"Good day to you, Miss Prescott." Mr. Fines bowed to her and the sisters before he popped his hat back on. "I must be going, but I assure you, I will see that justice prevails for all."

"Mr. Fines?" Caroline tucked her hand into his arm. "Might you escort me? I'm headed to visit with Mr. and Mrs. Salisbury."

"It would be my pleasure." He lifted his elbow, and Caroline threaded her arm through his.

They turned and strode toward the courthouse together.

"What was that about?"

"You know how Caroline talks." Judith pursed her lips. "Mr. Fines asked what we were doing in town, and she and I explained how Lord Granville had forbidden you from leaving so we snuck away while he was in the fields."

"You've overstepped. I don't appreciate you sharing personal information." Maggie frowned. "You made it sound as if I'm being held against my will."

"You're hardly a prisoner." Judith scoffed and snapped the reins. The horses leapt to a cantor. "You'll soon discover, that on an island like Antigua, gossip is a means of protection. Propriety is a front for hiding dark secrets, but hearsay gives a forewarning regarding the truth." She raised her chin and issued Maggie a sideglance. "Mr. Fines mentioned how Lord Granville has been exiled from England." Judith's voice lowered. "Rumor has it."

Judith's tone lightened, reminding Maggie of Caroline's giddiness for gossip, and the fine hair on the back of her neck prickled. Maggie had to lean closer to hear Judith over the clomping of the horses' hooves.

"Lord Granville didn't come to Antigua of his own accord. He was forced to come here due to some sort of scandal involving him and the peerage."

"He . . ." Maggie's chest heaved with the need to defend Samuel.

Judith perked up and leaned her ear toward Maggie. "Do tell."

Oh no, she wasn't going to become some gossipmonger. She knew all too well how it felt to be the subject of their sharp tongues and ridicule. "If Lord Granville would like his private doings made public, he will discuss them with you." If Caroline and Judith were indicators, Antigua was no different from England. Gossips and elitists existed in both places, and if Maggie turned out to be baseborn, she'd be as much at odds here as in England.

Cilla's voice rang in her head. *Christ followers weren't meant for this world. We're all navigating a strange land because this isn't our home. Our home is with Jesus.*

"He did something to fall out of favor." Judith shook her head. "Aren't you the slightest bit curious?"

Maggie tracked a bird flitting from one branch to another, no longer willing to participate in the conversation.

"If Mr. Fines is correct"—Judith flashed her a warning look—"then we must be careful around Lord Granville, for he's a dangerous man."

"Sam—er—Lord Granville."

Judith studied her with renewed curiosity.

Maggie chastised herself for using his given name. "He has been nothing but kind and generous. He took me in—"

"Because he shot you. We brought that to Mr. Fines's attention, but he already knew."

"The magistrate was about to shoot my uncle. Lord Granville grabbed the rifle and raised the barrel, not knowing I was hiding in the branches of the breadfruit tree. It was the magistrate who pulled the trigger."

"Well, he also hasn't kept his promise to discover your lineage. Don't you find that strange? Mr. Fines thinks he forbids you from leaving the house to prevent you from finding out your heritage and claiming rightful ownership of Greenview Manor. He's frightened you're here to claim his only remaining inheritance."

"Don't be ridiculous. I'm here to learn of my parents, not question Lord Granville's proprietorship." Had Samuel neglected to follow through on his word? Was Samuel deliberately withholding information for fear his ownership would come into question?

"It's not right," Judith slowed the wagon. They'd reached the far border of Greenview Manor. "But let's not get carried away. Lord Granville is my employer, and I don't want to cause a stir." She gasped and pulled Maggie down to the floorboard. "Speak of the devil."

In a break in the sugarcane field, Maggie glimpsed Samuel seated tall on his horse, talking to Cuffee like a commander to his general. Thankfully, he didn't look their way. Judith directed the team so the wagon's approach would be blocked from his view by the stables.

A groom aided Maggie down from the wagon, and a draft of air ballooned her skirts. Maggie's hands pressed against her stomach. "My mother's scarf." She twisted about, hoping to spy it lying on the ground. "It must have fallen off." She balanced on one leg and rose onto her toes to peer into the wagon, but it wasn't there.

Judith searched the floorboards and under the seat before descending. "I don't see it."

"It must have fallen off." Maggie pressed her fingertips to her temples. How could she have been so careless?

"I'm certain it will show up. I'll send a footman to Reverend Tynan and retrieve it for you." Judith hooked her arm into Maggie's. "Right now, we must get back to the house before we're discovered." She pressed a coin into the groomsmen's palm. "Do not mention our outing to anyone. Understood?"

The man stared at the coin and nodded.

More lies, more secrets, more people involved. Maggie chewed her lower lip. The deceptions must stop. The consequences always caught up with her.

Judith dragged Maggie around the side toward the garden path, her injured leg straining to keep up the pace.

The sound of galloping horse's hooves approached from behind.

"Ho there," Samuel's voice called.

Maggie turned to face the man she'd disobeyed. He dismounted and passed the horse to the groomsman and stalked toward them with long, sure strides. His brow furrowed with a troubled expression.

Thank you for believing me. Samuel's words from yesterday pricked her with guilt. He'd confided in her, and she'd gone and added her name to the list of those who'd betrayed him—in her case, by sneaking out.

How could she believe Mr. Fines for even a second when Samuel had gone out of his way to care for her? Despite the demands placed upon his time, he'd dined with her every night, dutifully checked on her wellbeing, even bought her slippers and a cane.

The man is dangerous. Judith and Mr. Fines had tried to convince her that Samuel's temper put her in peril. He'd snapped at her twice, once before he'd kissed her and once as her leg was being stitched, but Maggie hadn't feared his temper. Why?

She remembered the raggedness of his breath and the longing in his gaze. In the stairwell, he'd been as confused by his emotions as she. And she'd heard him pace behind the screen and saw the lines of strain on his face after hearing her cry in pain. His anger seemed born out of helpless frustration.

Because he cared.

A dizzying current raced through her.

But does he love you? Even if he did, what would it matter? She'd be stigmatized unless she found proof of her parent's marriage and her legitimate birth, but she'd met with only dead ends.

"What are you doing out of the house?" His hard expression demanded an answer.

Judith pulled Maggie against her side. "Just taking in some air." She straightened. "Unless that is forbidden also."

He released a weary sigh, and his gaze met Maggie's. "I merely ask that you not overly tax your leg. I want to see you well—back up and dancing."

He remembered that she loved to dance. The thought brought a weak smile to her lips.

He returned it with a shy, boyish grin of his own. Clearing his throat, he unlatched the gate and held it open.

Maggie passed, seeing only the passionate man who'd fiercely and loyally protected what he loved.

Could that be her? Could two societal misfits be a match?

Samuel nodded for the footman to remove his plate.

Mrs. Morgan picked at her dessert while Middleton focused his energies on wooing the widow. Middleton's ship had been delayed leaving due to the need for a minor repair, and Samuel prayed for speed. The sooner *The Windward* returned with water the better he'd feel.

"I do believe I hear your crew summoning you. Shouldn't you be running along?" Mrs. Morgan's numerous rebuffs became comical and added *thick-skulled* to Middleton's list of negative attributes.

Maggie stilled the footman with a gentle touch. She asked after John's family, listing his three children by name. John's face softened.

Her gaze flicked to Samuel, and a shy smile touched her lips, swirling a feeling of warmth in his stomach. Something had changed between them today. Her eyes held a different glow, and it spread like a fever through his limbs. He had to bite his tongue not to dismiss the entire room and bask in her full attention. Her hand still rested on the footman's arm, and Samuel gripped the chair to restrain from shoving the servant away from her. When had Samuel become jealous? He'd never felt this possessive of Lucy. He snorted. Maybe he should have.

I believe you averted disaster. More and more, he believed Maggie to be right. What if God hadn't been punishing him for not measuring up. Instead, what if God had saved Samuel from a doomed, loveless marriage? What if God knew something better was right around the corner?

Maggie was seated beside him, close enough that if he stretched his legs, they'd brush hers. Her lips curved into a natural smile as if she couldn't contain the joy within her. Her warm grin filled the empty corners of his heart.

He scratched his head and chuckled. If God had intervened, then Samuel actually owed Harry his gratitude. *How's that for ironic?*

Middleton downed the last of his drink. "*The Windward* is loaded and ready. My crew and I leave for Montserrat in a few hours." He eyed Mrs. Morgan. "Are you going to miss me?"

Judith pursed her lips. "As much as I'd miss a nest of racer snakes."

"Now, darling." He leaned back in his chair with a smug grin. "There's no reason to hide your true feelings. We're among friends."

She set her fork down and looked to Samuel. "Is it possible to send him someplace further? The bottom tip of Peru, perhaps?"

Samuel snorted. He didn't dislike the idea, but the cisterns were running dry—a new set of problems that weighted his shoulders. The holding pond had been reduced to nothing but cracked mud, and the sugar cane plants had started to yellow.

As if sensing his change in mood, Maggie said, "Fortunately, it's a fast trip. It should only take three days, and then we'll have water aplenty."

"That's right." Middleton waggled his eyebrows at Mrs. Morgan. "No need to despair. I shall return before your heart has a chance to wander."

Mrs. Morgan's eyes narrowed. "Your hubris rivals Narcissus in Greek mythology. Be careful you don't gaze too long in the mirror, or you may fall in love."

"So you're saying I'm beautiful like Narcissus?" His lips twisted. "Go on, you can admit it."

She exhaled a deep sigh. "Miss Prescott, it is past time you retired for the evening." Her nostrils flared, and she eyed Middleton. "It has been a trying day." The footman pulled back her chair as she rose. "Good night to you, captain. Don't drown on your voyage." She turned to Samuel and curtsied. "Good night, my lord."

He nodded. If the widow hadn't been so repulsed by Middleton, he'd have to consider hiring a chaperone for the chaperone.

Maggie stood, and he did the same. Her mother's gown may be twenty years outdated, but Maggie didn't need to wear the height of fashion to look lovely. She held a classic beauty made unique by her traditional style of dress.

Something, however, was different. "Your scarf is missing." He blinked at her. "Are you having it laundered?"

"I fear I've misplaced it." Her gaze lowered. "I think it slid off."

"While you were out walking?"

The cords of her neck strained as she swallowed and nodded.

She had adored that scarf, and its vibrant colors had suited her. "I'll have the men retrace your steps and hunt for it tomorrow." He glanced through the side window into the night. "I wish you had mentioned it earlier."

"All hands are needed in the fields. Don't put them out on my account." She lowered her gaze and coiled a loose lock of hair around her index finger. "I should have been more careful."

He lifted her chin with his knuckle until he glimpsed the golden flecks in her eyes. "Mistakes happen." The words his father would never say fell from Samuel's lips, but he meant them. "All is not lost. We will locate it tomorrow and return it to you."

Her teeth tugged on her bottom lip, but her eyes spoke her gratitude.

"Good night." He bowed and stepped aside so she could pass. "Rest well." The tangy scent of orange blossoms lingered after she left, teasing his senses.

Middleton stared after Mrs. Morgan. "I could use a drink."

Samuel inclined his head toward the sideboard. "I have work still to do, but help yourself."

The captain didn't hesitate in pouring himself a glass of Samuel's best port. "Women." He raised his glass in a solemn salute. "Praise God for making them, but God help the man who can understand them."

Samuel grunted and left the room, striding down the hall to his office. With the heel of his boot, he kicked the door shut and settled behind his desk. He pulled out a volume of Loretta Baxter's journals from his side drawer and flipped to the page to where he'd stopped last evening. The second volume had started with more mundane daily descriptions and streams of conscious thought. As he read the words, Maggie's image conjured in his mind's eye. Even though the two women lived different lives, they held similar personality traits. Both were overly optimistic, had a self-assurance that bordered on stubbornness, and acted on fanciful notions—like Maggie sailing to Antigua to learn of her heritage and Loretta Baxter's infatuation with a man nicknamed the wolf. Maggie's optimism was going to land her in a similar situation to her mother's. His jaw clenched. Some libertine like Harry would come along, cutting a wheedle with his flummery and slathered attention, and he'd seduce her to make her his mistress.

The sooner he got to the truth, the easier it would be to safeguard Maggie from such lecherous men. Then they could determine the best way to proceed for her future. He returned to reading.

April 4th, 1810.
A ship has sailed from England, with my betrothed aboard.

Samuel sat up straighter. Betrothed? Had Loretta Baxter been engaged to an Englishmen, not a French Captain? Which man was Maggie's father? Could Maggie have a rightful claim to Greenview Manor? He poured over the volume, jotting down notes for his investigators to research.

1. Banns posted?
2. Childhood betrothal?

He flipped to the next page. Loretta hadn't been opposed to the arranged marriage. Her father had offered a substantial dowry consisting of all of Greenview Manor for a titled match. Documents had been drawn. Samuel picked up his quill and wrote:

3. Locate particulars regarding dowry and marriage agreement.

Samuel settled back in his chair, his eyes accustomed to Loretta's slanted script and how she dotted her i's several letters down instead of above the i. On July 14, 1810, Loretta wrote:

Dear Reader,
   Today has been the most extraordinary day. I fight to hold back my smile. All the while, my stomach rolls like waves during a storm.

   She'd attended her father as he rode down to the bay to ensure the barrels of sugar were being properly loaded and stored. When he went below deck, she wandered down the beach and rounded a cluster of mangrove trees to discover a flock of seagulls circling above a man tied over a barrel. He'd been whipped, and his back had crusted over with scabs, baking in the island sun.
   She had written:

> I turned my head in horror at the wretched sight. The smell of blood and raw male hung in the air, turning my stomach, but curiosity got the best of me. I peeked over my shoulder to find the beaten man's head had lifted. His eyes pleaded for mercy. He whispered to me through cracked lips, but I couldn't make out his words. I had to quickly think, for we were in plain view of the ships, so I tied my steed to a mooring and used its body as a shield. My knees quaked as I knelt in the sand just close enough to understand him.

"L'eau," he'd whispered in a weak and hoarse voice.

Water. Samuel's ability to remember his French lessons had been tested lately. The man spoke French like the wolf from her letters. Was this him? Samuel rubbed his chin. In 1810, England had still been at war with the French. Loretta merely speaking to a Frenchman risked her family's reputation. He returned to his reading.

His parched lips struggled to form words. "Please, mademoiselle, water. Have mercy," he begged me. His accent was thick but understandable. My heart pounded against my breast. Would helping a man on the verge of death be a treasonous act? At my hesitation, his head slumped back against the barrel. Whether due to exhaustion or loss of hope, I could not be certain. I sent up a prayer for wisdom, and as if heaven above answered my plea, the words of Hebrews rang in my heart loud and clear. "Do not neglect to do good and share what you have, for such sacrifices are pleasing to God."

I have never been so nervous as when I reached into my saddle bag and offered him my canteen. His hands were bound, so I held the jar to his parched lips. He drank, quenching his dire thirst until not a drop of water remained. "Merci, mon ange."

Dear reader, if only you could feel my heart flutter as I still hear him calling me his angel. The sweetness of his voice and the glow in the depths of his hazel eyes warmed me to my very toes. A lock of his black hair had fallen over his eye, and I haven't the foggiest idea what possessed me, but I boldly brushed it back behind his ear. He smiled at me then, and I confess, the splendor of it left me giddy.

Good sense and breeding insisted I must go. If Papa had discovered me, he would have taken a switch to my hide, but I hesitated to leave him in such condition. If they hadn't left him to die, then he most certainly would have been hanged on the morrow. As I stood there uncertain what to do, a sparkle lit in his golden eyes, and he said to me in French, "A little assistance, my angel?" I couldn't figure what he meant until the sunlight caught on the blade of the knife he held in his bound hands.

I thought my heart would rip from my chest, my fear was so great, but I took the knife. Thankfully he'd already cut a good way into his bindings, for my hands trembled, and thrice the dull tip of the knife poked his skin as I cut the rope. I whispered my apologies. But he cared not once his hands were free. He untied my horse and handed me the reins. In a voice that spoke of a man used to giving orders, he instructed me to lead my horse behind the shelter of mangrove trees. He crouched beside my steed as we moved. I wanted to run, but he insisted it would draw unwanted attention.

Once hidden behind the trees, he mounted my horse. I thought he meant to ride off and leave me, but his strong arms pulled me up into his lap, clasping me to his chest. He spurred us into a gallop. I should have been afraid, but my heart stirred only with awe. We rode east toward the rocky bluffs of Old Road near Cactus Hill. We hadn't gone far before he yanked back on the reins. He aided me down and slid out of the saddle.

He asked my name and, despite my better judgement, I gave it to him. He bowed over my hand as a gentleman would and said, "Captain Sebastian Lowell Corbett of the French Royal Navy, at your service." His hands gripped my shoulders, and his gaze held mine. "It is not safe for you, Miss Loretta Baxter.

You must return before they notice your disappearance."

Like a ninny, I clung to his sleeve. "What will happen to you?"

"Ma chéri." He smiled at me in full. "Do not worry for my sake." He glanced over his shoulder, and his expression grew serious. His eyes searched my face, and his lips parted as if to speak, but then, to my utter shock, he crushed me to him, taking siege of my lips in a breathtaking kiss. God forgive me, for I enjoyed it immensely. I may be a wanton woman, for I succumbed to the ripples of pleasure his kiss sent through me. Only when my hands, of their own accord, slid around his back did he arch in pain and break the kiss. Heaven help me. I had forgotten his wounds.

He lifted me back into the saddle and promised, "I shall return in a week's time. I will find you, my angel." Those were his exact words before he smacked my horse's flank and sent me galloping to the bay and my papa.

Papa had noticed my disappearance and the missing French captive. He hugged me in a rare moment of affection and thanked God that I was all right. I was asked if I saw a fleeing pirate. I gasped, for the sentence for piracy was death.

I told them I had not. All the while, I prayed God would rescue Captain Corbett and forgive me of my sins.

When the gong of the hall clock stuck the first chime of midnight, Samuel startled. He flipped the cover closed and hid the diary under his desktop. Had anyone seen him? He'd been so engrossed that he'd not only lost track of time but also his surroundings. His chest tightened, and he rubbed it. Maggie would no doubt feel violated that he'd read her mother's personal journal before her, but he was doing so to protect her. The question that remained was, how to tell her?

The chiming ceased. Samuel stifled a yawn and ran his hand over his face. Dawn was only a few hours away, and Cuffee would be waiting for him to oversee the harvest of the east field. He closed the journal and set it back inside his desk drawer. He'd be lucky if sleep didn't elude him after the new revelations.

In the morning, he'd pen a letter to his investigators to look into the name Sebastian Lowell Corbett. He dipped his quill into the inkwell and added to his list.

4. Was Sebastian Lowell Corbett the wolf?

Samuel dimmed the lamp and rose. He opened the office door, and light from the hall lamp spilled into the room. *Drat.* He turned back into the dark room to retrieve the list from where he'd left it on his desk.

Soft footsteps padded down the hall, and Mrs. Morgan passed in a flurry, her coiffure askew. The stairs creaked as she mounted them.

"Wait. Don't go." Middleton followed her. The latch of her door clicked shut, and she must have evaded him for a telling mumble of curses were murmured under Middleton's breath.

Samuel crept up the stairs, avoiding the one that creaked, and caught the flash of Middleton's coat before his door closed behind him.

Was Mrs. Morgan as opposed to the captain's advances as she led others to believe? What he'd witnessed tonight was grounds for her dismissal, but exhaustion swept over him. The last thing he had time for was seeking out another chaperone for Maggie. At least Middleton was leaving in the morning. It afforded Samuel more time before he was forced to act. Tomorrow the Kellys would be dining with them. He would ask Thea for another recommendation.

Samuel lumbered to his chamber, and Carson aided him in his undress. After washing his face and brushing his teeth with tooth powder, Samuel stared up at the ceiling. Sleep was long in coming. His mind wrestled with the new turn of events, and fresh guilt pricked at him for his dishonesty. He should have told Maggie about her mother's journals and the letter he'd sent to her parents. He'd confide everything after his investigators discovered the truth about Captain Sebastian Corbett, and he'd tell them to be quick about it. His investigators would be discreet. Although Maggie acted as if the truth would set her free, he'd witnessed firsthand the damage wagging tongues could inflict.

Loretta Baxter had written that Corbett had hazel eyes and raven hair. Same as Maggie. The mounting evidence leaned toward ruinous. Loretta's words so far implied that some French Captain had wooed her while her intended, the poor bloke, sailed from England. He'd arrive only to find his betrothed in love with another man.

Samuel's chest tightened, and he tried to block the memory of Lucy and Harry wrapped in a lover's embrace. His hands scrunched the coverlet.

Had Maggie's mom done to the Englishman what Lucy and Harry had done to him?

Was it in Maggie's nature to do the same?

He rolled over and punched his fist into his pillow more to release his ire than to fluff it.

Could any woman be trusted?

Chapter 23

My love purchased a lovely scarf at Sunday market. He declared its color didn't hold a candle to my vibrant nature, its flowers to my beauty, nor its silk to the smoothness of my skin.

~ Entry by Loretta Baxter, September 21, 1810

Maggie savored the creamy bite of banana custard and let Theadosia and George Kelly's teasing banter envelop her like a warm sunshine, even though the sun had long set. Samuel loosened his cravat and even slouched a bit in his chair, leaning heavily on one arm. The lines of worry he often carried after Cuffee's briefings regarding the harvest, lack of water, or sugar production melted into an amused smile in the company of friends. His relaxed state enhanced a more boyish appearance, and Maggie fought to keep her gaze from lingering in his direction.

Theadosia eyed Samuel. "Just because you're the titled firstborn son of an earl doesn't mean you must take life so seriously. I'm glad to see you are living a little. I daresay, Miss Prescott has been a good influence on you."

Maggie relaxed in her chair. The lessened strain

could have been due to her uncle being gone and Judith claiming a headache and having supper brought to her room. Which was well enough, for Judith's presence would have set Maggie on her guard. She would hold her tongue lest she found herself the center of gossip.

"Will you and Maggie be attending the assembly ball in two weeks' time?" Thea's eyebrows rose.

Maggie's spoon froze halfway to her lips. A dance? Her gaze flew to Samuel, who twirled the stem of his glass between his fingers.

"It's the night before the assembly's vote." George pursed his lips. "I believe that date was set to either use the dance as an opportunity to persuade those who waffle or get them foxed so they oversleep."

Samuel peered at Maggie, and the heat in his gaze spread warmth up her arms and into her already full stomach.

He sipped from his glass. "I admit to being tempted."

Because of her? She swallowed.

"But it would depend on Miss Prescott feeling up for it—"

"Yes," she blurted too quickly.

"—with her leg and all." He chuckled.

The heat in her stomach moved to her neck and her cheeks. "It's improving every day." She twisted her napkin into a knot. "I should be getting around well by then."

George leaned back in his chair and rubbed his stomach. "Delicious meal. My compliments." The footman removed his finished plate.

"I will pass along the sentiments to our chef." Samuel pushed back his plate, and the footman cleared it. "It is high praise, knowing the scrumptious meals Thea prepares for you daily."

George wrapped his arm around his wife, drew her close, and pecked a kiss into her hair. "High praise indeed."

Maggie melted at the Kellys' apparent love for each other. Her gaze slid to Samuel only to find him studying her with an affectionate lopsided grin.

"You're in high spirits this evening." Thea peered at Samuel. "Harvest must be going well even after the fire?" She raised her glass in a mock toast to Maggie. "Or is it Miss Prescott we have to thank? I don't think I've ever seen you this relaxed. I do believe I even heard you laugh."

Maggie's hand stilled with a scoop of custard in her spoon. Did she raise his spirits?

George Kelly had ignored social customs and married a mulatto woman for love, leaving his life in London behind. His arm lay draped over Thea's chair, and his thumb lazily brushed up and down her shoulder. He didn't seem to regret his decision.

Samuel's gaze caught to the intimate gesture, then looked at Maggie. Her heartbeat quickened.

Could such a love be possible for her and Samuel? Would he be willing to overlook her unknown past? If he saw her sitting in an assembly room, would he ask her to dance? Would he stand with her in front of others?

His eyes twinkled. "I do have Miss Prescott to thank." He, too, raised his glass in salute. "And hibiscus blossoms."

Maggie burst out laughing.

George and Thea looked to each other and then to Samuel. George asked the obvious question. "Hibiscus blossoms?"

Samuel held Maggie's gaze with a broad smile until her laughter subsided. "It's a long story. Shall I explain it to you over a cheroot?"

"Indeed." George stood, and Samuel followed suit.

Samuel pulled out her chair. "I'm certain Miss Prescott will regale your wife with the details."

He escorted Maggie down the hall and stopped at the drawing room. George pulled Thea close for a moment as if unable to bear parting. An expectant pause lingered, and Maggie glanced up to find him noticing the Kellys. His gaze riveted on her, and he peered at her the same way Tobie looked at Cilla. She'd always longed for a love like her parents', but her unknown lineage had left her socially on an island, alone, just as her parents had found her.

Desire pulsed in the depths of his eyes, stealing

her breath. Now more than ever she craved belonging.

Samuel cleared his throat and patted her arm before striding down the hall and into the billiard room.

Thea eyed Maggie with a knowing look before pulling her down onto the settee. "I can tell Samuel adores you."

Truly? Maggie's lips parted, but her brain floundered. Should she deny the claim or demand further explanation? "He . . . No . . ." Maggie shook her head and smoothed the wrinkles from her skirt. "Pardon?"

Bubbling laughter erupted from Thea's lips. "Don't fret. When I first fell in love with George, every time someone brought up his name, I got flustered and would blush redder than a sunburn."

Love? Was that what she felt toward Samuel? Initially, she'd found him fascinating with his strict routines, lists, and the regimented way he ran the plantation. But living under his roof had shown her his softer side, the way he wanted to ensure that his workers benefited alongside him, the concern he felt for her wellbeing. Yes, he had a temper, but it appeared when he felt protective of something or someone. Knowing that only heightened her regard for him.

But love?

Love would explain why her blood zinged through her veins when he entered the room.

Why he frequented her thoughts. The way she'd responded to his kiss.

Good heavens. She was in love with Samuel.

"Tell me why hibiscus blossoms made you laugh."

Maggie pressed the back of her hand to her forehead. "It's ridiculous. A word trick my parents used that I thought might help Lord Granville." Maggie retold the tale and watched Thea scowl at the things Mr. Fines said in the hallway and cheer for Maggie's bravery in making Mr. Fines feel foolish.

"I know I'm supposed to have grace and mercy." Thea pursed her lips. "But that man makes it hard to be Christ-like. But don't get me started on him. It will turn our stomachs, and we don't want that after such a lovely meal." She scooted forward. "Samuel mentioned that you were orphaned alone on an island?"

Maggie explained what she remembered about her mother and why she'd come to Antigua to discover her lineage. She spoke of Tobie, Cilla, and her siblings, and a weighty homesickness fell over her. "They'll be so hurt when they find out I misled them. I believed that if I learned the truth of my parentage, I could move forward with my life instead of floundering between society's social classes."

Maggie kneaded her palm with her thumb of her other hand. "Now, I'm not so certain. I wonder if

I'll always be stuck, an outsider looking in, the lame animal who's forced to stay on the fringe of the herd. And to make it worse, I will have hurt the ones who loved and believed the best of me." She hung her head. "I don't mean to burden you with my problems."

Thea clasped Maggie's hands between her warm palms. "I'm glad you did. I understand what it's like to be between worlds. George and I moved to Antigua for a new beginning." Her brown eyes softened into a warm molasses color. "Lineage may be important, especially in society's eyes, but I've found it's not as important as the legacy you choose."

Maggie's heart jolted, her words hitting their target. Had she truly been stuck? She had a family who loved her and whom she loved in return. She'd sailed across the Atlantic and met amazing people like Samuel and Thea, who welcomed her as an equal and not an outsider. Had she let Mitchell and his mother allow her to feel less-than? Why? In truth, Mitchell wasn't someone she wanted to associate with anyway, certainly not after he revealed himself to be a libertine and despoiler of innocents.

"Besides." Thea patted the top of Maggie's hand. "You already know the identity of your father."

Did Thea know something? "I do?"

"Our Heavenly Father." Thea glanced up. "He

knit you together in your mother's womb. Do not forget you are His beloved daughter. His child. By His decree, you are royalty, and no one can take that from you."

Maggie grunted. "I hadn't thought of it that way."

"He has grand plans for you, Maggie Prescott." She smiled wide. "And if I'm not mistaken, it might have something to do with Lord Granville."

"Could God have brought me here so that our paths would cross?" Maggie shook her head. "It can't be. I deceived my parents in coming here, and God condemns such treachery."

"Yes, but God can turn all things around for His good."

"I hope so."

"I know so."

Maggie clung to Thea's words, letting them settle the restlessness in her heart.

"You said the Prescotts had to re-teach you how to speak." Thea leaned against the arm of the settee. "How did they discover your name?"

"They didn't. I still don't know my true name."

"Why did they call you Maggie?"

"On the island, where I was found, I used to horde things like a Magpie. I guess I reminded them of the bird, and they needed something to call me other than 'feral child.' " She shrugged. "Maggie stuck."

"Did they give you a middle name?"

"No. Just Maggie, but I always wanted one. I envied the other girls who'd be introduced as Miss Amelia Elizabeth Walker or Henrietta Sophia Maddox. The butlers would glance at my calling card a second time and clear their throat before briskly announcing Miss Maggie Prescott."

"Oh tosh. I would pray for my middle name to be skipped. Theadosia Kelly sounds much better than Theadosia Dorcas Kelly."

"Dorcas isn't half bad."

Thea burst into laughter. "You are a terrible liar." She pressed her hand over her heart and calmed herself. "I want to hear the song your mother sang." She stood and moved to the piano on the opposite side of the room. "Hum me the tune, and I will accompany you with the piano."

Maggie sang a few bars, and Thea's fingers moved over the keys, easily settling into the melody.

"You are an astute pianist."

"I played for years at my father's inn. If you can hum it, I can play it. Now sing the words."

Maggie closed her eyes, and the words poured from her heart as she felt transported back to sunshine, ocean breeze, and her mama's comforting presence. Her hands shook, but she unlocked a fourth and fifth stanza, awakened from a deep slumber to reveal their hidden secrets.

• • •

"You never thought twice about giving up your inheritance?" Samuel smacked the six-ball with his stick, and it dropped into the side pocket.

George rubbed his cue's tip with chalk and lined up his next shot. "My inheritance was small since my papa was a small gentleman farmer, and I was torn initially, but my heart and my spirit were in alignment. It didn't take long for them to get my mind in agreement."

"You didn't see your marriage as a sacrifice?"

A striped ball shot into the corner pocket, and George straightened. "The odd thing is, many see a sacrifice only as penance. But a sacrifice can be an exchange. Relinquishing something you value for something you love."

Samuel positioned his next angle, and Maggie's smile flashed through his memory. He pulled back and shot, but instead of hitting center, his cue stick nicked the side of the ball, sending it whirling. The same way the mere thought of Maggie swirled his senses.

George arched a questioning brow. It wasn't common for Samuel to miss.

"I confess." Samuel sighed. "I have sentiments for Miss Prescott, but there are more barriers than just her lineage."

"For example?" George leaned down and practiced an imaginary hit to the side pocket.

"Like she hopped on a ship, setting good sense

and reason aside, to pursue a featherbrained belief that the answers she sought would miraculously appear." He snorted. "She acts as though God will just"—he raised his shoulders in a slow shrug—"provide."

George leaned on his stick. "And how is that going for her?"

Samuel frowned. "Better than I would have guessed."

"We serve a God of the supernatural, yet we try to limit Him to the natural. Remember, Gideon battled the entire company of Midianites with only three hundred men. Moses raised his staff, and the Red Sea parted to allow the Israelites an escape. Five loaves and three fishes fed five thousand." George's face softened the way it always did before he imparted wisdom, and Samuel braced for his words to cut through bone and marrow.

"From what you've described of your father, it is rational for you to expect God to sit on His throne and cast down His approval or disapproval. But the truth is, God stands beside you, encouraging you to follow his path and whispering, 'This is the way. Walk in it.'"

George tossed his stick up and caught it with his other hand. "Perhaps God's using Miss Prescott to show you how to believe in something other than your own might. You'll work yourself to the death trying to do everything in your power. Maybe it's time for you to leave things in God's hands."

George slammed the white ball into the center of two striped balls, and they parted, landing in separate corner pockets. "I'm winning."

"Not for long." Samuel rubbed more chalk on the end of his stick and studied his options.

"Is that music I hear?" George leaned toward the door. "It sounds like the ladies are singing. Shall we join them?"

The lilt of Maggie's voice vibrated the air like a siren call. He set down his stick and eyed George. "You're merely looking to end the game while you're ahead so you can gloat about beating me."

"Precisely." George set his stick aside and opened the door. "I think I hear angels calling."

They quietly entered the salon, where Thea bent over the keys and Maggie stood beside her with her eyes closed and hands folded across her breast. Her voice filled the room with an ethereal quality, and for a moment, Samuel believed George was right, and they'd crossed over into the supernatural realm, the heavenly realm.

It was the song Maggie's mother had taught her. She sang a fourth stanza. He jolted and strode to the nearby writing desk, pulling out a sheet of paper and dipping his quill.

"Papa wouldn't give me away, and the assembly had much to say.

*The price was much too great to pay.
For our love continued to grow."*

He scribbled the words on the page.

*"A battle waged over cross and cane.
Underneath the stairs, I hid my pain.
As the young wolf and earl
   came to blows.*

*In a new world, we sought a new life.
A chance to love without the strife
But our battle was far from over.*

*A tempest swelled and a gale blew.
Only we survived a ship torn in two
Our wolf sacrificed his life,
   so we'd have moreover.*

*Little one, never forget, you were born
   out of love.
A gift most precious from up above.
We shall rejoice and not mourn
   a life well-lived."*

A sob tore from Maggie's lips.

Thea jumped up and wrapped her arms around her.

Samuel's desire to comfort Maggie outweighed his ability to finish jotting down the verses, but he forced his hand and concentration, knowing Maggie would appreciate the gesture. He scribbled the final lyric and stared at the words. *A life well-lived.* Could he say the same?

George loomed over him. "Her song was very moving, but I sense that I'm missing something."

He puffed out his cheeks and scratched his hairline. "It's a song her mother taught her, and those last stanzas came to her just now."

"She hadn't sung them before?"

Samuel shook his head.

Maggie pulled back from Thea and inhaled a deep breath. She shyly peered at Samuel.

He held up the paper, and she smiled, her eyes glistening with tears.

The Kellys departed not long after, for the hour had grown late. Samuel escorted Maggie to her chamber and opened her door.

She stifled a yawn.

Resisting the urge to kiss her goodnight, he said, "Sleep well."

"I'm getting so close to the truth. Both song and the letters agree. The wolf is my father, but who is the wolf?"

French Naval Captain Sebastian Lowell Corbett. His chest squeezed, choking off his breathing. Samuel swallowed and passed her the sheet of scribbled lyrics.

She raised onto her toes and pressed a kiss onto his cheek. "Thank you."

Her breath tickled his ear, sending a rush of sensation that paralyzed him.

She stepped into her room and closed the door behind her.

Samuel staggered back under the stab of remorse piercing his heart.

Her father was the wolf. She'd sailed to Antigua on a hunch, and it miraculously had come to fruition. She had faith in the supernatural to lead her to the truth, and Samuel was standing in the way.

He gripped the wall to steady himself and trudged to his chamber. Standing in front of the washbasin, he dipped his hands to wash his face but found only hard porcelain. He sighed. All water was being conserved for drinking.

Tomorrow he would confess and present Maggie with the diaries. He'd explain that he'd only wanted to have his investigators find proof so as not to get her hopes up if things didn't align. Perhaps he could pressure his investigators to hand over the information they'd obtained sooner rather than later. Then Maggie wouldn't be as hurt by his actions. Maybe the information would distract her from his deceit.

He asked Carson to give him a minute alone and knelt by his bed, something he hadn't done since he was a child. He folded his hands and prayed, "God, George is right. Maybe it's time I stop trying to do things in my own power and instead trust in You. I realize I deserve Your admonition, but please forgive me for what I've done and help Maggie to forgive me, also. I'm grateful that there is no threat to my inheritance of Greenview Manor, but I cannot celebrate when it adds proof to Maggie's illegitimacy. She deserves a good husband."

He rubbed the ache out of his chest.

"Lord, more and more I desire for that man to be me."

Chapter 24

My love and I have instituted plans of our own. May God be with us.
> ~ *Entry by Loretta Baxter,
September 21, 1810*

Maggie let her bonnet fall and turned her face toward the sun. She inhaled a deep breath, and the fresh salty air calmed her tumultuous thoughts. She and Judith sat on the hillside overlooking the grand house and cane fields down to the ocean bay. She had much to think about after last night, and her head always felt clearer outdoors.

The origins of her birth never felt so close, yet she'd been following a string and come to its end without reaching the source. What should she do now? She'd read and re-read the wolf's letters, scouring every line for any hint of his real name. She'd sung the newly remembered lyrics of her mother's song to both Dinah and Judith for their input. They were excited for her but couldn't add any pertinent information.

God, if it isn't Your will for me to know my birth father's name, then help me relinquish that need to You.

A brisk breeze tugged on her bonnet strings as if trying to fly it like a kite. Dark clouds hung in the distance, offering the hope of much-needed water.

"We are tempting fate." Judith clicked her tongue. "I'd prefer not to do anything to rile Lord Granville's temper, and you know he doesn't approve of you leaving the house."

"For the last time, I'm not being held prisoner." Maggie tightened her bonnet strings. "He is merely worried about my injury."

"Then us having hiked up a hill will surely send him flying to the rafters." Judith yanked on the corner of the blanket upon which they sat. "I don't want to witness such violence, especially if it's directed at me."

Judith had been in a dudgeon ever since Uncle Anthony's leaving. Was something amiss between those two? And if so, wouldn't she be happy that Anthony was gone?

"If the coming storm breaks, how are you going to make it back to the house hobbling on your injured leg without getting a good soaking?" Judith crossed her arms.

"I will be delighted for the good washing."

"You don't understand how fast these storms can roll in."

Maggie remembered quite well but smiled in an attempt to cheer up her grumpy chaperone. "I appreciate your concern."

The sound of horse hooves turned her attention to the north road, where a solitary man approached.

Judith rose and waved. "Mr. Fines. Good morning."

Maggie pushed to a stand as well, putting too much weight on her injured leg and gritting her teeth.

He slowed his horse's pace and tipped his hat. "Good day to you Mrs. Morgan, Miss Prescott. How fortunate to find you." He glanced about as if on the lookout for someone. "I was hoping to speak with you." His gaze leveled on Maggie.

Her spine stiffened. So much for relaxing and clearing her head.

He dismounted and sauntered over.

"Several things have come to my attention, and I fret over your wellbeing, Miss Prescott."

It was clear why Judith's sister found the overseer to be a handsome man. His teeth were even, and his coat stretched over his broad frame. He held a relaxed arrogance about him that reminded Maggie of her schoolgirl infatuation with Mitchell. Her inner warning alarm sounded.

A crease formed between his brows, but she didn't know him well enough to determine if it was out of actual concern or feigned. "I'm certain you've come to witness Lord Granville's severe temper."

"As I recall, Lord Granville wasn't the one displaying his anger during your last visit."

"I admit." He shrugged and stepped closer. "It was difficult to see how the new overseer has turned the men I used to command against me and the insolent manner in which to mock me . . ." His mouth tightened and nostrils flared, but he quickly regained his composure. "But this isn't about me. I fear for your safety. You don't know what that man is capable of."

Judith drew closer. "Whatever do you mean?"

Fines's gaze flicked over the grounds once more, and he lowered his voice as if someone might overhear. "Lord Granville didn't come to Antigua merely to check on his inheritance. I have it on good account that the House of Lords banished him."

Judith gasped. "Whatever for?" She stifled her loud voice with her hand and whispered. "What did he do?"

Maggie could feel coiled tension radiating from Judith as she waited.

"He bludgeoned a man almost to death—one of his peers."

"He's a murderer?" Judith's hand splayed over her heart.

Maggie crossed her arms. "I hardly think breaking someone's nose is considered murder or even a bludgeoning, and in truth, he had a justifiable reason."

"Is that what he told you?" Fines snorted. "That he broke the man's nose?" He shook his head. "The scoundrel. I should have known he'd lie to keep up appearances. The only reason the man is here and not in Newgate Prison is because of his family's connections." He clutched Maggie's shoulder and eyed her with a steady gaze.

She fought the urge to shrug his hand away so as to not appear rude.

"Think about it. Do you really believe the House of Lords would banish someone over a small skirmish?"

Her heart pressed into her throat, wanting to defend Samuel. But Fines had made a good point.

"His father held the same temper." Fines's vehemence blew hot breath in her face, causing her to blink and the heat of his palm burned into her skin. "It was the Earl of Cardon, Lord Granville's father, who drove your mother to flee the island."

"What?" Maggie jolted. "Where did you hear this?"

He released her. "Loretta Baxter had been betrothed to the ill-tempered Earl, but instead of marrying him, she'd preferred to take her chances in America. Her ship sank suspiciously, even though it was rumored the captain was the best sailor in the Caribbean."

The young wolf and earl came to blows. She backed up a couple of steps, shaking her head. "Where did you hear that?"

He cleared his throat and his lips twisted in a smug half-grin. "It seems Lord Granville has his lawyers and investigators snooping around for information regarding your birthright. They, too, came by the rectory, and I just happened to have been coming in as they were leaving and overheard them discussing the earl and your mother. Oh, and the reverend wanted me to give you this."

He reached into his breast pocket and removed a yellowed, folded sheet of paper. "Reverend Tynan read through his files on posted banns."

She opened the fragile page and it read in bold script:

> I publish the Banns of Marriage between Lord Henry Thurston Granville, the Earl of Cardon from Dursley, England, and Loretta Genevieve Baxter of St. Mary, Antigua. If any known cause or just impediment why these two persons should not be joined together in Holy Matrimony, ye are to declare it. This is the first announcement.

She read and reread the words, forcing her hands not to allow the paper to slip through her numb fingers.

What did this mean? Her mother had been engaged to Samuel's father? Could he have been the wolf? It didn't make sense. The wolf was a Frenchman and a captain.

Judith read the page over Maggie's shoulder. "Your mother jilted an earl? Why would anyone cry-off the chance of wealth and a title?"

"I did a little hunting on my own." Fines hooked his thumbs in his pockets and rocked back on his heels. "Paul Fredrick Baxter, your grandfather, arranged the marriage, and when his daughter disappeared without any known heirs, the Earl of Cardon coerced Baxter to honor part of the arrangement and will his lands and property to Cardon."

"The scoundrel," Judith spit the words.

"And his son is of the same ilk, that's why he was tossed out of England on his ear. I have it from a good source, if Lord Granville doesn't turn things around with the House of Lords, he'll likely be left with only Greenview Manor as his inheritance. Now imagine if he feels threatened that he might lose his only holding. Do you think he'll have any qualms about making you disappear, as his father did your mother before him? If he's wretched enough to attack a lord of the peerage—a scion of a noble house—would he not hesitate to do whatever it takes to protect his inheritance from the likes of a lone female whose lineage isn't established? He'll hold no regard for you. He's holding you close by his side to keep you out of public view so that your disappearance will go unnoticed. Doesn't it make sense now why he wouldn't let you ride into town?"

Maggie raised her chin. "My uncle and his crew know about me and my whereabouts."

"And where is your uncle now?"

"On a voyage to get water."

"And who sent him on this voyage?"

Samuel. Her lips refused to say his name, but it needn't be spoken.

Fines was a scoundrel and not to be believed. She stared at the document in her hands—actual evidence of her mother's betrothal. Could it be as Fines said? Was Samuel, who'd promised to help her discover the truth of her birth, protecting his interests instead? Was the paper she held proof of her illegitimacy? If so, then she would no longer pose a threat to Samuel, but her reputation would be ruined. Rumors would no longer be suspect gossip. There had always been a good chance of her being baseborn. She'd always believed she'd feel relieved, but that was before Samuel. Why had he withheld this information from her? What was the reasoning behind keeping secrets?

Her hand shook from the new revelations. She let it fall to her side and squeezed her eyes closed. Her nerves had worn thinner than the sheet she held in her hand.

"What is going on here?"

Maggie's eyelids sprang open, and she stuffed the paper into her pocket, hidden in the folds of her gown.

Samuel approached on foot, hoofing it up the slope with long strides. He stared at Fines with a wary look. As he drew closer, he peered at Maggie, and his brows snapped together. Stopping in front of her, his gaze searched her face, and he squeezed her hand. "Are you all right? You look pale."

The concern lining his face made her want to shove the troubling thoughts Mr. Fines had planted aside and slide her arms around Samuel, seeking comfort in his strength. But would she be seeking reassurance from someone who was working against her? Her thoughts whirled, and bile rose in her throat. She couldn't speak, so she nodded.

"What are you doing here, Fines?" Samuel's sharp tone sliced the air. He wrapped a protective arm around Maggie's shoulders and drew her to his side. She garnered her resistance against the scent of bergamot and lye soap that taunted her.

Fines held up both hands and backed up a step toward his horse. "I was merely passing by and saw the ladies." He reached into his saddlebag and pulled out a long, colorful object. "I wanted to return this."

He held out her missing scarf. *God help her.*

Samuel snatched the beloved object from Fines's clutches. How had Fines gotten this? Had he been trespassing, sneaking around Greenview Manor?

Judith inched away from Samuel, her gaze wary as if he might burst into flames.

Beside him, Maggie paled even more. The truth

hit him like a punch to the stomach—Maggie and Fines had engaged in a clandestine interlude. His grip tightened on her mother's scarf like a stranglehold.

"I look forward to our dance at the assembly." Fines dragged his knuckles down the side of Maggie's shoulder.

She jerked away.

Samuel pounced, twisting and wrenching Fines's arm behind his back. "I think it's time you left my property."

Fines winced and rose on his toes. "Ow."

"Samuel." Maggie's tone pleaded.

He shoved Fines toward his horse.

Fines rubbed his arm. "Your property?" A wicked smile curved his mouth as he backed away. "Can that be confirmed?"

Heat scalded Samuel's face, blurring his vision.

"As I recall, only property owners are allowed a vote at the assembly?" Fines mounted his horse. "It would be an utter shame if your vote were called into question." He clicked his heels and galloped back to the main road.

A drop of rain plopped onto Samuel's scalp, evaporating into steam.

Maggie called his name, but the word sounded far away and barely registered over the tumult screaming in his mind. He wanted to chase Fines down, yank him off that horse, and teach him not to threaten Greenview Manor. The quaking in his chest spread to his limbs. He crumpled the scarf into a ball, his control slipping. Could Fines legally call Samuel's possession of Greenview Manner into question? Could Samuel once again lose everything?

Was control merely an illusion?

"I'm sorry." Maggie's fingers curled around his arm. "We went to the parish annals even though you forbade us."

Even though he knew it was Maggie standing there, all he heard was Lucy's voice. All he saw was Lucy's hand clinging to his arm. He'd been betrayed again, and this time with his enemy.

"I need to know the truth about my family before I sail." Maggie stepped around to face him.

His chest filled with a howl of rage, and he struggled to keep it caged. What was the word Maggie said to distract him?

"My time is running out," she said. "If I'm not back by the pre-season ball . . ."

He pictured Maggie smiling at Fines and Fines kissing her pliable mouth as Samuel had in the stairwell. The roar of his blood increased in his ears. His chest tightened, and his breathing shallowed. He needed to get away before he turned into a monster.

"Samuel?" Maggie touched his cheek, her green eyes imploring him for understanding.

His jaw burned as if it might snap. A drop of

rain hit his cheek and ran down. He didn't bother to wipe it away.

Go, before you explode.

He threw the scarf on the ground at her feet and stalked away, bumping her shoulder as he passed. A gentleman would apologize, but his stride lengthened, his muscles straining to cover more ground. More drops of rain fell onto the parched earth.

At the moment, he was no gentleman.

Chapter 25

I cannot and will not pledge myself to such an egotistical, boorish man, not when my heart has already declared itself to another.

~ *Entry by Loretta Baxter, October 3, 1810*

Maggie paced in front of the salon window while Judith rested on the settee. Lighting flashed. A drenching rain pummeled the rooftop.

Was Samuel safe out there? Had he sought cover in the mill?

Thunder cracked, and Maggie jumped.

"You should sit." Judith beckoned her over. "For your leg's sake."

"It hardly pains me." Short durations of movement seemed to be helping the healing process, but she wouldn't be able to relax until she could make sense of all that had happened. Had Samuel's crime been more than he'd let on? Was he protecting his interests instead of helping her? Were his investigators involved in discovering who her father was or finding out if she could usurp his inheritance?

Was she going to believe Fines's word over Samuel's? Fines's actions had been none other than those of a scoundrel. She held no doubts that he'd waited until Samuel was present to hand over her scarf. She'd witnessed the gloating look on his face, making it seem as if they'd met secretly. He'd done it to rile Samuel, to goad him into a fight. She couldn't prove it, but she'd seen the smugness in Fines's gaze and heard it in his tone. Could anything truthful come out of the mouth of a person of such ilk?

Besides, Samuel's concern for her injury had been sincere. When he'd given her the cane and slippers, he'd watched her expression like a child hoping for a parent's approval. She'd been disappointed that he hadn't gone to the parish like he'd said he would, but she also understood the demands the plantation had placed upon him. If he were trying to prevent her from discovering the truth, then why would he have helped search for additional diaries? She pictured his expression when he realized his arm had become stuck, and a small chuckle escaped.

Maggie stopped pacing. Could the books still be there? Maybe he hadn't been able to reach them. Or, could he have pretended not to feel them?

"I want to look again under the floorboards." Her heart clenched at her disloyalty, but she needed to know for certain.

"You think he might have lied?" Judith stood.

"No." The word flew from Maggie's lips. "I

merely want to check again since his arm got stuck. He might have been distracted or unable to reach." She beckoned over a footman. "Please find the tallest, longest armed servant, preferably thin in stature. Have him meet me in my mother's sitting room."

He nodded and disappeared.

Judith aided Maggie up the stairs, but her leg felt much improved.

James and a lanky footman named Billy met them on the second floor, but their attempt revealed nothing but cobwebs and dust.

The ladies returned to the salon, and Maggie pushed aside the curtain to stare at the rain still pouring. Her chest tightened. She shouldn't have questioned Samuel's character. Only a foolish person would believe the doubts Fines had planted.

Thunder rumbled, and the wind bowed the palm trees low. Where was Samuel?

Maggie fingered her mother's scarf that was once again holding back her hair. "Do you think we should send someone after Lord Granville?"

Lighting flashed, illuminating a shadow near the garden. She blinked and tried to focus through the blurred rivets of rain running down the glass, but the shadow was gone.

The French doors opened, and the raging storm whistled inside the house.

Samuel.

Maggie darted into the hall.

Samuel ran the soles of his boots on the mud scraper before entering while the wind whipped his soaked jacket and flapped the drapes. He stomped into the narrow, back entrance foyer, and the door slammed closed behind him.

Maggie skidded to a halt in front of him, ready to wrap him in an embrace and weep at his safety. The deep scowl on his face stopped her. She clasped her hands to hold them down. "Praise God. I was worried."

Rain dripped down his face and off his chin, but he didn't wipe it away. His gaze searched hers as if to determine the truth.

Hawley pushed around her to aid him in shrugging off his jacket. The butler struggled with the wet fabric, and the snug fit didn't aid him. They peeled one arm free, but the material caught on his other shoulder.

"Allow me—" She tugged on the fabric, but Samuel jerked back as if she'd shocked him with a static charge.

His walk in the rain hadn't lessened his anger.

Hawley peeled him out of his other sleeve, and Maggie averted her gaze from the shirt plastered to Samuel's chest like a second skin.

Rain pounding the windowpanes filled the silence.

Hawley pulled up a stool for Samuel to sit while the butler removed his boots.

Maggie glanced out the window and attempted light conversation. "I've never seen such heavy rain. At least not that I can remember."

Samuel didn't bother to respond.

Hawley loosened one boot, removing it, but Samuel didn't wait for him to get the other. He yanked it off himself, handed it to Hawley who squeezed past Maggie to care for the mud-caked boots. Samuel rose.

Maggie stood in his way. "We need to talk."

"I must change." He attempted to step around her.

She blocked his path. "After you change then."

His jaw tightened. "I have work to do."

"There are things that must be said." She tried to catch his gaze, but he refused to look at her. "There's been a misunderstanding, and it's better to get it corrected right away than to stew over it."

He leveled her with a glare. The force of it caused her to retreat a step. "I won't be stewing on anything because I won't be thinking of you at all." He wiped away a trailing rain droplet from his cheek with a swipe of his arm. "When your uncle arrives, you will pack your things and return to his ship."

She gasped. Would he not allow her the chance to explain?

He attempted to move around her, bumping her shoulder, but she held her ground.

He growled and pulled back.

"Hibiscus." Maggie muttered the word and placed a gentle hand on his shoulder.

"Enough of your ploys, Lucy!" He flung his arm back.

Her hand dropped to her side. He hadn't appeared to notice the slip of his tongue.

She straightened to full height, raising slightly on her toes. "I. Am. Not. Lucy."

His voice lowered in a dead calm. "After your rendezvous with Fines, you might as well be."

He pressed forward, and this time she moved aside and let him pass.

He stomped up the stairs, the very spot where only two weeks ago he'd kissed her.

The door slammed, and Maggie flinched—inside and out.

The rain didn't let up. If Fines hadn't trespassed, Samuel would be celebrating the storm, for it was replenishing their water storage. He wouldn't have sent Middleton to Montserrat if he could have predicted the weather. Middleton had probably gotten caught by the storm and sought shelter. If they had to repair the ship due to storm damage, who knew how long it would be before Maggie was off his hands.

He raked his fingers through his hair, unsure how long he could endure having her so close, knowing she'd betrayed his trust. She'd knocked on his door on several different occasions. He knew she wanted to discuss what happened. Why she'd gone behind his back to meet with Fines, but he couldn't stomach it. The thought of her staring up into Fines's face or him touching her was like tossing gun powder into a campfire. History was repeating—like mother, like daughter. He battled against the generational curse of an angry temper, and Maggie would struggle with virtue, as her mother had before her.

The rain persisted, trapping them under the same roof. Still, Samuel successfully avoided Maggie for a day and a half. But his muscles had tensed every time he heard her voice, and his thoughts continued to stray to her whereabouts and what she might be doing at that moment—whether she thought of him or of Fines. He snapped a quill pen between his fingers, and ink splattered across his white shirt.

Blast.

Carson, even with his magic touch, would not be able to save this one.

He jerked open his desk drawer to locate another writing utensil and jostled Loretta Baxter's diaries. The contents of his stomach churned. Technically, they were his property. They came with the house. He could ship them to England after his ownership was established. Let her parents decide whether or not to reveal the information. The responsibility would be out of his hands as soon as she departed—*for good.*

The muscles in his legs twitched, restless to move, to work—anything to distract him from the black thoughts that bombarded him. He closed the drawer and moved to the window. Maggie had been a distraction. She'd taken his focus off getting the land to produce, driving his workers to harvest the cane so he could return to England. Even though the rain would restore the wilted, newly-planted ratoons, it meant nothing was being harvested. The men in the mill and the boiling house had caught up with their work and returned to the chattel houses. In the meantime, they were getting behind. If he woke up a little earlier, pushed the men a little harder, they could get back on track.

You'll work yourself to the death trying to do everything in your own power. Maybe it's time for you to leave things in God's hands.

He'd tried praying, but things had only gotten worse. Pinching his lips in a tight line, he fought the urge to scream, *God are you even listening?* but George's voice, once again, rang in his head. *Are you prepared for God's response, telling you this is the way, walk in it?*

Samuel wiped the glass pane to remove the condensation. The mountain towered in the distance, remaining strong even during a storm.

"I lift my eyes to the hills—where does my help come from?" A Psalm that he'd heard Thea repeat on several occasions floated through his memory. *How did the rest go?* "My help comes from the Lord, maker of heaven and earth. He who watches over Israel will neither slumber nor sleep. . . ." He squeezed his eyes tight and scratched his hairline with his index finger. *Something about the sun . . .* "The sun will not harm you by day, nor the moon by night."

He grunted. Since when had he started recalling scripture? He opened his eyes.

The mountain looked different—crooked. He squinted, but the palm trees were bent at a forty-five-degree angle.

He jerked away from the window.

"Mudslide!"

Chapter 26

His mind was muddled by drink, and I witnessed the true lengths of his anger. A shiver of fear ran through me, but I know my wolf shall rescue me from my bitter fate.

~ Entry by Loretta Baxter, October 5, 1810

Samuel darted into the hall, screaming, "Get to the roof!"

Outside, the alarm bell in the windmill tower gonged. *Thank God.* Cuffee would see to getting the workers to safety. *Please God, slow the mudslide until we can get to higher ground.*

Hawley gripped the wooden trim to round the corner and peered at his master.

"Mudslide." Samuel pushed a maid toward the butler. "Get everyone upstairs quickly. There isn't much time." Samuel ran down the hall and burst into the salon, looking for Maggie.

She and Judith peered out the window. Maggie turned. "What's wrong? Why is the bell ringing?"

"Mudslide." He waved them over. "Hurry, upstairs." They were running out of time.

Judith flew past Samuel, down the hall, and up the steps.

Maggie wasted no time, but she ran toward the kitchens.

"Maggie, there's no time." Samuel chased her.

Her raven hair whipped behind her. "We must warn the staff."

"I'll handle it. You get to safety." Samuel opened doors, clearing rooms and directing his staff upstairs.

A flock of scullery maids and cooks brushed by him. Maggie must have made it to the kitchens. A confused footman poked his head out of the storeroom.

"Upstairs, run!" Samuel pushed past him.

Maggie exited the kitchens. "I think that was everyone."

He grabbed her hand, and they hurried toward the stairs. The ground shook, and a low rumble rose into a thundering grumble. He yanked Maggie around the corner and mounted the first stair.

"Help." A young scullery maid peeked from the coat closet.

Maggie pulled away, and Samuel halted.

She tugged the maid from that closet and pushed her toward him, and he shooed her up the stairs.

The hall darkened, and window panes shattered. Maggie ducked her head to avoid flying glass. The floor beneath them moved, and Maggie tripped.

A wall of mud, rocks, and trees spilled into the house through holes and crevices.

Samuel's blood ran cold.

They weren't going to make it.

He hooked Maggie around the waist and flung her into the cramped closet amid coats and blankets. He dove in after her, but the impact of the mudslide smashed into the door. It banged against the lower half of his body, knocking him into Maggie and slamming the door closed.

The closet walls shook as the thundering continued incessantly. He curled his body around Maggie's small frame to protect her as muddy water oozed under the crack of the door. They huddled in an inch of muck in complete darkness for endless minutes before the thunder and quaking lessened, until it grew harder to distinguish the sounds of the mudslide over the pounding of his heart. He willed his pulse to steady through slow controlled breaths, but an eerie stillness followed. Had they been buried alive?

Maggie's puffs of breath stirred the fine hairs on his neck. Her hands clung to his upper arms, and she whispered into his collarbone, "Is it over?"

Samuel peered into the darkness, straining his ears for external sounds. "I believe so."

He felt her head rise, and her hair brushed over his hands, which clutched her back.

"That was close." The tension in her body relaxed, and she sagged against his chest.

His arms instinctively tightened around her. "Too close, and we're not in the clear yet."

She didn't move, and he didn't release her. A lump rose in his throat. What if he'd lost her? What if she'd been swept away, and he hadn't been able to save her?

He squeezed his eyes closed against the image of this woman, this incredible selfless woman, being swallowed by rocks and dirt. The gut-wrenching ache in his heart paralyzed him. He needed Maggie. Her smile made the day brighter. Her warmth circulated through him as part of his life-blood, and her enthusiasm for life offered hope. She made him believe that good would prevail. He had walked away from Lucy, but he couldn't walk away from Maggie, even if she loved another.

He stroked her hair. *God, I'm sorry. I've been distant and thinking only of myself, but I owe You my life for saving hers.*

She stirred in his arms. "What do we do now?"

He reluctantly released her and slowly rose. He tried the door, but it didn't budge. He pressed his shoulder into it. Nothing. He turned his back and pushed his feet against the wall for leverage. Still nothing. He banged on it with his fist. "Hello there? Anyone?"

Instead of a hollow echo, his knock resounded as a sequence of thuds followed by silence.

He tried again. Maggie added her voice and rose to pound her palm against the wooden panels. "Help! We're in here."

How deep had they been buried? How long could they survive in a closet without food or water?

Or air?

His hand froze mid-pound. Would they suffocate? He raked his hair. *Think.* There must be a way out.

Maggie pounded and yelled until he stilled her with a hand on her back. "Give it a minute. Everyone is probably still on the roof." He didn't want to worry her.

He leaned against the back wall, careful not to bump his head on the coat hook, and slid to a seated position on the filthy floor. Thankfully, most of the mud had drained or puddled in the far corner.

Maggie sat next to him and whispered.

Not able to decipher her words, he started to ask her to repeat herself.

"Lord, You are our ever-present help in trouble." She spoke louder into the darkness.

She was praying. Samuel leaned in to better hear the words.

"Thank You for being our front and rear guard and saving us from the mudslide."

He felt for her hand and gripped it, bowing his head.

"We boldly ask for Your grace and mercy to help us in our time of need. Nothing is hidden from Your sight. In Your wisdom, show us a way out. Come to our rescue. We ask this in Jesus's name."

"Amen." Samuel raised his head and released her hand.

Maggie exhaled. "They will find us."

"Indeed." He agreed, but to him, the word sounded hollow. *God, help me to have Maggie's surety.*

Silence stretched between them. He held no concept of time or duration in the darkness, except that his backside began to hurt and his legs needed a good stretching.

"Samuel?"

"Yes."

"Do you think the others survived?"

"Higher ground is the safest spot, and the house doesn't seem to have collapsed." His firm tone and sound logic helped his heart believe. "They've made it, and they will find us."

His men would dig them out, and then he'd survey the damage. The muscles in his back knotted. It was gone. Even if the manner house was salvageable, the destruction of the crop would set him back another year, which meant it would be another year before he could return home. If he were lucky.

All of his hard work had been for nothing. If the mud took out the north and east fields, they'd be fortunate not to starve. Maybe if he worked the men in double shifts? Offered more incentives to work harder? Drove himself past the point of exhaustion.

You can't do this in your own power.

He felt Maggie pull her knees to her chest and wrap her arms around them.

"And the workers?"

His heart dropped. What were the chances that they all lived? He swallowed his guilt. The loss of crops was nothing compared to the loss of lives. At least Cuffee had been alerted. He could have gotten some to safety, but it depended on the direction of the mudslide. If it had extended to the slave quarters, there wouldn't have been enough time. The image he'd seen a few weeks back—of the fieldworker returning from the field to his family cooking over the fire, his son jumping into his arms—stirred Samuel's heart. Had they survived, or would wild dogs someday dig up their bones?

He couldn't share his despair with Maggie. Neither would he lie. "It depends on the direction the mudslide took."

She rubbed her legs. "I'm believing for a miracle."

Perhaps God is using Miss Prescott to show you how to believe in something other than your own might. George's words rang in Samuel's memory. He stood, unable to resist the need to do something. Anything. He banged on the door and yelled until his fists ached and his throat felt scratchy. He searched the closest for any useful tools to help them dig out but found none. He even tried pulling apart the wallboards to see if they could escape through the other side, but stopped when he felt mud seeping through the lattice. The temperature in the closet rose by at least ten degrees and sweat dripped off his forehead.

Maggie touched his back. "Take a break for a moment."

A break? He refused to give up and die. His father may find him lacking and willingly pass his inheritance to Bradlee, but they would find his body in this closet with claw marks down the walls and know he did everything he could. He kicked the door, and pain shot up his leg, but he repeated it again and again, taking full vent of his rage. "Blast it all! I will not die like this."

Maggie, once again, bowed her head and prayed.

He returned to beating on the door with his fists until they bloodied. His chest heaved, and he sank to a seated position. Over his ragged breaths, he listened to her whispered prayer, only making out a few words.

She stopped and he heard her hair swish against the wall. "Are you finished?"

"Are you?" He hadn't meant to snap at her.

"For now."

"Well?" What did he expect God to tell her—confirm that He had punished them? This was justice for Samuel not reining in his anger and for her for deceiving her parents and him. They would die for their sins. "Did God answer?"

Her hand brushed her hair back, and the silky strands ran over his shoulder. "Yes."

Samuel jolted. He'd assumed that God wouldn't bother with sinners.

"What did He say?"

"That He is a God of the supernatural, and He is in control."

We serve a God of the supernatural, yet we try to limit God to the natural. Wasn't that what George had told Samuel a few days before?

Maggie shifted beside him, and the movement was followed by the sound of tearing fabric. "And He said to bind your wounds because He loves you."

What? How would Maggie know his knuckles had started to bleed? It was pitch black. He wouldn't even know she was in the closet with him if he didn't hear her. "God spoke to you . . . audibly?"

She felt for Samuel's hand and wrapped it with the torn cloth. "It's more of an impression on my heart or a clear thought that is accompanied by a certain boldness to face the task ahead." Her fingers wrapped his bruised and bleeding hands with such tenderness that a lump rose in his throat. Was she showing him God's gentleness? God's love?

Maggie attempted to shrug off Samuel's silent treatment after she bandaged his knuckles. He retreated to a different corner. Not that the closet allowed for much distance. He remained within arm's reach, but emotionally, a vast gulf grew between them. She tried to give him time to come to his senses, but questions continued to plague her until their cries could no longer remain silent.

She fought to keep her voice even. "I didn't come here to stake any claim to Greenview Manor. You must know that."

He stayed quiet.

Maggie swallowed, fighting for the right words. "Why did you keep me from going into town? Was it to keep me from discovering the truth?"

"I didn't want you further injuring your leg."

"Is that the full truth?"

Silence.

"You promised to help me." She swallowed around the thickness in her throat. "I didn't believe the things Fines said, but when you won't be open with me, it allows room for doubts to grow."

"You question my honesty when you're the one who ran off to meet with that scoundrel." He punched the wall.

Maggie flinched.

"What lies did he tell you?"

She couldn't see Samuel, but she heard his breathing and felt the heat roll off him in waves. *He bludgeoned a man. Do you really believe the House of Lords would banish a man over a small skirmish? I fear for your life.*

Maggie held her ground, though her insides quaked. "He said you were intentionally keeping me hidden here so that I couldn't learn the truth. He gave me a paper that showed wedding banns posted between your father and my mother. Did you know they were supposed to marry?"

"He showed you proof?" The darkness stilled, and after a long pause, Samuel spoke. "Are you certain it was correct?".

"I read the banns myself." It pained her not to be able to see his expression.

"My father was engaged to Loretta Baxter?" Disbelief rang in his voice. He hadn't known.

"Fines said that when my mother ran off with the French captain, your father made her disappear, and if the truth got out, you'd do away with me like your father did my mother."

She felt him reel back.

"You believe I'm a murderer? That my father was a *murderer?*"

The hurt in his voice sliced her chest. All she could picture was his face in the garden. How vulnerable he'd looked when he'd spoke of Lucy's betrayal. She heard the pain in his voice when he'd mistakenly said, *Enough of your ploys, Lucy.* With her accusations, she betrayed him too.

"No." Her verbalization only firmed the resolution in her heart. Samuel wouldn't hurt her. She'd known it all along, but it took her voicing it to erase the doubts planted by Fines. Samuel had risked his life to save her. She crawled forward and placed her hand over his heart and felt its tempo quicken. "I know you would never hurt me, but Fines easily sways others who have witnessed your temper."

He placed his hand over hers, and his voice rang with hurt. "Why him? You haven't taken the scarf off since I brought your mother's chest down from the attic."

"I promise, I didn't meet with him. Judith and I snuck out only to go to the rectory and search the annals. Fines saw us when we were leaving and aided me up into the carriage. That was all. My mother's scarf must have fallen off. He could have returned it to me earlier, but he waited until you arrived because he wanted you to see it and think the worst of me."

Her voice cracked. "I realize my part in the blame. I should never have snuck away when you forbade it. I understand that Lucy and Harry hurt you, but I'm not Lucy."

"Your mother betrayed my father. How do I know you won't do the same?"

"Because you know me. I may be like my mother, but I'm not her, just as you are not your father. I'm sorry Lucy left you bitter, but you are clinging to your bitterness as if it will save you from drowning."

"You don't know what you're talking about."

"Don't I?" She crossed her arms. "Are you driven to push harder to create a future for yourself or to spite Harry for what he did?"

"What does it matter?"

"Pride can blind us." She rested her head against the wall. "My pride blinded me. One boy thought that my adopted status allowed him the right to take liberties. I stopped him with the cutlass Tobie gave me, and I lied. I told him my father was a pirate and I'd run the boy through if he tried anything again."

She felt Samuel tense beside her.

"Instead of confessing my mistruth, I let the gossipmongers have their day. In a single moment, I tattered my reputation further and ruined my chances at marriage. I came here to find out about my birth because I don't want to be a burden to my parents, continuing to live off them as an on-the-shelf spinster."

"What will you do if you're found to be illegitimate?"

"Perhaps I'll go to America and become a schoolteacher, or return to England to be a governess. I trust God's will for my life. He has taught me recently that He loves me not because of where I came from or what I've done, but merely because I'm His daughter."

She sighed. "I've been like Jonah from the Bible since coming here. I'd left with my own agenda, disobeying God and my parents. But God has been understanding."

She chuckled a hollow laugh. "And more than forgiving. God used my getting shot, a fire, and now a mudslide to direct me back to His way. It took coming here for me to understand Cillia's explanation on why she kept wooden plates in the cupboard."

"Wooden plates?" Confusion was clear in his tone.

"She told me fine china is valuable but weak. A wooden plate isn't fancy, but it's strong. Both serve different purposes. God values both weakness and humility. Even if I'm not fancy or from good stock, God still values me."

"Maggie." Samuel wrapped his arm around her and pulled her to his chest. "To me, you are a treasure beyond value." They sat there for a long moment in silence, holding each other. At some point, Maggie dosed off and awoke still in his arms. She stirred, easing the pain of the wooden floorboards on her hip.

Samuel didn't release his hold even though she rested so close that when she blinked, her lashes brushed his cheek. Instead, he gently stroked her hair, and she reveled in the feeling. He continued brushing her hair with his fingertips for some time until he inhaled a ragged breath. "I drove Lucy away."

Chapter 27

Papa sees only the man's good qualities. His dear friendship with my betrothed's father blinds him to any faults.

> ~ Entry by Loretta Baxter,
> October 5, 1810

Samuel waited for Maggie to recoil, but she remained completely still, as if not wanting to interrupt what he was about to say.

"You were right about pride blinding me." He faced the darkness, peering into it. "It hadn't been just Harry's silvered tongue that lured Lucy away from me. I'd placed my duties above Lucy. I didn't pay her the attention she deserved. She'd tried to get my opinion on the wedding, but I couldn't be bothered, for I had more pressing matters. She begged for me to take her to parties and the opera, but I offered excuses, and when she persisted, she witnessed my quick temper. I can still see the horrified look on her face."

Maggie's hand slid to his chest and rested over his heart, but she didn't say a word.

"I didn't want to admit my blame to anyone, not even myself. If Lucy's betrayal wasn't due to Harry's vile libertine ways, that meant she never loved me—that she chose his arms instead of mine—disgrace over the protection of my name."

"We've all made mistakes." She snorted. "I've learned the hard way how our sins allow the enemy to sneak in and steal, kill, and destroy."

Reliving his past had always stirred his anger, but Maggie's faith comforted him. Instead of tensing, he continued to stroke her hair. How many times had his anger allowed the devil an opportunity? He exhaled a sigh. *God, I repent of my anger and mistakes. Help me to change—to be a better person.*

Her finger traced his collarbone. "What Lucy disregarded, I would have cherished."

His hand stilled.

"I'm not certain whether I'm baseborn. I'm not sure of my future nor whether we'll live to see tomorrow, but I believe Jesus came to break the chains of sin. He came so that we can have life, but not just to survive but to enjoy life to the fullest." She brushed her knuckles along his jaw. "I might have gone about things the wrong way, but I'll always be grateful to have known you."

His hands reflexively pulled her closer. She'd voiced the words in his heart. He cupped her face for a brief kiss to prove his love, whispering her name before lowering his lips to hers. He pressed into their velvety softness that fit so perfectly against his as though she'd been made for him. They were as different as England and Antigua, yet somehow, they were right together.

She softened his edges, but he added stability. His fingers curved deeper into her silken tresses, releasing the scent of orange blossoms.

She pulled away. "I can't. I love you but . . ."

She loved him. He fought to even his breathing and calm his racing pulse.

"I wish . . ."

"Maggie." He tried to pull her back into his arms and hold her, but she moved to the other wall.

"Until I discover my father—"

"I know." They were perfect together, but societal divides walled them apart. *My help comes from the hills.* A mudslide had drawn them together. No doubt society would question their time alone together. Maggie's already tentative reputation would be sullied.

Unless he married her.

The thought cleared away a dense fog that had cluttered his mind since the night he rode through the barley fields with his papa. His father and the House of Lords might never be able to see Maggie as a suitable match, but they'd have to agree that due to the circumstances, Samuel took the proper actions. He very well couldn't have allowed a young woman to die nor could he stand aside while her reputation suffered. A plan started to form.

"I just wish I knew something with certainty." Maggie sucked in a sob.

The sound of it wrecked him. He lowered his head into his hands. *God, is this what you would have me do?* In the small still confines of his heart, he felt God's hand on him. George's words rang in his mind. *Sometimes a sacrifice can be an exchange—relinquishing something you value for something you love.*

"Maggie." His voice rang with assurance. "You can be certain of my love for you." He exhaled a deep breath. "We'll trust God to handle the rest."

A sob lodged in Maggie's throat as she dreamed of Cilla weeping, *Why did Maggie leave us?* while Tobie consoled her.

The creak of a floorboard stirred Maggie from a nightmare where she'd been buried alive. She squeezed her eyes tighter to block out her guilt and pressed her forehead against a firm, warm surface. Something pulsed under the palm of her hand. A heartbeat?

Wait. A grave wouldn't be warm.

With a gasp, she lifted her head, but the rest of her was pinned under the weight of Samuel's arm. She must have drifted to sleep, but in the darkness of the closet, it was impossible to know whether it was day or night. Her stomach rumbled, her throat parched.

The air had slightly cooled. She gently tugged on Samuel's sleeve to extricate herself without waking him, but he nestled closer, and his other hand slipped about her waist. They lay in a bed of coats, her nose to his chest, with only the thin cambric material of his shirt separating her cheek from the touch of his bare skin. This wouldn't do.

She prayed the Lord would keep her from temptation, especially after Samuel's confession. *You can be certain of my love for you.* What was she to do with that statement? It didn't change their situation. He was still expected to become an earl, and she was expected . . . Well, she didn't know quite yet, but she was sure God had a plan.

A creak sounded from up above.

Was the roof collapsing? Would the house crumble down on top of them?

"Samuel, wake up." She shook his shoulder.

He jolted. One of his hands hit the wall while the other squeezed her close as if to protect her. He attempted to sit up. "What is it? What's the matter?"

"The house is creaking."

He released her and sat up fully. Neither of them spoke as they waited and listened.

A distant muffled sound reached them. Maggie gripped Samuel's hand. Were those voices? This time, a squeak of a floorboard sounded more like a footstep, someone passing overhead.

Samuel jumped up and banged on the ceiling. "Down here." He pounded, and bits of plaster dust sprinkled on her forehead. "Help! We're in the foyer closet."

The creak came again. "Milord? Is that you?" Carson's muted voice called from above.

"Yes. We're trapped down here."

"Praise the Lord above." The floor groaned and footfalls moved. "Over here. I heard them. They're alive."

Samuel grabbed her around the waist, lifting her into the air in a tight embrace. "It's a miracle."

It took an entire day to shovel them out. Every abled body came to aid in the process, and Carson yelled down from the floor above to keep them abreast of the progress made. By nightfall a servant was able to pass water through a small crack and by early morning, he and Maggie wedged out of the closet through the partially opened door. Never had it felt so good to wash, change into clean clothes, and fill his famished stomach.

Miraculously, no one had been killed in the mudslide. The sliding earth had shifted down the natural gully of the lane after hitting the main house, missing the slave quarters. Samuel reminded himself of that miracle repeatedly. After they broke their fast and regaled their harrowing tale to the staff, he and Cuffee surveyed the damage. Mud caked their boots, and each stood with a shovel in hand.

"Da north field is gone, and da main house

was knocked off its foundation by a good two feet. Da structure seems sound enough, but I've been havin' da staff sleep en da slave quarters ta be safe. Anyting on da second floor is clean and untouched, but da first floor is either ruined or in need of a good washin'." Cuffee raised his hat and scratched the top of his head. "We've got a lot of work ta do."

"I don't know, Cuffee. Maybe it's not God's plan for me to make this land profitable. It certainly doesn't seem like He wants it that way after the fire and now a mudslide. The land has beaten me."

"If dere is one ting I know is dat da Lord works in mysterious ways." He jabbed the point of the shovel into the packed mud. "But He turns all tings around fer His good. Mudslides are part of island life. I've seen dem wipe out whole farms, but in da years ta follow da crops sprout up better den ever before. I've seen fields burn, but in a year or two ya never would hav known dere ever was a fire."

Samuel rubbed his temples. "I don't know if I can manage another couple of years. While my attention is here, issues go unresolved at home. There have been squatters and border disputes and tenant negotiations. My plan was to have the plantation profitable in a year and then deal with the rest in England, but the plan falls apart if I'm here more than a year."

"Da heart of a man plans his way, but da Lord establishes his steps." Cuffee's gaze shifted.

Samuel followed his gaze to Maggie carrying a bucket out of the house. Mud stained her gown, and dirt marked her face where she'd attempted to wipe away errant strands of hair that had slipped from the colorful scarf containing it.

He remembered her words. *What Lucy disregarded, I would have cherished.*

"Hoy, there." George, with Thea beside him, picked their way over the debris. Their wagon stood at the end of the lane, unable to bring the baskets of provisions and shovels closer.

Cuffee whistled, and men moved to help them unload.

Thea veered in Maggie's direction and George approached. "What else do you need?"

"Could Maggie stay with you and Thea until the house is habitable?" Or until her uncle returned, and they sailed back to England . . . along with his heart.

"Of course, Thea would be delighted." An affectionate smile lit his lips. Thea already fussed over Maggie to get her to stop, rest, and eat.

The wind whipped Maggie's skirts, accentuating her slender shape. She instructed what used to be Greenview Manor's kitchen staff to carry the recently dug-out dining room table and chairs to a shady spot under the trees for everyone to sit and eat. She may believe she didn't understand etiquette, but she'd make an excellent wife.

George cleared his throat, catching Samuel staring.

Samuel quickly hid a smile he hadn't realized he'd allowed.

"The two of you were in that closet alone for two days." George's voice held a warning, and Samuel knew the direction of his thoughts. "Social standards are looser on the island, but tongues will wag, especially knowing the widow Morgan's propensity for it. Miss Prescott's reputation will be ruined."

"The mudslide didn't care if we were properly chaperoned." Samuel raised his chin. "I wasn't going to let her die. She saved the lives of our entire cooking staff. Is that the thanks she'll get?"

"I understand, but society won't. There's a chance the fickle lot will make an exception, but I doubt it."

"It doesn't matter." Samuel allowed confidence to ring forth in his tone. "I plan to offer for her anyway, if she'll have a son of an earl who may no longer hold any inheritance and who, try though he might, can't make a sugar plantation profitable."

"No one could have predicted a natural disaster. You're too hard on yourself."

"The mudslide was an awakening. My pride was blinding me to who ultimately is in charge and what is truly important." He shifted in a circle, scanning the damage the mud had created. "I can choose to be bitter, or I can choose to be better."

George smiled. "If Jesus can turn bitter water into wine, think of the great work he can do with you."

"God is refining me through these hardships. I'm not the same man who first arrived on these shores."

"Might as well change into the person you want to become." George slapped Samuel on the back. "Because one way or another, we're changing."

Cuffee cleared his throat. "If you don't mind me sayin' "—he nodded to the workers shoveling out the main house—"Lord has already been doin' a great work through you."

"They'll be even more powerful as a married couple." George's expression grew serious. "How are you going to inform her parents?"

Samuel blanched. "My word. Between the fire and the mudslide, I completely forgot." He gripped his lower jaw. "I wrote to let them know Maggie was all right after being shot. They could be on their way here now."

"Well, it would be convenient if they could arrive before the wedding."

"It may not be a happy reunion. Maggie never told them she'd sailed here. They believed she was at finishing school, and I haven't mentioned to her that I wrote them." Samuel pressed his palms to his eye sockets. "And depending on what rumors of my past still circulate among the *ton*, they may not be happy to meet me, especially not as a potential future son-in-law."

"Lord Granville and Captain Middleton are riding up the lane now."

Maggie's stomach flipped inside out.

Judith, who'd arrived ten minutes earlier, let the curtain fall, blocking their lovely view of the lane and the distant cove with waves forming whitecap lines that extended into the bay.

Judith smoothed errant strands of hair into place.

Maggie wished she'd spent more time in front of the looking glass instead of tying her hair up in her usual manner. She'd dressed in her mother's high-waisted gown trimmed with lace on the hem and bodice.

Thea reassured her that she looked stunning, but Samuel had been around proper and fashionable women in England, and for the first time, she wanted to measure up to them and not be found lacking. Had he meant what he'd said when they'd been trapped in the closet? Or had he merely said those words—*you can be certain of my love for you*—because he believed they were going to die and wouldn't have to see them through?

Although Maggie adored Thea and George, a week away from Samuel had felt like an eternity after spending so many days at Greenview Manor. She'd wake, expecting to hear Samuel's early morning routine of sipping his coffee while the staff updated him on the day's requirements. She yearned for moments like when he looked up at her window before he went about his rounds or how he'd relaxed around her, allowing them to venture into all sorts of dinner conversations. She even missed the way he stirred his soup and scratched the peak of his hairline when thinking.

A knock sounded on the door, and the maid answered it. Maggie arranged her skirts and straightened her posture to emulate Judith and the years of training Cilla had attempted to ingrain. Why hadn't she paid more attention?

Thea's gaze bounced from Maggie to Judith to the door with an amused smile. George read news from England, oblivious of the women fluttering about, fussing over appearances.

The door opened and the maid entered and curtsied. "Madame, Lord Granville and Captain Middleton have arrived."

Maggie pressed her palm to her stomach to keep it from flipping.

"Send them in." Thea shot Maggie a reassuring smile.

Uncle Anthony entered first with hat in hand.

He nodded to Thea and Maggie before his gaze landed on Judith and held.

A niggling in the back of Maggie's mind found that strange, but her companion and uncle were forgotten the moment Samuel stepped into the room.

His boots were polished, and his trousers snugly fit. He filled the doorway with his broad chest and commanding demeanor. His gaze flew directly to her, and a smile spread across his lips like welcoming an old friend. She could only hope she meant more to him than that.

Thea offered them both a seat.

George greeted his friend and monopolized Samuel's attention to determine how the estate progressed in its restoration efforts. Maggie scooted to the edge of her seat and gripped the cushion to keep herself from doing anything improper, like jumping into Samuel's arms.

Thea prodded Uncle Anthony for information regarding his voyage to Montserrat. He regaled his tale of battling the unexpected storm and his delay with much ado. In typical Uncle Anthony's style, he depicted himself as a grand hero. Maggie humored him, forcing a smile even though inwardly she knew of his exaggerations. He'd become known for his Canterbury tales.

Samuel shot a glance her direction, and the fire in his blue eyes warmed her to her toes. For a second, she wished it were just the two of them alone in the closet. Did he remember his words? Had he meant them?

Dinner was served, and Thea had a way of making all her guests relax, enjoying the food and delightful company. She teased Samuel over his routine and George for his bent toward politics. Laughter filled their cozy home.

"I tell you." She raised her glass in a salute to the men. "This island would be back to its prime in a heartbeat if the three of them were in charge."

The dessert plates were taken away, and Samuel rose, holding Maggie's gaze. "Would you care to take in the evening air with me?"

Thea jumped up. "You may borrow my shawl." She snapped her fingers at the maid. "Run and grab the garment."

"Splendid idea." Uncle Anthony pushed back from his seat and aided Judith to rise. "I shall be happy to accompany Mrs. Morgan."

Samuel pulled out Maggie's chair.

Thea draped her shawl over Maggie's shoulders and squeezed her elbow before shooing them into the evening air.

The brisk ocean breeze kept the mosquitoes at bay. She and Samuel, with Uncle Anthony and Judith in tow, drifted toward the path to the beach.

"How fares your leg?" Samuel's gaze swept down the length of her and rested briefly on her injured limb.

"Almost as good as new." She fought not to wrap Thea's shawl tighter to hide her outdated gown. Samuel was a meticulous dresser, and she had always been . . . shabby.

"Are you well enough for a stroll along the water?" The swirl of heat darkening his gaze met hers, scattering her insecurities into bits of ash that floated away on the night breeze.

She cleared her throat, which had become dry as hot sand. "Indeed. Thea says I no longer even limp, that I shall be ready to dance a least a set or two at the assembly."

He maneuvered her around a rock that jutted out of the ground. Blades of sea grass and purslane brushed her gown's lacy hem. "I hope you'll save a dance or two for me."

She squeezed his arm. "So you'll be attending?" She couldn't hide the hope in her voice. "I didn't know with the mudslide and all that needs to be done at Greenview Manor if it would seem frivolous to take a night to dance."

He stopped, and she did the same, turning to face him. He touched her cheek with his finger. Her breath hitched, and he hooked his finger around a few strands of hair that had gotten stuck to her lips. His eyes searched her face as if memorizing her features. "I wouldn't miss it."

A nervous half-snort, half-laugh pushed its way through her lips. "Truly?"

"You love dancing." He tucked the hair behind

her ear, and the light graze of his fingertips sent a rush of tingling sensation to her core. "Nothing on earth could stop me from being there if only to witness the joy on your face."

Heat rose into her cheeks, burning them hotter than the hazy orange sun that set the distant ocean waves and clouds ablaze with color.

His gaze flicked to Uncle Anthony, and Samuel's Adam's apple bobbed above his loosened cravat. He turned, and they continued down the path to the water's edge. Would he truly move heaven and earth for her, even if she were of illegitimate birth? He couldn't have meant what he said in the darkness. Could he?

Uncle Anthony and Judith slowed their steps and allowed the gap between the couples to widen.

Samuel appeared deep in thought. He leisurely kicked up sand with his casual pace. Was he wondering how to make good on his word? Or if she would hold him to a promise made under duress? Would she awaken each morning questioning if he loved her or whether he had merely done the duty expected of a gentleman?

She stopped and rounded on Samuel, taking his hands in hers. "I meant what I said when we were alone." She stepped closer. "I won't take it back, and I'll never be ashamed of what I feel for you, but you are the heir to an earldom. Your every word is weighed and measured, and I won't hold you to anything you said that you might not have meant."

"Maggie." He clasped her wrists, and only then did she realize her hands had slid up his arms and her palms rested on his chest. She caught the rapid beating of his heart before he pulled her hands away. Instead of releasing them to drop back to her sides, he lifted one to his lips and placed a kiss on her knuckles.

"You have changed the way I see others." He kissed her fingers on her other hand. "You've changed the way I see my future."

Samuel cradled her palm against his cheek, and despite the lovely feeling of his clean-shaven jaw, her body braced for the *However* . . .

He slid her hand over his lips and pressed a kiss into her palm. "You changed the way I see myself."

Maggie's toes curled in her slippers, and she swayed toward him.

His arm circled her waist to steady her, and her head tilted back. The heat of him scorched the bodice of her gown.

"This last week has been torturous—utter agony—because you were not with me."

Although she might remain an unknown nobody with no future prospects, Samuel didn't see her that way. She meant something to him, and that made her heart soar like a line of pelicans gliding over the waves.

He cupped her face in his hands. His lips hovered so close to hers that they stole her breath and ability to think.

"Maggie, I—"

Judith's squeal doused them like a cold wave. Their heads jerked in the other couples' direction.

Maggie felt Samuel stiffen, and she stepped out of his embrace. How could she have forgotten her chaperone's presence?

"Yes. Of course, yes." Judith jumped up and down.

Uncle Anthony stepped aside, his arm extended as though presenting the queen. "Judith Morgan has done the impossible." His eyes glittered, and a wide smile spread his lips. "She's gotten a notorious bachelor, Captain Anthony Middleton, to settle down and take a wife."

Chapter 28

I heard his call and crept out into the night, running down to the shoreline. Our breaths mingled as we made plans for a life in America.

~ *Entry by Loretta Baxter, October 16, 1810*

Samuel's jaw clenched, and he stuffed his hands into his trouser pockets to keep from reaching for Middleton's neck. The jeweled ring he'd planned to place on Maggie's finger cut into the backside of his hand mocking him for not getting the words out sooner.

He couldn't propose now.

Blast. How could this have happened? He'd spent all week planning for this moment.

Maggie hugged Judith and her uncle, congratulating them, and turned back to Samuel.

He quickly forced a smile and his own felicitations.

She looped her arm around Samuel's in that natural way of hers. "I can't believe it." Her long lashes swept up and down as she blinked, and he remembered their light and feathery feel when they'd brushed his cheek. "I had no idea, especially since they bickered at each other so, but they're in love. Cilla and Tobie will be astounded. I don't think they ever believed he'd settle down."

Her tone wobbled a bit when she mentioned her adoptive parents. He must tell her about the letter he'd sent and soon, before her parents arrived and beat him to it. His insides squirmed. The storm had likely set them back. He counted the days in his head. If they'd set out immediately upon receipt of the letter, it probably would be another week before they arrived. Samuel would propose to her tomorrow at the assembly dance. Within his pocket, his fingers curled around the ring with renewed determination. It would be perfect. She loved dancing, and he'd hold the honor of escorting her onto the floor. He'd claim the socially acceptable two dances, propose to her on the terrace, and then shock everyone with a third dance, publicly declaring his intentions. Afterward, he'd tell her about his letter.

To pull this off properly, he would need to enlist help, and Thea was just the person to ask.

Maggie folded her hands in front of her to keep them from shaking. Thea and her maid fussed over her hair and gown as if she were debuting before the queen instead of attending a dance. They'd altered one of her mother's dresses to give it a modern flare. The soft gauzy peach material had been taken in at the waist and puffed at the sleeves. The flowing skirt swirled about her ankles. Her long hair had been pinned and curled into an elaborate coiffure with a matching peach ribbon woven in and out of her curls.

Cilla's voice rang in her head. *Hold still, my little magpie, almost finished.*

Maggie had never understood all the primping efforts that young women went through just to attend a ball. Now, though, she wanted to appear her best—not for London's patronesses who could request or deny the coveted invites to Almacks, not for a group of strangers who'd ogle her and decide if she were worthy, definitely not for a bunch of marriage-mart-mothers who'd never see past her questionable birth—but for Samuel.

As much as she loved dancing, the prospect of a proposal fluttered and somersaulted her stomach like a windmill's sail. Not only did Samuel say he would be there, but he'd told her to reserve him a dance. For the first time, she would be led onto the dance floor, not out of obligation by a family member, but by someone who desired her company.

The maid held up a mirror. Maggie's lips parted in a silent gasp. A lovely but strange woman stared back in her reflection.

Thea peeked over Maggie's shoulder into the mirror. "If this were London, you'd be deemed an incomparable."

Maggie's mouth quivered. "Am I a fraud?"

"What would make you say that?" Thea clasped Maggie's cold hands between her warm ones.

Unwanted tears pricked the back of her eyelids. "I'm illegitimate. I will never regret that my birth parents truly loved one another, but look at me." She fluffed her skirt. "I'm pretending to fit in among society—looking to reach above my station and dance with an earl. Won't everyone see through this disguise? What if I let Samuel down? What if I make a fool of myself or him?"

Thea led Maggie over to the bed and guided her to sit, settling beside her. "You are a child of God. He loves you, not because of who you are or what you've done, but because you are His. That is the only lineage that matters."

Thea squeezed Maggie's hands.

"Remember, you are royalty. Samuel sees it, and it's time you showed society that you are a princess." She scooped up the matching satin gloves she'd loaned to Maggie.

"Let's put these on and not keep your prince waiting."

Samuel lifted his chin for Carson to knot his cravat. In his mind, he ran over every detail of his plan again. He had the ring. Thea and George were to escort Maggie to the assembly hall, and he would arrive shortly after on his own accord. He'd ask her to dance and then propose to her on the balcony. The last thing he needed was another delay like the blow Middleton had accidentally pulled.

Who was Samuel kidding? His Maggie was full of surprises. Since the day she fell from the tree, she'd upended his plan. Her zest for life set his tightly regulated one into a state of disarray. Often she simultaneously infuriated him and calmed him. This week had felt lackluster without her. How many times in the past few days had he wanted to ask her opinion, tease her about hibiscus blossoms, feel her touch, see her smile?

He grinned. *His Maggie.* He liked how that sounded.

"What has you grinning like a schoolboy?" Carson walked around Samuel for one last inspection, brushing off lint from his best suit.

"The future." Samuel exhaled. He couldn't make Maggie his soon enough. He'd never envisioned his future with joyful anticipation as he did now. His life had been determined for him. The pressure of a firstborn's responsibilities and meeting his father's expectations had made his fate seem daunting.

And then the House of Lords had hinged his prospects upon making a go of an island sugar plantation—not an impossible task but formidable. He'd been crushed by the weight upon his shoulders until Maggie had him questioning why he'd work so hard to meet society's expectations. Why did he think he had to do it all in his own power? Why not trust God for help, guidance, and direction? Did his future have to be in England? Couldn't he feel just as fulfilled in Antigua or America?

The answer was clear. With God in his heart and Maggie by his side, he could be content no matter whether his father passes Samuel's rightful inheritance to his brother or whether the House of Lords prohibits him from returning to England. Life will have its challenges but with God's help, Samuel will grow wherever he is planted.

He checked his pocket watch and headed downstairs. Outside, he nodded to Hawley. "Lovely evening, isn't it?"

"Indeed, my lord." Hawley didn't crack a smile. "A Mr. Pierpont and Mr. Stanhope have arrived. They said it was pertinent and await you in your office."

"Very good." Samuel strode down the hall to his office with sure steps. He opened the door and his attorneys rose. "Greetings gentleman." He sat behind his desk and gestured for them to sit as well. "You have new information for me?"

Pierpont removed a folder from his briefcase and opened it. "You'd requested we check into one Sebastian Lowell Corbett. He was born in France in 1789 and moved up the ranks of France's navy, *La Royale*, to a naval captain. He fought for Napoleon during the war and distinguished himself to the point of being awarded a viscountship and earning the nickname, The Wolf. He was stationed in Guadeloupe and was captured by British naval forces stationed in Antigua, but escaped. On his return to Guadeloupe, his ship disappeared during a storm and was never heard from again."

Their findings lined up perfectly with what he'd discovered in Loretta Baxter's diaries. "Did you uncover any evidence of Sebastian Corbett's marriage to Loretta Baxter?"

"We're still searching, but so far nothing has been documented at any of the Antiguan parishes."

Stanhope pushed his spectacles up and peered at an open folder he'd placed in his lap. "Regarding Greenview Manor, Paul Fredrick Baxter disinherited his daughter after she spurned his choice for marriage to a one,"—Stanhope cleared his throat and eyed Samuel—"Lord Henry Granville, Earl of Cardon, and also your father."

Pierpont studied Samuel's reaction, but Maggie had already relayed this information. She'd told him the whole truth. He hadn't done the same with the diaries, but he would make it right.

"We haven't yet located proof of their marriage, but rumor has it she ran off with a French lover and drowned at sea when the ship sank during a storm. We suspect that same ship that capsized during the storm was captained by Sebastian Corbett."

Stanhope flipped a page. "Since Paul Baxter no longer had an heir for Greenview Manor, he agreed to will it to the Earl of Cardon for his silence regarding Miss Loretta Baxter, saving both families from his daughter's disgrace."

Samuel pictured a woman similar to Maggie in spirit and demeanor with Samuel's father. Had Miss Baxter's despotic father driven his daughter away as her diary alluded, or had Samuel's father's anger pushed Loretta Baxter into another man's arms like Samuel's temper had Lucy?

Lord forgive me for my part in hurting Lucy. Thank You for Maggie who had the courage to face my temper and remain steadfast.

"As it stands"—Stanhope closed his folder—"Greenview is yours without question, even if Miss Prescott is the legitimate heiress, her mother forfeited her birthright."

That was it. His ownership was no longer in jeopardy. He checked his heart, but it didn't change his feelings toward Maggie. "Thank you, gentlemen. You have been a great help. That will be all. I'll submit payment for your services immediately."

The men filed out, and Samuel leaned back in his chair and stared out the window. Funny how God worked. He'd ask Maggie to marry him and then Greenview Manor would return to the Baxter family line. However, his attorneys' inability to locate hard proof of Maggie's legitimacy would condemn them to reside in Antigua as George and Thea had. His shoulders slumped at the thought of not getting to know his niece or nephew. News was probably on its way that Bradlee and Hannah had brought their first child into the world. Would Maggie regret missing out on seeing her siblings grow into adulthood?

"Lord Granville?" Dinah stood in the doorway beside a hunched-backed woman with white hair peeking out from her turban. "I beg your pardon, but may I have a word?"

"Of course." He checked his pocket watch. "I have forty-minutes before I must leave for the assembly dance." He beckoned for them to enter.

Dinah guided the elderly maid into the room. "Dis is Melinda. I thought she might help wit more clues from Miz Prescott's song. Melinda was Miz Loretta's lady's maid."

"Indeed." Samuel straightened. Could the woman have the answers they sought? "Please, come in and have a seat."

Dinah aided the hobbling woman over to sit in his reading chair. Samuel pushed over a lowback seat for Dinah before settling at his desk. Dinah rolled the hem of her apron between her fingers. "Her mind switches back ta da old language on occasion, but I can help out."

She patted the old woman's leg, and the elderly maid spoke in a thick African accent. "I served Miz Loretta back 'n me day. Miz Loretta was a good woman wit ah good okan." She looked at Dinah.

"Heart." Dinah nodded. "Okan means heart."

The old woman licked her lips and continued. "Her . . ." She touched her turban with both hands.

"Head?" Samuel guessed.

She nodded. "Her head full of ala."

"Dreams," Dinah translated.

"She fell in love wit a man her father no like. So she . . ." The woman moved her hands like an ocean's wave and blew air through her lips.

"She sailed?" Samuel knew this part. She sailed off with The Wolf, and the ship capsized.

"Ta Guadeloupe."

Samuel scooted forward in his seat. "Guadeloupe?"

"Yessir. Ta marry in da ijo ta Monsieur Corbett."

"A church?" He stood to his feet and peered at Dinah.

She nodded.

Of course. He should have thought of it. Without her father's permission, Loretta Baxter would have needed to marry where no one would object when the banns were posted. "Are you certain?"

"Yes, ijo—church, Michael ká Ijo."

Could he find proof of Maggie's legitimacy in Guadeloupe? How fast could his attorneys sail to search the church records there? His mind buzzed through the implications.

"Dinah, you are a Godsend." He pecked a kiss on her forehead and bent and kissed the elderly woman's forehead too. "You have done what the best paid attorneys couldn't figure."

The women stood and shuffled out of his study. Samuel yanked a piece of paper out of his desk drawer and scribbled instructions to Stanhope and Pierpont. He stuffed it into an envelope and sealed it with wax.

He rose and strode into the hall. "John."

The footman stood at attention.

"Please take this letter to my attorneys' office. They are to pack their bags and meet you at the docks at first light. Send another footman to the harbor and commission a ship to Guadeloupe. Tell the captain I will pay whatever it takes to expedite their journey."

"Yes, milord." John accepted the letter and nodded to Calvin, who emerged from the dining room, and the men hustled to do their master's bidding.

Samuel opened his pocket watch. He still had ten minutes before it was time to leave. Pulling down on the cuffs of his sleeves, he paced the length of the hall carpet.

Could the elderly maid be correct? Was Maggie

legitimate? What did that mean for Greenview Manor? Did it even matter anymore? He planned to marry her, legitimate or not, but her having been born under the sanctity of marriage meant they could return to England someday.

Life was coming together splendidly. Perhaps a little too nicely. It seemed surreal to have such a boon when everything he'd done thus far had nearly killed him with effort.

God will make a way. Maggie's words rang in his head. *If God opens a door, no one can shut it.*

He sent up a silent prayer, *Lord I would be the happiest and grateful man to hold the honor of marrying Maggie. If it is your will, let nothing stand in our way.*

"My lord." Hawley cleared his throat. "It is time to leave. I've had your carriage brought around to the front."

Hawley helped him with his coat and hat. Samuel patted his pocket with the ring and bid the butler good evening. Hawley didn't look at Samuel but stepped aside for him to pass, and Samuel wasted no time bounding out the door with a tiny skip. He was ready to lead Maggie out onto the dance floor and propose in front of all those gathered, ready to begin a new chapter—one filled with adventure if Maggie had her way.

The sun stood low on the horizon. The humid air held promise, and even the tree frogs chirped their excitement. He frowned at the wagon pulled in front. That wouldn't do. The groomsman was supposed to bring his carriage. He'd waste precious minutes waiting for them to hook up the horses. Samuel simultaneously reached for his pocket watch and hollered toward the stables for a groomsman, but no one appeared. Strange. Would they have accompanied his footman on their trips?

He strode toward the stables.

Two shadows launched out of the bushes.

A rough burlap sack was thrown over his head. "Hey!" His vision blocked, Samuel swung in all directions. He connected with something and heard a grunt. A loud crack resounded, and pain sliced through Samuel's head, blurring his vision white. He fell to his knees, fighting the blackness.

Maggie . . . the dance . . .

A kick to the gut pushed the air from his lungs and the excruciating pain plummeted him into darkness.

Dancers whirled around the assembly floor to the lively music of reels, cotillions, and the occasional waltz. Maggie sat in a chair up against the wall with a view of the entrance, tapping her toe. The doors opened, and a young man about Samuel's size strode into the warm ballroom.

Thea craned her neck for a better view, but the man sauntered in the opposite direction, tossed back a drink handed to him by one of his acquaintances, and blended into the crowd.

Definitely not Samuel.

The hour grew late as the ball progressed into full swing.

"I shall be right back." Thea rose with pursed lips and stomped off to speak to her husband.

Where was Samuel? Did he change his mind about attending? Had something happened at the plantation to detain him?

She welcomed the reprieve of not having to force a cheerful disposition for Thea. Her newfound friend had obstinately sat by her side, ruining her own evening of dancing out of loyalty to Maggie. But it wasn't necessary. Maggie had spent her entire life relegated to wallflower status. The same young men who played stickball and mock jousting festivals with Maggie swung a wide berth when the opportunity to dance arose. Their disapproving Mamas issued them stern warnings that Maggie's unknown bloodlines could taint them by a single twirl about the floor.

A woman dressed in a yellow gown smiled and curtsied at her partner before taking his hand and following his lead down the center of two lines of onlookers awaiting their turn. Judith and Uncle Anthony were up next. Maggie swallowed around the lump forming in her throat. Why had she ever thought she would be among them?

A young dandy glanced Maggie's way before elbowing his friend. The pair burst out laughing before he pushed away from the wall and sauntered over to the Kellys, asking for an introduction from Thea. "Miss Prescott, would you care to dance." The man ogled her as if he were a seaman who just sailed into port, searching for the nearest brothel. He bowed over her hand.

Gossip regarding her predicament of being trapped with Samuel in the closet must have spread. Maggie glanced at the smiles on the faces of the dancers as another couple promenaded down the line. This was her opportunity to be merry, but without Samuel, it would be like scaling a mountain for the lovely view only to have it obscured by fog, or saving to purchase a ticket to the opera to discover the lead singer was out sick.

"Shall we?" The man held his elbow up for her to take.

Something about him reminded her of Mitchell, and she hadn't brought her cutlass tonight. Besides, she wanted to save her leg strength for dancing with Samuel. "I apologize." She shook her head. "I am recovering from an injury."

Thea sat beside Maggie and attempted light-hearted conversation, but her gaze kept flicking to the entrance and the clock.

The man walked away.

You had your chance, but it wasn't with Samuel.

"Something must have happened." Thea's lips

thinned into a tight line. She stood once more and excused herself.

He's not coming. Maggie fanned faster. Hadn't he asked her to reserve a dance? Did he change his mind? Was he embarrassed to be seen with her?

Keep your head about you. He'll show. She lifted her chin and sat as regally as she could manage. More gazes flicked in her direction and more heads leaned to whisper in each other's ears. Her throat and chest constricted much like it had the other times she sat at a local dance, relegated to the status of wallflower. She bit the inside of her lip until she tasted blood. This time was supposed to have been different. Samuel wasn't like the rest. Or was he?

Uncle Anthony sauntered over with Judith on his arm. "As much as I loathe to leave your side, I cannot change tradition. I must dance with my beautiful niece."

Her insides caved in at the pity in her uncle's eyes. She should be grateful. He was only trying to protect her sensitive heart. He and Tobie had done so many times over the years by asking her to dance. She tilted her head, pretending to be considering his request, and used the opportunity to blink away odious tears that continued to plague her. Regaining her composure, she offered him a smile. "Thank you anyway. I'm still resting my leg, but perhaps I'll get in one dance before the evening is over. I've never danced the waltz. I thought that might be a lovely one to choose. What do you think, Judith?"

"Indeed. The waltz is lovely." She cast a coy smile at Uncle Anthony before returning her gaze to Maggie. "If you need introductions, I'd be happy to comply. I'm acquainted with most of the men here."

"Thank you, but that won't be necessary."

"Where is that scallywag anyway?" Her uncle glanced at the door. "Granville should be here."

Judith turned to follow his gaze. She leaned closer to Uncle Anthony, lowering her voice so that perhaps Maggie couldn't hear, but she caught every word. "He must show. Rumors are already spreading that she is his wanton cast-off."

Thea returned, dragging George on her arm, and the two of them also frowned at the entrance.

Maggie's head throbbed with the cadence of the music.

"Her reputation will be in tatters." Judith stepped aside. "And so will everyone's who stands with her."

Chapter 29

I fear our love will be the end of me.
~ *Entry by Loretta Baxter,
October 17, 1810*

Samuel's head thundered with every jolt of the wagon. The pain forced him into consciousness. His back ached and his left arm and both legs had gone numb in his hunched position. The sack blew his hot breath back into his face and kept him in darkness. When he tried to move, he met with hard wood on all sides.

A swell of cold sweat ran over his skin. Where was he? Buried alive in a wooden coffin? No, he'd be laying, not scrunched in a ball. He inhaled a deep breath past the feed odor of the burlap bag to the smell of sugar. His attackers had dumped him in a sugar barrel. Was the container airtight? How much air did he have? He wiggled his hand nearest his head and had enough movement to peel the sack off. A small light shone near his shin. Thank heaven, they'd drilled an air hole.

"I say we shoot him and dump him in the ocean."

The air hole turned dark, and the distinctive cocking of a gun stilled Samuel's breathing.

"You fool. Put that away," a raspy voice said,

and the light returned as the barrel of the weapon was knocked away. "You shoot a member of the peerage and this whole island will be crawling with the authorities. Abducting him until the vote is taken will cause enough of a stir as it is."

His abduction had been all about control. If Fines and his followers wanted the vote to go their way, they could have gone after any dissenter. But of course Fines had a vendetta against him, and Samuel's pride had made him an easy target. Maggie's words rang in memory, *I know you would never hurt me, but Fines easily sways others who have witnessed your temper.* He believed he could handle the situation, but he'd given Fines the chance to pay a pair of thugs to make him disappear.

I do believe we've made some enemies today, George's warning elevated the throbbing pain radiating from the back where Samuel had been hit. Why hadn't Samuel prayed for God's protection against his enemies? *Pride.* Once again, he'd proved he couldn't do it all himself. He'd be lucky to make it out of this mess alive.

And Maggie . . . He inwardly groaned, thinking of her standing at the assembly, the gossipmongers closing in like a pack of wolves as she stared at the door, waiting for him. Maggie would once again suffer for his desire for control. *Oh, Lord. Forgive me of my sins. I need Your divine intervention. My enemies are many and they hate me with a cruel loathing. Deliver me for I put my trust in You.*

"Fines better make good on his payment," the younger voice spoke. "Hennion said Fines reneged on his last deal. Blamed it on the fire and lazy good-for-nothing slaves, but I heard Fines passed 'em the match himself to stir up the islanders and get revenge on Granville."

Silence fell between his two captors.

Where was he? Should he scream for help? Draw attention? He scrunched into a tight ball, trying to move his head low enough to determine if he could see out of the knot hole, but he couldn't reach. *Blast.* He strained his ears to listen for sounds of other people, but nothing could be discerned over the creaking of the wagon and the rumble of the wheels. Inside a barrel, his options were limited, and with armed abductors, if he made a wrong move, he could wind up dead.

Raspy Voice cleared his throat. "To the devil with Fines. I have a plan. One that's guaranteed to be lucrative."

To help hold her emotional state in check, Maggie squeezed her folded hands together in her lap. She'd survived being alone on a deserted island, sailed across the Atlantic, broken into a house, gotten shot, fought a fire while wounded, and endured being trapped in a mudslide. How could one assembly ball leave a lethal wound?

But the longer Samuel remained absent, the longer the doubts chipped away at her heart, killing it piece by piece. The voices that had plagued her all her life rose to a deafening chant. *You don't fit in. Samuel doesn't want you. No one wants you. No one will have you. You're all alone, again.*

The orchestra struck up a waltz and the guests gathered with their partners to dance, except for the cluster staring at the door willing it to open. Her head throbbed, growing into a loud buzzing until she could barely hear the music. *Dear Lord, don't let me embarrass myself further by fainting.*

The hour had grown late, and with each new set, the truth became abundantly clear.

Samuel wasn't coming.

Maggie gulped back the pain of her crushed spirit. She was foolish to come here and think she could blend in with society. What a ninnyhammer she'd been to believe Samuel loved her. Now her poor judgment would hurt the Kellys, her uncle, and Judith.

More gazes slid her way and more heads bent to whisper. The weight of one stare lay heavy upon her, and Maggie glanced across the room to see Fines nudge the magistrate. Langham pushed off the pillar he'd been leaning on and sauntered in their direction.

"Mr. and Mrs. Kelly." He bowed to the couple. "Good showing for the dance. I think the whole upper crust of the island attended, but you seem like you're looking for someone."

Thea and George exchanged looks but didn't say anything.

Langham exhaled and he stuffed his hands into his pockets with a forlorn look. "It's part of my job to deliver bad news, and it never gets easy."

Maggie stiffened. Did something happen to Samuel?

"If you're looking for Granville, I don't think he's coming. He was dipping deep at the Black Parrot, just him, the barkeep, and a couple solicitors clanking glasses and tossing back rum." The magistrate shook his head. "I don't know what he was celebrating, but it must have been important to miss the assembly dance."

Langham's words weren't to be trusted, especially when he had Fines's urging. He must be lying, but three hours of watching the door and fighting to hold a tumult of past emotions pushing to the surface left Maggie like a piece of thin glass. All Langham had to do was chip the glass and watch as a spiderweb of cracks grew. The room blurred before her eyes, her ridged backbone kept her from becoming a puddle in her seat. *Solicitors.* Had Samuel only planned to marry her as a backup in case Greenview Manor did fall to her? Were they cheering because he'd found documents to prove her illegitimacy?

Did he toast to his narrow escape of being leg-shackled to someone's bi-blow?

The hole in her heart hurt ten times worse than the shot to her leg ever had. She gripped the arms of her chair, her fingers turning white from the effort of not tipping over and collapsing on the floor. Why did she have to love a man who'd not only take a machete to her heart, but not be finished until he ran it through the vertical rollers that crushed the sugar cane and squeezed out every last drop of sweetness.

Thea placed a hand on Maggie's shoulder. The mounted pressure of tears and welled-up sobs strained and stretched the seams of Maggie's throat and chest, choking out her ability to breath. Her entire body started to shake. She needed to leave before she made a scene. Turning to Thea, she implored her with her eyes to help her make an escape, since she was unable to trust her voice.

The thick oak doors to the ballroom burst open, and a man stood in the center, his demeanor tall and commanding. He scanned the room until his gaze landed on Maggie.

"Hounds teeth." Uncle Anthony straightened. "I'll be beggared."

The familiar face broke the dam, unleashing the tears she'd kept at bay. He crossed the room with long strides straight to Maggie and stopped abruptly within arm's reach.

Maggie rose with tears flowing, ready to cling to his pillar of strength.

"I'm sorry, Tobie."

The wagon jerked to a stop, and Samuel bumped his chin on his knee cap. He bit the edge of his tongue, and the metallic taste of blood seeped into his mouth. Clenching his jaw against the pain, he listened for any sounds.

The wagon rocked as his captors descended. "Let me do the talking," said Raspy Voice.

Samuel sniffed. Was that the sea? Had they stopped at a dock of some sort?

Muffled voices murmured. Was that English, Creole, or some other language? He scrunched to lower his ear closer to the knot hole. Booted footfalls approached. The wagon shook. Samuel tilted, the barrel abruptly tossed on its side, and he hit the back of his head. Stars floated in his periphery. He squeezed his eyes shut against the pain and fought to remain conscious. A hand slapped the side of the barrel, and it started to roll, jostling Samuel's head and body until his fight to remain cognizant failed.

Tobie opened his arms, and Maggie ran to her papa. He wrapped her in his strong arms, and she clung to him, weeping into his shirt front.

"Thank heaven you're safe." He squeezed her

tight and didn't release his hold for some time. "Thank you, God."

Homesickness washed over her in jarring waves. Her body ached with how much she'd missed Tobie, Cilla, and her younger siblings, Sophia and Michael. She wanted to ask about them. Were they well? Had Sophia started her tutoring with the new governess? Was Michael still determined to race boats in the stream every day? Was Cilla still planning for Maggie's season? But most of all—would they forgive her for what she put them through?

She couldn't compose herself enough to speak. People were starting to stare. She was causing a scene, but she couldn't bear to unclasp her arms from the man who'd wiped her tears, taught her to sing and dance, bandaged her scrapes, and rescued her from her messes.

But even Tobie couldn't save her from this debacle.

He eased her toward the exit, away from onlookers, and urged her into a chair in the front vestibule just outside the ballroom, where they could talk privately—at least as much as a group would allow. Thea, George, Uncle Anthony, and Judith had accompanied them. They peered at Tobie and her with perplexed expressions, except her uncle, who stared at his boots, looking contrite.

Tobie crouched in front of Maggie and passed

her his handkerchief to wipe her tears and nose. "You gave your mom and me quite a fright, Magpie."

She blew her nose with a loud inelegant sound but remembered her manners and gestured to her friends for the introduction polite society demanded. "Papa, may I present to you Mr. and Mrs. George Kelly. They've become good friends of mine. And this is Mrs. Judith Morgan, soon to become Mrs. Judith Middleton."

Her papa's gaze flew to Uncle Anthony, both eyebrows raised.

Uncle Anthony shrugged. "It's about time I settled down, and I found a beautiful woman who set me straight and convinced me to reform my ways."

"Don't think announcing your engagement will get you out of Priscilla's blistering tongue lashing. I had to keep her from sending a British brigade after you when she discovered you'd taken Maggie to the Leeward Islands."

"Maggie was going with or without me." He folded his arms. "At least this way, someone could keep an eye on her."

Was that why he'd agreed? He had let her believe she'd coerced him to come with a promise to put in a good word with some lovely woman Middleton had set his sights on. "Anyway." Maggie gestured to her papa. "This is my father, Captain Tobias Prescott."

Judith and the Kellys' tight expressions relaxed. Papa rose and bowed to the new acquaintances. "It's a pleasure. I only wish it were under different circumstances. I must beg your pardon, for my daughter and I have a lot to discuss, and I'm anxious to hear her side of this story." He gently guided her to stand. "Anthony, she'll be taking your cabin this night. You and I can bunk with the crew."

"You didn't bring your own ship?" Uncle Anthony frowned as if put out.

"Your old friend, Nathaniel Winthrop, happened to be in London and offered me passage on his ship, but he's eager to return to his family."

Uncle Anthony's smirk showed he was still bitter about Captain Winthrop confiscating Uncle Anthony's ship by knifepoint to rescue Lottie Winthrop, a close friend of Cilla's.

"I, too, am in a hurry to return to my wife." Tobie gently pulled Maggie to a stand. "Say your farewells because we'll be sailing after the crew finishes loading the supplies onto *The Windward*."

Maggie nodded, turned to Thea, and wrapped her in a big hug. "Thank you for letting me stay with you and for being a friend when I needed one."

Thea hugged her back and whispered in her ear. "Samuel had planned to propose tonight. He told me so himself. I don't understand why he's not here, but George sent a footman to look for him. Don't believe the worst just yet. Not until we find out what happened."

Maggie chewed her bottom lip and nodded before bidding George and Judith farewell.

Tobie escorted her down the staircase into the humid night air, where a hired hack waited. "We will have the entire voyage for you to explain your actions." He wrapped his arm around her and drew her against his side. "Tonight, I just want to thank God for keeping you alive."

She was grateful for the reprieve. She climbed into the carriage and took one last peek around in hopes of spying Samuel in the lantern light.

Thea had said he planned to propose. Why then did he not make an appearance? Had he changed his mind about marriage? Did he get a little overzealous building his courage to ask for her hand. Wait. Hadn't he once told her that he didn't care for spirits?

He had. Which meant Fines must be up to something, but what?

And where was Samuel? Was he lying in a ditch somewhere, injured or worse . . . dying?

God, keep Samuel safe. Please don't let him be hurt or injured. Don't let anything disastrous have befallen him.

Her mind tossed doubts around like a wave blown by the wind. Had he been using her to settle the plantation's ownership? Had he found a way out and celebrated that he wasn't required to marry a tainted-bloodline orphan? *The only reason the son of an earl would marry someone like you is for money, land, or both.*

Tobie slid into the seat beside her. He'd be looking for explanations tomorrow, and she didn't have answers.

You can be certain of my love for you. Samuel's declaration of love professed alone in the dark rang in her memory. Could his words be true?

Her fingers clenched the edge of the seat. *God, help my unbelief.*

Samuel awoke with a throbbing pain in his head that rose bile into his throat. From his cramped position, he'd lost all feeling in his legs and couldn't even shift positions with the poor blood flow to his extremities. At least, he hadn't been set in the barrel upside down. Perspiration beaded his forehead and soaked his cravat, and his swollen tongue stuck to the roof of his parched mouth. He tried to swallow, but his throat was as dry as a cracked cistern.

A warning squeezed his chest. If he didn't get water soon, he could die from dehydration.

The world shifted, and dizziness swarmed his head. Was that him or had the floor tilted? Boots stomped overhead and wood creaked. *Thunder and turf.* He was on a ship. How long had he blacked out? How far had they traveled?

No matter whether his captors were armed or not, he had to get out of this barrel.

"Hey!" The cramped space didn't allow for much thrust, but he beat his fist against the wooden side. He waited but nothing happened. Samuel tried again. This time, he tilted his head to the side and punched up. Something creaked open.

"Help! In here." Samuel jarred the top of the container with all the force he could muster. His knuckles would probably bleed again, and this time Maggie wouldn't be here to bandage them. Was she worried about him? Would a search party be sent to look for him?

He hunched down to listen, but the only sound was the lapping of waves against the side of the boat. How far out to sea had they ventured? If he wasn't back by day's end, would the plantation keep running? The north field needed to be replanted and the south field harvested. What if he wasn't back by week's end, or month's end? Would there be a plantation to return to? Would his workers desert, thinking their master had died? Would Maggie sail with her uncle, believing the worst of him?

Samuel pounded until excruciating pain shot down his arm. An anguished roar erupted from his gut.

Hibiscus blossoms.

Maggie's face floated in his memory. She'd

always had a calming effect on him. Sure, she caused some of his anger, but she could diffuse it with a mere touch. He closed his eyes and rested his head against the wooden slats and inhaled the oaky scent mixed with molasses. All he could picture was Maggie the way Middleton had spoken of her. A young girl waiting on the outskirts of the room, watching others enjoy themselves, putting on an optimistic face, hoping for a single name on her dance card, longing to fit in—to be wanted.

He'd wanted to right the past wrongs done to her by asking her to dance, but he'd only made it worse by not showing up.

Something hit the barrel, scraping the top. Creaking wood whined in resistance. Someone was prying open the lid. Lantern light blinded Samuel, but he squinted to assess his captors. A litany of French curses slashed the air. The light moved away, and a hefty kick knocked the barrel over. Samuel braced for the impact.

He spilled out of the empty molasses container among stacked crates and other loads being transported by a merchant ship. A waft of his sweaty stench merged with the dank air that reeked of fish, mildew, and unwashed bodies. Unfettered circulation pushed blood into his legs, which seized in painful cramps. He crawled on his elbows, dragging his uncooperating lower body out of confinement.

Two French-speaking men spoke in rapid irate sentences that Samuel's sluggish brain couldn't decipher. One paced back and forth, waving his arms in wide swaths. His face reddened and his fists clenched. He punched the wall and cursed some more.

Was that how Samuel looked when he let his temper get the best of him? Did that same ugliness spew from him as it had his father, the merchant, and Mr. Fines? Samuel slumped on the plank floor, but he kept a watchful gaze peeled on his new jailors. The red-faced Frenchman's hair was pulled back in a cue, his long bulbous nose scrunched in a snarl. He slammed the younger Frenchman with dark circles under his eyes up against the side of the hull and pointed at Samuel. "*Donnez-moi mon argent.*" Then climbed the small ladder above deck and slapped the portal door closed after him.

Get me my money, Samuel translated in his head. It seemed his initial captors must have received a lucrative sum while his new overseers got a surprise. Samuel's legs burned as if stung by a thousand bees, but movement returned, and he grabbed the corner of a nearby crate and pulled himself into a seated position.

The younger Frenchman raked his hair and muttered under his breath. He turned and gripped the ladder.

"*Attendez!*" Samuel signaled for him to wait by raising his palm.

The man shifted to face him. "*Parlez-vous Français?*"

"*Oui, un peu.*" Samuel fought past the fog of his joggled brain. "I need your help. *J'ai besoin d'aide.* I need to return to Antigua. *Je dois retourner à Antigua.*"

The man ran his hand down his face and peered up at the overhead as if overly taxed. He exited the same as the other Frenchman.

"Wait!" Samuel attempted to stand, but his knees crumpled.

The younger Frenchman returned a few moments later with a mug of watered ale and some hardtack bread. He clanked the plate and ale down on a nearby crate and stopped in the portal. "*Vous devez effectuer le remboursement de votre dette et vous allez devoir travailler pour le faire.*" He closed the door and slammed down the latch.

Work off his payment? How long would that take? What price had been paid? He needed to get back to Maggie. He needed to explain. She'd be crushed by his disappearance. Islanders would assume the worst after hearing they'd been trapped together alone in a closet for two days, especially when he didn't bother to stand up with her at the assembly. Her reputation would be ruined. She'd no longer be acceptable company for Thea or Judith without stirring the derision of planter's wives.

He must do something. He rose on unsteady legs, ate the stale bread, and washed it down with the sour ale. However foul tasting, the substance returned his strength. He climbed the ladder and tried the door.

Locked. He pounded on it as he had the lid of the barrel and shouted to the crewman to let him out, that he wanted to negotiate, but there was no answer. He searched the small hull for any other means of escape before returning to the portal door and pleading for mercy in French and English. He tried his best to convince the crewmen of the injustice and how he'd been set up. He could hear men moving about and the occasional grunt, laugh, or words, *Who does this Englishman think he is?*

I'm a man desperate to get back to the woman I love. Pressure built in Samuel's chest and the jeering taunt pushed him past the bursting point. Every inch of his being raged against the injustice until Samuel blew his temper in the true form of his father, using empty threats of societal censure to no avail. The only things he intimidated were the rats, who steered clear of him, their beady eyes watching him from the far corners.

It's not by our strength. God is in control, and His will shall prevail.

Maggie was right. Samuel climbed down and

sat on a crate. He should be grateful he was still alive. He bowed his head and prayed, without trying to sound like a pious man of the clergy, letting the words spring from his heart. *Lord, forgive me for my outbursts of anger and for thinking I could control outcomes. I understand full well that I can't battle my rage and this wretched debacle on my own power. I give this over to You and trust Your will to be done. Help take this anger from me and replace it with self-control. Protect Maggie in your care. I can't thank you enough for bringing her into my life, but don't let my failings hurt her or her reputation.*

He'd instructed her to sail with her uncle upon his return. Hopefully their time trapped together proved his heart had changed, but would his disappearance have her questioning his sincerity? Would she leave Antigua with her uncle thinking he'd spurned her?

Lord, I've been a cad, but don't let her believe I rejected her. She's withstood enough ridicule, don't let me add to the hurt.

After a fitful night's sleep and no word from Samuel, Maggie asked permission to visit Greenview Manor. Her spirit needed answers to be settled. After some debate, Tobie allowed her to go on the condition that he rode with her. He paid a local for the use of his curricle, and they bounced up the palm-tree-lined lane into the verdant landscape of Samuel's home.

As they approached the area where the mudslide had flowed down the lane, he pulled over. "I can't maneuver the carriage over this mess. We'll have to walk from here."

"It's not far." Maggie put her hand in Tobie's, and he aided her descent. The once wet mud had dried into hard-packed clay under the hot Antiguan sun. They picked their way around uprooted trees, rocks, and cane stalks poking out of the ground. Tobie remained quiet as if understanding the solemn magnitude of this moment. She inhaled a deep breath, girding her emotions for the truth—whatever it might be.

The path was no longer centered, and the porch's front steps slanted at a slight angle. Hawley swung the front door open before she could knock.

"Good morning, Hawley. Is Lord Granville home?"

Hawley kept his gaze peeled on Tobie and didn't look at her. "I'm afraid not, miss. He had important business in town this morning."

So that was the truth of it. Langham hadn't lied, and Samuel wasn't injured. Samuel had chosen not to attend the ball. Hawley's words stung more than the pellet bullet she'd taken in the leg, and she staggered back a step.

"Are you all right?" Tobie's steadying hand

came to rest on her lower back. "We can turn around."

She'd mentally prepared for this, but hearing that Samuel had chosen not to be with her held more finality than merely thinking it. "I need to do the right thing." *And maybe someday, he'll realize what he gave up.* She tilted her chin higher, refusing to dwell on Samuel's decision until later. "I was hoping to say farewell to him and some of the staff. May we come in?"

Hawley hesitated, but she brushed past him, not waiting for an answer.

Tobie followed her but turned and stared down the butler while Maggie mounted the stairs.

"Dinah? Carson?" No response.

Hawley leaned to the side of Tobie. "They aren't here, miss." He pulled down on the bottom of his jacket. "Er . . . the house has not yet been deemed habitable. I stayed and the master, but everyone else . . . they have sought accommodations elsewhere."

Maggie entered Samuel's chamber anyway. "Surely Carson would have stayed with his master." The scent of bergamot nearly brought her to her knees. She didn't want to love him, but her heart couldn't help it. Not even after all he'd done.

As usual, his bed was neatly made, and everything appeared in its place even though a mudslide had knocked the house off its foundation. A piece of paper rested on his nightstand. His daily to-do list. Only one task had been written, unlike his usual list of five to seven. Her fingers slid the paper around to face her so she could read his neat script.

•*Propose to Maggie.*

Her lips parted in a silent gasp. When Samuel didn't show she figured Thea must have misconstrued his intentions, but the list proved he had planned to propose.

Apparently, he'd thought better of it.

The item hadn't been crossed out because last evening he'd chosen not to. Funny that he hadn't discarded this list and written a new one today.

Fresh tears burned, and she dashed from the room. There was one more chamber she needed to visit.

She stopped in the doorway of her mother's old room and rested her head against the frame. Her mind memorized the layout, for it was unlikely she'd return, not with Samuel residing here.

"Goodbye, Mama." She spoke to the air. "I'm grateful that I was able to get to know a little about who you were. Reading about you has helped me to understand more about myself. We both may have struggled to conform to what society expected of us, but I will never be ashamed that you took a chance on love. I'm just sorry it was so brief"—Maggie's voice cracked—"for the both of us."

She took in the room one more time before turning and descending the stairs.

Tobie eyed her, probably noting her red eyes. "How are you faring?"

She sniffed. "I only need a second." *To leave a note.*

Hawley protested, but Tobie clasped a hand on the butler's shoulder and spoke over him. "Take however long you need. Hawley and I are having a nice chat."

The butler fell silent.

She slipped into Samuel's study and searched his desk for paper. Finding none, she pulled open the middle drawer. It contained the manor's ledger. She closed it. Greenview's finances were no longer any of her concern. The right and left drawers were both locked. He must have paper somewhere. She turned in a circle. Her gaze briefly fell on the landscape outside and quickly returned. The windmill sails hadn't been raised, and no smoke rose from the boiling houses. Where was Cuffee? Surely, the workers would be busy. The slave quarters had been spared. They hadn't needed to find other lodgings, and there was still cane to harvest.

Hawley's voice rose from the doorway. "There is something of yours you may want to take with you." He removed his keys from his belt and walked around to the opposite side of the desk. "He said it didn't matter anymore." His stern flint gaze eyed her. He unlocked Samuel's desk drawer and removed a book, handing it to her.

Strange, the cover looked familiar. She accepted it and turned it over. Her mother's loopy handwriting jumped off the cover. She flipped to the first page of the book, where it read, *Diary of Loretta Genevieve Baxter, Volume 2.*

"How long did he have this?"

Hawley glanced toward the ceiling as if calculating. "Several weeks, maybe longer."

Samuel had lied to her. She shook her head in an attempt to comprehend. He'd had the second diary all along.

"My lord was reading it yesterday and said it confirmed his decision." Hawley's lips twisted into a wry smile. "He was going to have me toss it into the fire, for it has no value, but to me, it seemed a waste of paper. Perhaps you'd enjoy it."

She clutched the book to her breast. Her legs unable to hold her, she sank onto the chair cushion.

It had all been an act. Samuel had only pretended to care for her to solidify his right to Greenview Manor. He'd only planned to marry her if her birth had been legitimate, to gain back possession of his property. How fortunate for him to have learned the truth before he had to make such a horrible sacrifice. She hugged the diary tighter and stood.

If he thought so lightly about tossing her mother's memory into the fire and throwing aside Maggie's love, then she was fortunate as well, for he'd saved her from a disastrous marriage.

"Magpie." Deep lines of concern furrowed Tobie's brow where he stood in the doorway.

Her stomach heaved with nausea.

Her mother betrayed Maggie's grandfather and Samuel's father, and Maggie betrayed Tobie and Cilla, who only wanted to protect her. Lucy betrayed Samuel, who then deceived and betrayed Maggie. Sin proliferated more sin, trapping people in a whirlpool of lies and sucking them to the bottom of the ocean.

Her gaze fell on a paper weight in a rectangular basket. Inside it held a stack of blank paper. She pulled out a piece, dipped a quill into the inkwell, and scribbled.

I came to bid you farewell.

She paused, wanting to rile at him for his betrayal, to blast him with the anger and hurt that burned like acid in her chest. *If any of you has a grievance against someone, forgive as the Lord forgave you.* The hurt and betrayal needed to end with her. Her hand hovered over the white sheet and shook.

I was hurt by your not showing at the assembly and keeping the other diary from me, but I will find it in my heart to forgive you.

Her mind battled with her heart over whether she meant the words, but she chose to call them into existence. At this moment, forgiveness felt like a large wave to crest, but someday she would. She signed her name, set the pen down, and left without looking back.

Tobie fell into step beside her, and she gripped his hand same as she had as a young girl. How many times had she clung to her papa's strength? Right now, she needed his comforting presence. *Thank you, Lord, for Your timing.*

She may have taken the diary, but she left her heart behind, splintered into more pieces than the trees broken in the mudslide.

Chapter 30

Papa's temper has been fierce of late. I fear he senses our plans, and it sets me in deep torment. I cannot help but jump at every sound.

~ Entry by Loretta Baxter, October 19, 1810

Samuel awoke with an aching neck, having slept sitting up against a crate. The rats decided he was no longer a threat and sneaked out of the corners to lick the remaining crumbs from the moldy bread he'd been given for supper. A single sunbeam crept across the floor, allowing him some concept of time. He rubbed his jaw, and stubble pricked his palms. Everything he'd been through rushed into his memory, Lucy's betrayal, his banishment, disease in the crops, the fire, a mudslide, and now his abduction. How much was he meant to endure? What more could he withstand?

He shook off the grim thoughts. What had Maggie said? *Consider it joy when trials come because they develop character and perseverance.* He wanted to wallow in his self-pity, write off the Bible verse and Maggie's voice in his head. But he couldn't. Maggie had survived on an island as a small child without anyone, and she still remained optimistic. She still trusted God, her Lord and Savior, the One who saves.

He leaned his head back on the crate and stared at the amazing amount of light that permeated the small crack in the wood. Jesus had been whipped, beaten, mocked, donned with a crown of thorns, hands and feet nailed to a cross, and pierced with a spear. He hadn't deserved such punishment, but Jesus withstood it for all—for Maggie—for him.

Waves crashed against the side of the boat, but to Samuel's mind it sounded like the crowd chanting, *Crucify Him. Crucify Him.* Samuel inhaled a ragged breath. Jesus understood what it was like to have enemies—religious leaders wanted to kill Him over the fear of losing their power and control and for doing the will of His Father.

Consider it pure joy when trials come because they develop character and perseverance.

The scripture hit Samuel in a way it never had before.

Could his trials—betrayals, fires, abductions—have been a struggle for power? He'd thought being sent to Antigua was punishment, but images ran through this mind. Of Cuffee, George and Thea, the worker whose child ran into his arms, and others who Samuel felt responsible for their care. And of course Maggie. He'd changed their working conditions and he had tried to make a difference in island politics—righting an injustice—and ran into opposition. Maybe God allowed him to be sent to Antigua to develop his character and to do God's work.

He rose, stretching his aching muscles, and paced as he prayed. *God, give me Your wisdom. Help me to do what is right. Show me how to persist and do Your will, but God, don't allow Maggie to believe she's unwanted. Please give me an opportunity to return to her and let it not be too late.*

The latch clicked and the portal door swung open. The young Frenchman carried in a mop and bucket and thrust it in Samuel's face. "*Mangez.*"

Samuel obediently followed, more to get out of the damp hull and learn about his whereabouts than to appease the Frenchman. He squinted in the early morning light. The merchant ship was smaller than he'd originally thought. A small single-masted sloop. He counted five men aboard, not including himself. The red-faced man appeared to be the captain, always barking out commands while the others grumbled and scurried about the deck.

A short burly man in wide-legged pants stopped in winching the sail and nudged the man next to him. He circled his finger near his temple and said, "George."

The other sailor with a curly beard burst with laugher and made angry stomping gestures as if he was throwing a tantrum and pointed at Samuel.

Samuel could only assume the George they were referencing was England's King George the third, who'd battled insanity in his final years. The young Frenchman beside Samuel chuckled over their joke. He moved to the bow and pointed at the desk. "*Tu laves*." He showed him the hook to haul up seawater and shoved Samuel as if to say, *Get going*.

Still donned in his elegant, but dirtied, evening attire, Samuel swabbed the deck, but the grunt work offered him time to get his bearings. They weren't near land, at least not close enough for him to swim to shore, but he could make out what looked like the cloud-topped islands of Nevis and St. Kitts. While he couldn't understand everything, he did catch a good portion of the crew's conversations. They were merchants who traded locally among the islands, as far north as Haiti and south to French Guiana.

The young Frenchman named Pierre was the newest member of the crew and the lowest in rank. Every time he passed by one of the other sailors, they either nudged him or gave him a light slap on the back of the head, as if to set him in his place. Pierre hauled up a net of fish and, instead of swinging it over to the part of the deck Samuel hadn't washed, he yanked the catch the other direction and spilled fish over the area he'd just cleaned.

Samuel's grip on the mop handle tightened. *Getting angry isn't wrong, it's what you do with the anger that matters.* He prayed a short prayer for peace. The stout crewman named Louis knocked Pierre's brimmed hat off, and it landed amid the flopping fish. Samuel's grip on the mop relaxed. He picked up the hat and handed it to Pierre, who swiped it. It seemed the recruit enjoyed having someone he could badger for a change.

The boat angled toward its port side, and he caught the word *Guadeloupe* from the captain's mouth. Samuel held his breath and concentrated on the captain's words. A storm was brewing from the southeast, and they would dock in Guadeloupe for cover and to restock supplies and trade goods.

Guadeloupe.

That was where he'd sent his solicitors to investigate Maggie's lineage based on the elderly maid's information. *God, You are good.* This was his chance. Maybe he could somehow escape and get to his lawyers or send them a message of his capture.

"*Arrêtez votre nettoyage paresseux.*"

A wet fish hit Samuel on the cheek and dropped to the floor. Every muscle in his body tensed, and his skin burned hotter than a full day's exposure to the Caribbean sun. He had half a mind to show Pierre who was the lazy one.

The other crewman laughed at Samuel.

A flash of eagerness in the young Pierre's eyes doused the inferno about to explode within Samuel. Pierre desired the crew's approval. He merely wanted to be seen as in control. In a way, he wasn't all that different from Samuel longing for his father's approval.

"*Aidez à trier le poisson.*" Pierre waved him over and pointed to the buckets in which he'd been commanded to sort the fish.

Samuel wiped fish slime off his face with his sleeve and knelt among the flopping fish beside Pierre, sorting them into different buckets. The tiny ones were thrown overboard. Sun beat down on Samuel's back, soaking him with perspiration as the two of them worked side by side. The ocean breeze offered some reprieve from the heat and the stench of fish.

By day's end, Samuel's back and knees ached something fierce. Pierre pointed for Samuel to sleep in the hold with the barrels filled with their new smelly catch. He tossed Samuel a piece of hardtack and a wedge of cheese that rivaled the fish in pungent odor. Samuel removed a mealy worm from the hardtack and ate both it and the cheese, too weary to care about ingesting bugs or mold as long as it put something in his stomach to ease the churn of hunger. He lay on the hard

plank floor and laced his fingers behind his head.
God, You work in mysterious ways. I might not be good at considering trials pure joy just yet, but thank You for humbling me, not giving up on me, and changing my heart. Thank You for putting Maggie in my life. Keep her safe in the Kellys' care.

The sound of crates sliding across the wooden planks toward Samuel woke him from a dead sleep of sheer exhaustion. He flinched and protected his face with his arms, but the noise stopped with the sound of netting stretching. He reached out into the darkness and bumped the corner of a wooden container inches from his face.

The boat shifted and the sliding sound reversed in the opposite direction. Liquid sloshed along the edge of the hold, not reaching him yet, but somewhere the boat was taking on sea water. He scrambled to stand so he wasn't hit by the next moving crate. Lightning flashed through the small crack in the boards, illuminating the beady eyes of rats lurking in the corners. He counted to eight before the boom of thunder followed. Had the storm arrived early? How close was the ship to Guadeloupe? *God, don't let me miss my opportunity.*

He climbed the ladder and pounded on the door. The boat rocked and sea water poured under the crack of the portal. His foot slipped and he gripped the ladder tighter.

Blasted formal attire. What he wouldn't give for his Hessian boots.

He pounded again and Pierre swung the door open. His face tinged green in a flash of lightning. Wind-driven rain soaked Samuel in seconds. Pierre passed him the winch and pointed for him to help lower the sail, then brushed past him and cast up his accounts over the rail.

The slippery deck and sudden dips made walking straight a challenge, but Samuel maneuvered to man Pierre's station. He owed Harry gratitude for having brought him on his father's sailboat on the Thames those weekends at university. Samuel helped lower the sail with the other crewmen. A bolt of lightning sliced across the sky, and he froze mid-turn of the winch.

Guadeloupe.

They were so close, he could make out the spires of a church, but also so close the storm could toss the ship onto a reef. The French captain and the stout crewman struggled at the helm to turn the rudder, and they'd already lowered the anchor, attempting to hold the boat offshore. The two other seamen prepared the storm trysail.

Now was his chance. *God, guide me and make my path straight.*

A large wave tossed the boat starboard, and Samuel stumbled backward. Pretending to lose his balance, he hit the rail and flung himself up and over, dropping into the rough seas below. Tepid water surrounded him, and he kicked with all his might toward shore, staying below as long as his screaming lungs would allow.

He broke the surface and gulped down air before a large wave crashed over him. He pressed on, swimming toward the shore. The current and swell of the waves stole his shoes and made it hard to discern the distance traveled. His arms and legs burned, and he rose periodically to catch his breath and listen for sounds of the crew. He thought he heard a shout, but a rumble of thunder drowned out the sound. Lightning flashed all around as the storm raged.

Lord, protect me from the storm. Don't let me get struck by lightning as I flee. He stayed closer to the surface now, trying to keep his focus on the church steeple. He choked out water and swam until his arms and legs could barely move, but the steeple appeared as far away as ever. Was he not making any progress? He would have been better off on the boat instead of drowning in a foolhardy attempt. What had he been thinking?

Trials develop perseverance.

He forced his legs to kick and his arms to scoop through the water over the next wave and then the next. A large crest picked him up and tossed him into the crashing surf. His knee scraped against something. Was it sand?

Another swell pushed him, and this time his feet felt solid ground. Almost there. He would make it.

He trudged through the swirling water, the ferocious currents knocking him to his knees and sending him tumbling amid the surf. Several times, rough waves pinned him to the sandy bottom, where rocks battered and bruised his bones. Coral ripped his clothes and skin and threatened to not let him up for air, but he persisted.

Another wave tossed him into a clump of mangrove trees. He used the branches to pull himself closer to shore, past the breakers. He crawled onto the sand and collapsed on his back, allowing the drenching rain to wash away the blood from his scraped knees, chin, and hands. He'd escaped. A bark of a laugh erupted, shooting the rain and seawater off his lips in all directions. *That was by the work of your hands. Thank you, Lord.*

The storm began to let up, and a streak of sunlight peeked over the dark clouds. He had to get up. Had to find his solicitors or someone else who could help him. He gripped a nearby mangrove tree to pull himself up. He wasn't in the clear yet. *God, give me the strength.*

His movement sent sand crabs plunging into their newly dug holes. Every muscle in his body ached as he trudged up the shoreline. He had no idea where he was on the island of Guadeloupe or even if this *was* Guadeloupe. His stomach growled and his skin and clothes felt stiff from the drying saltwater. How did Maggie survive alone as a mere child?

He needed to remember his mission and stay on task. Best to create a list.

Number one: Stay alive.

Number two: Find his solicitors.

In order to find his solicitors, he'd need to locate an islander who could direct him to the church where Maggie's parents had been married. Then he'd need to find proof of their marriage and hurry back to Antigua to tell Maggie and ask her to marry him. He pictured her smile and the way it transformed her whole face, brightening her eyes and turning her cheeks rosy. Would she think him a hero for finding her answers? She might be upset initially about him not showing at the dance, but after his explanation, she'd easily forgive him. That was her nature and he loved it about her.

But would she be as forgiving about the diaries?

He gulped, despite the dryness of his throat, and stepped over a large piece of driftwood washed up on shore from the storm. Why did he keep her mother's diaries from her? He'd believed he'd been doing the right thing at the time. Trying to control the information and circumstances as if he knew best.

He'd find a way to make it up to her. *God, please help her find it in her heart to forgive me.*

Samuel rounded a corner of the beach to a small bay. His chest lifted. Boats lay anchored, islanders milled about unloading and loading, crewmen assessed damage from the storm. Perhaps one of these people could direct him to the church of Saint Michael.

"*Vous!*"

From the boat now anchored in the cove a man pointed at Samuel. *Pierre.*

Samuel turned and ran headlong inland, into the cover of the mangrove trees.

"*Arrêtez!*"

Samuel didn't stop. He grabbed branches to pull him through the wetland and balance over roots. He could hear shouts behind him, and he plunged deeper into the tropical foliage. His feet, unused to treading rough terrain without boots, added cuts from the sharp dried leaves to his bruises and scrapes. He winced, stepping on a jagged root, and emerged into an open area where a sugar field began. The cane was too thick for him to maneuver through, so he skirted the edge of the farmland. His lungs burned from exertion, and he struggled to draw in enough breath.

Another shout rang from behind. Were they gaining on him? How many people pursued? Had they split up?

A small path between fields caught his eye, and he veered up the lower side of La Grande Soufrière Mountain. He glanced back over his shoulder and only saw tall blades of cane grass and the narrow dirt path.

Good. Perhaps he'd lost them or they'd given up.

His ankle rolled, and Samuel toppled into a gully, somersaulting twice before skidding over roots and rocks on his back. If he'd had more breath, he would have groaned. Instead, he lay there, chest heaving, staring at the clearing blue sky. How did Maggie survive?

The tip of a machete blade pointed under his chin.

Samuel didn't dare move, but his gaze followed the long knife up to the dark arm and bare-chested man who carried it.

"Why are white men chasing after another white man? What have you done?"

Samuel translated the man's French in his head. The more familiar creole accent made it easier to understand than the French merchants. "Nothing. I was abducted."

A low rumble of laughter vibrated the air. "So now, white men are also taking white men as slaves?"

"Not quite." Samuel raised his palms in a position of surrender. "They snatched me for control and power to keep my voice hidden."

"Isn't dat da truth." He lowered the machete.

"To where are you running?"

"Saint Michael's Church."

"Da ruins?"

"Ruins?"

"Tat church burnt down seven years ago."

Samuel pressed his palms to his temples. The church had to still be there. *Please let it not be so.*

"Come." The man extended his hand and aided Samuel to rise. "You are at least headed in da right direction. Follow da gully up to da road, den take a left and stay on da road until . . ." He glanced up at the sun in the sky. "Until its mid-aftanoon. You'll pass da old stone ruins of Saint Michaels, but if ya keep walkin' another field's length, you'll see da spire of St. Paul's. Dat's where ya can have yer sins confessed. Da priest dere used ta hear sins at St. Michaels."

Samuel's breath hitched. Would that priest know of Captain Sebastian Lowell Corbett, better known as The Wolf? "Thank you."

The islander removed a coconut tied like a satchel and handed it to Samuel. "Drink."

Samuel guzzled three big gulps. The freshwater rich with a mineral taste slid down his throat, cooling his overheated body, quenching his thirst, and restoring the hope he could escape his pursuers. He gasped in a breath. "Thank you."

The man nodded. He glanced left, and his

forehead wrinkled. "Go." The single word punctured the air.

Samuel turned to see the sugarcane waving in the lower field.

"I will send them off your trail."

He returned the coconut and grasped the islander's hand surprised to find it solid of flesh and blood for the man seemed like an otherworldly guardian angel. He pumped it. "Bless you, my friend. Your kindness will not be forgotten."

Refreshed by the drink of water, Samuel followed the islander's directions to the end of the field and up the road. His feet throbbed with each step and the sun blazed heat down upon his back. Rabbits and cane toads hopped back into the shelter of the cane. On his left, vines nearly covered the skeleton of an old cathedral being drawn back into the earth.

Saint Michael's Church. It must be.

He paused in the road just long enough to honor the place where Maggie's parents married. One day he would bring Maggie here to see it.

The spire of St. Paul's Church rose above the cane, and Samuel pressed on, entering the church through its main doors. His eyes adjusted to the dim light, but could make out the white robes of an elderly priest kneeling at the alter in prayer. Samuel limped down the aisles of empty pews.

The father crossed himself and peered up at the

newcomer, then flinched. *"Notre Père qui est aux cieux, aidez-nous!"*

Samuel lightly chuckled at the translation. *Heavenly Father full of grace, help us.* What a sight he must appear, covered in dirt, sweat, cuts, and bruises, dressed in ripped evening formal attire.

The priest gripped the rail and warily rose. "How may I help you, my son?" he said in French.

Samuel spoke slowly, searching for the proper words in the foreign language. "My name is Lord Samuel Fredrick Granville and I was,"—he didn't know the word for abducted—"taken from Antigua. I need help in getting back there."

"I see." His eyes scanned Samuel's torn clothing. "The church excels in aiding lost sheep."

"Also, I'm looking for information." He rubbed the scruff on his lower jaw. "Specifically, any information you may have on a man who resided on Guadeloupe by the name of Captain Sebastian Lowell Corbett, or a woman named Loretta Genevieve Baxter."

The French priest scratched his temple. "You are not the only one to ask about these people." He held up his index finger. "Two lawyers were here earlier."

Samuel sagged against the end of the pew bench, and a weak smile curved the corners of his mouth. *Thank you, Lord.*

"They left when I told them that all the records burned in a church fire." The priest crossed himself once more. "They filed out so quickly, I hadn't the time to tell them that I was the one who married the couple. I remember it clearly because I've never seen a couple so in love."

They were married. Samuel fell to his knees. Tears burned the back of his eyes. "Father, I need your help."

Chapter 31

It has happened! Vows were taken before a priest and in the presence of God and witnesses. I am now Sebastian's, in mind, body, and soul, but I can't bear for us to part. I must return to Antigua and put off Lord Cardon until my husband and I may sail to America.

~ Entry by Loretta Baxter,
October 19, 1810

The carriage stopped halfway up the lane, due to the rough terrain left from the mudslide. Samuel got out and trudged over the hard-packed mud toward the house. The lawyers had agreed to reconvene tomorrow to plan a strategy, and to entertain the priest in the meantime.

George met him at the door and welcomed him. "Praise God you're alive. When I received your missive, I raced over here. You were abducted?"

"It's good to see you, George. Is Maggie with Thea?"

George shook his head.

"She's here then?" Samuel's ears listened for the lilt of her voice. "Maggie?" He called for her and held his index finger up to George. "Hold fast one second."

Samuel mounted the crooked stairs and entered through the door Hawley held open. "Maggie," he called. "Maggie, I'm sorry about the dance, I need to explain what happened."

"She's gone."

Samuel spun to face George. "Gone where?"

"England. Her father—er adopted father—showed up the night of the ball and set sail with her several days ago."

Samuel gripped the newel post to stay upright and felt the blood drain from his face. "Please tell me she doesn't believe the worst."

There was a long pause. "Thea told her you had planned to propose."

God, please, don't let Maggie doubt my love.

He wanted to run down to the harbor and commission a ship to sail after her. With their week's head start, he'd likely not outrun Middleton's schooner, and he wasn't free to set foot in England—not yet.

He could write her and explain what happened, but would she understand? He despised being separated, but he had no choice. The land must produce so he could redeem himself to his peers and return to Maggie to see for himself if she forgave him. A list of tasks that needed attention lined up in his mind. Debris needed to be dug out of the lane so vehicles could pass, but he couldn't afford to pull the men away from the fields when the cane was to be harvested. Yet if he didn't have them dig out the broken trees and rocks, then they wouldn't be able to get the sugar barrels to the bay to be shipped. He didn't hold the patience to wait that long.

Maggie's voice rang in his head, *Trust God. He'll make your paths straight.*

In a dazed state, he glanced out the window and said the first thing that came to mind. "The north fields haven't been harvested."

George followed his line of vision. "Don't blame Cuffee. The morning after the dance, he and I decided it was best to form search parties to hunt for you. We didn't know if you'd been robbed and left for dead or injured. Every abled body went looking except for Hawley, who stayed to oversee the house. We searched the entire island."

That meant they'd lost five days of work, but their concern for his wellbeing touched him. If it had been the other way around, would he have stopped work to do the same? He clamped his hand on George's shoulder and locked gazes. "Thank you, my friend. It means a lot to me to know you and Cuffee have my back. I know your being away from your plantation is costing you too."

George snorted with a crooked grin. "Don't think of it."

Samuel pointed George in the direction of his office. "Why don't you have a drink in my office while I change." Pierpont had given him something from his wardrobe to wear, but the pants and shirt hung on him.

"Carson will be cross as crabs to hear your evening wear was ruined," George said, making his way down the hall.

"Indeed." Samuel chuckled, but it sounded hollow, reminding him of how Maggie laughed with her entire being, bringing joy and life to any room. Had she truly vanished from his life? Had her hurt kept her from saying goodbye? He pivoted to face Hawley. "Did anyone come calling in my absence?"

"Only Mr. Kelly, my lord."

His heart deflated as he trudged up the stairs. Carson greeted him with a wide smile that faded when he glanced at Samuel's clothes. He quickly laid out fresh attire and supplied a second washbowl to rid Samuel of all the filth he'd picked up during the voyage.

Samuel washed and donned the clean clothes. He lifted his chin for Carson to tie his cravat and spied his list facing a different direction on his nightstand. It still read, *propose to Maggie.* He'd failed in his task, the one item he'd put on his list that day. The only item important enough to write down. How confident he'd been as he'd written it. How sure of himself and his future. One would think he'd come to realize that nothing was certain.

I just want to know something with certainty, Maggie had whispered in the dark, and he'd replied. *You can be certain of my love for you.*

A lump formed in his throat, and he blinked away the burning sensation in the back of his eyes. *God, please let her remain confident of my love.*

The note taunted him, a reminder of his failings.

Carson stepped back. "All finished, sir."

Samuel reached out to crumple the paper but hesitated. Something was off. "Did you move my list?"

"I learned long ago that you are particular of where things go and it's best not to alter them."

His list had been moved. It was facing the wrong way like the list had the first day Maggie had arrived. Had she been there? Had she snuck in to collect her things? No, that didn't make sense. She'd taken her mother's gowns and other items with her to the Kellys' house. Had she come back to say goodbye only to find him missing?

He strode from his chamber, stopping to peek into her old room and her mother's, hoping for any other clues but finding none. He descended the stairs and stopped Hawley, who was instructing Dinah to have some scones or finger sandwiches brought up for their guest.

"Lord Granville." Dinah curtsied. "Praise Gawd dat you are well. Let me know if dere is anything you need."

"Thank you, Dinah." He faced Hawley. "Are you certain no one came calling? Not even Miss Prescott?"

A muscle in Hawley's jaw twitched. "No one, my lord. Like I said, only Mr. Kelly."

"Very well then." Samuel rubbed his face and exhaled.

Samuel joined George in his office.

George, instead of taking a seat and helping himself to a drink, stood stiff in the center of the room with a sheet of paper in his hands. "This was lying on the floor near the waste bin. I think it's from Miss Prescott." He handed the paper to Samuel. "I'm sorry."

Samuel read her scribbled handwriting. The words, *I will forgive you,* jumped off the page. He opened his desk drawer to find the diaries missing. Pain seized his chest, squeezing his heart and dragging the air from his lungs. Maggie must believe him to be a monster. He sagged against the wall. Why hadn't he told her about the diaries?

"Maggie is an understanding sort." George poured a drink from the decanter of cognac Samuel kept for guests and handed it to Samuel, but he turned it down. "You can write her and explain." He set the drink on the desk.

Samuel groaned. "I should have been honest. I wanted to have all the information. I wanted to be the hero, but I ended up being the villain."

"It's never too late to do the right thing." George aided him to rise. "Trust God. If it's His will then no one can shut that door. Not even us with our own mistakes."

I visited to bid you farewell . . .

She'd thought well enough of him to come say goodbye. Samuel frowned.

Hawley had told him no one paid him a call. How did she obtain the diaries he'd locked in his desk drawer?

A knock sounded on the door, and Hawley entered with a tea tray and finger foods.

"Set it down on the end table." Samuel pointed toward his reading chair in the corner. "Hawley, you said no one came calling while I was out."

"No one of importance, my lord." He set the tray down and turned to face his employer. "Perhaps a few deliveries brought around back."

"Miss Prescott didn't come visiting?"

George eyed Samuel with a questioning gaze, but Samuel cast him a look he hoped said lets-see-how-this-goes.

The same muscle in Hawley's jaw twitched. "No one of importance called except Mr. Kelly."

"You stayed with the house?"

"Of course." His eyes widened as if affronted. "It's my duty."

"It's also the duty of the butler to inform the master of the house of any visitors."

His face reddened, and his body stiffened. "My

father and my grandfather before him served and protected your family for several decades, and I continue to do so."

Hawley was the last person Samuel saw before he was abducted. Had Hawley been in on the plans? Samuel stepped toward the butler, pushing his edge. "Not telling me of Miss Prescott's visit is your idea of protecting me?"

Hawley's nostrils flared. "I'm not about to lose Greenville Manor to some little minx whose traitorous mother ran off with a Frenchman. She deserved to die, and so does her menacing daughter who doesn't fit among polite society."

That familiar red mist clouded his vision, but he closed his eyes to it.

We live in a broken world. Anger is going to rise in us. It's how we act on our anger that matters. Samuel emptied himself and let the Lord do a work in him. *I give this to you, Lord.* A peace he hadn't known before set aside his rage to defend Maggie's honor in order to shed light on the truth.

"You read the diaries, didn't you?" He took another step closer. "It's the only way you'd know that information."

"I was there." His mouth curled into a snarl. "I was young and kept out of the way in the kitchens, but I overheard the gossip. I saw the affect Miss Loretta Baxter's marriage had on her father. He grieved himself to death, probably because he was so ashamed of his daughter's traitorous actions and his disgusting French-swine son-in-law."

"You knew all this time Loretta Baxter and Captain Corbett had married?" Samuel clenched his jaw. What he'd and Maggie endured with their search and his scoundrel of a butler had the information all along.

"Her disgrace in marrying a Frenchman wasn't public knowledge and her father meant to keep it that way."

"Why then did you give Miss Prescott the diary?"

"I knew it would drive her away and good riddance. I found Miss Baxter's diaries in the room under the stairs long ago. I should have burned them but figured they were harmless. Then she showed up."

"So you took matters into your own hands." A twinge of conviction twisted Samuel's heart. Was this the path he'd been heading down, trying to control situations?

Hawley's eyes darkened. His fists clenched, and he began to shake. "I was protecting what will rightfully be yours from the despicable Bonaparte lovers. Those French think they own the Caribbean."

"You believed you knew better than your employer." Samuel swallowed the acid burning his throat.

Much like you thought you knew better than your Heavenly Father.

"I knew enough not to give her the one that proved her lineage. That one I burned."

"Burned?" Samuel jolted. Maggie will never get to read her mother's last diary.

"And thanks to me, there's no evidence to prove Miss Prescott's legitimacy."

Cuffee appeared in the doorway.

Samuel stepped toward Hawley, his fingers itching to ring the man's neck.

Hawley backed up a step. "You should be grateful." His eyes grew wild. "I was protecting your lands."

"Take him away." Samuel exhaled and relaxed his clenched fists. How had he not seen Hawley's bitterness toward the French—toward Maggie?

"I saved you. You would have nothing if it weren't for me." Hawley eyed the door and lunged in that direction, attempting to dodge Cuffee.

George jumped behind him and grabbed the butler's arms, pinning them behind his back.

"What are you doing?" Hawley tried to shake free, and Cuffee gripped his other arm.

Samuel unlocked his jaw. "Letting you get a look at the inside of Antigua's jail cell."

"You're making a terrible mistake," Hawley yelled. George and Cuffee dragged him out, his heels sliding across the wooden floor. "My family has served Greenview Manor for centuries, and this is how you repay me?"

Lord willing, the generational curse of pride, deceit, and anger would be cast out from this moment forward. "Add Hawley to the list of Fines's accomplices."

Maggie fidgeted with the sleeve of her taffeta gown, adjusting the gauzy lace overlay. She attempted to hold still even though, having been on land for over two weeks, the floor still tilted as her sea legs adjusted. During their five weeks at sea, a few storms had tossed the ship about, but Anthony proved a capable captain.

Her lady's maid circled her with hair pins sticking out of her mouth like a dragon with sharp teeth. Cilla smiled at Maggie in the full-length mirror.

"You look lovely." Cilla's hand cupped the mass of dark pinned curls piled on top of Maggie's head. "When did my little magpie get so grown up?"

Maggie turned, despite the maid's protest, and layers of petticoats and light coral taffeta swirled about her feet. "I can't do this." Maggie bit her bottom lip. "Not even a team of duchesses will change the marriage-mart-mamas' minds about me. They will call me a fraud."

Cilla's nostrils flared. "Then they will be daring to defy not only the Duchess of Linton, but her daughter-in-law, the Marchioness of Daventry, the Countess of Cardon, and Lady Etheridge—because no one crosses her sharp tongue. I brought in all the reinforcements to ensure your debut was a smashing success. Which I know it will be."

Maggie's stomach dove, taking cover in her slippers. "Lady Cardon will be in attendance?"

"Indeed. She and her new daughter-in-law, Mrs. Hannah Granville. Perhaps you've met her?"

Samuel's parents, brother, and sister-in-law would be among the guests. Maggie strained to drag in air, but her stays felt tight, restricting her breathing. She had only spoken of Samuel by his given name, and Cilla didn't know the relation. "I haven't had the pleasure."

"Delightful young woman. She and her husband were a last-minute reply since she'd just given birth several months ago. You'll adore her. You two will have much in common. She's from the island of Nevis." Cilla bent and fluffed out Maggie's skirt. "I will be sure to introduce you."

The rush of air helped fan away the heat that continued to rise in Maggie's body. Cilla stood, and Maggie saw the strained lines that hadn't marked her forehead before Maggie left for Antigua. Guilt formed a lump in her chest. Had her disappearance created the creases of worry on her adopted mama's brow?

Maggie had barely set foot off the gangplank

when Cilla wrapped her in her arms and squeezed her. They both cried tears of joy that morning. Maggie had to explain her actions and endure Cilla's stern lecture, but in the end, Cilla forgave Maggie and showed her unconditional love, and for that, Maggie would be forever grateful. She'd told Cilla of Samuel. Her heart still hadn't healed. What if she mentioned Samuel's name by accident or broke into tears in front of his family? Or worse swooned.

"What if I make a fool of myself."

Cilla squeezed her hand. "Your etiquette tutor had only high marks for you. She called it a 'miraculous change,' especially with so little time."

Tobie and Cilla had decided to allow Maggie's maid to finish out the semester at boarding school and hire a tutor to ensure Maggie mastered the etiquette rules she'd never taken seriously. This time, Maggie threw herself wholeheartedly into learning, but whether her new zeal was to please her parents or some deluded attempt to prove herself dance-worthy to Samuel, should she ever see him again, she wasn't sure. Her conscience poked at her. She was no better than Samuel, who'd wished to demonstrate to Lucy that he would have been the better choice.

How many more times would she replay what happened with Samuel in Antigua in her mind? The only logic for why he'd withhold her mother's diaries from her was to control the information they contained. Although he'd betrayed her trust and broken her heart, hadn't she done the same to her parents when she'd sailed to Antigua? She'd feared they'd say no, and so she'd deceived them.

That didn't explain why he didn't show at the assembly dance.

You can be certain of my love for you.

His actions *certainly* hadn't backed up the sincerity of his words.

Cilla looked Maggie over, and a wistful smile touched her lips. "I love you, magpie. You are and will always be my daughter, and I would move heaven and earth for you." She brushed Maggie's cheek. "I just want you to be happy."

"I know, and I know you could have brought out the reinforcements to get society to accept me all along, but I needed to try things on my own. I wish I could explain why I had to sail to Antigua, why it pressed on my heart so. I needed to understand who Loretta Baxter was so I could better understand myself. It didn't and never would diminish who you are to me and all that you've sacrificed to make me who I am. I hope you understand."

"I merely want you to realize it doesn't matter if your lineage is good, bad, or plain awful. What matters is the legacy you choose. Your earthly heritage isn't as important as your heavenly one.

You are Maggie Prescott, child of God. We have been blessed to have you in our care because God willed it to be."

Maggie hugged her mama. "I love you. I'm so sorry that I caused you to worry."

"I love you too." Cilla pulled back, holding her at arm's length. "I'm just glad you're safe." She frowned and stared at the ceiling, blinking away tears. "Now, I don't want you entering the ballroom puffy-eyed from crying after we spent hours perfecting your appearance." Cilla pulled a dance card from the bookshelf and handed it to Maggie. "Lady Brennan and Lady St. Martin have hinted that their sons will be requesting a dance."

"They're willing to overlook my unknown lineage?"

"The Duchess of Linton's backing has removed any doubts. And a rumor has begun to spread, superseding the ridiculous one of you being spawned by a pirate. The *ton* now declares what they claim to have suspected all along, that you were the legitimate daughter of a French nobleman."

Maggie raised her eyebrows. "And where did they hear that?"

"I have no idea, but it started last week and had impeccable timing."

Maggie snorted and stared at the dance card. This was her chance to show polite society's upper crust that she was one of them.

Why then did she feel like sobbing?

"I don't know if I can dance. My heart's not in it anymore."

Cilla rubbed her arm. "Darling, God sent your papa and my ship way off course so that we could find you, and He will go out of His way to ensure the right man waltzes into your life. Trust me." She smiled. The worry lines disappeared, restoring the youthful beauty that attracted Tobie to her mama. "Better yet, trust God."

Samuel followed the Duke of Linton's butler down the highly polished marble floor. He had one chance to make this work, or else everything he'd set in motion this past week would be for naught. Maggie's debut ball was his best and only chance, but if the House of Lords prematurely learned of his return, he'd be shipped back to Antigua for the rest of his days. When he'd stood before his peers and had refused to publicly apologize to Harry, the Duke of Linton had been the only one who'd looked at Samuel with mercy. He'd called for a stay instead of issuing immediate sentencing. Now, Samuel hoped the duke would, once again, offer compassion because Samuel needed His Grace's help.

The butler tapped on a door.

"Come in," The duke's deep voice rang out.

Swinging the door wide, the butler announced Samuel's presence.

A large red bird swooped overhead. Samuel ducked a second before the parrot seized the opportunity of the door's opening and flew into the room.

"Blasted bird, get out of here." The Duke of Linton stood behind his large mahogany desk and shooed it with a swipe of his hand.

In a flurry of beating red wings, the creature turned around. Samuel ducked once more, and the bird exited with a squawk.

"Pardon my son's pet." The duke exhaled and shook his head. "That dumb bird is going to outlive us all just to spite me."

The bird croaked from somewhere outside in the hall, "Rawch, dumb bird."

The Duke of Linton grunted. "I was surprised to hear you defied the ruling of the House of Lords and returned to England before your summon at the end of the year." He gestured toward the chair in front of him.

"I can expl—"

"Sit." The duke's tone rang with authority.

Samuel dropped into a nearby chair, but his palms itched while the distinguished man took his time removing a file from his desk drawer.

Samuel's lips parted with the need to speak in his defense, but the duke silenced him with a sharp hiss and one raised finger. His grace opened a folder, read the top sheet of paper, and peered at Samuel.

"It seems you continue to draw quite the controversy—showing up in England without being summoned, involving your brother by taking up residence at his lodging instead of your parents as if in hiding, and spreading rumors about a French heiress in our midst."

Word spread fast. "I can explain." Samuel cleared his throat. *Please, give me a chance.*

"I assumed you would after appearing at White's for a single hand of cards. You are either a calculated genius for arriving when my son and I enjoy our weekly card game and, in doing so, forcing me to summon you for a private meeting. Or you are a complete imbecile for such brash behavior."

"I—"

The Duke of Linton raised his hand and silenced him again. "Who's the rightful heir to Greenview Manor?"

"It should be Miss Maggie Prescott, your grace."

He frowned and stared at the paper once again. "It says here that the rightful ownership was given over to your father and thus shall be your inheritance. Your brother's attorneys sent these papers so I'd know the full truth of it."

Bradlee. He should never have approached his younger brother. Why was Bradlee interfering in his life?

"You'd willingly sacrifice your inheritance"—

The Duke closed the folder and leaned on his desk—"knowing full well that you need that land to prove your worth to the peerage and resume residence in England?"

"I would and I do."

The duke rubbed his index finger under his nose. "Why?"

"Sacrifice means giving up something you love for something you love more, and Miss Prescott is worth more to me than any inheritance."

The Duke of Linton eyed him carefully as though weighing its truthfulness. He pursed his lips and nodded. "You love her, but does she hold you in the same regard?"

"No, your grace. She believes the worst of me. I wronged her by holding back the truth. I returned to attempt to rectify the situation."

He snorted. "And how do you plan to pacify the fury of a woman scorned?"

"I will apologize for my wrongdoing."

"Truly?" The duke leaned forward onto his elbows with his fingers laced in front of him. "As a public gesture?"

"With every wagging tongue in attendance."

The duke's eyes were gentle—the same expression he held when Samuel had faced him with the order to apologize to Harry. And when Samuel had refused, he'd appeared disappointed, but his expression wasn't condemning, as everyone else's had been.

"A risky endeavor. Might I suggest a room full of key influential people rather than a large crowd. Your presence will cause enough of a stir. I'd prefer not to turn the ball into a circus."

Samuel nodded. "I took a chance coming back to prove the legitimacy of her birth and that her father was of noble descent. She deserves to take her rightful place among the *ton*."

"And a public display will force society to publicly acknowledge the truth. At the time of her mother's marriage, England was at war with France. I can understand why her grandfather didn't want his inheritance to fall into French hands, but much has changed."

"Maggie—er Miss Prescott"—he winced at his gaff—"has been raised in England from a young age. She's as much an Englishwoman as your wife and my mother."

"You are asking to overwrite the will of her grandfather." He folded his hands and leveled his gaze with Samuel's. "I suggest you make amends with Miss Prescott as quickly as possible, and if she'll have you, then you can sacrifice your inheritance as a wedding gift. I'd prefer to have documents drawn for Greenview Manor to be part of her dower estate."

Samuel fought to keep his shoulders from sinking. "Me too, but I have much to be forgiven."

The duke removed a pen and scribbled notes on a sheet of paper. His hand stilled. "Your sacrifice proves you measure up to the title of earl you will one day inherit. On the morrow, I will meet with the House of Lords and see that your banishment is overturned for a lesson learned. You will have to evade the public eye until then. Shall I have the papers sent to Yvain Manor?"

"Y-yes." Samuel jolted. "Thank you, your grace. I don't know how to repay you for such kindness."

"Express your gratitude by setting things to right with Miss Prescott. My own son, Maxwell, was recently married to a sweet young woman named Evelyn." His gaze grew warm and distant as he seemingly reflected. "Marriage has a wonderful way of maturing a man.

"That being said . . ." He pulled out a card and wrote something on it. "My wife is sponsoring one Miss Maggie Prescott this evening at our London townhome."

He passed the card to Samuel. "It's an invitation. My wife can be a show of force when she sides with someone, especially someone she feels is disadvantaged. Come prepared to woo Miss Prescott, my wife, and all of society. Do not fail me in persuading them."

"I can't afford to fail, your grace. The stakes are much too great."

Chapter 32

A ship has been readied and I am overly zealous to be reunited with my husband, captain, and wolf. I'm afraid, dear diary, that you must be left behind. Perhaps someday you will be discovered, and the truth revealed.

~ *Entry by Loretta Baxter, November 2, 1810*

"Priscilla, you are pulling off the ball of the century."

Maggie swallowed. If only she felt as confident as the Duchess of Linton seemed by her words to her mother. However, standing next to the duchess's daughter-in-law, Lady Evelyn Weld, Marchioness of Daventry, who'd whispered that she, too, was relatively new to London's social scene, allowed Maggie to at least not feel alone.

Tobie and Cilla greeted guest after guest, and Maggie curtsied so many times in a row that she felt like a windup doll. The couples acknowledged her but moved to the Duke and Duchess for introductions. A group of young bucks bowed as they passed.

"Maggie?"

A chill ran up her spine at the familiar

sound of Mitchell's voice. She turned from greeting Lord and Lady Navarro to face her old friend.

He gripped her fingers and bowed. His bold gaze raked over her. "You've changed." He flashed the same charming grin that would have melted her knees back in the day. "Congratulations on being a French heiress. I do hope you'll save me a dance."

He believed the rumors? He awaited Maggie's response, but she blanked. She certainly wasn't going to dance with him after his past proposition, but how did one go about declining a dance?

"I daresay, her dance card is already full." Cilla saved her. "If only you'd taken the opportunity at one of the country dances." She waved him off like a young school lad. "Run along now, Mitchell. I think your mama is beckoning you."

Maggie suppressed a whoop, and Mitchell trailed off in his mother's direction.

Cilla touched her daughter's arm. "And may I present Lord Harry Reginald."

Maggie choked on air but recovered quickly. The man before her reeked of arrogance and conceit, but Samuel hadn't exaggerated his good looks. He held the face of an angel—except for his crooked nose.

The rogue's gaze ignited with a smoldering flame and unprincipled delight. "The pleasure is mine, Miss Prescott." He bowed with impeccable manners. "I do hope we can further our acquaintance."

Not likely.

Evelyn caught her watching Lord Harry Reginald saunter over to a group of young ladies and nudged Maggie with her elbow. "Be careful of that one. I know the type, and they're not good enough to lick the heels of your slippers."

Maggie nodded. "Oh, I plan to give him a wide berth."

Not long after, Miss Lucy Tilly was introduced to Maggie, but she seemed distracted craning her neck, likely searching for Lord Reginald. Her face paled the moment she found him, leaning over the shoulder of a young debutante and whispering in her ear. It seemed Lord Reginald had already sailed on toward fresher waters.

"Maggie, dearest."

Maggie turned to the next person, and Cilla made introductions. "May I present Lord and Lady Cardon and their son Mr. Bradlee Granville, and his wife, Mrs. Hannah Granville."

Lady Cardon surprised Maggie by scooping up both of her hands. "I'm delighted to meet you. I'd love to call upon you in the near future so we can get to know one another better."

Lord Cardon bowed, saying it was a pleasure to meet her, and started for the card room. Lady Cardon redirected him. "Come along, dear." He frowned and grumbled something under his breath, a small indication of the temper Samuel had mentioned.

"Don't mind him." Samuel's brother addressed her. He held a similar look to Samuel around his eyes but didn't resemble him in stature. "He's just angry that he had to give up holding his grandchild to come here."

His wife, Mrs. Hannah Granville, smiled at Maggie, and she admired how lovely and vibrant a couple they presented. "I plan to come calling with Lady Cardon," Mrs. Granville said. "From what I've heard about you, I know we are going to become fast friends."

What she'd heard? People honestly had been discussing her—in a good light? This was going to take some getting used to. She took Mrs. Granville's hands in her own. "Congratulations on your new little one. I hope you bring him when you visit." Maggie chuckled. "That is if you can sneak him away from his grandpapa."

"That will be a feat, but I'm certain Hannah will figure a way." Bradlee led her down the line, and the Duchess kissed both of Mrs. Granville's cheeks. Maggie had heard both had lived on the island of Nevis for a time and were close friends.

Maggie swallowed around the lump in her throat. Samuel had a lovely family, one she would have adored to have been a part of. The constricting of her chest made it painful to breathe.

She turned to greet the next round of guests. Uncle Anthony and Judith had arrived, and they paused to see how Maggie fared under the inquisition.

Maggie peeked over her shoulder. "Thank goodness the line had dwindled."

The increasing rumble of the crowd of guests made introductions harder to hear, but the ear-piercing voice of Lady Etheridge rang above the din.

Uncle Anthony blanched and tried to pull Judith away.

Maggie bobbed a polite curtsy and faced Lady Etheridge, who'd held a grudge against Uncle Anthony ever since he was forced at gun point to aid in rescuing her daughter, Lottie Winthrop, from the hands of smugglers.

"Middleton." Lady Etheridge speared him with a glare. "My prayers for you to be eaten by an alligator have yet to be answered."

Judith crossed her arms and squared off with the dowager. "Alligators would only spit out such a salty character."

"Touché." The older woman arched an eyebrow.

"Lady Etheridge." Maggie attempted to intervene before blood was drawn. "You are already acquainted with my uncle, but may I introduce to you Mrs. Judith Morgan, his fiancée."

Lady Etheridge's lips twisted into a wry smile.

"Mrs. Morgan, take a turn about the room with me." She took hold of Judith's arm. "You remind me of a younger version of myself."

"Wait." Uncle Anthony trailed after them. "No, she doesn't."

Maggie grinned at the trio's backs. So far, tonight had been full of surprises. Who would have thought her debut would draw so many people. Oh, to tell Samuel about all that had transpired.

Maggie's smile fell. She must put him from her mind. The objective of tonight was to introduce her to society so she'd catch the eye of England's eligible young gentlemen.

And marry one who would want her.

Samuel was never late, except, it seemed, for when it counted. He hadn't expected one of his horse's hooves to pick up a stone and become lame or the need for the carriage to turn around for a different animal.

By the time they reached the ball held at Mendon House where Maggie resided, most of the guests had likely arrived, and carriages lined both sides of the street.

Samuel burst from the carriage without waiting for the footman to open the door and yanked the poor priest onto the front walk. Music floated on the night air. Brightly lit windows illuminated the front face of the sprawling two-story Georgian manor home more so than the torches set along the way. He traversed the brick path with vigorous steps and stopped to allow the priest to catch up so they could review their plan.

"We'll stay along the perimeter of the room, trying not to draw attention. Once I locate my sister-in-law, she will draw Maggie over, I will explain what happened, and you can verify everything. I'd like to keep it to a small group of witnesses, preferably not in the main ballroom, but in a room off to the side. Let's explore our options before waltzing into the hullabaloo."

"May God be with us," the priest said in his thick French accent.

Samuel bounded up the front steps two at a time and paused at the door to summon his courage. *God, give me the strength to make things right.* He tugged on the bottoms of his sleeves before knocking.

Two footmen swung the double doors open, and an austere butler stepped in front, blocking their way. Samuel removed his invitation from his front pocket and passed it to the manservant, who looked it over and stepped aside to announce their names.

"Hold." Samuel stopped him mid inhale. "We had a long drive and would care to freshen up a bit before making our entrance."

"Very well. Right this way, my lord." He ushered Samuel and the priest down the hall to a washroom. Samuel waited for the butler to return to his post before stepping out and opening a few doors, seeking a place where he and Maggie might speak privately. He rapped lightly before poking his head into a dimly lit room and waiting for his eyes to adjust.

"What do you think you're doing here?" Middleton stepped out of the shadows, his hair askew and the candlelight illuminating the blaze in his eyes. "Don't you even think of ruining this night for Maggie."

"Anthony," a woman said. "Don't make a scene. Please."

Samuel recognized Judith's voice, and then her face as she fumbled to fix the pins in her hair.

Middleton's strides ate up the distance between them. "If you think you can show up here after deserting her the way you did, you have another thing coming."

Samuel recoiled from the scent of alcohol that hung heavy on Middleton's breath. "I just need a moment—"

Middleton's fist planted one wallop of a facer into Samuel's nose, snapping his head back. Blinding white pain lit up the back of his eyelids.

Judith screamed, and the priest shouted in French.

Blood poured like a faucet out of Samuel's nostrils, and he cupped one hand over his nose and yanked out his handkerchief with his other to staunch the bleeding.

Judith burst into tears, and Middleton seemed to waver between comforting his fiancée and fending off a priest bent on lecturing him in French on the sin of casting stones.

The Prescott butler opened the door and cleared his throat. "The water closet's the second door on the left."

"Beg your pardon." Samuel mumbled from under the bloodied cloth and found the washroom to clean up.

Precious time was lost as Samuel clenched his jaw and pinched his nose to staunch the flow of blood that had already stained the front of his snowy white shirt and cravat. If only he could have borrowed a change of clothes, but he had little time before Middleton would make Samuel's presence known. Best to stick with the plan. He exited the water closet, and the priest rose from his kneeling outside the door.

They were going to need all the prayers they could get.

If he hadn't been so desperate to locate Maggie, he would have laughed at the shocked expressions of the footmen, opening the doors to the ballroom. Noise and heat slapped Samuel in the face, causing his eyes to water once more, but he blinked the moisture away and scanned the guests' faces. Stick to the perimeter, locate Hannah, don't draw attention.

He stepped into the ballroom, and heads swiveled in his direction. Ladies stared at him and whispered behind their fans, young men elbowed their friends and inclined their chins toward the door, older men raised their monocles for a better look, and dancers crashed into one another, stopping to stare. Even the musicians stopped playing.

So much for going unnoticed.

Middleton had a head start, pressing through the crowd. He headed toward the far corner, where he whispered to a man, whom Samuel suspected was Maggie's adopted father.

A hushed silence hung over the room. Samuel stepped forward, and a sea of skirts parted, the women who wore them issuing audible gasps. Ladies and their partners stepped aside as if afraid of what a crazed mad man would do. He bowed to the Duke of Linton on his right. The duke's gaze dropped to Samuel's shirt front, and he frowned. He didn't comment, though. Instead, his grace raised his glass in a silent salute and inclined his chin, directing him to Maggie's location. The duke's prior words mocked Samuel. *Come prepared to woo Miss Prescott, my wife, and all of society. Do not fail me in this.*

He wasn't off to a great start.

Samuel pressed forward, and the crowd

retreated until Maggie was in his line of sight, a horse length away. The light pink gown Maggie wore accented her curves and trim waist. The color set a healthy glow to her cheeks and contrasted nicely with her glossy, dark hair piled in curls on her head like a regal crown. Maggie smiled at something the duchess said, and he stumbled a step, his knees weakening. The sight of her smile had always had that effect on him.

He loved her.

God only knew how much he'd missed her, how sleep had evaded him, and how everything reminded him of her. He heard windchimes and thought of her laugh. He ate soup and remembered how she teased him about his three stirs. Sunsets and sunrises reminded him of her beauty and the light she brought into the darkness. Where he was regimented, stuffy, and vengeful, she was carefree, welcoming, and forgiving.

He prayed she was as forgiving as he'd need her to be.

Maggie spied him, and their gazes locked. Her smile faltered, and those green eyes widened. "Lord Granville?" Her chest rose and fell at an alarming rate, to the point he feared she might swoon, and she hated swooning. "What happened?"

"Miss Prescott." He'd remembered what a sight he must appear and tentatively stepped forward. "May I have a moment?"

A barricade of silk gowns closed rank around her.

The Duchess of Linton stood front and center, blocking his view of Maggie.

A woman who fit Maggie's description of her adopted mother stood beside the duchess, along with his mother and sister-in-law and a few other women he didn't recognize. All of them stood like a row of sentinels, all frowning at him.

"Samuel." His mother pursed her lips. "How dare you show up looking such a fright. What in heaven's name happened?"

His hand gently touched his broken nose. "I had my cork drawn." He glanced at Middleton.

"I'll do it again." Middleton puffed up his chest as if ready to start swinging, but Judith and the Duke of Linton grabbed his arms.

Samuel raised his palms in surrender. "I daresay it was well deserved, which is why I'm here."

"It's best that you leave." The Duchess of Linton reached back to ensure Maggie stood behind her before crossing her arms. "You were not invited."

Samuel clasped his hands in front of his chest, ready to drop to his knees. "Please, I don't mean to intrude—"

"I invited him." The duke moved to stand next to Samuel but frowned and lowered his voice. "I'd hoped not to be involved."

A confused expression flittered across the

duchess's face. "Harrison, this cad, he had the audacity..."

Maggie straightened. Surely her grace wouldn't expose how he rejected her to the entire *ton*?

"I owe Miss Prescott an apology." Samuel's voice rose above the din.

"Haven't you done enough?" Maggie's mother raised her chin the same way Maggie often did.

Hannah turned to address Maggie and the influential band of women. "Please, hear him out." She opened her palms. "In the name of love and all that's holy."

God bless Bradlee for marrying such a considerate woman.

"It better be quick"—Mrs. Prescott's tone could have frosted Antiguan crops in summer—"and good."

"Maggie." He tried to lean to the side to see her face, but the ladies blocked him. "I'm sorry if I hurt you." Samuel raised his voice above the din of whispers. "I had every intention of coming to the assembly ball, I promise you, but Fines detained me."

Maggie's mother's mouth dropped open. "You were arrested?"

He stepped aside to gaze straight at Maggie. "Abducted and impressed on a merchant ship to keep me from having a say in a crucial vote coming up the morning after the dance. It took four men restraining me to keep me from you.

It was island politics, and it had nothing to do with my feelings toward you. I knew what that dance meant to you, and I ranted and screamed at my captors, but to no avail. I'd planned to propose."

"To ensure Greenview Manor stayed in your possession."

The pain in her voice squeezed his chest like a vice.

"No, I already knew that Paul Baxter had signed paperwork giving Greenview Manor to my father."

The crowd gasped and circled closer to listen. He'd be making the headlines of the *Morning Gazette* for certain.

Maggie stepped forward, nudging her way between her mother and the duchess. "Then why hide my mother's diaries from me?"

"It was wrong and prideful. I wanted to control the information and protect you, but I ended up hurting you." He opened his jacket, pulled a rolled paper from his pocket. "I racked my brain for a way to make amends and only came up with one solution. It doesn't make up for my mistakes, but I had to start somewhere."

He handed it to the duchess, who scanned the contents. "It's the deed to one Greenview Manor in Antigua." She held it over for Maggie's mama to examine. "And it's signed over to Miss Maggie Prescott."

• • •

Maggie's gasp was swallowed up by the crowd's.

"Arrest this man."

Harry Reginald pushed through to the edge of the guests. "He's been banished for brutal assault and attempted murder on a member of the aristocracy."

Two men strode to apprehend Samuel, and a cacophony of murmurs rippled through the room, but Samuel's gaze remained steady upon her. He didn't refute Harry's accusation or defend himself, merely let his love for her shine in his eyes.

"Wait!" The slice of Maggie's command silenced the room. She turned to the duchess. "Please, your grace. I'd like to hear this out."

The Duchess of Linton eyed her husband and, upon a nod of his head, the two men standing behind Samuel backed down.

The weight of the guests' gazes fell back upon her, and Maggie swallowed and focused on Samuel. "Greenview Manor is your only means to return to England."

"Was." A weak smile flickered on the corners of his mouth. "Now it belongs to you."

Her mother passed the paper to Maggie. She read it and covered her mouth with her hand.

"You showed me people weren't a means to an end and that relationships are more important than position and prestige. I believed I could protect

525

you from what I thought was in the diaries. But then you taught me how to laugh, love, and trust God. Although they were still wrong, my motives changed. I still tried to control the situation, but because I wanted be the one to discover your lineage so I could be your hero." He clasped his hands. "I'm sorry."

She blinked away the blur of unshed tears to see him clearer.

"My attorneys didn't come through." He grunted, and his smile grew. "But Dinah did. She discovered your mother's lady's maid still resided on the premises, and she explained that your mother, Loretta Genevieve Baxter, and Captain Sebastian Lowell Corbett, nicknamed the Wolf, were married in Guadeloupe." He waved the priest forward. "The church in which they were married burnt down, but Reverend Brissett is the priest who married them."

The Duchess of Linton's lips parted. "You dragged that poor priest here from Guadeloupe?"

The priest stepped forward and took Maggie's hand, speaking in French. Tears ran down Maggie's cheeks, and she choked back a sob. Someone from the crowd shouted, "What did he say?"

The duchess raised her voice for all to hear. "He said that her parents were very much in love, and he was happy to marry them in front of God and his congregation on October 19, 1810."

Mitchell's mother nudged her son, "I knew it all along."

"I know I don't deserve your forgiveness after keeping secrets from you." Samuel lowered to his knees.

A convulsive sob choked her. He was humbling himself and honoring her in front of the peerage.

"I wanted you to know that I am truly sorry. I never meant to hurt you. You have my heart, now and always, even though I don't deserve to kiss the ground you walk upon."

Harry sneered. "He's right. He doesn't deserve to step foot in this ballroom much less British soil."

Maggie's spine stiffened.

Rising, Samuel said, "I actually owe you an apology." He pivoted to face his former friend.

Harry gripped his lapel with a smug snort and glanced about the room with an it's-about-time-look. "Now that you failed at making a go of it in Antigua." He nodded his chin at Maggie, "And made a mess of things with the duchess's new protégé, you want to apologize."

He was attempting to goad Samuel into a rage, same as Fines had tried to do in Antigua. Maggie's fist clenched with the desire to rearrange his nose to have it crook to the other side.

"I also owe a debt of gratitude to you and Miss Tilly."

Lucy pushed past another woman and slid her hand into the crook of Harry's arm.

"I have been blessed beyond what I could ever have imagined by having met Miss Prescott." Samuel glanced back over his shoulder at Maggie before addressing Harry once more. "It took Miss Tilly's and your betrayal to save me from making a lifelong mistake."

Samuel didn't succumb to his temper. Instead he acted calm and collected—with a supernatural peace despite the accusations.

Maggie held back her urge to cheer for him.

He shifted to peer at Maggie. "It took Fines's anger to expose the ugliness of seeking vengeance and a mudslide to reveal my love for you. Disasters can be blessings from a different perspective. God hadn't been punishing me. He'd been protecting me."

"Well, I never . . ." Lucy huffed at the strange apology and glared at Harry, nudging him with her arm.

Samuel gestured between himself and Lucy. "We are very different people and were never meant for each other." He issued her a sheepish smile. "I take responsibility and blame for not giving you the attention you deserved. For that I am truly sorry."

Lucy's lips puckered into a frown, and her offended look melted into an expression of regret.

"Perhaps . . ." Maggie couldn't resist the urge

to bring Harry down a notch, for Samuel's sake. "Lord Reginald should make an honest woman of Miss Tilly."

Harry's eyes widened, and his jaw quivered. He backed away, and Miss Tilly scowled at his reaction.

Mr. Tilly met him half way through the crowd and grabbed him by the collar.

The guests turned to watch the exchange, murmuring about a scandal.

But Samuel paid the spectacle no mind. He stepped closer to Maggie, his eyes pleading. "Can you ever find it in your heart to forgive me?"

She raised her chin and, although she'd already forgiven him, she wasn't letting him off that easily. "I'm disappointed in you, Samuel."

His head lowered like withered sugar cane during the drought.

"You never checked off that last item on your daily list."

His head snapped upright, and his gaze flew to her. "You would have me?"

Her pulse stuttered before racing through her body. "You won't know unless you ask."

He fumbled in his pocket for the ring and lowered to one knee to extend the offer toward her. His gaze flicked to the crowd, and his Adam's apple bobbed.

Was he wondering if she might exact revenge by rejecting him? She bit the inside of her lip, her heart clenching.

"Maggie." His shoulders pulled back and his eyes held a determined glare, proving that, to him, the risk was worth it. "You hold my heart. Would you do me the much-undeserved honor of becoming my wife?"

She squeezed her mother's and duchess's hands before letting them go. She stepped forward. "Yes." Tears ran over her cheeks and dripped off her chin, but she graced him with a smile. "I will marry you."

He jumped to his feet and cupped her face in his hands. "Truly?"

She nodded.

Samuel swooped down and pressed a kiss to her lips meant to seal his promise.

Hoots and applause rose from the crowd, but a man cleared his throat behind Samuel, and Samuel broke the kiss.

Maggie chuckled to discover Tobie, standing over them with a watchful eye.

Samuel stepped back, and Tobie shook his hand. "I think you're just beginning to understand the treasure you have in my daughter. I hope we get to find that same treasure in you."

"I would like that very much." Samuel nodded to his future father-in-law.

Maggie hooked her arm around Samuel's and

leaned her head against his shoulder. "You still owe me."

"Name it and I will do it. I will prove my love even if I must sail to the moon."

She didn't want him to sail to the moon, just a chance to love one another, be together, and share a future, something her birth parents never had. And maybe one more thing. "I've been waiting a very long time to dance."

The duchess raised her hand and flicked her fingers, and the orchestra struck up a waltz.

He stepped back and bowed over her hand. "Miss Prescott, would you do me the honor of this dance." He pressed a kiss upon her knuckles.

The look in his eyes tripled the pace of her heartbeat.

He led her onto the dance floor and swept her around the perimeter with graceful steps and a firm hold. Even though she'd never waltzed publicly, she'd memorized and practiced the steps for this moment. Eyeing his stained front, she teased him with a grin. "Carson's going to have your head for ruining another shirt."

A burst of laughter erupted from deep in Samuel's chest. A couple of the most pretentious dowagers, including Lady Etheridge, pursed their lips at such an inappropriate display of emotion.

"Welcome to the club, older brother." Bradlee Granville winked at Samuel before leading his wife into the dance and matching her and Samuel's movements.

Samuel quirked an eyebrow. "Which club?"

His brother swept Hannah away but chuckled over his shoulder and said, "The one for hopelessly smitten men."

Samuel lifted his chin in acknowledgement before returning his attention to Maggie. "He's right, you know."

She glanced at Cilla encircled by the duchess, Lady Cardon, and Lady Ethridge, each growing more animated as they spoke. Maggie giggled. "It appears the ladies have already started planning our wedding. My mother, your mother, and the duchess will be looking to pull off the wedding of the century in three months."

"Three months." His words dragged out with a tone of impossibility. "I'm weighing the option of obtaining a special license. Tell them they have three weeks."

She flashed him a broad grin. "I will give them one."

"I love you." His expression softened. "You've added color, laughter, and joy to my life."

"You have given me everything I have ever wanted, a dance, love,"—her heart swelled—"even a middle name."

His head tilted in a questioning pose.

"I'll soon be Mrs. Maggie Prescott Granville."

His fingers reflexively squeezed as if to pull

her into his embrace, but he peered about the room and released a low groan resounding with frustration.

"When I thought I'd lost you, everything turned dark." The intensity in his eyes stole her breath. "I had veered off God's path and taken my own way, but God was gracious enough in His mercy to offer me a second and third chance." His thumb stroked her spine, sending tingles up her back. His tender gaze softly caressed her cheek. "God lighted the way one step at a time, making my path straight. And I'll be forever grateful that He led me back"—he flashed her a broad smile—"to dance with you."

She gazed at the man whose nearness whirled her senses in a pirouette, amazed that God had orchestrated this dance, but also a way for her and Samuel to be together. Although his shirt was bloodied, his nose slightly crooked, and a purple circle had formed under his left eye, she'd never been prouder of the man who humbled himself before God, her, and by tomorrow's gossip columns headlines, all of England.

About *The Heir's Predicament*

Maggie first appeared in *The Captain's Quest* as the feral child shipwrecked on a deserted island. Readers fell in love with her character and emailed me, hoping to learn more of her story. It didn't take much coaxing for my imagination to delve into how a child, who'd lived outdoors and struggled with daily survival, would adapt to Regency England's intricate social conventions of the *le bon ton* as a grown woman.

Like Maggie, my grandfather and mother-in-law were both adopted. Each felt a disconnection from their roots and a natural yearning to fill a void by learning their origins. The thriving industry of Ancestry.com and 23-and-Me exists due to this pervasive desire to understand one's background. Understandably, Maggie longs for answers, but the guilt of being disloyal to the family who accepted her into their loving home tempts her to fabricate a lie and cover up her journey to the island of Antigua.

Another driving force for Maggie is that in Regency England, questionable heritage could hinder an adopted child from marrying within the upper social ranks. Unknown lineage could taint noble bloodlines, and many aristocrats wouldn't dare align their families with someone of uncertain origins. Maggie's marriage prospects would have been limited unless she uncovered her past. She'd have been considered too risky to wed among the gentry but raised too highborn to marry within the lower classes.

The Heir's Predicament is the last installment of the *Leeward Islands* series, and I will miss immersing myself in the rich cultural history of the Caribbean. I loved exploring different isles and island-hopping with readers through various settings. The island of Antigua, where *The Heir's Predicament* is set, boasts of ninety-five miles of scalloped coastlines, white and pink sand beaches, a tropical but arid climate, windmills and plantations, and a sugar and spice history complete with Caribs and pirates. Island tensions create a lively setting and weave their way into the characters' stories, for instance, the push and pull between the island's calming beauty and battering storms, water abounding but not much of it drinkable, a laid-back culture of hearty survivors, and a legacy of slavery versus colonization.

The journey, however, isn't over, my next series will take place in the rolling hills and quaint towns of England's Cotswold, but there's hope of a *Windward Islands* series in the future.

Acknowledgments

Thank you, readers, for allowing me this incredible journey. I'm sad to see the Leeward Islands series come to a close. It has been a joy to be transported to white-sand beaches, crystal-clear turquoise waters, and colorful island villages to learn about the rich West Indian culture and its association with England during the Regency Era. Each story and its heroines were a blessing because I was able to dig deeper into life's lessons on love and the best love story of all—that God first loved us.

I'm so grateful to my publisher Misty Beller and Wild Heart Books for believing in me, encouraging me, and offering their wisdom and expertise. The whole team has been amazing, from their administration (Sherri—always on top of things) to the design, marketing, and promo team. You make magic happen.

I can never say enough about Robin Patchen and her editing. As busy as she is writing and publishing her incredible suspense series, family, weddings, and other projects, I'm so blessed to have her watchful eye to fine-tune every detail and correct all those mistakes my brain doesn't see. Thank you for grabbing a shovel and helping me fill in any plot holes and brainstorm alternate solutions. Your wisdom is invaluable. I'm so grateful for you and our friendship that has developed over the years.

To my friend and freelance editor, Robyn Hook, thank you for being my sounding board and pointing me and my characters in the right direction. I appreciate your input, knowledge of the craft, and helping me chip away at the coal to get to the diamond. Also, special thanks go out to Nathalie Parenee for her knowledge and kindness in helping me with my French.

I can't thank my beta readers enough for their encouragement and for catching all those last-minute changes, Shannon, Lori, Kristin, Liz, and Louise. I can't forget the great women who make up my critique group, Tammy, Barbara, and Megan. Reading your manuscripts has been a pleasure, and thank you for helping hone mine. A big shout-out goes to my launch team for posting reviews and pictures of you reading my books on social media. Your efforts contributed to making this series a success.

My family deserves a big round of applause for putting up with me talking about my characters as if they were people. I'm so blessed to have such a supportive family—from my aunts, uncles, and cousins, who not only read my books but forward my blog posts and encourage their local libraries to pick up several copies, to my mom and dad, who proudly announce my book launches to their

Sunday school class and who speak to local book clubs. I'm so proud of my three boys, who have grown into fine young men during this writing journey, and my supportive husband, who has helped carry the weight around the house so I can finish that last chapter.

About the Author

Lorri Dudley has been a finalist in numerous writing contests and has a master's degree in Psychology. She lives in Ashland, Massachusetts with her husband and three teenage sons, where writing romance allows her an escape from her testosterone filled household.

Connect with Lorri at http://LorriDudley.com

Center Point Large Print
600 Brooks Road / PO Box 1
Thorndike, ME 04986-0001 USA

(207) 568-3717

**US & Canada:
1 800 929-9108**
www.centerpointlargeprint.com